'Jones' debut novel uses his experience as a journalist to reprise a series of events in the early 1970s . . . the action of the novel is deftly strung together [and] the research is palpable on the page.'

The Australian

'*The Twentieth Man* is a political thriller in the Robert Harris mould . . . Jones cleverly weaves fact and fiction—and has great fun painting "real" characters like the wilful Lionel Murphy.'

Jennifer Byrne, *The Australian Women's Weekly*

'An engaging political thriller . . . Anna [Rosen's] key role serves to remind us of the importance of investigative journalism in a democracy.'

Spectrum, The Sydney Morning Herald

'Alongside the hefty doses of political and bureaucratic intrigue, there [are] romantic complications, family tensions and a nearly pitch perfect feel of time and place . . . Extremely readable, fascinating and very cleverly done, *The Twentieth Man* is unfortunately a bit of a rarity in Australian fiction—an historical political thriller covering our recent past.'

AustCrimeFiction.org

'*The Twentieth Man* is an incredibly assured debut novel and Jones has delivered a pacey and original historical thriller. While historical detectives seem to be everywhere, historical political thrillers are not a genre we have seen much of in Australia. And this one shines a light on a fascinating period of Australian history, contemporaneous with Watergate, in an engaging and interesting way.'

PS News

About the author

Tony Jones was still at school when Lionel Murphy raided ASIO. After an ABC cadetship, he joined *Four Corners* as a reporter in 1985, and then went to *Dateline* at SBS in 1986. He subsequently was an ABC foreign correspondent, for a time in London and later in Washington. Inter alia, he covered the war crimes in Bosnia. Today he hosts *Q&A* on Monday nights. He is married to fellow ABC journalist, Sarah Ferguson. *The Twentieth Man* is his first novel, to be followed in November 2019 by his new book, *In Darkness Visible*.

TONY
JONES

the
twentieth
man

ALLEN&UNWIN
SYDNEY · MELBOURNE · AUCKLAND · LONDON

This edition published in 2019
First published in 2017

Allen & Unwin
83 Alexander Street
Crows Nest NSW 2065
Australia
Phone: (61 2) 8425 0100
Email: info@allenandunwin.com
Web: www.allenandunwin.com

A catalogue record for this book is available from the National Library of Australia

ISBN 978 1 76052 815 7

Set in Minion Pro by Midland Typesetters, Australia
Printed in Australia by McPherson's Printing Group

10 9 8 7 6 5 4 3 2 1

The paper in this book is FSC® certified. FSC® promotes environmentally responsible, socially beneficial and economically viable management of the world's forests.

For Sarah

1.

Saturday, 16 September 1972

The figures on the platform blurred as the train gathered speed through Central Station.

He saw women in spring dresses and men in short sleeves. Sea Eagles' fans in maroon and white, and others in the Roosters' tricolours heading out early to the rugby league grand final. A platform guard, a Chinaman in a white shirt, mothers and children.

Mothers and children! A girl's face flashed by. No matter how many times he had steeled himself against this thought, these people were real.

Two boys skylarked in the open doorway of the red rattler, holding on to the poles and leaning out of the carriage as it rushed towards the tunnel. They laughed as the wind lifted their hair. Their mother yelled at them and at the last moment they ducked back inside before the tunnel closed around them.

Upright columns loomed and passed one after the other— *whoosh, whoosh, whoosh*—and he blinked at the assault on his eyes, forced to look away. It was an odd, nostalgic discomfort: he remembered looking through these windows as a child on his way to the city, the warm bodies of his father and mother pressed close on either side of him.

The train rattled and bucked and he tightened his grip on the two shopping bags, cradling them between his legs against the movement. He glanced again at his old wristwatch. 10.50 am.

He looked at the other passengers in the carriage. Had they noticed anything about his movements, something furtive? No, no one was watching him.

Several of the men on the other side of the carriage were reading newspapers; the woman directly opposite was clasping a handbag on her lap, avoiding eye contact, as if in a doctor's reception, waiting for some shameful procedure; a boy and his girlfriend whispered to each other, heads together. They were all preoccupied, enclosed in invisible fields of disregard.

Save the mother, who followed her boys' every move, ready to intervene to prevent catastrophe. She hadn't noticed the man with the shopping bags sitting next to her, though he was surely her worst nightmare. He whose senses were so completely engaged and raw and—yes, he could say this—*primitive*. He registered that, despite her alertness to the obvious dangers to her children, her instincts were dulled. She saw the cliff's edge but not the lurking predator.

In the close confines of the tunnel, the racket through the open doors and windows drowned out all other sound. As the noise peaked, the carriage lights suddenly flickered off. The ensuing blackout was accompanied by shrieks and howls as the straining mechanics and couplings, the metal-on-metal scrapings and the electrical contacts produced the sounds of a torture chamber while the decrepit red rattler barrelled through the darkness. If all the passengers screamed at once they would barely be heard above the din. He truly felt like screaming, actually, but he suppressed the urge as though holding back a sneeze.

When the lights came back on he glanced again at his watch. He told himself not to but it was irresistible. Its imperfect mechanism was like a heart beating too fast. The damn thing was gaining time, moving ahead of itself, ahead of the schedule. He sensed an acceleration of the coming events and took out a handkerchief, wiping sweat from his face. He shouldn't do that either, but the faulty watch was making it all worse.

There was a long squeal of brakes, the noise confined and then cavernous as the train thrust out of the tunnel and into the urinous light of Town Hall Station. Green tiles and dark bodies. A muffled station announcement as people rose in the carriage around him. So did he, jerkily in the sudden deceleration.

He had a shopping bag in each hand and stumbled against the mother, who was now beseeching her sons to wait. The boys ignored her, springing off the still-moving carriage and letting the momentum carry them through the crowd and straight on to the escalator. The mother caught his eye, and he saw a panicked look before she bustled her way to the door.

He moved in her wake through the parting crowd, which opened as if in response to the mother's distress. He used her momentum to drag himself along and on to the escalator, saving time now, gaining on his watch. The woman's thick hips rolled in a steady rhythm as she stomped up the moving stairs.

The boys were waiting at the top and she rounded on them, grabbing the younger one by the ear and slapping the older one's cheek. He kept walking, registering a small shock as he passed them. His own mother had never hit him. She'd had a dark mist around her, disappearing before he was the age of either of these boys.

Not now! Put that memory away . . .

He switched the bags to one hand, pulled out his ticket and passed through the barrier before rebalancing his load.

The underground concourse was full of people and he joined the flow before peeling off to the public toilet. Once inside he edged past men facing the stinking urinals and moved along the row of cubicles to the furthest empty one. He locked himself inside, sat on the toilet seat and took a deep breath. The door in front of him was scored with obscene messages and a crudely drawn cock above a phone number. He grimaced, pulled out his handkerchief, wiped his brow again and dried his hands. He held his right hand out on a horizontal plane. Steady, no shakes.

He opened one of the shopping bags, took out the old towel that covered the contents and laid it on his knees. He reached down and gently removed a heavy brown package swathed in tape. Attached to the top, and wired to batteries and detonators, was his most accurate watch. Now he set the timer, put the live bomb back in the shopping bag, and covered it up again. Then he repeated this procedure with the bomb in the second bag.

When he stood up it was too quickly. Dizziness. He sat back down, closed his eyes and took slow, deep breaths.

He visualised the timing devices. He had constructed them himself with utmost care. A perfectionist and highly skilled in this art, he had repeated the procedure of setting the timers in training. But despite all his precautions, his mind turned to Tomislav Lesic. He thought every day about Lesic, whose legs had been blown off when a bomb he was carrying exploded in a quiet street in Petersham.

Lesic had been an amateur and a fool. His own method was infallible.

He opened his eyes and checked the time. 11.08 am. He stood again, slowly this time, and flushed the toilet. He picked up the shopping bags. He felt the weight of them down into his boots.

*

No one took any notice of the man with two shopping bags climbing the stairs out of the station. He blinked in the sunlight, adjusting his eyes before looking up at the Town Hall clock. 11.12 . . . That can't be right!

He set off briskly through the shoppers and sightseers. Everything had an odd intensity. Families and groups of young people on their way to the cinemas, to Chinatown, to Paddy's Markets; heavy traffic on George Street; crowded buses throbbing beside him; impatient drivers trying to beat the lights; children teetering along the edge of the footpath.

He walked downhill towards Haymarket, focusing so intently on the journey that his vision narrowed to a tunnel. He had taken the route before and timed it. It was only a block and a half to number 668, the Adriatic Trade and Travel Centre, his first target.

He knew the proprietor, Josip Martin, would be there. The man's real name had been Marijancevic, before he changed it. He had watched him working in the agency, had mapped his work habits.

He had set his mind to kill Martin.

His motivation was simple enough. Tito's regime was evil. Martin was a tool of the regime—a communist who made a living from party contacts in the Belgrade bureaucracy. Martin's job was to facilitate connections between Australia and Yugoslavia: to arrange tickets, visas, permissions and political contacts for businessmen and tourists.

For such activities they had designated Martin an enemy. In November last year a splinter group had planted a bomb outside his agency. It exploded in the middle of the night, but it failed to bring his business to a halt. Today the Brotherhood would settle the matter once and for all. They had chosen him to do it. The honour outweighed his fear.

Josip Martin was busy with a customer and didn't pay much attention to the man who came into the premises carrying shopping bags, only to leave soon afterwards with only one. Nor did he notice that the missing bag was now concealed behind a chair at the front, next to the shelves displaying tourist brochures for the different regions of Yugoslavia.

The man walked out of the centre with a colour pamphlet. He tucked it into his coat pocket, checked his watch again. 11.14. He was behind schedule and quickened his pace towards Haymarket. It was two hundred and fifty metres to 736 George Street, his next target. His mission half-complete, he was anxious to be rid of the second shopping bag.

He reached the Adria Travel Agency and went straight inside. The Serb, Risto Jadorovski, sat at a desk, talking on the telephone. Jadorovski waved to him, indicating that he should take a seat. A young woman was behind the shop counter. She smiled at him. She was a pretty young thing. He hesitated, staring back at her. Then he put down the shopping bag, turned and walked back out through the glass door.

Jadorovski finished his call and looked up to see the man leaving. He got to his feet, surprised to see the fellow quicken his pace. The puzzled proprietor instinctively felt there was something wrong and rushed to the front of his shop, peering up the street at the retreating figure. The man had started jogging towards Chinatown.

Out of the corner of his eye, Jadorovski noticed the shopping bag leaning against the large plate-glass window facing the street. He picked it up and ran outside, calling to the man. But he did not look back.

Jadorovski was still standing on the footpath when the first bomb at the Adriatic Trade and Travel Centre exploded. He turned as the flash and roar rushed towards him. The shock wave almost knocked him off his feet. Building materials arced over George Street within a cloud of smoke and dust. Panicked drivers wove about as rubble pelted their cars, thumping the bodywork. Shards of shattered glass, from the high windows on either side of the street, rained on to the footpaths.

Those in the middle of this deadly downpour covered their heads. A woman was knocked to the ground by falling objects. Other bodies lay prone on the pavement. As cars reached the outer edge of the blast zone, some accelerated past Jadorovski towards Railway Square. Other vehicles pulled over close to where he was standing and spilled wide-eyed occupants on to the street. As the cloud began to dissipate, Jadorovski found himself staggering towards the blast site. His ears were ringing.

It was then that he realised he was still carrying the shopping bag. He stopped, frozen in the middle of the street. He was covered in a film of dust. Slowly, he put the bag on the ground and bent down to look inside. An old towel concealed the contents. He lifted it and saw a watch, wiring, a brown package.

His mouth opened in horror. He wanted to run away as fast as he could, but there were people everywhere. At last Jadorovski found his voice.

'Get back! Get back, all of you!' he screamed. 'It's a bomb!'

The effect was immediate. People ran headlong in every direction away from the locus of the panic. An explosion, a madman with a foreign accent, another bomb. Where are the police? The abandoned shopping bag, so banal in any other context, was now an object of fear and revulsion.

Jadorovski heard a shout and turned back towards the agency.

His young assistant was running towards him. Without warning she plucked up the bag and carried it back into their doorway.

'Jana, what are you doing?' Jadorovski yelled, chasing after her.

'We have to put this away from the people,' she said, hurrying through the shop and out the back door. She placed the bag down on the empty footpath in the rear lane and came inside again, pale and shaken.

'Thank God it didn't explode.' Jadorovski took her by the shoulders and hugged her. 'That was very brave.'

'We should tell the police,' she said, her voice quavering. 'Before anyone walks past it.'

'The children from the ballet school upstairs,' Jadorovski cried. 'We must get them out. I'll go up there. You find a policeman.'

They ran back into the chaos on the street. From different directions came the sounds of approaching sirens. The wounded on the ground at the site of the explosion were now being attended to. A group of men were carrying a bloodied body out of the building on what looked like a blown-off door.

'There!' Jana called, pointing to the flashing lights of a police car. She ran towards it.

Jadorovski rushed to the street entrance of the ballet school and bounded up the stairs. He arrived breathless at the top, pushed the doors open and found inside a band of tiny angels staring back at him. There were more than twenty young girls in white leotards and frilled skirts, but the wall mirrors seemed to duplicate their numbers.

The teacher had her back to him, staring out the window into George Street. There were other windows at the back of the studio. Right over the lane.

'Hello,' he called to the teacher. 'I'm from the shop downstairs.'

Jadorovski lowered his voice when he reached her.

'That was a bomb that went off up the street and there is a second one behind this building,' he rasped in an urgent whisper. 'We have to get the girls away from those back windows and to a safe place.'

'My God! How do you know?'

'There's no time to explain. It could go off at any time.'

'But it's terrible out there. Where can we take them?'

'Let's get them into the stairs first, away from the back of the building. The police will be here soon.'

They moved the excited, chattering angels into the stairwell and sat them three by three on the steps. Jadorovski told them to wait there and ran back out on to George Street.

A police car was now parked in front of the agency. Jana was speaking to a policeman while his partner shouted into the car's radio receiver. Other police arrived and Jadorovski showed them where the girls were sheltering.

After a radio call to Headquarters, the tiny ballerinas were swiftly evacuated over George Street. An unmarked police car pulled up next, disgorging two detectives. By now a small crowd of onlookers had gathered, having heard news of a second suspicious device.

One of the plain-clothes men positioned his car across the entrance to Parker Lane and ordered the area to be cordoned off. The elder of the detectives pulled the uniformed men aside and issued a series of instructions. Two constables climbed back into their car and set off at high speed with the siren screaming.

The old detective beckoned to Jadorovski. 'A word with you, mate. Your name is?'

'Risto Jadorovski.'

'Yador-offski, you say? Tell me how you spell it.'

The detective, taking a note as Jadorovski spoke, scrutinised the older man suspiciously.

'Where you from, mate?'

'I came here from Yugoslavia many years ago. I run the travel agency here. We were targeted. A man was behaving strangely in the office. Then I found the shopping bag inside and I saw the man running away.'

'We'll talk to you about all of that soon enough, but it sounds like you're the only one who's seen inside this thing. Is that right?'

'Yes, well, I think my assistant, Jana, might have seen it too. She's the one who put it in the back lane. Away from the people.'

'I'll get to her in a minute. First, tell me exactly what you saw in the bag.'

As Jadorovski recounted his story, ambulances began arriving at the bombsite. Paramedics and police had set up a triage and the worst cases were rushed from the scene.

'It's just awful,' Jadorovski told the detective. 'We can't let this happen again.'

The detective looked at him grimly. 'I want you to try and think back. Did you see anything at all on the watch—a metal pointer, something like that, which might show what time it was set to explode?'

Jadorovski paused. Tried to bring the image back.

'No,' he said at last, putting both hands to the sides of his face. 'I can't remember anything like that. I was so shocked.'

The detective nodded. 'That's normal. Don't worry. We've called the bomb squad, but who knows if they'll get here before it blows.'

They heard a siren returning. A police car, at speed, skidded to a halt next to the unmarked vehicle.

'Stay here,' the detective instructed. 'I'll need to speak to you again.'

Two young constables threw open their doors, ran to the back of the car and opened the boot. They began hauling out heavy sacks, which they each hefted on to their shoulder before jogging into the lane. Jadorovski realised that the sacks were 30-kilogram bags of potatoes.

'Sent 'em to Paddy's Markets,' the detective explained, before running over to help the others.

The policemen stacked the potato sacks around and over the shopping bag with panicky haste and ran back around the corner to safety.

'There's no way I'd ever do that again,' said one, breathing hard. There was no bravado. Their faces were drawn and bloodless.

'No, mate, no way,' his partner agreed. 'I was sure it was gonna blow. Nearly shat meself.'

'Go and have a smoke, fellas,' the older detective told them. 'Forget the rules.'

A fire engine arrived and the police stopped it short of the entrance to Parker Lane.

The two detectives were hovering at the lane's entrance when the bomb exploded. Smoke and flames erupted as they dived behind a car. Jadorovski, ducking behind the fire engine, heard chunks of shrapnel clanking on its roof. Windows in the nearby buildings and on the other side of George Street shattered, showering the footpath with glass.

As light flotsam rained down on him, Jadorovski heard a woman screaming. He felt winded. His ears were ringing again. There was something wet on his face. Blood? He wiped at it, looking at his hand. Mashed potato was smeared across his fingers. In spite of everything, he laughed.

When he stepped out from cover, the shopping bag and the sacks were gone, and smoke drifted over a blackened crater. Along with the chemical stench of the explosives, the homely smell of cooked potatoes lingered in the air. All around him people were moving again. Firemen unrolled a hose and sprayed water on the gaping hole in the ground. Police entered the rear doors of buildings in the lane to check on the safety of anyone inside.

It was over.

2.

Earlier that morning Anna Rosen had woken in a strange bed in a strange room. A warm body lay against her, back to back.

The fog in her mind cleared as if whipped away by a strong southerly.

Fuck! Fuck! Fuck!

She turned to look at the man. The old rogue was smiling in his sleep.

Daylight did him no favours. It picked out the white stubble on his hawkish face, the tangled salt-and-pepper mop, the long grey hairs curling on his chest.

She sat up carefully and searched around until she found her knickers hiding under the covers at the foot of the bed.

Had they crept down there in shame? She pulled them on and moved around the room on her tiptoes, collecting her other garments from where they'd been thrown, and retreated silently from the bedroom.

The apartment had high ceilings and tall windows. The living room was full of light. It was elegant and spacious, lined with bookcases. She remembered it differently—lit by side lamps and stubby aromatic candles, two of which now sat, hollowed out and extin-guished, on the low, beaten-copper table that squatted in the centre of the room on a large Afghan carpet.

Beside the candles were discoloured glasses of different sizes, along with two empty wine bottles and a depleted decanter of Armagnac. A brown resinous lump lay in a crumpled nest of tinfoil next to an engraved brass pipe. It was a tableau of debauchery.

Anna had partaken willingly, of course, caught up in the flow of his entertaining discourse. Even as she had observed his little ritual—the heating of the hashish over the candle's flame and then crumbling its outer edges into tobacco before packing the pipe and offering it to her—she had understood the likely consequences. She had watched the reddening glow as she inhaled and felt the familiar easing of the mind, the soft stone that enhances desire.

Now she dressed quickly.

'You're leaving?'

She looked up. McHugh was in the doorway, wrapping a Balinese sarong around his waist.

'I didn't mean to wake you,' she said.

He rubbed his face, smoothing his pouched eyes, or attempting to. 'Stay. I'll make you some breakfast.'

'I've got to go.'

'No, you don't.'

'I do, Peter.' Anna looked down, shook her head. 'This is crazy. I really don't know . . . what was I thinking?'

'We weren't thinking, either of us,' he said. 'That's a good thing, isn't it?'

'Screwing the boss?' Anna scooped up her old leather bag and slung it over her shoulder before meeting his gaze. 'We've just turned the gossip into reality and, honestly, I wouldn't blame them for looking down their noses at me.'

'Let them think what they like, they don't need to know.'

Anna moved in, kissed him on the cheek, and stepped back. 'But *I* know. That's the problem.'

McHugh made a plaintive expression. 'It was nice, wasn't it?'

'You were great, boss.' She gave a brittle laugh and turned on her heel. 'I've really got to go.'

Anna felt a spasm of sadness as the door closed behind her, and then relief. She left the building, walked out into morning sun and headed home.

Anna lived under a witch's hat in a turret with bay windows overlooking Glebe Point Road. It was a big room with a brass bed, an immense colonial wardrobe, overflowing bookcases and an old cedar desk with a creaking captain's chair.

The windows were open and the noise of Saturday traffic filled the room. Anna lay on top of the duvet, restless. She watched the rice paper lantern shift in the breeze, an inverted dirigible, tethered not to the earth but to the plaster rosette in the ceiling. She was angry with herself.

Anna was not much given to regret, but now she dwelled on her poor judgement. McHugh was not only her boss, he was her mentor, having plucked her from the newsroom to join his team. Even worse, his long friendship with her father gave the night a faintly incestuous edge. Then there was the nagging sense, quite unreasonable under the circumstances, that she had betrayed the one man she really wanted to be with.

She hated that feeling most of all because he was no longer part of her life. She knew that Peter McHugh was no answer to her longing. But so what? Yes, she'd made a mistake; but in the end no one had died, just let it go . . .

Anna jumped from the bed—time for a coffee. She found Pierre in the kitchen watching the Atomic spurt steam from its release valve.

'Ah, the kwaken wakes,' he said. 'I heard you come in this morning. Holding your shoes when you cwept down the hall, were you?'

There was something disarming about her friend's mild rhotacism that made his intrusions seem more acceptable. Anna ignored him nonetheless.

'I'd love a coffee, thanks.'

Pierre raised his eyebrows, quizzical.

'The silence of the sphinx then,' he said and turned his attention back to the juddering machine. 'Lucky I made enough for two.'

Housemates in the ramshackle old place had come and gone, but Pierre Villiers had been her constant companion for three years. He had found the house and was her co-signatory on the lease. For two years he had been Anna's deputy editor at *The Tribe* until she left to become a trainee at the national broadcaster. Having now succeeded her as editor, Pierre showed every sign of becoming a permanent student.

The Atomic reached maximum pressure and quivered over the gas flame, as sinister as an unexploded bomb. Pierre shoved a steel pan under the spout and released the roaring steam into the milk. He poured the frothy liquid into his coffee and passed Anna a long black.

He sat down and pushed a copy of *The Tribe* across the table. 'Latest edition,' he said.

Anna scrutinised the front page. The artwork showed the FBI Headquarters with J. Edgar's head as a bas-relief. Emerging from multiple apertures in the building were swivelling TV cameras and men with hats and trench coats carrying Tommy guns. The headline was intriguing.

'*Total surveillance*?'

'Yeah, I bought the piece from *The Daily Cal*,' Pierre explained. 'It's about how the toys the Pentagon made for Vietnam are now being used against civilians back home. Orwell saw this coming. Hundweds of camewas feed images into a single control centre where a computer scans each one at thirty sequences a second and compares the feeds to images stored in its memowy circuit.'

Anna read the article, sipping her coffee while Pierre made them eggs and toast.

'Great piece,' she said eventually. 'The ABC should be doing stuff like this.'

'You should.' Pierre nodded. 'And get me in to do it, don't you think?'

'We can try, but it's a miracle they let me in.'

'You're the vanguard.'

'They think I'm an anarchist.'

Pierre gave her a stern look. 'Come off it, Anna! An anarchist? You're just a social democwat with a Marxist dad. On that twajectowy, your childwen will vote Libewal.'

'Fuck you too,' Anna muttered, flicking through to the entertainment section. 'Hey, we should go to the movies tonight.'

'What's on?'

She ran a finger down the page. '*Ballad of Joe Hill* at the Valhalla? *The French Connection* is on at the Academy. What do you think?'

'I don't know.' Pierre shrugged. 'Joe Hill gets shot by a fiwing squad and Gene Hackman busts a dwug-smuggling syndicate . . . So they both have unhappy endings.'

Anna rewarded him with a laugh. 'Let's see *Joe Hill*.'

'Sure, why not?' But then Pierre returned to gnawing the old bone he never managed to bury. 'Where *did* you get to last night?'

Anna was about to tell him to mind his own business when the phone rang. She jumped up to answer it, her face flushing when she heard Peter McHugh's voice on the other end of the line.

'Anna. Thank God you're there.'

She caught her breath.

'I'm not ringing about last night,' he said quickly.

'I didn't think . . .'

'We can talk about that another time.'

'Okay,' she agreed cautiously. Maybe he accepted it had been a mistake.

'So,' he said. 'You haven't heard?'

'Heard what?'

'You need to turn the radio on right now!'

'Pierre!' she called out to the kitchen. 'Quickly. Can you put the radio on? What is it, Peter?'

'There's been a huge explosion near the Town Hall,' he exclaimed. 'Dozens of people down on George Street. Someone blew up a bloody Yugoslavian travel agency.'

'God, that's unbelievable.' Anna's mind was racing. 'Is anyone claiming responsibility?'

'Not yet . . .' McHugh paused. 'But you'd have to think it's your Croats, wouldn't you?'

From the radio in the kitchen she heard snatches of high-tension reporting from the scene.

'Peter, let me go listen to this,' Anna said. 'I'll make some calls and get back to you.'

'Good, do that as soon as possible. I'm going in to the office.' McHugh hung up.

She walked back into the kitchen where, despite the volume, Pierre was leaning in close to the radio speaker. He looked up. He was well aware of what Anna had been working on over the past two months.

'I guess the movies are off,' he said.

In Canberra, Inspector Harry Harper was putting his golf clubs into the boot of his car when Helen hailed him from the doorway.

'Harry? A call for you.'

Harper put his hands on the rim of the boot and dropped his head. He looked at the clubs lying there expectantly, the irons shiny and clean, the woods neatly capped with numbered leather covers.

'It sounds urgent,' Helen said. 'Headquarters.'

He sighed, pushed the boot shut and went back inside.

'Harper,' he said emphatically into the receiver.

'Colin Reynolds, sir.'

Reynolds was the weekend duty officer.

'What is it, Sergeant?'

Reynolds spoke fast. 'Big flap in Sydney. A bomb's gone off at Town Hall, multiple casualties. Just got a telex, marked urgent, for your attention.'

'Read it to me, please.'

'Jesus, Saturday morning!' Reynolds babbled. 'George Street'd be full of women and children. I took the wife there just last . . .'

'Sergeant,' Harper interrupted, 'the telex!'

'Sorry, sir.'

Harper didn't think twice about tugging the reins on his subordinate. He was a stickler for protocol, British military police pedigree, Northern Rhodesia, known to take no prisoners.

The telex spelled out that a large bomb had exploded inside a Yugoslavian travel agency on George Street, causing dozens of casualties. The exact number, the nature of their injuries and the question of fatalities were still to be confirmed. Ray Sullivan had sent the communication within half an hour of the explosion. Harper was grateful Sullivan was on duty in Sydney. The detective sergeant was one of the sharper knives in his drawer.

There was more. An unexploded bomb had been found in another Yugoslavian travel agency a short distance away on the other side of the street. Police had contained that device.

Sullivan's assessment: a high degree of certainty the bombing was politically motivated.

As head of the Bureau of Criminal Intelligence, Harper was at the top of the list for notification of a suspected terrorist attack. He thanked Reynolds and hung up.

Helen was lingering in the hallway.

'Sounds bad,' she said.

'It is, darling, but I don't have time to explain,' Harper said. He walked past her into his study, closed the door, flipped open the teledex, found the commissioner's home number and dialled it.

'Harper here, boss.'

'What is it, Harry?' asked Jack Davis. 'I've got people here for lunch.'

Harper briefed him.

'Christ, it's the Croats again,' Davis summed up. 'A terror attack. There's no real doubt, is there?'

'No, sir.'

'State police'll have operational control. What can we do?'

Harper paused. Time to jump in.

'Intelligence and extra manpower, to start with. Offer them all our available resources in Sydney. On the intelligence side, I'd like to send Al Sharp straight down.'

'Righto, Harry. I'll ring the NSW commissioner. He'll be grateful for the help, I'm sure. But we can't tread on their toes. You liaise directly with CIB. I'll make that clear.'

'Yes, sir,' said Harper. 'And Sharp?'

'Send him by all means but he'll have to operate under their authority. I'll make the call straight away. I want a full briefing at the end of the day.'

Harper hung up and rang Sharp.

'Al, sorry to interrupt your weekend.'

'The bombs?'

'Where'd you hear?'

'It's all over the news. I just lit the bloody barbecue.'

'And I was about to head off for a round of golf.'

Sharp chuckled at this familiar trope. 'That'll never happen, Harry. You should know that by now.'

'Why do I bother? I don't even like golf. Did they name the targets on the news?'

'Two Yugoslavian travel agencies. Is that right?'

'Yes,' Harper confirmed. 'Sounds like your old mates are at it again.'

Sharp was Harper's senior intelligence officer. He'd once been an ASIO agent, now he was the best analyst of Croatian extremist groups in the BCI. Harper rated him highly. His threat assessments were a thing of joy. Despite the disparity in their ranks, he tended to treat Sharp as an equal.

'What do you want me to do, Harry?'

'Quick as you can, put together your files on the Croats. I want you on the first plane to Sydney. You'll be my eyes and ears on the investigation. The NSW coppers will run it, but they're way behind us on intelligence. You'll brief their investigators on the likely suspects. Sorry about your lunch.'

Sharp sighed. 'I had a few mates coming to watch the grand final.'

'I'd completely forgotten about that.'

'Typical Pom.'

'I don't even know who's playing.'

'Seriously? Manly and Easts, you heretic—battle of the silvertails.'

'Right,' said Harper. He'd stopped listening and was mulling over the timing. 'Imagine planning a bombing on grand final day.'

'The bloody Croats don't give two hoots. Soccer fanatics, all of them,' Sharp said. 'I might make the 2 pm flight if I get a wriggle on. Anything on the bomber—anyone taking credit?'

'Nothing yet.'

'I don't get it. Bombs in the middle of the city . . . That's a major escalation. Got to be a new group, hasn't it?'

'You know these mad bastards better than anyone. They're going to need you in Sydney.'

'Do I have to stay in that same crappy hotel on Castlereagh?'

'Don't complain,' Harper said. 'It's a short walk to the bombsite and a few blocks away from the CIB. Go straight there. They'll be expecting you. Call me at the office.'

The venetian blinds were all closed to the light except for one broken slat, which was twisted against the grain and allowing a single beam of sunlight to burst through the opening. It landed between a pair of legs shrouded by a sheet.

Tom Moriarty, whose legs they were, was lying on his back, watching the beam climb towards his groin.

In his fevered imagination it was the laser in *Goldfinger*, accompanied by a loud soundtrack.

BANG bang BANG bang BANG bang . . .

The drumbeat came from behind his bloodshot eyes, sickening and relentless. Strauss's 'Also sprach Zarathustra', with the timpani section on a loop. It seemed to be generated by his pulse, which was at least a sign that he was still alive. But that fleeting thought brought no comfort.

He kept his head still on the pillow, fearful that any movement might produce more of the ghastly pain. He'd been through this many times before, so he knew from experience that this sense of being locked-in would pass. Yet nothing seemed certain in this particular phase of the torment.

How long before Brown sent over some heavies to break down the door? Would he even hear them over the infernal racket? *BANG bang BANG bang BANG bang.*

There was a dull gleam in his peripheral vision, but he didn't dare turn his head to confirm the suspicion. He searched his last conscious memories as the laser beam edged towards his genitals. How had 007 avoided fiery emasculation? Painfully, but with fine mimicry and no sign of a stutter, Moriarty spoke the immortal lines:

'Do you expect me to talk?'

'No, Mr Bond, I expect you to die.'

Think, Tom, think . . .

Gradually the gleaming object consolidated into a memory. It took the familiar shape of a bottle and eventually he visualised a single word in his native tongue.

STOLICHNAYA.

The fingers of his right hand twitched. With a superhuman effort, he raised his arm and swung it towards the object. When his fingertips brushed against glass, he opened his trembling hand to caress the thing. Grasping it by the neck, he brought it into his line of sight and was relieved to see an inch of viscous liquid sloshing in the bottom.

When had the black curtain come down last night? The vodka seemed to stir up fractured memories. Glimpses of the lost night forced their way through the incessant drumbeat. He was cutting a swathe through the patrons of the Press Club like a dodgem car. Elbows repelled him, drinks were spilt. Angry faces. A woman at the bar was briefly entranced; then she was hostile, mouthing at him with fierce intensity. The sudden materialisation of a man— her boyfriend? A fist rattled his cheekbone. A view from the floor of legs dancing around him, faces leering. The lurch to the door. Streetlights and car beams. An impressionistic cab journey, his face smeared against the window, drooling . . .

All of this swirled in the bottom of the bottle before Moriarty pulled it to his mouth and gulped down the contents, heedless of the fragrant burning in his throat and nostrils, until it steadied his hand and dulled the pain. Poison as antidote, a familiar thought.

He threw the empty bottle aside, wiped his moistened lips.

'*N-Na Zdorovie*,' he said. A toast to no one.

He looked down. The laser was about to scorch his balls. In a burst of energy, he swung his skinny legs out of the bed and staggered to the bathroom. In the mirror he saw a face like a painter's palette. There was a shiner in shades of purple around his left eye; both eyes were red; his skin had a greenish pallor, darkened in places by stubble. His black hair stood up like the worn shoe brush in his old army footlocker.

Would you trust this man with the nation's security? He splashed water on his face, pushed wet hands back through his hair and addressed the creature in the mirror: 'Stirred but n-not sh-shaken.'

The disreputable fellow staring back did not reply, so he pulled the mirror open and rummaged in the shelves for aspirin. He threw a handful into his mouth and bent to suck water out of the tap, drinking and drinking with no thought of dignity. Gideon would never have chosen him as one of his Brave Three Hundred. But that was nothing to be concerned about. That's not what spies do anyway.

He was wondering whether to shave when the phone rang. He ignored it, but it just started again a moment later, and this time he snatched up the receiver.

'M-Moriarty.'

He listened without interruption as the urgent disembodied voice cut through to the functioning core of his brain. The Croats had gone rogue.

'F-fuck me roan,' he told the caller. 'I'm on my way.'

3.

Anna Rosen spent almost an hour on the phone tracking down contacts while monitoring the radio coverage of the bombing. Then she rang McHugh at the office.

'Hi, Peter, I've made some calls—'

McHugh interrupted. 'What are you hearing?'

He sounded jittery and Anna registered something else in his voice. She knew that journalists were not the most admirable of creatures. Their first reaction when broken bodies and severed limbs were strewn through the city was not revulsion; it was excitement. She heard it in Peter's voice now and was surprised to find that she felt the same impulse.

'It's hard to get on to people because of the panic,' she explained. 'But I've spoken to a few close to the Croats. Most are too scared to say much, but no one's in any doubt who did it. I got through to Marjan Jurjevic and he straightaway blamed the Ustasha.'

'Jurjevic?' McHugh said, scrolling back through a long list of Balkan names in his head. 'The whistleblower?'

'That's right, he's in Melbourne. Marjan Jurjevic. He's not a neutral commentator. A left-wing Croat who hates the Ustasha;

he's the one they keep trying to kill. They've branded him a traitor.'

'I remember now—brave bastard.'

'Yes, he is. Anyway, Marjan told me something very interesting. He got information last night, obviously before anyone had a clue what was about to happen in Sydney, that Ustasha terrorists had just hijacked a Scandinavian airliner in Stockholm. They're demanding the release of the six Croats held in Swedish jails.'

'What, the same fellows you've been looking into?'

'The same ones. The men they want the Swedes to set free are all members of the cell that assassinated the Yugoslavian ambassador in Stockholm earlier this year. Now, remember what my Commonwealth Police source told me?'

'That there's an Australian connection?'

'Exactly. The Swedes contacted our police months ago to pass on intelligence that the embassy killers have links to the Croatian Revolutionary Brotherhood in Sydney.'

'Okay,' said McHugh, considering the implications. 'So are you saying the Sydney bombs and this Swedish hijacking are connected?'

'Not me; Marjan Jurjevic is. He's convinced of it because of the timing. And listen to this. First thing this morning he rang Special Branch in Melbourne to warn them to keep watch up here because something could happen. Then the bombs went off in Sydney.'

She could hear McHugh breathing heavily as he contemplated the new information.

'Have you spoken again to your police source?' he asked.

'No, I only have his office phone and it just rings out. It's Saturday of course, but I'll bet he's on his way to Sydney.'

McHugh had heard enough. 'Okay, Anna, this is what we're going to do. I'm going to bring your program forward to Monday night. That gives you forty-eight hours. We'll open a slot at 9 pm. We can't sit on this material. Too many other journalists will be crawling all over this story and right now you're ahead of them.'

Anna bit her thumbnail. This was what McHugh was famously good at: backing his judgment, setting the agenda and trusting his people to do the job.

'So, what do you think?' McHugh pressed. 'Can you do it?'

'I can, Peter, but I'll need to go down to Melbourne as soon as possible. The attorney-general has agreed to do a fresh interview with me tomorrow morning and I want to get Jurjevic on tape while I'm down there.'

McHugh paused. He realised she had anticipated his decision. 'You've spoken to Greenwood's people already then, have you?'

'Yeah, I figured you'd want me to do that.'

'You're right, well done. Let's get you on a plane tonight. We'll organise flights and a hotel for tonight, and book you a Comcar for tomorrow.'

'Sure.' She tried not to sound overwhelmed. 'I can't just do the government, though.'

'Right, we'll need the opposition. What about Cairns or Murphy?'

'Yeah, Lionel Murphy, I reckon. As Greenwood's shadow he's the one who's been asking him the toughest questions about Croat extremists. He's all over this stuff.'

'Do you know Murph?'

'I've never met him, if that's what you mean.'

'You're in for a treat.' McHugh chuckled. 'And I *know* he'll like you.'

'What do you mean?'

'You'll find out.'

'Come on, Peter, what are you getting at?'

'He's a very charming man, that's all.'

'Right,' Anna said, her suspicions aroused. 'I was going to

27

interview him anyway. But he's in Canberra so I'll have to go there from Melbourne on the way back. What do you think?'

'I think you're going to have a busy weekend. Do you need help with the script?'

'No, I can handle it. I'll need someone to get dubs for me of the actuality from the bombings.'

'I'll get that done, transcribed and left on your desk while you're on the road.'

'All right. I'll top and tail it with news of the bombings, and weave Greenwood and Murphy into it.'

'Anna?'

'Seriously, I can do it. Sunday will be an all-nighter, but I'm up for it. We can go through the changes on Monday morning.'

'Good girl. Off you go then.'

Anna wanted to tell him not to patronise her, but she held her tongue.

By 5 pm Al Sharp was alongside the prime minister at the site of the first bombing as they picked their way through the rubble of the Adriatic Trade and Travel Centre. Half-blinded by the spotlights from a bank of cameras, Sharp almost stumbled.

Then the media scrum shuffled backwards and questions were shouted from it: 'Prime Minister, do you know who did it? Do the police have any leads? Did Yugoslav terrorists do this?'

Prime Minister McMahon paused and blinked at the lights, squinting as he gave his prepared answer: 'Ah, it's, ah, too early to say, ah, at this time.'

Sharp, drifting out of the camera's gaze, rolled his eyes as he listened to Billy McMahon's expressionless voice. The man was deaf as a post and wore hearing aids in both of his outsized ears.

Sharp might have had sympathy, even a degree of admiration, for someone who had overcome such a handicap to lead the nation, but having now met him for the first time he was inclined to agree with the popular view that McMahon was a supercilious and treacherous little prick. He found himself ruminating on the coup McMahon had successfully orchestrated against his predecessor. He had been on a trip to Italy, on the Isle of Capri no less, when he made the critical telephone calls to organise the numbers against Gorton. Gough Whitlam later nailed McMahon in parliament, dubbing the new prime minister 'Tiberius with a telephone'.

To that small piece of recent political history Al Sharp now added his own dim assessment. After his admittedly short briefing, Sharp was angered to have the prime minister reject his advice out of hand. 'I most certainly will not be pointing the finger at our Croatian friends. That's an outrageous suggestion,' McMahon had droned in his infuriating monotone. 'Tito's goons are everywhere. This is most likely the work of an agent provocateur.'

As the press conference continued, Sharp noted that McMahon was not foolish enough to make that case publicly. The prime minister stuck to formulaic non-answers, mumbling condolences to the injured people and their families. He stumbled over details, such as the number of casualties and what had happened to them, and delivered the stock words of praise to police, emergency workers and doctors.

As McMahon droned on, Sharp spotted a spectral figure in dark sunglasses off to one side. He made his way over to the man.

'Tom,' he whispered, leaning in close. 'I didn't expect to see you here.'

'All hands to the p-p-pump, lad.'

Sharp reeled back. 'Christ, you smell like a brewery. Don't get close to the PM, whatever you do.'

Moriarty cocked his head and grinned. 'Fucking little f-fairy—that's the last thing I'd do.'

'So, what are you up to?'

'What do you think, Al?'

'You tell me. I'm here to advise the local coppers.'

'Good luck with that.' Moriarty smiled. 'Like teaching ch-chimps to write poetry.'

Sharp couldn't see Moriarty's eyes through the dark glasses. 'Late in the day for sunnies, isn't it? You look like the manager of a rock band.'

'Incognito.'

'You still haven't said what you're doing here.'

'Intelligence gathering, son, n-nothing for you to worry about. You're not in the loop, now that you've departed the f-fold.'

'Don't put up those walls.' Sharp sighed. 'This is too big for secrets.'

Moriarty moved in close, belching stale vodka fumes. 'The bigger it is, the b-bigger the secrets. You should remember that much from your time at the Organisation.' Moriarty paused, before adding, 'I'm here to c-catch up with an old mate.'

'How can I contact you?'

'You can't.' Moriarty straightened and stepped back. 'You staying at that same shithole the f-feds use?'

Sharp nodded. 'And I'll be working out of CIB.'

'See how things g-go. I m-might get in touch with you there.' The stuttering spy tapped him on the shoulder. 'Better get back to the f-fairy queen. His detail's looking nervous.'

Sharp turned and saw the protective services team manoeuvring the prime minister out to the waiting limousine. Tom Moriarty slipped away.

*

Later that evening the bomber sat alone, watching the news on television. All the footage was devoted to the chaotic aftermath. Police on megaphones, warning people to stay off the streets. Sirens wailing. Ambulances tearing past; the destroyed buildings and their shattered interiors; firemen and police searching through the rubble for casualties; people spilling on to the street from the Capitol Theatre, which had been evacuated while police sniffer dogs searched for the other bomb.

A reporter, talking to the camera, said that a man with a foreign accent had called the *Sydney Morning Herald* after the explosions and warned that if the 'Yugoslavian situation' did not improve in the next week two hospitals and Central Station would go up next.

At this news the bomber stirred, puzzled. Who had made that threat? It was mad. But, then again, who was he to accuse someone else of madness, having brought the world down on their heads?

There was footage of the prime minister inspecting the site with Commonwealth Police. The floppy-eared pixie was wearing a fawn suit and a dark skivvy as he stepped daintily through the wreckage. The bomber grimaced. How was such a creature chosen to lead a country?

A news anchor read out the casualty list. Two victims still in hospital in a critical condition. Doctors had amputated the leg of one of them. Sixteen taken to Sydney Hospital and St Vincent's with serious injuries, cuts and burns.

The bomber poured another large brandy and gulped it down. There was none of the elation he expected. He felt hollowed out, as if someone had reached into his chest and scooped out his soul. He wondered if his father had felt like this after one of his missions. He thought about his brother.

The telephone rang. He waited for it to stop. He snatched at his jacket and pulled out from one of the pockets the tourist pamphlet he had retained, opening it at a colour picture of Zagreb. He had never been to the city; he was sure he would never see it. The pamphlet shook in his hands.

The telephone rang again. He left it. It rang and rang.

4.

On Sunday afternoon Anna Rosen boarded the TAA flight from Melbourne to Canberra with a growing sense of unease. She had completed her work in the southern capital and her interviews had yielded nothing new. She had known this might be the outcome. She could have almost written the transcripts without the interviews. Marjan Jurjevic had virtually repeated word for word what he had told her on the phone. No surprise there. It was her encounter with Attorney-General Ivor Greenwood that had set her on edge, and not because of anything he'd said on tape.

There had been a strangeness about the encounter from the moment she arrived at the senator's office. His staff had treated her with barely disguised contempt. They put her in a small conference room, told her to set up her recording equipment and then made her wait for almost an hour. Anna assumed their hostility was payback for her first interview with the attorney-general. It hadn't gone well, especially when she had accused him and his predecessors of importing war criminals with whitewashed backgrounds into Australia.

When Ivor Greenwood was finally ushered into the room, straight-backed as usual, clear-eyed and immaculate, not a hair out of place, he sat without speaking. He remained silent while his acerbic press secretary explained that Anna had precisely fifteen minutes with the attorney-general before he had to go to an important meeting. Anna knew that his enemies referred to him as 'Ivor the Terrible' and assumed she was about to learn why. She was wrong about that.

Greenwood answered her questions with a polite, if cold, formality. With regards to the bombings he displayed a legalistic determination to say nothing at all about the likely culprits, as she had expected. When she cross-examined him, he repeatedly claimed, but without rancour, that nothing could be deduced until the police had completed their investigations.

She decided that this was the performance of a man unfazed by something as trivial as a few bombs being set off in the centre of the nation's largest city. Nothing about yesterday's events would cause him to alter his previous statements that there was no evidence of an organised Croatian terrorist threat.

Only when Anna thanked him and turned off the tape recorder did something interesting happen. Instead of rushing off to his appointment, Greenwood put his elbows on the table and leaned in closer, indicating he had something to say.

'I understand,' he said slowly, 'that you were, until recently, the editor of a student newspaper.'

'That's right, Senator. I joined the ABC at the beginning of last year.'

'*The Tribe*, was it?'

'Yes.'

Greenwood's expression darkened. All traces of the mild academic barrister were erased.

'What a dreadful, subversive, pornographic rag.'

'I'm sorry you—'

34

'That's just my view, of course. I blame the Liberals on campus for allowing you free rein. In my day we would have rallied and taken control of the paper from you.'

'In your day?'

'Melbourne University, 1947. We won back the SRC and wrested *Farrago* from the left. That's democracy in action.'

'In your day, Senator, there was no Vietnam War.'

'That's true enough.' Greenwood gave her a sardonic smile. 'But we did have men like your father to deal with, taking his orders from Moscow.'

Now it was her turn to remain silent. Anna was face-to-face with one of the most powerful men in the country, and he was radiating personal enmity.

Then Greenwood smiled, clearly aware of her growing discomfort. 'Don't worry, my dear. I may disagree with everything you stand for and, judging by the tone of your questions, I will certainly disagree with the conclusions I expect you to reach in your radio show. But I don't dispute your family's right to believe whatever they want.'

'Prime Minister Menzies certainly did,' Anna countered.

'Go back and check. You will find that I opposed Menzies when he tried to outlaw the Communist Party. I said publicly that the referendum was contrary to everything liberalism stands for.'

As the attorney-general stood to leave, Anna gathered her wits and said, perhaps too loudly, 'Senator, you shouldn't assume that I am a simple-minded follower of my father's politics.'

'Oh,' he responded, 'I don't believe that you are simple-minded. Not at all. You're a much bigger problem than that.'

*

On the flight to Canberra, Anna reflected on the interplay between the personal and the political.

In Ivor Greenwood's mind her father was an ideological enemy. To Greenwood's credit, he did not countenance the idea of outlawing his political enemies; but that didn't lessen his contempt for them. So what about the devil's spawn? His final comment had been intimidating, to say the least, and Anna pondered what Greenwood had meant by 'a much bigger problem' as she flew towards his most serious political enemy in the Senate.

Shadow Attorney-General, Senator Lionel Murphy, had agreed to meet her late in the afternoon at his home. Her cab brought her to a nice house on a large block in Forrest, one of Canberra's most affluent suburbs. Anna rang the doorbell, waited for a while, and was preparing to ring it again when it swung open.

In front of her was the famous man she had often seen on television. Murphy had always impressed her as a relaxed, laconic character with the incisive mind of a Queen's Counsel. She had only seen him once before in the flesh, from some distance as he spoke at an anti-conscription rally. His had been the most rousing speech.

'Senator Murphy, I'm Anna Rosen,' she announced, shaking his hand.

'Good of you to come,' he said.

'Thanks for seeing me on a Sunday.'

'Not at all, it's been an eventful weekend. Shocking, really.'

Lionel Murphy stood back from the door. 'Come in. I'm sorry I took a while to get here. I was out in the greenhouse.'

Anna smiled at him as she walked into the entrance hall. Murphy wore a crumpled white shirt with the sleeves rolled up and dark woollen trousers, which appeared to belong to a suit. Long strands of grey hair had fallen across his face and he pushed them back behind his ears.

'I didn't take you for a gardener,' she said.

'Oh no, I'm not a gardener at all. My wife does all of that.'

He laughed and, as he did, his homely face was transformed. His eyes creased, the two dark arches of his eyebrows lifted and his ponderous nose was nicely balanced by a wide grin. Anna warmed to him.

'I'm more of a scientist really.' Murphy's nasal voice had a deep, pleasing resonance. 'Ingrid had the idea that we should grow our own strawberries and I've had a hydroponic system installed. Do you know what that is?'

'No, I don't,' said Anna, although she did have a vague memory of hearing about hydroponics on a science program.

'Well, I'd be happy to show it to you later if you have time.' Murphy touched her elbow and led her further into the house. 'Come through to the kitchen. Ingrid has gone out, but she left us some things for afternoon tea.'

They sat in an alcove next to the kitchen, surrounded by windows overlooking a large, well-tended garden. It was not a house she would have associated with one of the leaders of Labor's left.

Murphy heated the pot of coffee and poured it into cups for each of them. There was a fresh strudel on the table and she accepted a slice at his urging. Murphy sipped his coffee and looked at her over the cup. 'So, you're Frank Rosen's daughter.'

Anna looked back at him. Was this to be the theme of the day?

'That's right,' she said cautiously. 'Do you know him?'

'No, we've never met.' Murphy smiled regretfully. 'I'd like to meet him. Frank's an interesting fellow. I suspect we'd have a few things in common.'

'He's an internationalist. You have that in common.'

Murphy nodded. 'Yes, we could certainly agree on the need for world peace. But I mostly admire his stand against the Stalinists.'

After the strange conversation with Ivor Greenwood, Anna was reluctant to go down this path. Long experience had taught her to clam up about her father. Frank Rosen had warned her too many times to be wary of being wooed by security agents, informers and journalists for her to ever be comfortable speaking to strangers about him or his role in the Party.

She tried defusing it. 'If you'd like to meet him, it could be arranged.'

Murphy took another sip of his coffee and put it down.

'And what about you, Anna?' he asked at last, his voice oddly seductive. 'Are you a Party member?'

Anna's hackles rose. 'You mean, am I now, or have I ever been . . .?'

Murphy laughed and his face lit up. He reached across and took a slice of strudel.

'I really shouldn't eat this. Do you like it? Ingrid made it. A recipe from her German mother.'

'It's very nice,' said Anna, confused.

'As it happens, my first wife was born in Russia,' Murphy explained. 'I tell you this so you understand that I have more than a passing interest in communism. And it does strike me that being a communist and working at the ABC would not be without its challenges.'

'I'm not a member of the Party,' said Anna. 'I was in the Junior Eureka League when I was a kid. Does that count against me?'

Murphy laughed again, ignoring her prickly response. His face radiated a puckish pleasure. 'It doesn't as far as I'm concerned,' he said. 'I know plenty of fellows educated by Jesuits who didn't join the DLP.'

Anna found herself warming to this oddly personable man. So much so that she was being drawn into a conversation about her least favourite subject: herself.

'It was more about raising political consciousness than indoctrination,' she said, thinking back to the Eureka League camps. 'But what I mostly learned was how to play table tennis.'

'Oh,' said Murphy. 'Will you teach me one day?'

'Senator . . .'

'Call me Lionel.'

'Lionel, would you mind if I set up my tape recorder?'

'Of course, of course.' Murphy sounded apologetic. 'You must be on a deadline.'

'Well, I do have to get back to Sydney tonight.'

'Go ahead and set up your machine,' he said. 'But I have something here for you. You'll want to read it before the interview.'

'Something . . . on the bombings?'

'On the Croats,' he explained. 'It's a document. I think you'll find it very interesting. I have a copy for you to take away. You can read it first, and then I'm happy to answer questions about it.'

Anna sat there bemused, until Murphy stood up. He touched her shoulder and she felt a jolt of electricity pass between them.

'I'll go and get it,' he said.

Tom Moriarty sat in the late-Sunday darkness, watching the house. His car was parked under a tree that offered some concealment in the poorly lit street. There were lights in the back of the house, but none on the front porch.

He held a Starlight Scope up to his eye. The whine of its machinery brought back memories of the blackest nights in Vietnam. The faint noise made the scope an imperfect tool for spies, but the targets were too far away to hear anything. Two visitors were still inside.

He unscrewed the lid of a miniature whisky and downed it, probing the bruise around his right eye. As the swelling subsided, the shiner had matured into an ugly black ring. For two days he'd worn dark glasses.

He tried to recall the woman whose boyfriend had king hit him. He was missing something there. His photographic memory was fogged by drunkenness. Her image was indistinct. Who was she? Why the sense of recognition? God forbid that she might be the wife of a colleague. Or a surveillance target . . . Could that be it? She had been Eurasian. A thought crossed his mind. Oh no! Junie Morosi? Could it have been her? He definitely had a thing for Junie, but then so did every man with a pulse.

A light came on at the front of the house. He sat up and grabbed the scope as the door opened. The whine began again as its motor powered up and then three glowing green faces appeared in the doorway. The middle one was Ivo Katich. The other two were younger; they were strangers to Moriarty. Katich was a big man, but one of the others was a barrel-chested giant, taller and broader than him. Moriarty was sorry now that he hadn't brought a camera.

The men embraced Katich before leaving him at the door and walking out through the front gate. Moriarty sunk down in his seat, but they turned away from his direction. He followed them with the night scope as they climbed into a car at the end of the street. As it pulled out he memorised the numberplate and then wrote it down.

When he turned back to the house the front door was closed, the porch light off. He unscrewed the lid from another miniature and settled back to wait.

Eventually, all the lights in the house went out. Moriarty sat for another hour in the car, topping up with miniatures from time to time. Then he got out, slinging a small satchel over his shoulder and checking both ends of the street with the night scope. Nothing.

He crossed the road and entered the front gate, stopping again to survey the yard through the scope. He crept around the side of the house and waited at another gate he encountered there. Soon he heard the dog sniffing around it. He took a plastic bag from the satchel, removed a bloody piece of steak and slid it under the gate. The dog yelped once, but curiosity quickly overwhelmed its instincts. He heard it sniff and paw at the meat before gulping it down.

Moriarty sat for a further ten minutes, and then stood and slid his hand over the gate to release the latch. The dog lay unconscious on the concrete path. He examined it through the scope. It was so still he wondered if he might have overdone the dose. He hoped not—he liked dogs.

After scoping the path to make sure there were no obstacles, he crept along the side of the house, stopping at the corner to check the backyard for any surprises. When he reached the back door he took the picks from his pocket, gently opened it and entered the house.

He stopped in the kitchen, listening to the hum of the fridge and the juddering second hand on the wall clock. Then came a sudden noise from within—a broken snore, so loud that it seemed to leave silence in its wake.

He reached into the satchel and felt the cold steel of the stubby revolver. He pulled it out; the weight of it was reassuring. It was an unauthorised weapon, but this whole operation was unauthorised.

He scoped the space ahead for obstacles and then crept into the corridor, feeling with his toes for loose floorboards. When the loud snore started up again, he took quick steps to the bedroom door and opened it. Ivo Katich's large green body was splayed out on the bed.

He put the scope in the satchel and moved fast to the bedside. Pointing the revolver at the man's head, he flicked on the closest lamp.

Katich's eyes flew open, blinking. 'What? What is . . .?'

'Stay completely still.'

'What the fuck!'

Katich struggled to sit up. Moriarty gave him a sharp hammer blow on the temple with the gun butt and he fell back on to the pillow.

'Don't move!'

Despite the blow, Katich regained his senses quickly.

'It's you? Tom! What the fuck you doing?' he roared.

'Shut up or I'll blow your brains out.' Moriarty watched the man go still as he focused on the weapon. 'Roll on to your stomach,' he ordered calmly. 'And put your hands behind your back.'

'You're making big mistake!' Katich shouted.

Moriarty's hand whipped out and gave him a second hammer blow on the head.

'*Ahhhh!*' he cried. 'Stop! I do it. I do it!'

Katich rolled over and put his hands behind his back. Working fast, Moriarty took a roll of gaffer tape and a knife from the satchel and bound the big man's wrists before standing back. 'Roll over so I can see you.'

Katich twisted back around and propped himself on the pillows. He was remarkably composed.

'Are you fucking crazy, Tom? What is it you want?'

'Who did the bombing?' Moriarty asked quietly.

'Go fuck your mother!'

Moriarty cracked him on the head again, harder this time.

'*Ahhh!* You bloody cunt!' Katich shouted.

'Answer my questions or this is going to get much worse.'

A thin line of blood trickled down Katich's forehead and into his eye. He turned his head, rubbed it into the pillow and looked back at Moriarty. 'Someone beats you,' he said. 'Now you beat me. What is this?'

Moriarty paused.

'Your eye,' Katich said.

'What?' Moriarty touched his hand to the swelling and realised what he meant. 'Oh, that was about a woman. Forget it.'

Katich regarded him slyly. 'Why you're not stuttering anymore?'

'It goes away when I'm ready to kill someone.'

'You don't have balls for that.'

Moriarty reached forward and pulled the bloody pillow out from under Katich. He wrapped it around the revolver and stood back, pointing the cumbersome thing at the man's head.

'Who did the bombing?' he asked again.

'Fuck you, cun—'

A muffled explosion, mid-expletive, then a cloud of feathers filled the air between the two men. The bloodstained pillow had blown apart. Katich stiffened on the bed; there was a black hole in the wall beside his head. His eyes widened and fear had replaced the anger in them. Smoke and the stench of burnt feathers irritated the nostrils of both men.

Moriarty dropped the pillow and sat close to Katich on the bed. He reached over and gently brushed stray hair from the man's eyes. Katich flinched and pulled away.

'Who did the bombing?' Moriarty asked, almost sadly.

'I don't know.'

'You're lying.' Moriarty suddenly perked up, cocking his head and smiling. 'How about this?' he suggested. 'How about we play some Croatian roulette?'

He cracked open the revolver and tipped the bullets out on to the sheet. 'Old Ustasha game, isn't it?' he asked, placing a single bullet back in and spinning the barrel. 'Get the boys together, bottle of *sliva*, some poor f-fucker who crossed himself the wrong way.'

Moriarty beamed a wild grin down at Katich.

'Come to think of it . . .' He pulled one of the miniatures from his coat pocket, twisted it open and downed it in one. 'That's better,' he said, putting the empty back in his pocket. 'Can't be leaving evidence all over the place, can we?'

There was no smugness in Katich's expression now.

'You're crazy, Tom.'

'That may be.' Moriarty gave him the stare. 'Off the r-reservation, anyway. Thing is, I've had it with you, Ivo. You've pushed it and pushed it, and now you've gone too far. B-blowing up civilians. You know what they say, mate? When the dog goes m-mad, you put him down.'

Moriarty rummaged in his pocket, pulled out another miniature, downed it and again pocketed the empty. He winked at Katich and tapped him on the forehead with the barrel.

'Who did the bombing?'

'You know I can't—'

Moriarty pulled the trigger.

CLICK.

'*Ahhhhh!*' Katich screamed.

'Oh, sh-shit.' Moriarty burst out laughing. 'I really didn't mean to do that. Hair t-trigger! I was going to give you another chance. That would've been so embarrassing.'

'You're drunk . . .'

'Not at all, just a bit tipsy.'

Moriarty unscrewed the cap from yet another miniature and took a long pull. Still holding the bottle, he pressed the gun hard into Katich's head. 'Let's try again,' he said. 'Who did the bombing?'

'Croatian Youth,' Katich answered quickly. 'Is a new group. Crazy men. I don't even know them.'

'You can do better than that.' Moriarty took a sip and tapped Katich's forehead again. 'Don't want to test this trigger again, do we? Who were those two blokes you had here tonight? That them?'

'First time they come here. I never see them before.'

'Come on, Ivo, mate. That's bullshit.'

'No bullshit. I've done nothing since Bosnia. Nothing. That was fucking disaster, Tom. Marin is still missing. You know that.'

Moriarty considered this. 'Marin. He volunteered, so I heard,' he reminded Katich. 'Anyway, he knew the r-risks.'

'Only God knows if he's capture now, maybe in prison in Belgrade.' Katich had real tears in his eyes; the big head lolled around in self-pity. 'Only God knows. Maybe they torture him. What do you know?'

'Nothing. Not a word. He's gone. It's down to you.'

'You're the same like them.'

'Not even remotely, mate.' Moriarty waved the bottle at him, clearly drunk now. 'They always have someone w-watching over their shoulder, some c-colonel or c-commissar. I'm here on my own r-r-recognisance, lone wolf or whatever. So don't fuck with me!'

He threw his head back, downed the rest of the bottle and dropped it clinking into the pocket with the others. He pulled the gun from Katich's head and pressed it against the man's left knee.

'Anyway, jolly good for you. You're talking at least, so we'll ch-change the st-stakes. Off the head; on to the knee.' Moriarty was slurring words. 'But you're still bullshitting me. So, one last ch-chance. Give me the names of those two blokes.'

'I told you I don't . . .'

Moriarty pulled the trigger.

CLICK.

'Fuck, fuck!' Katich cried.

'Oooo, lucky, lucky, luck*eee*.' Moriarty almost sang the words. 'Still walking. For now. So, one last chance. Who are those two blokes? Start with the big one.'

Ivo Katich's face was deathly pale, save for the line of blood running down his forehead. Beads of sweat stood out on his fore-head. He started talking.

'They're from out of town. The big one, that's Kavran. Blaz Kavran. He's from Canberra, but his network is Melbourne. The other is Matic. Simo. He's a Melbourne guy.'

'Better, that's better.'

'Maybe they did bombing, maybe not,' Katich went on. 'They are madmen and liars. From me, they want money, weapons. Want me to sing praises for them. I want nothing to do with them.'

'These cr-creeps don't do anything without your s-say so.'

'That's not true. Not anymore. Since Bosnia, the young ones have taken over.'

'I don't believe you.'

'Listen to me, Tom. Listen. Open drawer.' Katich gestured to the bedside table. 'Yes, that one. There's black book inside.'

Moriarty found the book. 'What about it?'

'Inside the first page. There's a number at the top. See it?'

Moriarty looked at the number.

'Ring that one number,' Katich said. 'You know him. He will tell you. Leave Katich alone. He will tell you.'

Moriarty stared at Katich and back at the book. Time to go. He knew the number very well.

5.

The lift doors started to open, then stopped halfway, shuddering with indecision. Then an arm pulled the inner safety doors open and attempted to prise the outer doors. With a terrible sigh they parted, revealing a dark-eyed, irritated-looking woman.

Anna Rosen had been on the road all day. After the Murphy interview her flight from Canberra had been delayed. She'd had nothing to eat but a stale ham roll and a bag of chicken chips. Her slim frame was weighed down on one side by a Nagra tape recorder and on the other by an overstuffed leather bag. Adjusting the burdens on her shoulders, she stepped through the still-quivering doors and into the late-evening gloom of the vinyl-tiled corridor, avoiding the worn patches that had tripped her up before. Maintenance was not high on the priority list of the cash-strapped broadcaster, and this floor, where the studios were located, resembled the lower decks of a decommissioned warship.

Anna didn't care. Fading glamour had its own appeal. After eighteen months she still hadn't come down from the high of being chosen as a trainee reporter. Only recently had her vague uneasiness—the sense of being an intruder in an exclusive club—begun to dissipate. Tonight she really felt she belonged here.

As she moved almost robotically through the maze of empty studios, her mind was preoccupied with the new information she'd picked up throughout this long Sunday. When Anna finally reached her office, she shut the door with a flick of her backside, and set down her tape recorder and bag.

Inside she was surrounded by ranks of battleship-grey filing cabinets and bookcases filled with reference and history books. On the floor around her desk were piles of specialist works, bearing the stamp of the Fisher Stack, at Sydney Uni, which would give a visitor the impression she was preparing a thesis on Balkan history. All of them were months overdue and somewhere on the overflowing desk was an increasingly desperate series of letters from the library demanding their return.

From the bottom drawer of one cabinet she pulled out a fat folder, opened it on the desk and took out her makings: a packet of ready-rolled tobacco, cigarette papers and a plastic bag of weed. She pulled out two papers, licked the side of one and stuck them together. Then she took a pinch of tobacco and a larger ball of the resinous grass, mulched the two piles together. She deftly rolled a thin joint, before licking the adhesive. She ripped a narrow strip from the Tally-Ho packet and made a filter from it, tamping it in.

Finally, flicking open her stainless-steel lighter, she fired up the joint. Seeds crackled as she drew deep and waited for the THC to hit her bloodstream, which it did quickly. She had figured out years ago, through trial and error, that working stoned—well, slightly stoned, at least—was not a hindrance to her concentration. Rather it enhanced it.

Now she unpacked the contents of the leather bag on to her desk: marked-up tapes in their boxes and notebooks and pens and a folder of news clippings, along with crumpled sticks of chewing gum and . . . Yes, yes, yes! A full packet of Maltesers. She put a small handful into her mouth and sucked on them gratefully as she took from the top drawer a thin square box marked: *The Ustasha Files— Edit Master 1.*

From the box she removed the large tape and fitted the spool on to the Tandberg editing machine on her desk. Next to her, on a metal bench on wheels, sat a second Tandberg, and on the workspace beside it she piled the boxes containing the new taped interviews from her trips to Melbourne and Canberra.

Swivelling back to the machine, Anna pulled out the edge of the tape on the edit master and threaded it in a pattern over the sprockets and heads and through to the empty spool on the other side.

She pulled the lever into play and, as the tape ran across the heads, she heard her own voice, recorded in a sound booth, coming loudly from the speaker:

'*Tonight on* Agenda *we ask: Is Australia home to an organised right-wing terrorist group known as the Ustasha?*'

She hit *Stop.*

'No doubt about it. As I will now prove to you, dear listeners . . .' Anna paused and laughed. 'Who are you speaking to, girl? Get a grip!' She laughed again. 'That's enough of you,' she told the joint as she ground it out in the ashtray.

Anna loved the simple craft of cut editing. For a person like her, with an impractical mind and few manual skills, it was a soothing discipline. The broadcaster's conservative enemies liked to refer to the 'basket weavers' in the backrooms of the ABC and she was happy enough with that metaphor. How could the bastards know that the work itself really was a form of therapy?

Anna sorted through the smaller boxed tapes until she found the one labelled *Lionel Murphy Sunday 17/9/72*, opened it and fitted the tape on to the second Tandberg, spooling through it until she found the shadow attorney-general's answer to the rhetorical question she had posed at the beginning of the documentary.

She cut out his answer from the interview and draped the long strand of tape that held it around her shoulders while she cut it into the master reel, securing the edits with adhesive tape.

'*There is ample evidence of well-organised terrorist activity for those who wish to act on it, but the government is sympathetic to this group, no matter what it does, because it is anti-communist. Yesterday in the centre of Sydney we saw the fourteenth bomb explosion in Australia by the Ustasha criminal movement. How many more are they going to get away with?*'

She knew her instincts were right. It was a powerful way to start. But now she needed the government response. She consulted her interview notes for the attorney-general, lined up the Ivor Greenwood tape and played the grab:

'*As to whether or not I still maintain that there is no Ustasha terrorist movement in Australia, I stated in July that intensive police investigations had revealed no credible evidence that such a terrorist organisation existed. As far as the incidents on Saturday are concerned, one must surely await the outcome of these police investigations before expressing any judgement.*'

Anna shook her head. It was still incredible to hear it. Two bombs explode on a Saturday morning in the heart of your biggest city and that was not 'credible evidence'? Surely no one was going to buy that line now. The attorney-general repeating it after such an outrage sounded at best deluded, at worst like he was covering something up.

She put together three sheets of A4 with two of carbon paper, rolled the bunched pages into the typewriter and began rewriting the script. As she did she shuttled back and forth through the new taped material, consulting her notes. She had to re-edit the beginning of the master tape, incorporating the news of yesterday's bombings and analysis of the implications.

The program's researcher had left tapes of actuality recorded by reporters in George Street and Anna cut together a sound montage from this material:

Policeman on loudhailer: *'There is a live bomb in the street! Everyone except emergency workers must move immediately behind the police barricades. I repeat: there is a live bomb in the street.'*

Witness 1: *'We'd ordered lunch when the bomb went off. There was a bar along the wall—it just disappeared in flames.'*

Witness 2: *'There was blood everywhere. People were lying around bleeding—it was terrible.'*

Witness 3: *'The proprietor came into the shop and walked over near the door where the bomb was. His legs just disappeared.'*

Witness 4: *'There was smoke everywhere—the ceiling had come down. I saw my brother lying there on the floor. He had lost his right leg—it was blown off at the knee.'*

As she'd expected, the raw eyewitness accounts of blood and smoke and flames, of severed limbs and prone bodies, immediately rendered the attorney-general's lame, legalistic rhetoric incomprehensible. Surely any listener would be asking: Where's his sense of outrage? Where's his angry determination to track down the terrorists, no matter who they turned out to be? Why this pig-headed determination to claim there is no evidence of a terror-ist organisation?

Anna turned to the document that had only come into her possession today. As she read it carefully, she began to regret that she had not had it before her interview with Attorney-General Greenwood because it completely undermined his repeated state-ments that 'intensive police investigations had revealed no credible evidence' of the existence of a Croatian Ustasha terrorist move-ment. The document was a memo from the Commonwealth Police Central Crime Intelligence Bureau sent to the attorney-general in July. It detailed more than fifty serious incidents in Australia over nine years, including bombings, murders and assassinations. The memo stated the belief that these violent incidents were planned and carried out by Ustasha-controlled organisations.

Anna began scripting quotes from the leaked memo into the top of the documentary. She had a long night ahead of her, but she felt a sense of elation.

Al Sharp felt a prod on his shoulder.

'Can you shift down the back, mate? You're in my way there.'

The irritated voice belonged to Nigel Daltrey, a small, thin man who moved around the dark, narrow van the three of them shared like a twitchy guinea pig in its burrow. Sharp felt oversized in here. He lifted his big arse off the bolted-down metal chair, stood and bent over.

'Sorry about that.'

'Don't be sorry—be gone.'

Sharp did a dance around Daltrey, trying to change places without hugging him. He winced at a twinge in his back, the old injury still playing up. He resolved to ignore the little man's insubordination.

He could've been a dickhead and pulled rank, but he needed to get on with these blokes. There weren't too many electronics specialists in the CIB and it looked like he was going to end up spending a lot of time with the pair of them in this cramped tin box on wheels.

'Over here, Mr Sharp,' said the other man, indicating a chair on his side of the van, in front of the bank of tape recorders. 'There's more room here while we're working.'

'Thanks, Bob.'

If Daltrey was like a guinea pig, Bob McCafferty was a bear moving with ease inside his cave. McCafferty was polite without being welcoming. These two odd creatures were used to occupying the same small space, but Sharp was an intruder. He'd only met them a few hours ago. Now they were under his orders and it didn't sit well with them.

Their task was to bug the upstairs room of the Hrvatska Restoran, which was straight across the road from where they were parked, and tap its phone. The room was the regular meeting place for the leaders of the two most radical Croatian groups and where they came together to plan joint actions. Sharp had brought that particular piece of intelligence to the investigation.

He watched Daltrey wire up a listening device to a transmitter and prepare the bank of batteries to charge it. The man worked with an agitated, obsessive intensity, twitching as he did so.

'Fuck,' he said. 'This shit's so old, it's falling apart.'

'Maybe they'll give us a proper budget for this op,' McCafferty said, turning to Sharp. 'We get some new equipment? What do you think, Mr Sharp?'

'Give me a list of what you need,' said Sharp. 'I'll see what I can do.'

Daltrey snorted. He'd heard shit like that before.

'I'll take two of these in with me, Bob. Christ knows where we'll put them. A bloody restaurant, never easy.'

'You'll find somewhere,' McCafferty replied in soft, measured tones. 'I'll give you that list, Mr Sharp.'

'Call me Al.'

'Yeah, right,' said Daltrey. 'We're all just mates.'

McCafferty stared daggers at his partner. 'Give it a break, Roger!'

Sharp looked up, confused for a moment until he recalled Nigel Daltrey's nickname. One of the smart-arse detectives had dubbed him 'Roger', after the lead singer of The Who, and it had stuck. An ironic jibe, no doubt, but Daltrey really did resemble the stuttering rock star.

Sharp knew that the troglodyte wing of the NSW coppers, especially the old-guard detectives, had a deep distrust of these technical bods. They hated all the other smarties too, including people like Sharp who might have been to uni or whatever, and so were completely up themselves—wankers and poofs, barely a rung up the ladder from the student trash they'd obviously mixed with.

The head of the Special Breaking Squad, Jim Kelly, had given Sharp pen portraits of the two men he'd be working with.

Daltrey: A bit of a genius, but a maddy who has issues with authority. ('He might give you a bit of trouble. Let me know if he does.')

McCafferty: A big kid who reads comic books and technical magazines, and is most likely a poofter. ('He's good at his job, though, I'll say that for Bob McCafferty. The best bugger in the force.')

Kelly had grinned at his own wit.

Sharp put such thoughts aside and returned to practical matters. The two buggers wore Post Master General uniforms to avert suspicion and he could see that they had already erected a PMG tent around the junction box. It was close to the entrance to the restaurant.

'How hard is the phone going to be?' he asked McCafferty, whose job it was to tap the line.

'I think I've got the pairs for that number,' McCafferty replied. 'But it would help if you could find the phone when you go in there and talk on the line, just so's I know for sure.'

Sharp knew the drill. McCafferty had attached alligator clips to the two wires he believed serviced the phone; when Sharp said a few words on that line, McCafferty would listen through a set of headphones to confirm he had the right ones. Then he'd connect that pair of wires to a transmitter, which would send the signal back to the tape recorder in the van, and Bob's your uncle. The trick was to find a place nearby to park the van for long periods, concealed from the targets.

'I can do that,' said Sharp.

Daltrey suddenly looked up from his fiddly work. 'Fuckin' Manly, eh! Didn't deserve to win. That fuckin' Keith Page is a deadset crook. We should be tapping *his* phone.'

McCafferty groaned. 'Come off it, Roger, you can't blame the ref.'

'Two fuckin' Easts tries disallowed. Manly awarded two dodgy tries. Do the maths. You don't have to be Hercule-fuckin'-Poirot. The fix was in.' Daltrey turned to Sharp. 'What do you reckon, mate? We get a warrant to do Page's phone?'

Sharp smiled, pleased to be included. 'If you can establish a link between Keith Page and the bombings we might be able to swing it without a warrant.'

Daltrey winked at him. 'Like this job, eh?'

'Yup,' said Sharp. 'Off the books.'

'Well, mate.' Daltrey smacked both hands on the metal

workbench. 'It's fuckin' obvious, isn't it? The bombings were a diversion. Fixing the grand final—that was the main game.'

Sharp nodded. 'You might be on to something, Roger. You just might be.'

When the devices were ready Sharp and Daltrey went around to the back of the restaurant, using a small torch to light their way between the ranks of over-full garbage bins in the rear lane. When the torch beam picked out rats gnawing through rubbish bags, the rodents swiftly flitted away.

Daltrey scampered up a short set of stairs and crouched before the back service door. Lock-picking was another of his talents and he made short work of this one. They were inside in moments, quietly closing the door behind them.

'No alarm,' Daltrey whispered. 'Your bloke was right about that.'

Sharp had a mental map of the layout based on the briefing he'd received from his informant. They went through the kitchen, out a door, around a long counter and into the main dining room. It was full of tables, with upturned chairs on top of them. They moved carefully through this obstacle course to the staircase at the side of the room.

At the top of the stairs were several doors. The one on the left Sharp knew to be a storage room. He opened the door on the right and they went into a smaller dining room with a central table. It was flanked on one side by a pinball machine and on the other by a television set.

'A fuckin' pinny—that's all we need.' Daltrey gave up any pretence of whispering. 'That'll be a fuckin' nightmare if anyone's playing during the meetings.'

'Yeah,' Sharp said. 'I didn't know about that. Can we disable it somehow?'

'How paranoid are these blokes?'

'They'll be pretty nervous if they're the ones who ordered the bombings.'

'Up to you, then. Might scare the horses, though.'

Sharp pondered the problem before asking, 'Can you do it so it looks like some piece of equipment just gave up, like every piece of electronics I've ever bought?'

'Let's have a look.'

Daltrey opened up the back of the machine and spent some time working on its innards before reappearing with a smile.

'I reckon that'll do it. Try turning it on.'

Sharp found the wall socket and pushed the plug in. Nothing happened.

'Dead as a dodo,' he said.

'Righto,' said Daltrey. 'It'll take a while to repair that. I've been thinking about where to put the bugs.' He tapped the side of the pinball machine. 'Can't put one in this because someone's gonna have to open it up to repair it. They've got fluorescent lights in the ceiling, so there's nothing hanging down I could rig up on. There's no pictures or anything on the walls to hide a bug. It'd be pretty bloody obvious if I drilled a hole anywhere.'

'So, what are you thinking?'

'I'm thinking the TV set. But, of course, we'll be fucked if they turn it on as a countermeasure. Wanna take the risk?'

Sharp thought about it for a moment. 'Do we have any choice?'

'Nup.'

'Okay, you're the expert.'

'Buggers can't be choosers.'

'Okay. Get going. I'm going back downstairs to find the phone for McCafferty.'

Sharp located the phone behind the counter on the ground floor. He put the receiver to his ear and listened. Heard static and electronic scraping sounds. He spoke softly: 'One two, one two, are you reading me, Bob?'

More static. More scraping. Was he sending a signal? He repeated his first question, then started counting slowly. He reached twenty-four.

'You can stop now.' McCafferty's voice was in his ear. 'I've got you on my handset. The wires are tapped. We're ready to go. I'm gonna turn the transmitter on and close this thing up. How's it going upstairs?'

Sharp gave him a quick account.

'Well, Roger knows what he's doing. If he's gone for the TV, it must be the only option.'

'Right.'

'I'll see you back at the van.'

The whole operation took thirty minutes. Both the phone and the room were now live. McCafferty had found a place for the van beside an abandoned warehouse nearby, concealed behind a gate and a fence.

'This should be right for a while,' he said. 'We'll lock up and leave her here tonight. So, back on shift tomorrow. What time?'

'The problem is this meeting Jim Kelly's called for 9 am,' Sharp said. 'He wants the whole team there, including us. I reckon the owner'll be here around nine to prep the restaurant . . . We want his phone calls, obviously, in case someone rings to set up a meeting.'

'Well, the recorders are voice-activated. How about we start at 11 am? Roger and I will rotate shifts in the van, but we'll need that translator, right?'

Sharp nodded. 'That's all set to go.'

'We could be here for a long time,' Daltrey said. 'Hope he plays cards.'

'It's a woman, Roger,' Sharp said.

'Never put a woman on a surveillance op,' Daltrey said. 'Too distracting.'

'No choice, I'm afraid,' Sharp consoled him. 'But I don't want you two falling out over a woman.'

'Oh, Bob won't be bothered.' Daltrey smirked. 'He don't care for 'em.'

'Shut it,' McCafferty snapped.

'Foreigners, I meant.'

'Pull your head in.'

Sharp cut them off. 'All right, let's call it quits for tonight. Good job. Now we wait.'

6.

A persistent ringing woke Anna Rosen on Monday morning. She rolled off the office couch on to her knees and picked up the receiver.

'At the third stroke it will be 7.45 precisely. *Beep, beep, beep*.'

She yawned, lay back down again and closed her eyes, trying to reconnect with the lingering images of her dream.

Marin Katich again. He was still there, deep in her subconscious. She didn't need an analyst to tell her that she hadn't shaken him off. But this dream had been the strangest yet. Marin had worn a black uniform as he walked across a field through long grass. And there had been something in his hand. A gun? A knife? The image had slipped away before she could recall the detail—something definitely bad there.

She rubbed her face hard. The image had left her disturbed because it was so anachronistic. Marin had never worn the black uniform. That was his father, Ivo, the murderous old Nazi, and it had been way back in 1942.

Thoughts of Marin Katich raised the same questions she'd been asking herself for two years. Why had he disappeared? Where the hell was he? She had strong suspicions. If they were right, he was most likely dead. Perhaps his ghost was haunting her dreams.

Anna had decided early on not to tell her boss that she had a personal motive behind her interest in the Ustasha. Even before her indiscretion with him, she'd known Peter McHugh well enough to know he'd distrust her for it and might even pull her off the story.

She looked over at her desk. The edit master was still there in its box. No gremlins or spies had run off with it in the night. At 4 am she had gone to the trouble of making a copy and had locked it away in a filing cabinet just in case. She wasn't paranoid—no, ASIO really could be utterly ruthless. Anna and her whole family had ample evidence of that. They'd been targets of the security agencies her entire life, and ASIO came out of her story very badly.

She held the box in her lap, her painstakingly gathered evidence. How harmless it looked—just a cardboard container holding a tape full of recorded words. Maybe Pandora had had the same thought.

Sunken-eyed and bedraggled, Anna made her way back through the lower corridors. Shoals of dayshift workers were coming the other way. Some of them glanced at the dark apparition weaving through them like the last survivor of a rock concert.

As daylight glimmered at the end of the final corridor, Anna put on her sunglasses. The morning sun lit her up like a spotlight as she stepped outside and met the unflappable old guard at the door to the car park.

'Reginald.'

'Up all night, love?'

'Pretty much. Going for coffee. Want one?'

'I'd kill for one, love.'

'No need for that,' she said, flicking him a peace sign.

He had probably killed a few people in his time, old Reg. He was a veteran, like most of the guards and front-desk boys, all of them recruited by the same tough old bastard, a retired sergeant major who ran the Commission's security. Reg once gave her the drum on his war in the minimalist way of real veterans: *New Guinea. Lost some good mates. Fucking nightmare.*

She liked him.

The car park sat above Darlinghurst, surrounded by a high chain-link fence. If the broadcaster were a hilltop fortress, these would be its ramparts.

Anna descended a steep stairway to the lane below, where she stepped warily into a carpet of syringes. The smack freaks had scuttled off to dark places before the sun caught them out in the open. Now the bright light picked up swirls of red in the discarded fits, the counter flow of their life's blood sucked back into the hypodermics.

In her early days as a trainee Anna used to come in by cab at 5 am for the morning shift, lounging in the back seat and marvelling at her unfamiliar entitlement to a taxi docket. The hookers had still been around at that hour, shivering in the pre-dawn chill beneath the stone steps down to William Street. They'd stir listlessly at the cab's arrival, hoping it might deliver them one final john. Simultaneously relieved and disappointed, they'd peer at her through pinned eyes and veils of smoke, then they'd cast their gazes downwards again, tapping ash into empty Tango cans. One might offer a desultory greeting: 'G'day, love. Spare us ten bucks?'

Anna always smiled and shook her head, climbing the stairs between them, as if part of the sisterhood. Their miniskirts were hiked over bruised legs, mascara melted on their anaemic faces, and she clocked their blank looks, their purple lips and their shuttered hearts. She hated that this life had fucked them up so badly.

This morning, as she stepped over the evidence of last night's misdeeds, Anna rehearsed, as she always did, the obvious questions. Who fed their habits? Where were the cops? The corrupt bastards were all on the take—most of them, anyway. So many stories, so little time.

She walked up the laneway to the junction of William Street and Darlinghurst Road, gateway to the closed-down carnival of Kings Cross. Exposed to daylight, the Cross had a squalid beauty. The vast wall of neon, so diverting at night, now revealed as nothing more than vacuum tubes and scaffolding, tacked on to conceal the crumbling buildings. The upper floors were left to peel and rot above rusty awnings that shaded stinking chicken shops and milk bars and padlocked strip joints. A few US servicemen still lurched about these establishments, looking for sustenance at the butt end of their shore leave. Morning traffic rolled slowly through the newly washed streets. Kerb-crawling cabs scooped up the remnants of the night.

Anna made her way through back lanes to the Piccolo on Roslyn Street, where Vittorio gave her a nod from behind the ancient Gaggia.

'*Ciao*, Anna.' He produced an espresso in a little white cup. '*Se non fossi cosi snella saresti una bella ragazza.*'

'Too early, Vittorio. I need subtitles.'

'If you weren't so skinny you'd be beautiful.'

'*Una bella rag-azza?*'

'*Si, buono.*'

'*Mille grazie*, I guess.'

'*Prego*. But I need to feed you up.'

'An omelette, a small orange juice, and another one of these in a moment,' she said, holding up the coffee.

'Go sit. I make you breakfast.'

There was a copy of the *Herald* on the bar. Anna unfolded

the paper and scanned the front page: *'Yugoslavia to Protest on Bombings.'*

This was about Belgrade's anger that so little had been done to stop Ustasha extremists. Ambassador Vidovic would meet senior government ministers today and deliver that message to his host country.

Anna knew Vidovic well. He was a useful contact. The Yugoslavs ran their own network of agents and kept detailed intelligence files. Not exactly untainted information, but their knowledge of the Croat extremists was sophisticated. They considered them an existential threat.

The *Herald* confirmed that detectives on the bombing investigation were convinced it was the work of right-wing Croats. Anna sipped the espresso. Well, that was blindingly obvious, unless you were the prime minister or the attorney-general. Sure enough, further down, she found the stock denials from Ivor Greenwood, the same old lines he had peddled in his interview with her: there was no evidence of a Croat terrorist organisation; the police had investigated every allegation of terrorist training camps and found no evidence of those either; if Labor had additional information they should just pass it on to the police . . .

Anna was relieved. The paper had nothing new. Nothing that undermined her story and none of the fresh evidence she would air tonight.

She flicked through to the inside coverage: *'Croat Leaders Deny Bomb Plot.'* Again, the standard reaction from community leaders: if Croats were responsible for Saturday's blasts, they could only be 'sick individuals'.

'Jesus-fucking-Christ,' she muttered, shaking the paper so angrily that she spilt coffee on it. If you included the indoctrination of children in special schools, the widespread fundraising for

Ustasha operations in the community, the secret training camps, the bomb-making classes, the men recruited here to join armed guerrilla incursions inside Yugoslavia and the covert backing of Ustasha priests in the Catholic Church, that was one hell of a lot of sick individuals.

Then she discovered something she had missed. While she was travelling between Melbourne and Canberra, four hundred marchers had taken to the streets in Sydney for 'Captive Nations Week'. Reading the account of it, Anna let out another cry of outrage.

Vittorio arrived with her breakfast. 'What is it?' he asked, placing the orange juice and the steaming omelette on her table and handing her the cutlery. 'Nothing to make you lose your appetite?'

'No, no, I'm starving. This looks great.' She smiled at him and pointed to the paper. 'It's a story about the Town Hall bombs. Two federal ministers are saying the whole thing's a communist plot, that's all.'

'That's what they do, Anna.' Vittorio leaned in, *sotto voce*, a Renaissance conspirator. 'Remember the Reichstag fire? That was a Jewish plot, right? Nothing changes.'

'If you leave out the Holocaust.'

'That's why we got to stop the Nazis before they get going.'

'Good point,' she conceded.

Vittorio raised a theatrical eyebrow to confirm the great significance of his comment and returned to the bar to serve a new customer. Anna drained her orange juice and started in on the omelette. Vittorio had never let her down and today was no exception. She felt her strength returning as she ate, enough to go back to the newspaper article.

Accompanying the story was a picture of the marchers' spokesman, the minister for Social Services, William 'Billy' Wentworth.

Anna snorted. True to form, the crazy old bastard had emerged as the leading proponent of the conspiracy theory on the bombings: simply blame the evil communists, Yugoslav *agent provocateurs* who'd bombed their own country's travel offices to blacken the name of the poor benighted Croats.

'We recall that the communist terror had its origins in individual acts of civil violence,' Wentworth had told the crowd. Anna effortlessly conjured up his maniacal, lisping delivery. 'There is likely to be a parallel here with the Australia First Movement in the 1940s. That was a communist plot, but was presented as a right-wing group.'

Then there was fellow marcher Dr Malcolm MacKay, minister for the Navy and another senior member of the government peddling the same conspiracy theory. MacKay claimed that people were 'sitting ducks' for the communists. By 'people' he meant good anti-communist Croats.

'I am far from convinced,' MacKay opined, 'that the causes are solely or mainly on the area most obvious of blame.' He demanded the police turn their investigation in the direction of the communists.

Anna sighed. Captive Nations Week had once again flushed out the lunatic fringe. She was all for demonstrating solidarity with those people trapped behind the Iron Curtain. Even she, the daughter of a leading communist, could sympathise with that.

Her father had led the push inside the Party to reject Moscow's leadership after the Soviet tanks rolled into Budapest way back in 1956. It wasn't until new squadrons of tanks rolled into Czechoslovakia to crush the Prague Spring in 1968 that Frank Rosen won that argument. It was one outrage too many, and most of the comrades finally sided with Frank. The Party severed its ties with Moscow, but it was irretrievably split as a result.

Anna despised the pro-Soviet nutters who'd torn the Party apart as much as she hated the right-wing nutters who'd hijacked Captive Nations Week. There were fascists at either end of the spectrum. But this was too much!

She threw the paper down. Less than twenty-four hours after the worst terrorist attack in the city's history, and despite the irrefutable logic of who was responsible for it, the hard right was already looking into the wrong end of the telescope.

Anna was still fuming when Vittorio returned with her second espresso. She asked him for another coffee in a paper cup for Reg. Time to get back and knock this nonsense on the head once and for all.

Detective Sergeant Jim Kelly, the head of the Special Breaking Squad, was a wily old coot. That was Al Sharp's assessment of the man running the investigation into the Sydney bombings. Kelly was tall with a long, lugubrious face, like Chips Rafferty. He looked as if the sun had burned all the fat off him, like he was made out of wood and leather.

Sharp had shaved and climbed back into the rumpled suit he'd worn on the surveillance op earlier that morning. He still felt shabby when he knocked on Kelly's door to give him a quick briefing before the meeting at CIB Headquarters.

'Morning, boss.'

Kelly looked up from the pile of reports on his desk. He wore a crisp white shirt with braces, metal sleeve garters and a two-tone tie with a silver clip. His hair was slicked back. Sharp caught whiffs of Brylcreem and Old Spice.

'Nothing here from you, Mr Sharp,' said Kelly.

'We finished at 3 am. I thought it best to brief you personally.'

'Convenient, you mean?'

'Expedient, I'd say.'

Kelly produced a thin smile. 'At risk of being a smart-arse?' When Sharp didn't respond Kelly continued: 'So, brief me.'

Sharp explained that the restaurant was now live for surveillance, with a listening device in place and a tap on its only phone.

'How'd you go with the two eggheads?' Kelly asked.

'They're pros,' Sharp said. 'As good as I've worked with. But their equipment's old. If we're going to be doing more of this, someone needs to spend some money fast to update their gear.'

'They put you up to this?' Kelly stared at him for a moment, considering the request. 'Very well,' he said at last. 'Get me a budget in writing as soon as possible. It'll be approved. The top brass is ready to throw everything at this.'

Kelly stood up and grabbed a well-pressed grey jacket from a hanger on the back of his door. On its hook he left the black pork-pie hat with its colourful feather. Hanging below it, Sharp could now see, was an empty shoulder holster. He assumed the revolver was locked away somewhere in the office.

Kelly shrugged into the jacket and turned to Sharp. 'I'd like you to join me at the briefing and meet the whole squad. How soon can you organise your own briefing for the detectives?'

'On the Croats?'

'Obviously.' Kelly looked at him as if he were an idiot.

'Sorry,' said Sharp. 'I thought you might have been talking about the surveillance op, but I imagine that'll be on a need-to-know basis.'

'Why?'

'We didn't have a warrant.'

Kelly flashed a sly smile. 'Don't you worry about that, Al . . . What I want you to do is to brief the detectives on the targets, the main suspects and their organisational links.'

'I've asked for a projector. I'll be ready as soon as it arrives.'

'Good,' said Kelly, pleased. 'Make that a priority. Let's go—they're waiting.'

The hubbub from the squad room went instantly quiet the moment Jim Kelly's wide shoulders cleared the doorway. Several dozen men were positioned around the room, sitting on chairs and tables, or standing with tea mugs and cigarettes in each hand. Smoke hung in the air.

Typewriters, telephones and notebooks littered the tables, along with ashtrays, dirty mugs and takeaway-food wrappers. A man with a napkin tucked into his collar was munching on a Chiko Roll. In the open space in front of the desks large noticeboards were pinned with photographs of the bombsites and charred parts of the devices. Enlarged street maps indicated the targets and the distances between them. Mugshots of suspects, some of whom Sharp recognised, were also stuck up in neat rows.

He scrutinised the front ranks of the Special Breaking Squad and implacable faces stared back at him. They wore the habitual expressions of detectives: uncompromising and cynical, or else blank and unreadable. He sniffed at the air. The collective odour was not sweet, like Kelly's Old Spice—it was something chemical that leeched from their pores, the hormonal stench of latent violence. They'd been recruited from the toughest and best investigators in the homicide and armed hold-up squads. Some of the younger ones had been brought over from 21 Division, the training ground for hard men.

At the back of the room, separate from the detectives, he saw his team from the Electronics Unit, Daltrey and McCafferty. They looked tired and pissed off, but neither of them had the intimidating aura of the detectives. Sharp caught Bob McCafferty's eye and nodded to him, receiving only the smallest jerk of the head in response. Around them was a small collection of other men who, either by their manner of dress, their hairstyle or their demeanour, faintly radiated eccentricity. These, Sharp reasoned, were perhaps from forensics.

Jim Kelly took up a central place in front of the noticeboards and addressed the room in a booming voice.

'On Saturday morning, some cunt walked right into our patch, waltzed down George Street with two huge fucking bombs and set them off without any regard for human life,' he roared with a real anger. 'It's a miracle no one was killed. There's a ballet school above one of the targets. It's a miracle none of those little girls was blown apart. Any of you have daughters?'

A few of the men mumbled assent.

'When this murderous cunt blasted those people and those buildings, he also blew a huge hole in our credibility. We didn't see it coming. We don't know who did it. The lunatic is still at large. If we don't catch him, he could do it again tomorrow. As far as the public is concerned, and as far as the press is concerned, we were caught with our pants around our ankles, our dicks in our hand and our thumb in our mouths. Does anyone disagree with that?'

Kelly stared around the room belligerently. No one said a word.

'I didn't think so . . .'

He picked up the cudgels again, effortlessly shifting into the blistering anger of a coach whose team has let him down badly.

'We are all in fucking shame. All of us. And we will be in fucking shame until we catch this cunt. That's why you're all here now. You're supposed to be the best of the best in whatever squads you belong to. From now on, until we lock these bastards away, you are all members of the Special Breaking Squad. Whatever else you've been working on, drop it! Put it aside or hand it over to someone else, because this is your only job from now on. We will find this cunt and we will break him, and we will find the cunts who ordered this cunt to do it and we'll break them too, and then we're going to break the cunts who donated money to run their murderous fucking organisations and we're going to break those organisations. They have no right to bring their evil to our country. No fucking right. It's un-Australian! Any questions?'

One of the younger detectives spoke up. 'We're assuming this is political, are we? All other motives ruled out?'

Kelly peered down at him, not unkindly. 'I'm not ruling anything out, son. If you come to me with evidence of another motive, I'll take it seriously. But this fits a pattern. There've been sixteen politically motivated bombings against Yugoslavian government targets in the past few years. That's got to be our starting point. I'll have more to say about that shortly.'

Now one of the front rankers piped up. Sharp recognised him from press coverage of his antics as Bill Lonergan, a notorious homicide detective.

'I've dealt with some of these Yugos before,' said Lonergan. 'They're hard nuts. Fucken tribes that stick together. Never come across a reliable informer among 'em. You accuse 'em of something, they act like they don't understand the language, or they say some other wog in a different tribe done it.'

'Well, Bill, first things first. It's obvious that no one will talk to you at all if you call them wogs.'

'Wog's a wog, isn't it?' Lonergan called back insolently. 'Like a spade's a spade.'

That drew a few laughs from the front rank until Kelly cut them off. 'Carry on like that, Bill, and you'll be out of this squad on your ear. Want a neutral term? Call them cunts!'

That brought more laughter, and even Sharp found himself chuckling.

'On your other point: it's true, they are hard nuts to crack, so we have our own operating instructions, right from the top. Not to be repeated outside this room. From the commissioner himself, the instruction is to do Whatever It Takes. We are going to get these cunts under the Whatever It Takes rule.'

Sharp stared at Kelly. A chill went through him. What the hell was he talking about?

Lonergan, who seemed to be the unofficial spokesman for the older detectives, piped up again. 'Short of murder, right?' he cried out. 'Some of us are paid to investigate those.'

Kelly reined him in again. 'Yes, Bill, short of murder. And short of fitting up some poor bastard . . . You, of all people, know what I'm talking about.' He stared pointedly at Lonergan, whose reputation in that regard was legendary. 'The last thing I want is to turn some dumb migrant into a patsy, like the bloke they pinned for Kennedy.'

'Oswald!' someone called out.

'That's right,' said Kelly. 'So what do I mean by Whatever It Takes?'

Sharp leaned forward. His future in the squad now hung on Kelly's answer to his own rhetorical question.

'I mean that we will not wait for warrants before questioning a suspect. I mean that with these hard cases the normal rules of engagement do not apply. We need to rattle their fucking cages. On my orders we will pick people off the street or take them out of their homes, and we will interrogate them under my rules. We will tap their phones and we will bug their homes and their meeting places, and we won't wait for warrants to do it. Our authority to do this comes from the commissioner and, beyond him, from the minister.

You should know that surveillance is already under way—operations began last night.'

Sharp caught his breath. That was *his* operation or, more precisely, *his* unauthorised operation—the one he thought was meant to be top secret.

'We're not alone in this investigation,' Kelly continued. 'Mr Sharp, will you come forward?'

He beckoned and, with no option, Sharp walked over and stood next to him, facing the whole squad, focusing his eyes on a point high at the back of the room.

'Al Sharp has been seconded to the Breaking Squad from the Commonwealth Police—'

An audible groan came from the front rank.

'He's their leading expert on Croatian terrorists and I've asked him to give you all a briefing later today on the organisations, their links to criminal violence and the individuals who give the orders.'

Bill Lonergan could not restrain himself. 'You're fucken kidding,' he called out. 'We'll be doing Whatever It Takes and the Feds will be here watching us from the inside? I don't know about the rest of you blokes, but I haven't got a suicide wish.'

'As always, Bill, I can rely on you to be the naysayer.' Kelly addressed the detective with undisguised condescension. 'So let me put your mind at rest. Yesterday Mr Sharp came to me with information about a key premises where leaders from the most suspect Croat organisations conduct regular secret meetings. On my authorisation, he led a bugging op last night. It was our first action under the Whatever It Takes rule. So, Bill, Mr Sharp here is not an outsider in this squad. He's well and truly one of us.'

Sharp looked down at Lonergan and met an expression of undisguised contempt. He glanced at the head of the Special Breaking

Squad, who beamed back at him. All's well with the world, Kelly seemed to imply.

Sharp was left to reflect on the prophetic accuracy of his initial assessment. Jim Kelly was a wily old coot, that was for sure. And now he had Sharp by the short and curlies.

Anna Rosen raced back from the Cross to Forbes Street, careful not to spill Reg's coffee. The commissionaire took the paper cup gratefully, holding it in two hands as if the receptacle itself was designed to warm him.

'Bewdy,' he said. 'Nuthin' better. This from the eye-tie?'

Anna narrowed her eyes. '*Si, Regiano*,' she said. '*Uno espresso Italiano*.'

'All right, love. No need to go all continental.'

'*Eye-ties*, Reg? Really?'

'It's what we called 'em in the desert war. They were the enemy.'

'And now they make the best coffee.'

'Can't argue with that, love.'

Anna left the old soldier contemplating national migration policy and made her way back to her office. The plan was to meet Peter McHugh at 9 am to review the final cut of her program. She hadn't seen him since she'd left his apartment on Saturday morning and she wasn't looking forward to it. She had put the whole messy business out of her head while she had been engrossed in the edit, but it came back to her now and made her tense about the meeting.

As head of Talks, McHugh had commissioned the Ustasha project and mentored her through the two months of investigation. He was a risk-taker, one of the few editors who would even consider commissioning an untried reporter to do a major investigation.

His decision to pull the program forward for broadcast tonight had compounded the risk.

Perhaps it had all been about getting into her pants, but Anna also knew that McHugh was prepared to back obsessive pursuits when their goals lined up with his own political philosophy. He seemed impressed with the body of evidence Anna had assembled to show that Croatian extremists had thrived for decades under the secret protection of ASIO. McHugh had long believed the organisation was an illicit branch of conservative politics.

Anna looked up at the wall clock in the common room. 9.20. Peter McHugh was late. She recalled his comment about the charming Murphy. *I know he'll like you.* You know what we call that, Peter? Pots and black kettles come to mind.

'Anna!' A boisterous call broke her reverie. 'How did you go?'

She looked up to see McHugh bounce into the room like an excited labrador. She was surprised to find she was pleased to see him; the tension dissipated.

'Very well, especially with Murphy,' she said. 'But I am a bit concerned about that.'

'How so?'

'He gave me a document which completely undermines the attorney-general. It makes Greenwood look like a liar or a fool, or both. The question is, can I use it?'

'What's the document?'

'It's a memo to Greenwood from the Commonwealth Police Bureau of Criminal Intelligence. It's dated July last year and details more than fifty serious incidents in the last ten years—bombings, murders and assassinations. The BCI concludes that all of them were planned and carried out by Ustasha-controlled organisations.'

'Well, you have to use it.'

'This has come from the Labor Party.'

'It could also have come from your police sources.'

'But it didn't.'

'So what, then? You left it out?'

'No, Peter, I put it in. But I feel like I've been used.'

'Get used to it, Anna. He'll only give it to someone else if you don't run it,' said McHugh, and then he grinned. 'I told you he'd like you.'

'I'm not too comfortable you keep saying that,' she snapped back.

'You're a sexy girl, get used to it . . .'

'Stop calling me a girl or we're really going to have a problem.'

McHugh put up both hands, a gesture of surrender. 'Is this about Friday night?'

'Of course it is, you idiot.'

'I didn't mean anything by it—'

'Then stop talking about me like I've become an in-joke.'

'You mean Murphy?'

'You make me sound like a whore to be passed around middle-aged men!'

'For Christ's sake, Anna, that's the last thing I meant!'

'I've told you what I think. Let's forget about it.'

'I think we need to talk.'

'No, we don't. We really don't. Let's go listen to the edit.'

Anna watched him walk off. He was offended. Well, he'd get over it soon enough. There were plenty of women who seemed to hang on his every word, though not so many of them close to his own age. Perhaps they knew where his predilections lay.

She felt a wave of sadness again. At the core of it was this deep, unfathomably deep, sense that she had betrayed something—the invisible something with the invisible man.

But there was sadness too for what she knew was going to be a lost friendship with McHugh. She should never have fucked him. And she knew she'd gone too far in what she'd said just now and probably screwed up her working relationship with him as well, but it had had to be said.

That thought bothered her because she had plenty of reasons to be grateful to McHugh. He had helped her out of the doldrums after two excruciating years.

7.

Nineteen-seventy was the worst year of her life. That year could have broken Anna Rosen. She sometimes thought it very nearly did.

It had been her final year at university. Alongside her extra-curricular work for the anti-war movement and the many hours she devoted to editing *The Tribe*, she was working on her honours thesis—an analysis of the betrayal of the Vietnamese independence movement by the imperial powers after World War II. 'Fucking Churchill,' she'd rail at anyone who would listen. 'He rearmed the surrendered Japanese troops and used them to fight off Ho Chi Minh's independence forces until the French arrived to reclaim their colony. He should have been tried as a war criminal!'

She was dealing well with these competing demands, and it all would have been fine had she not managed to fall in love at the same time with a young man of Croatian heritage called Marin Katich. Her housemate Pierre Villiers, who regarded Marin as a right-wing thug, called it the 'most counterintuitive love affair in human histowy'.

But how could Pierre ever understand what had happened, what unfathomable alchemy of chemistry and fate had come together that day when Marin stormed into the office of *The Tribe* demanding to see the editor? There was an irony to this too, since it was Pierre, as Anna's deputy editor, who had sent an insulting note rejecting the article submitted by one M. A. Katich. Marin's piece was a *cri de coeur* denouncing the anti-war movement's open worship of 'Uncle' Ho Chi Minh. Marin had detailed Uncle Ho's purges of party enemies; his suppression of political opposition; of religion; of landowning peasants and small-business people, as a consequence of which hundreds of thousands had fled south to escape his communist regime.

'So you're the editor against free speech?'

Those had been Marin's first words when she looked up to see an imposing figure looming over her desk, He was tall, straight-backed and well made, with the bearing of an athlete.

'Sit down if you've got something to say to me,' she said, refusing to be intimidated.

He did so meekly enough, and she caught something in his green eyes, amusement perhaps? Certainly not the rancour or the outrage she would normally associate with an ideological enemy. She admitted she had not read his article, although she recalled that Pierre had mentioned it in disparaging terms. And so began a debate between the editor and the author that went on for hours, thrust, parry and feint, but without anger. They were like a pair of fencers who found themselves entranced at the contest, unwilling to end it.

Against her own preconceived judgements, Anna was warming to the young man's brain. Marin was a contrarian, a quality she had long admired in others. His central argument was against communist totalitarianism, and that strand, at least, she had sympathy with. At some point she rolled a joint, and as they got stoned the debate unravelled. Of course she would publish his article. She might not agree with a word of it, but he was entitled to make his case. They found themselves laughing together, both recognising that the spark of attraction was mutual.

And so it began, against all odds.

For his part Pierre tried hard to persuade her to end it.

'His father is a wabid anti-communist,' he said reasonably. 'He's a sworn enemy of Tito. And his son's no better,' he went on, less reasonably. 'Your own father's their pwoberbial wed under the bed. What could possibly go wong?"

As a rational thinker and a dialectical materialist, Pierre, Anna knew, had a tin ear for the poetry of romantic love. But he was proven right about one thing. It did all go terribly wrong.

Anna was not much prone to superstition, but had she been so she would have marked 18 September 1970 as her own Black Friday. That was the day of the second Vietnam Moratorium march in Sydney, a far more violent event than its predecessor, and by the end of it Anna lay in a coma, wired up to a life-support system in St Vincent's Hospital.

On the other side of the world on that fateful day, her idol, the psychedelic rocker Jimi Hendrix, died in London of a drug overdose. And on that very same day her lover Marin Katich had vanished, without a word and without a trace, into thin air.

It was the strangest day in her brief life. All her subsequent efforts at detective work would prove fruitless, not least because Marin's father refused all communications—refused, even, to acknowledge her existence. All she had been able to piece together from that day was that she had been found unconscious in a lane in the city centre in the aftermath of the march. It was believed that she had been beaten over the head with a police billy club. Some tried to tell her, Pierre among them, that it was surely Marin who had attacked her and then run away in shame. Anna knew that this was not true, but Marin's disappearance left her bewildered, confused and angry. The sense of loss and the ongoing mystery might have overwhelmed a less resilient person, but Anna forced herself to finish her thesis and won first-class honours.

She then faced the inevitable question of what to do with the rest of her life.

The New Year came around and Anna responded, without much optimism, to a newspaper ad for trainee radio journalists at the Australian Broadcasting Commission. She assumed that her record of political activism, not to mention the publicity around the Moratorium incident, would rule her out. However, after a series of interviews, voice testing and a general knowledge exam, she found out that she was on the shortlist of candidates. The final hurdle was a cross-examination by the notoriously conservative News chief of staff, Charlie O'Brien, known in the division simply as 'The COS'.

When the day of the interview arrived, Anna was shown into a conference room where two men—one of them older, O'Brien obviously, and a bearded younger man—sat behind a table cluttered with manila folders and notepads, an overflowing ashtray, some empty teacups and a jug of water.

O'Brien drew deeply on a cigarette, a habit clearly against his better interests—his brick-red face was a topographical map of burst blood vessels and veins that writhed across his temples like swollen creeks. His pulsating head rested on dodgy foundations: a thickened neck and a bloated torso that strained at his shirt buttons. By contrast, the younger man was lean and roguish-looking, and were it not for his old Harris Tweed jacket and badly knotted woollen tie, he might have just come from pirating on the Spanish Main.

O'Brien ground his cigarette into the ashtray and slowly raised himself to shake Anna's hand. The younger man followed, introducing himself as David Ireland.

From the outset O'Brien ran the interview courteously. Anna had been ready to fend off accusations of leftist affiliations and for scrutiny of her many campaigning editions of *The Tribe*. Instead O'Brien confined himself to straightforward questions on the technical side of her work putting a weekly paper together, about which he, as an old newspaperman, seemed genuinely interested. The bearded pirate, somewhat lasciviously, probed her on the paper's explicit content—about how she chose it, where she had sourced it and if she thought pornography was the real secret of *The Tribe*'s notoriety.

'You won't have that kind of freedom if you end up working here, you know,' Ireland remarked with a wink.

'Well, I never thought . . .'

'It's all left to the imagination in radio,' he said.

'Stuff and nonsense,' O'Brien interrupted. 'We don't rely on imagination in radio news, just facts.'

'Of course,' said Anna. 'I just want the chance to learn how to be a proper journalist.'

The interview proceeded in this manner. The flirtatious younger man and the gruff older one sparred from time to time, and Anna became cautious, wondering if this was a good cop, bad cop routine designed to get her to reveal some tragic flaw. She appeared to have reached the end of the interview unscathed and was beginning to relax when things took an unexpected turn.

'Will you stand up, please?' said O'Brien, making the request sound like an order.

Anna sat there, puzzled. Did he want to check out her figure? She glanced over at Ireland, hoping he might reveal the intention, but the pirate seemed amused and raised an eyebrow as if to say, *He's the boss, what can I do about it?* So Anna stood up.

'Now,' said O'Brien, 'please pick up the chair you've been sitting on and hold it at arm's length out in front of you.'

'I beg your pardon?' She stared at him, astonished.

'Just do it, Miss Rosen,' O'Brien barked.

Ireland was smirking now and gave her a small nod. *You better do as he says.*

Anna picked up the chair and held it in front of her, glaring at O'Brien. Unperturbed, he peeled back his shirtsleeve and stared at his watch, timing out a full minute before he spoke.

'You can put it down now,' he said. 'Please sit.'

Anna sat. But she was so humiliated and angry she couldn't hold her tongue. 'I'm not a performing dog, Mr O'Brien.'

'Did I ask you to roll over, Miss Rosen?' he retorted. 'Did I ask you to jump through a hoop?'

When Anna didn't reply O'Brien ploughed on relentlessly: 'I simply asked you to hold up that chair. Do you want to know why? No? Well, I'll tell you. A Nagra 4.2 tape recorder is standard equipment for our radio reporters. With batteries and tape, it weighs fifteen pounds. When you add the microphone, spare tapes and other items, you'll be expected to carry around more than twenty pounds of equipment for hours on end. That's more than the weight of that chair. I need to know you're capable of doing that. Any questions?'

'Only one.'

'What is it?'

'Do you make the men do that?'

Ireland guffawed. But O'Brien leaned towards her menacingly, his belly pushing at the edge of the table.

'Has it occurred to you, Miss Rosen, that the very reason you're here now is precisely because you *are* a woman? There's a push on to hire more of you, and it just so happens that you're the most qualified of the female applicants, no matter what inflammatory and pornographic trash you filled your little paper with . . . You'll soon learn that leftist rhetoric won't wash here, or you'll get your marching orders. To be honest, I've got my doubts about you. But others tell me that the sins of the father should not be visited on the daughter. We'll soon see who's right.'

Anna stared at O'Brien for a moment, trying to comprehend what he had just said.

'Does that mean I've got the job?' she asked at last.

'We could say you'll be on probation,' said O'Brien, before showing her the door.

Anna had gone away pondering that phrase, 'the sins of the father'. Her upbringing had imbued in her what might best be described as a siege mentality.

Her earliest memories were of existential threats to her father and, by extension, to her family. Frank had tutored all of them never to say anything about him or his movements, certainly not on the telephone, or to strangers, or even friends for that matter. He was ostentatiously cautious on the phone. He had the habit of putting on loud music when meeting Party officials in the house. He would point out to his children the men in suits who sat for hours in their sedans just over the road from the house, and Anna became used to the ones who came knocking at the door, dressed like Mormons, to inquire after Frank during his many absences.

All of this was a constant reminder to Anna that her family inhabited a treacherous world, a world of conflict, and that this made them fundamentally different to others. Frank's revolutionary principles, and her mother's unwavering support for them, bound them into a conspiracy of belief. Anna learned from childhood that the state was their enemy and that its agents regarded them, in turn, as enemies of the state.

All this made it hard for Anna to make friends at school. She was jeered at and taunted by some children who seemed to have learned red-baiting from their parents by osmosis. From a young age she became used to being denounced in the playground as a *commo*, which incidentally taught her empathy for the other abused minorities—the *wogs*, *wops*, *dagos*, *reffos* and *abos*—who were still outnumbered in those days by the offspring of white Christians. The Christians, especially Archbishop Mannix's lot, really had it in for them. But her father dismissed them as bigots.

'Some of them are dangerous bigots, mind you,' he once told her. 'It's one thing to be a communist. To be a communist and a Jew— that's double jeopardy.'

Frank himself had abandoned any religious belief when he was a boy. That was only logical because, as Trotsky put it: 'He who believes in another world is not capable of concentrating all his passion on the transformation of this one.'

But as Anna grew older she came to understand that her father's commitment to the revolutionary transformation of the world was not so far from the religious belief that he shunned in others. That he clung for so long to the corrupted citadels of communist power would be the cause of the deepest rift between father and daughter; but she had always, even when she doubted him most, admired his stubborn bravery.

When Anna was a small child, a bushfire had rushed up to their back fence like a raging beast. She saw its power for herself when a stand of eucalypts exploded into fireballs ahead of its onslaught. Sinister formations of white-grey smoke glowered over the land. The sun was a red ball behind it.

When burning ash dropped on to their roof from the swirling

oven in the sky, Eva Rosen sprayed it with a garden hose while her daughter clung to her dress, two puny humans in the face of an apocalyptic force. Anna wished her brothers had been there, but they were away at a Eureka League summer camp. Frank was in the scrubland beyond the fence line with other men from the street. Among them was Laurie McManus, the father of her friend Katie, who had forbidden his daughter to set foot in the house of the 'Godless communists'.

Frank was stripped down to his old army boots, khaki shorts, a singlet and a broad-brimmed hat. His mouth and nose were masked like those of a bandit, with a bright red scarf soaked in water. The men fought the fire together with gunny sacks and rakes, desperate to protect their homes and families.

Finally the wind changed direction and the fire turned its fury away from them. The exhausted, smudge-faced veterans passed around cold beers, joking together with relief after the shared danger. Then they went back to their houses and closed the doors, and resumed their ostracism of the Rosen family.

That night Eva cooked a baked dinner. Frank chose a Mozart symphony and put the record on the radiogram before falling into a deep slumber in his armchair, a bottle of dinner ale at his feet. Anna helped her mother by peeling the potatoes.

'Wash them first, darling.'

'Dad's fast asleep—will he be having dinner?'

'He'll be hungry when he wakes up.'

Anna got on with her chore, looking out the window at the blackened skeletons of the trees that once whispered and rattled in the breeze. The birds were gone. The smoke stench was still in the air. The horizon glowed with distant fires.

'Are we safe now?' she asked.

Her mother looked up from dressing a leg of lamb. 'The wind

turned the fire around, but it's always there for us, Anna, smouldering away.'

'What do you mean?'

'I mean that, for your father, the danger never goes away. It's no
wonder he's exhausted.'

Anna always remembered these words from her mother, who
retained a faint German accent. Eva understood the encroaching
danger better than any of them. She knew that great murderous
firestorms could rise up out of nothing and burn civilisations to
the ground. Eva had narrowly escaped being turned to ash herself.

Every year on 22 September, the Rosen family had an anniversary
dinner to celebrate the vote in 1951, which had so narrowly saved
Frank from prison, or a life on the run. Prime Minister Menzies'
referendum to outlaw communism had seemed destined to pass
and, on the night before the vote, a car had come to take Frank into
hiding. He hugged his young sons, picked up his baby daughter and
drew Eva into his arms for a farewell kiss before driving away with
his comrades. Frank had been jailed as a communist once before, in
1940, during Menzies' first prime ministership, and he was determined not to let that happen again.

The Party's most secret operative, Wally Clayton, had set up the
networks of houses and sympathisers that would allow its continued existence and for the comrades to operate underground. But
by some miracle, which Frank could never explain, the Menzies
referendum was defeated. Perhaps it had something to do with the
fact that even their implacable enemy, Archbishop Mannix, had
voted against it.

Frank returned home the next day and resumed his life. From
her earliest days Anna had absorbed the family lore that, were it not

for a handful of voters in three states, she may never have known her father. She certainly would not have grown up with him.

For Anna this past was much more than a foreign country; it was the smithy in which she and her beliefs had been forged. Her political activism at university had been the logical extension of this, but university life had also tempered her by focusing her on opposition to the Vietnam War. That, in turn, had deepened her alienation from the state. It was only when she won a student election to become editor of *The Tribe* and began obsessively working at it that she discovered journalism was her calling.

For her first year at the ABC, working under Charlie O'Brien's supervision, Anna applied herself to the technical skills of voice work, sound recording and editing. She found O'Brien's authoritarianism and his perverse chauvinism a constant trial, but she learned to live with it just as army recruits do with their drill sergeants.

No doubt O'Brien considered himself an equal opportunity bastard. He referred to all the trainees, male and female, as 'pixies', and they were all used to hearing his shouted commands, 'Send me a pixie! I've got an edit that needs doing!', and his complaints, 'These pixies are as useless as tits on a bull!' It was all done with ironic humour, but the idea was clear enough. They were lower-order creatures until they graduated into the reporters' ranks, which comprised a kind of 'officer class' inhabited mostly by men.

Within the O'Brien hierarchy women were never destined for the top ranks. Any thought that the ritual humiliation would magically end for Anna with her elevation from pixie status was put to rest one morning when she saw 'The COS' turn on his one female senior reporter after she made a factual error on air.

'Rita!' he yelled across the newsroom, heedless of who was listening. 'My office, now! And you better put an exercise book down your panties because I'm going to spank you with a ruler.'

As the only female trainee in her group Anna was outraged, and her anger was not diminished when O'Brien pretended it was all an ironic joke. She resisted any thought of quitting because that would notch up another win to the bully. Instead she resolved to get out from under his thumb.

The following year, having graduated from pixie to reporter, Anna found herself chafing under O'Brien's conservative news agenda and his mantra: 'If it's not in the papers, it's not a story.' She began chasing leads that came to her from contacts she'd nurtured as editor of *The Tribe* and covering stories that O'Brien's newsroom had long ignored: police actions against Aboriginal activists; random violence against gay men; sexual abuse of women in their workplaces; police corruption and connections to organised crime.

Where she could, Anna skirted O'Brien's authority by taking her ideas to other editors, but he soon got wind of what she was doing and demanded she clear every idea directly with him. So she began working on stories in her spare time.

In July she was tipped off by a contact in the Yugoslavian Embassy, an old friend of her father's, that a group of Croatian extremists with links to Australia had been killed or captured in Yugoslavia attempting to raise a rebellion against Tito's government. Her contact, whose diplomatic post she assumed was cover for something far more interesting, told her that the story of the incursion had deeper implications for the government and for the security service.

When she took this information to Charlie O'Brien and asked his permission to pursue the lead, she didn't mention her own Croatian connection, nor her immediate suspicion that Marin's father, Ivo Katich, might be somehow involved.

O'Brien scoffed at the idea, rejecting her request out of hand.

'Sorry, Rosen, I'm not going to send you gallivanting around after a bunch of Yugoslavs.'

'Croats.'

'Whoever they are, we don't have the resources,' he said, digging his heels in. 'You're a news reporter. Stick to the news.'

O'Brien's implacable refusal to even listen to her arguments was the final straw. In her frustration Anna went outside proper channels and set up a meeting with Peter McHugh, who as head of Radio Talks had a reputation for backing fearless journalism. She pulled the one string she had and McHugh agreed to a meeting.

Entering his office, she was confronted by a fierce-looking man with a hawkish face sitting behind a large, untidy desk. McHugh stared at her over the top of half-rim glasses before speaking.

'It's hard to believe you're Frank's daughter,' he said finally. 'I was expecting someone as ugly as him. Your mother's genes must be dominant. Lucky for you.'

'Right, well . . .'

'Tell him this from me: a man as ugly as him does not deserve such a pretty daughter.'

Anna was momentarily lost for words.

'And tell him he owes me a lunch.' McHugh smiled for the first time. 'Actually, you better say that first. It's been a while. Sit, sit, sit!'

'Thank you.'

'Frank says I should hear you out. Usually I fob off old friends when they contact me about their children.'

Anna wondered if McHugh was a Party member. It hadn't occurred to her until then. Her father hadn't mentioned it; but, then again, he wouldn't.

'He tells me you're after some advice,' McHugh said. His tone was mild, but she was still intimidated by his exceptionally bright eyes. 'You've been working in news for, what, a bit more than a year?'

'That's right,' said Anna.

'So, tell me, did Charlie O'Brien give your group "the speech" when you started?'

'You mean "geometric points"?'

'That's the one.' McHugh laughed, switching to an imitation of O'Brien's rasping voice with its tones of rural Queensland: '*If you want to be a news reporter for the ABC, there's one bloody rule you have to remember . . . You, you and you . . . You are geometric points . . .* There follows a long pause, right?'

Anna smiled and nodded, recalling the punchline: '*You have position, but no magnitude!*'

McHugh laughed again. 'Position, but no magnitude. You've got to hand it to him. No one ever forgets it.'

Anna laughed too at the memory and McHugh's perfect mimicry.

'Charlie O'Brien,' he went on. 'He's old school.'

'He is that,' Anna agreed. 'He once told us to imagine ourselves standing on a soapbox in front of a million people, and then he asked how we'd feel about giving the crowd the benefit of our personal opinions. He said that's the size of the audience for the national morning programs, and if you're the kind of person who wants to tell the world what *you* think, you might as well bugger off now.'

McHugh nodded. 'Do you find that idea restrictive?'

'No,' she said carefully. 'I'm not interested in my own opinions. I'm interested in stories and I've got a good one.'

'Go on then,' he encouraged her. 'Tell me a story.'

And so she began: 'You'll know from what's already been reported that nine Australians were killed or captured in Bosnia by the Yugoslav Army in June. They were part of a group of nineteen or twenty men sent in as guerrillas to start an uprising against the communist government.'

'Yes, well, *Four Corners* did a program about it.'

'Last month the Yugoslavian ambassador sent the attorney-general an *aide-mémoire* on the Bosnian incursion, with a list of Croatians in Australia they claimed had orchestrated the raid and other terrorist acts.'

'That's right,' McHugh said. 'I know that a bunch of homes were raided in Sydney and Melbourne. We followed the story closely. Where are you going with this?'

'I've found out that ASIO has advised the attorney-general that he should disregard the Yugoslavian document. But the Commonwealth Police believe it contains, and I'm quoting here, "a core of irrefutable fact".'

McHugh interjected. 'Whoa! What's your source for this?'

Anna paused. 'A Commonwealth policeman. Working in intelligence.'

'How senior?'

'He's senior enough to read direct communications between the police commissioner and Attorney-General Greenwood.' Then she added, 'But I don't want to identify him.'

McHugh made a placating gesture with his hands. 'Sorry to interrupt. Please continue.'

'I should have said that the insurgents in Bosnia were killed by the Yugoslavs, but not all at the same time. Some of them were shot dead in running battles with the army and some were captured. I understand that those caught have all been executed. All of them were ethnic Croats living in Australia or Europe, but the Commonwealth Police believe the incursion was planned in Australia, the largest group was recruited here, they trained here, and most of the funding came from here.'

McHugh leaned forward, engrossed now. 'Did your source give you any Commonwealth Police documents about this?'

'Not yet,' Anna said. 'But I think he will.'

'Without a document it's all unsourced and off the record.'

'Yes,' she agreed.

'Easily dismissed by Ivor Greenwood.'

'I know. That's why I need some time to develop this. But there's more.'

'Go on.'

'The police know who the culprits in Australia are. They're all part of a network of the wartime Croatian fascist movement, the Ustasha. They have a clear leadership structure here—'

McHugh interrupted again. 'This has all been speculated on in the press.'

'Yes,' said Anna curtly. 'What hasn't been reported is that the Commonwealth Police believe these Croatians are being protected by ASIO. If that's true, it's outrageous. The Ustasha are a protected species of terrorists able to plot and plan unhindered, while our security services look the other way.'

'Your source has told you this?'

'Yes, that's the point. The police are ropeable, absolutely incensed by it, at daggers drawn with ASIO.'

McHugh stared at her, considering the implications. 'Well, if you can make this stand up—and that's a big *if*—then it is a serious story with significant political repercussions. Before we go on: how did you manage to put all this together while working for News?'

Anna had thought about how to answer this. 'I got to know about the Ustasha when I was at university.'

'Frank tells me you were editor of *The Tribe*.'

'I'm pretty sure that's why they took me on here.'

'Now you're impatient to get on with things?'

'You said yourself: this is a big story.'

'Potentially,' he emphasised. 'Only if you can stand it up.'

'They won't even give me a chance to do that in News. Charlie O'Brien thinks I'm some kind of radical upstart. That's why I came to you. You're not afraid to upset the government.'

McHugh smiled at the implicit flattery. 'What's ASIO's supposed motive in protecting these people?' he asked. 'Just because they're anti-communists?'

'It's more complicated than that.' Anna drew a breath. 'It goes back in time.'

'Go on.'

'To the end of World War II.'

'I'm still listening.'

'After 1945 Western intelligence agencies started recruiting agents among the war criminals hiding out in DP camps in Europe. They already knew the next big conflict would be with the Soviets. No one knew then if that was going to be a hot war or a cold war. They were just preparing for the coming conflict. They wanted anti-communists who already had networks in communist countries. Who better than Nazis and fascists from puppet regimes like the Ustasha in Croatia? Many of them had been indicted for war crimes, but the spies decided it was better to make use of them than hang them. In many cases their crimes were covered up; they were given clean papers and safe haven in countries like Australia. And once they were here they set up their own fascist networks.'

'People have been making allegations like this for years, your father among them. Do you have any proof?'

'Yes,' Anna said. 'I do.'

8.

George Negus jogged up the stairs two at a time. Lionel Murphy was the leader of the Opposition in the Australian Senate, but that still didn't entitle his press secretary to a proper suite of rooms in the rabbit warren of Canberra's Parliament House. It rankled Negus that he was housed in a basement office that was little more than a cupboard. It was blatant disrespect, not just for him personally but also for the Labor Party.

He thought about this every time he ran up and down the stairs. He ran because everything was urgent now. There was an election coming!

The born-to-rule Libs and their oafish country cousins would soon get their comeuppance. Their long ride on Pig Iron Bob's coat-tails was over. McMahon was a fuckwitted prime minister. The whole country was on to him. There were some things you just couldn't hide in front of a TV camera.

The smarter Libs knew they'd made a monumental mistake giving him the leadership. Halfway up the stairs Negus got his mantra going: *Fucking Liars, Fucking Liars, Fucking Liars.*

He turned down the corridor, accelerating now. Under his arm was a manila folder full of the parliamentary questions Murphy had demanded he prepare. They were good questions, a bucketload of hard questions, a bucketload of shit to tip on Greenwood's head.

The attorney-general had locked himself into a series of lies. The Ustasha? They're just a myth. Organised terrorism? My word, there's no evidence of that! Bombs in Sydney? It's an inconvenience, to be sure, but let's wait and see what the police say.

Fuck me dead! What choice did the man have but to lie and lie and lie again? All the way up to election day.

Fucking Liars, Fucking Liars, Fucking Liars.

The office door flew open and Negus strode in. Daphne Newman stopped typing and looked up. She imagined that Negus had styled himself on Dennis Hopper in *Easy Rider*, without the slouch hat. But he did have the long hair, the drooping moustache, even the tasselled suede jacket, plus a kind of wild-eyed Hopperian madness that the senator seemed to appreciate. All of it played in a lower antipodean key.

'Morning, George.'

'G'day, Daphne. Where's Maureen?'

'She just took tea and bickies into the meeting.'

'Oh, right. Who's in there with him?'

'Senators McClelland, Gietzelt and Wheeldon.'

'The Three Musketeers.'

'You can put it that way, George.'

'That's what Arthur Gietzelt calls them, anyway. That kettle still hot?'

'Have a look, you might need to heat it up. Have you got something for us there?'

'Yeah.' Negus took a sheaf of carbon copies from the folder and handed them to Daphne. 'These are the questions Lionel wanted for today, still unallocated. I did them in a bit of a hurry. Could you check for mistakes and type them up properly for the tactics committee?'

'He's expecting you in there,' said Daphne. 'Should we wait until after the meeting for changes?'

Negus was annoyed at the question. 'I wrote these. They won't change.'

He was waiting for the kettle to boil when another door opened into the narrow office space and Maureen Barron appeared carrying a big teapot on a tray. Lionel Murphy was behind her. When he spotted his press secretary, he held the door open.

'George, you're here,' he said with a smile. 'Will you come in and join us?'

'Sure, I've got today's questions. I'll just grab a cuppa.'

'Don't leave us waiting,' Murphy said and pulled the door closed.

'God forbid,' Negus replied.

Armed with a tea mug, a biscuit and his sheaf of papers, Negus entered Lionel Murphy's office to find the four senators engaged in passionate discussion. John Wheeldon was talking. The man didn't like being interrupted, so Negus quietly took a seat at the side of the room.

'Someone needs to stop that bloviating buffoon Billy Wentworth.' There was cold anger in Wheeldon's voice. 'Did you see that rubbish in the *Herald*? He wants us to believe this was all the work of communist *agents provocateurs*.'

'Tito wouldn't do that,' said Arthur Gietzelt. 'Blow up his own people? No way. Yugoslavia is a model of tolerance. Have you seen their nude beaches?'

'Oh, for heaven's sake, Arthur—nude beaches?' John Wheeldon had the ascetic look of a clever priest and the manner of a professor. He turned to his friend, not unkindly. 'Leave off with the hero worship. Tito holds that damned country together with an iron fist.'

Gietzelt adjusted his thick-rimmed glasses. 'He's a maverick,' he said. 'We should look to him as a friend. That's all I'm saying.'

Negus regarded Gietzelt with caution. The man looked like an old-fashioned shop steward, but his bumbling manner concealed the hard core of a zealot. These senators, who gathered here regularly, constituted Murphy's political brains trust. Arthur Gietzelt couldn't match the intellectual firepower of the others, but he was a tough left-wing factional operator and Lionel Murphy's numbers man.

'We need to be careful who we declare as friends, Arthur,' Jim McClelland counselled. 'Whatever else he might be, Marshal Tito is an out-and-out dictator.'

Gietzelt shrugged, but refused to let the issue go. 'Do you know my great-grandfather was a corporal in the Austrian army? He told his son that there'll always be wars in the Balkans, they'll never stop. He said to him, "You must leave. Find a place to live where there are no wars." That's why my grandfather came to Australia ninety years ago. Whatever you think about Tito, he stopped the wars. While he's in power Yugoslavia won't be torn apart again.'

McClelland sighed. 'And how do you think he keeps all the nationalists in check? Why do you think so many of them ran away to Australia? They're still coming.'

'You're both right,' Lionel Murphy pronounced, bringing the discussion back to the matter at hand. 'Tito stamps on nationalist dissent, and some of those who ran away and ended up here are extremists, prepared to do acts of terror. But here's the political reality. We are months away from an election and the government has left itself seriously exposed by the way it has responded to the Sydney bombs. They will carry this albatross around their necks all the way to polling day. We must be relentless. We can't give them an inch.'

John Wheeldon jumped back in. 'That's exactly what I was saying before we spun off on to the Tito tangent. There are dangerous ratbags in the ministry, right up to the prime minister himself. They refuse to accept there's a problem, and that idiot savant Billy Wentworth has modelled himself on Joseph McCarthy!'

'That's a bit strong, Senator,' Negus blurted out. 'He seems like such a duffer.'

'Don't underestimate him, George,' Wheeldon retorted. 'Wentworth's on an anti-communist crusade. Do you know he went privately to ASIO and convinced them to give him a list of every communist on the Vietnam Moratorium Committees? Then he persuaded them to conduct warrantless searches and surveillance on all those people. They tried to pull the whole anti-war movement apart. Of course, he'll be out on his arse after the election. The ones we really have to worry about are the unelected spies who'll still be there. Our real unfinished business is with ASIO.'

Lionel Murphy stood up behind his desk, a theatrical gesture. He walked to an old bookcase and pulled from it a legislative document—the *ASIO Act*, 1956.

'Well, John, I agree we should be angry about that,' said Murphy, flicking through its pages. 'But if you're suggesting that laws were broken, they were not. Under its own Act, ASIO does not require warrants for searches and surveillance, only for telephone intercepts. It's all in here. We'll never be able to prosecute them for putting our friends under surveillance or breaking into their houses. That was all legal. What we *must* do is to make them accountable to government, *to our* government. That will be our priority when we win. We'll make them transparent. I'll force them to open all their secret files on anti-war protesters and politicians. The Sydney bombs will focus the minds of voters. Why did ASIO devote so many resources for so many years to chasing peaceful anti-war protesters while dangerous terrorists were left free and unmolested to plot and plan their next outrages?'

Arthur Gietzelt could barely contain himself. 'John's right!' he interjected loudly. 'ASIO is run by our ideological enemies. It is literally riddled with them. They operate as a branch of conservative politics; they collect information on us for our political beliefs—on everyone who's against the war, for God's sake. Even the mothers in Save Our Sons! We can't leave them be. Heads must roll. Why should they even continue to exist?'

Murphy put up a hand to stop him. 'We had that debate at the party conference, Arthur,' he said evenly. 'You have to let it go. ASIO must be reformed. But we need it to exist precisely to stop the kind of events that happened in Sydney on Saturday. Our priority right now is their political masters—the attorney-general, in particular.'

'That's right, Lionel, but we need to consider our approach to Greenwood.' McClelland spoke judiciously, his brain calibrated to the courtroom. 'Greenwood's constructed an elaborate legal argument. Simply put, he's saying that no facts can be asserted until the police complete their investigation into the bombing.'

'He's just a bullshitter!' Negus cried out. 'That must be obvious to everyone by now.'

'George, I disapprove of everything Ivor Greenwood stands for. Of course I do,' McClelland countered. 'His argument is a charade, but he does have a point. We *believe* the bombs were set off by Croatian extremists—all logic points us in that direction—but where is the proof? No one has been caught. No one has confessed. There is no concrete evidence.'

'We do have the material from the ABC last night—Anna Rosen on *Agenda*,' said Negus. 'The mainstream press still haven't picked up on it yet.' He turned to Murphy. 'She's the one I arranged for you to talk to on Sunday, Senator.'

'She is indeed,' said Murphy. 'Anna Rosen. Frank Rosen's daughter.'

Arthur Gietzelt looked up in surprise. 'Frank Rosen? Really? His daughter works for the ABC?'

Murphy nodded. 'She says she's not a Party member. I believe her.'

'I didn't know that she was part of the Rosen dynasty,' Negus said thoughtfully. 'I might have thought twice about sending her to see you.'

'Frank's a good man,' said Gietzelt. 'I'm just amazed the ABC gave her a job. The Commission's in the hands of reactionaries, starting at the very top. Duckmanton runs a very tight ship and he's an out-and-out Liberal, an old mate of Menzies.'

'We have plenty of friends in the ABC, Arthur,' Murphy responded. '*This Day Tonight*'s not afraid to stir things up.'

'I know that, Lionel. *TDT* is very trendy, but it's not serious— just undergraduate stuff, pranks and what not. Private schoolboys trying to get attention,' said Gietzelt, hitting a raw nerve with Negus, who harboured ambitions to join the TV show.

'That's not true, Senator,' he interjected.

Gietzelt ploughed on, oblivious to dissent. 'But hiring the child of a leading communist, that's another thing altogether. I might even call it progress.'

'She's working for Peter McHugh,' Murphy explained. 'In the Talks Department.'

'Right then.' Gietzelt nodded. 'That makes more sense. He's one of us.'

'Don't make that mistake, Arthur,' John Wheeldon said with unexpected passion. 'I wouldn't trust any journalist, ABC or otherwise.'

McClelland touched his friend's arm. 'You don't have to trust them, John,' he said. 'Sniff the prevailing wind. Most of them want change in this country as much as we do. Right up to the election we need our arguments heard by a mass audience.'

Wheeldon turned to him and smiled. 'Peter McHugh's an old Trot, isn't he, Jim? I imagine you have a bit of a soft spot for him.'

Negus wondered how Jim McClelland would respond to such a calculated slight. After the briefest pause, McClelland chose to laugh.

'I'm a mug as a politician, John. I've always had this simple idea that we have to change the country. When I was young, I thought only radical change would work. So I became a Trot when I was at uni, and so did Peter McHugh. A lot of us swallowed Marxism whole and believed in it in the way others believed in God. There was no questioning any aspect of it.'

Negus liked McClelland's self-effacing frankness. The senator was a handsome man with a sharp mind and a gift for words, a potential future leader. Lionel Murphy was beaming. He loved it that his office operated as a kind of political *Salon des Refusés*.

But Negus was growing impatient. This was all about to get self-indulgent and, sensing a McClelland speech was brewing, he tried to impose some discipline.

'Senator, we should really—'

'Hold on, George,' McClelland cut him off. 'This needs to be said. Back then, if you were a Marxist, you were a Marxist through and through. But there was no way a thinking human being could go along with the corrupted Soviet version of Marxism after the invasion of Hungary. So some of us were inevitably drawn to the dissident Trotsky. It's true, John, that I do have a bit of a soft spot for Peter McHugh, but think about your own youthful indiscretions. You were a young Liberal, weren't you? Same period. I imagine you must have had a soft spot too ... between your ears.'

'Come on, Jim,' said Wheeldon quietly. 'You know why I quit the Liberal Party.'

Against his better judgement Negus was drawn in, his curiosity aroused.

'Why's that, Senator?' he asked. 'I've never heard this story. I didn't even know you'd switched sides.'

Lionel Murphy spoke. 'There is some irony in this, George. John turned his back on Menzies when the old reprobate tried to ban the Communist Party. A great principle was at stake. The freedom to believe what you want, the freedom of association, the freedom to join whatever political party you like. The freedoms that make us what we are. Another reason we need a Bill of Rights.'

'That's all true,' Wheeldon agreed. 'And those freedoms are terribly fragile, especially if security agencies don't respect them. You won't know this either, George, but ASIO tried to stop my wife coming to Australia because her father was a prominent communist in America.'

'I didn't know that.'

'That was a terrible story,' Murphy explained. 'The great spymaster Charlie Spry went to John Gorton with a file on Judith's background and advised him to block her application. To his credit, Gorton sent him packing. A Liberal prime minister, but even he thought ASIO was a law unto itself.'

McClelland chuckled. 'There's more to that story. Gorton had a personal grievance. Spry had kept a secret file on him and made the terrible mistake of trying to tell him who he could and couldn't fuck.'

This rang bells for Negus. 'Was that about who I think?'

'Far be it for me to besmirch a maiden's honour,' McClelland said wryly. 'Though I can't imagine what she saw in him.'

This was the kind of scuttlebutt that Lionel Murphy loved. 'So you think it was true?'

McClelland shrugged. 'Where there's smoke,' he said with a thin smile. 'In that case it was billowing out of the PM's office.'

Negus considered this. He knew his own boss was the regular subject of such gossip. He had been forced more than once to throw cold water on press gallery speculation about Murphy. Despite the senator's homely countenance and the great snoz, Murph had an eye for the ladies. It helped his cause enormously that he also had unfeigned charm—a way of talking to women, of engaging with them as if they were the only interesting person in the room.

'All in all,' said Murphy, 'it's probably a good idea for a prime minister to avoid intimate relations with his own staff.'

'Especially when big brother is watching,' McClelland quipped. 'Anyway, no need to worry about the next PM. Gough's a strangely sexless messiah.'

'Sexless?' Murphy was dubious. 'Do you really think so?'

'I don't think it even enters his head,' McClelland responded. 'He's almost Christ-like.'

'Except for the ego,' said Murphy.

McClelland smiled. 'Some things are beyond measure.'

When the laughter subsided, Negus seized the opportunity to get the conversation back on the rails.

'Just returning to Anna Rosen and her radio program. I'd love to know how on earth she got hold of that Commonwealth Police document on the Ustasha in Australia. That's something we were holding back for Question Time.'

Lionel Murphy shifted. 'I can't imagine,' he said disingenuously, and Negus knew immediately that his suspicion was right. The boss had tried to impress another pretty girl.

'She must have friends in high places.' Negus sighed.

Murphy looked for all the world like a naughty schoolboy. 'No doubt,' he said. 'In any event, it's out there now.'

Negus decided to let him off the hook. 'It's lucky that even ABC News isn't running with it. The Rosen program was on late, so it's possible that Greenwood's people haven't even heard it.'

'I expect you've made use of it in some of the questions you've drafted?'

'I have, Senator, of course. We need to go through them now or you'll be late for the Tactics Committee. If we handle this right, you'll have Greenwood dancing around on hot coals from the first question.'

'Thank you, George,' Murphy said. 'Let's do that.'

So Negus opened the manila folder and began his briefing.

Negus was watching from the gallery at 2 pm when the president of the Senate halted debate and called for Questions Without Notice. The first was the one he'd written. It was asked by a Labor barrister—not Jim but Senator Douglas McClelland, no relation.

'My question is for Senator Greenwood. Does the attorney-general still maintain that there is no organised Ustasha terrorist organisation or Croatian Liberation Movement in Australia?'

Ivor Greenwood stood up and strode to the dispatch box, looking dapper in a pin-striped suit, his dark hair swept back from his forehead. When he started speaking, there was no indication whatsoever that Negus could see of the pressure he must surely be feeling.

'As to whether or not I still maintain that there is no Ustasha terrorist Croatian Liberation Movement in Australia, I think the Honourable Senator is aware that I stated in late July, after intensive investigations had been made into allegations that there was a Croatian terrorist organisation in Australia, that the police investigations, State and Commonwealth, had revealed no credible evidence that such a terrorist organisation existed. As far as the incidents on Saturday are concerned, one must surely await the outcome of police investigations before expressing any judgement on whether or not that will alter a view. I think that is the prudent course to take. We do not know who planted this bomb.'

'Bombs!' Jim McClelland interjected loudly.

'We do not know who planted those bombs,' the attorney-general corrected himself. 'We do not know what the motivation was and, until we have that report, I believe one should not pass judgement, one way or the other, on what happened in Sydney.'

Negus smiled grimly. He could have written Greenwood's answer out in full this morning. He returned to his mantra.

Fucking Liars, Fucking Liars, Fucking Liars . . .

9.

On Tuesday afternoon Al Sharp, assisted by a police technician, set up a projector in a meeting room with raked seating. He stacked the carousel with slides from his intelligence file and turned on the projector, then he sat back and lit a cigarette while he waited for his audience to arrive.

He watched the smoke drift through the projector's beam until it swirled in the light, film noir style. He clicked the remote control and the carousel shuffled around to the first slide. It was a black-and-white photo taken clandestinely at a closed meeting of Croatian extremists.

The subject was leaning forward, one arm holding the bunched weight of his heavy shoulders, the other raised up and ending in a fist. The face still held traces of the handsome man he must once have been, but it was now thickened with age and alcohol and contorted with a passion that might, in another context, be mistaken for hard, unyielding pain. In his dark, deeply recessed eyes there was a wildness that could easily inspire fear.

'Who's that dickhead?'

Sharp looked up in surprise, recognising the sardonic voice. It belonged to Bill Lonergan, the homicidal homicide detective.

'Lonergan! I didn't expect you to be the first one here.'

'Don't get your hopes up. I didn't bring you an apple. So, who's the dickhead with the crazy eyes?'

'His name is Ivo Katich. Take a seat. I'll explain who he is when we get a quorum.'

Other men were arriving now, filling up seats in the back of the auditorium, and Sharp called to them. 'Move down the front if you can, fellows, so the latecomers can take those seats.'

Most moved grumbling to the front.

'A quorum? *Quor—umm*,' Lonergan mimicked a posh accent. 'Never heard that one before. A pack, a herd, a bunch of cunts or whatever—but a quorum?'

'A pack? That's for dogs, isn't it?' Sharp said. 'A bit disparaging. I suppose we could say a *murder of detectives*.'

Lonergan squinted at him. 'What's your fucken point?'

'No point. Let's go with a quorum of cunts. And we just about seem to have one.' Sharp stubbed his cigarette out. 'I think I'll get started.'

The front seats were almost full now and the flow through the back doors had slowed. Sharp stood up, grimacing from a spasm of back pain.

'Thanks for coming. Detective Lonergan here asked the obvious question a moment ago.' Sharp gestured to the screen. 'Who's the dickhead with the crazy eyes?'

A few people laughed. Lonergan had slumped with his feet on the barrier between them. Sharp glanced down. The Balinese regard pointing your feet at someone as an insult. He assumed in this case it was mere coincidence.

'His name is Ivo Katich and he's definitely a dickhead, but make no mistake: he's a dangerous one. This photo was taken at a secret meeting. The man who took it was working for us—an informer we had on a string for a short time after we picked him up with two pounds of heroin. He was one of the few ins we've ever had with these blokes. But he disappeared a few months ago; we assume he's dead. They have a habit of murdering informers.'

Sharp hit the button once and the carousel clattered on to the next image. It was Katich again, but a younger version, wearing a black uniform with a peaked hat. The letter *U* was emblazoned on both the cap and the shoulder of the uniform. The young Katich was smiling into the camera, his right arm bent and holding a pipe, which he was about to light.

'This is Ivo Katich in 1941,' Sharp told them. 'It was taken in the city of Sarajevo, which you may know is in Yugoslavia but which wasn't called Yugoslavia at that time. Back then Sarajevo was part of the newly formed Independent State of Croatia.'

There was an audible groan from some detectives.

'Don't worry, I'm not going to give you too much of a history lesson. Just to say this: the new Croatian state was set up under the authority of Adolf Hitler. Historians describe it as a Nazi puppet state. And that black uniform young Katich is wearing tells us he was an officer of the Ustasha. That's the military arm of the wartime Croat state, a force so brutal that even the German SS considered them to be inhuman killers. During the war Ivo Katich commanded a group called the Mobile Court Martial in the region of Bosnia. Their job was to travel the countryside and murder suspected enemies of the new state. This photo you're looking at—of this happy, pipe-smoking fellow—was taken at an execution site where he had just hanged twelve people.'

There was a swell of angry chatter and Sharp paused. Many of the policemen in the room, like Lonergan, were homicide detectives, and he understood their outrage.

'How did a monster like this get to Australia?' a man called from the back of the room.

'That's a good question,' Sharp said. 'It's a long story. To start with, our immigration authorities never looked too closely at good anti-communists. In Katich's case, we know that he was indicted for war crimes by the Nuremberg Tribunal in 1946; but he never stood trial and somehow his papers got cleaned up. He emigrated to Sydney with his wife, Samira, in 1953 and got a job as a rigger on the Harbour Bridge.'

'You're fucken joking!' Lonergan exclaimed, swinging his feet back to the floor and sitting upright.

Sharp looked down at him, pleased to at least have his complete attention. 'I'm not joking,' he said. 'He's still there. He's got a bigger job now, managing the bridge maintenance crews.'

'That's fucken sacrilege.' Lonergan's outrage was unfeigned. 'A Nazi wog workin' the Bridge. Shouldn't be allowed. Are you telling us this is the bloke we want for the Sydney bombs?'

Sharp didn't answer immediately. He pressed the remote control again and the carousel shifted, throwing up another slide.

This time three men were pictured together, inside a large nineteenth-century hall. Behind them were banners and tricolour flags with an odd chequerboard design. The man in the middle was Ivo Katich, older and considerably thicker set, but unmistakably the same man as in the Ustasha uniform. His arms were draped over the shoulders of the men who flanked him.

Sharp glanced back to the screen. Hard, ferocious faces; big bodies locked together like the three-headed dog, Cerberus, at the gates of hell.

He gave the audience a more prosaic assessment. 'It's Ivo Katich again in the centre. The big thug on his right is Branko Kraljevic and the scar-faced fellow on his left is Vlado Bilobrk. These three:

Katich, Kraljevic and Bilobrk are revered among extreme Croat nationalists because they were actually there in 1941 when the Ustasha formed their first independent state. They had their own führer, who was called the *Poglavnik*.' Sharp paused and pointed back at the screen. 'See that portrait up high in the right-hand corner of the room? That's him.'

He clicked the remote again and a close-up of the portrait appeared. A haughty, hatchet-faced man stared out from the screen, wearing a more elaborate black uniform with the familiar *U* insignia.

'The *Poglavnik*, Ante Pavelic,' Sharp explained. 'Another indicted war criminal, who escaped to Argentina with the help of the Catholic Church. Pavelic is dead now, but the reason this history and these connections are important is that the command structures of the old Ustasha are still in place in Australia.'

He clicked back to the shot of the three men. 'Katich, Kraljevic and Bilobrk were all members of the *Poglavnik's* Ustasha bodyguard during the 1940s. They were members of the Ustasha's Black Legion. They are hardened warriors. Fought alongside the German Wehrmacht against the Soviet troops during the siege of Stalingrad. Today they make every new recruit take a blood oath of loyalty to the Ustasha and its permanent obsession, which is to overthrow Tito's communist Yugoslavian government and create again an independent state of Croatia. They are fanatical believers in a cause that we can barely comprehend. This is what we have to deal with when we try to track down the Sydney bombers— fanatics who will remain silent on pain of death when we question them, and whose leaders don't think twice about executing suspected traitors.'

Sharp paused again to let this sink in. 'Now, I know this is a lot to take in at one time, so are there any questions before I go on?'

'Was that photograph taken in Sydney Town Hall?' called a man from the front row.

'It was,' Sharp replied. 'They've been building their Ustasha networks for more than two decades right under our noses. The city council rents the Town Hall to them every year for their independence day celebrations.'

There was a palpable sense of outrage in the room and Sharp knew he had them. He clicked the remote again, and the carousel clattered around and threw the next slide up on to the screen.

It was a naked woman draped across a chaise lounge. She was busty, with rouged nipples and a dark triangle of pubic hair. She winked at the camera, blowing a lascivious kiss to the audience. A roar came up from the roomful of detectives—whistles and cheers.

Sharp turned to look at the screen; Manet's *Olympia* she was not. He feigned embarrassment.

'Oh shit, how'd that get there?'

He fumbled for the remote and clicked on to the next image, an organisational flowchart. Boos and jeers came from the audience now, and cries of 'Bring her back!' and 'Show us your tits!'

'I'm so sorry,' Sharp said. 'I can't imagine how that happened.' He waited for the booing to subside. 'But at least you're all sufficiently awake now to study this chart. By the way, a file of all this material will be available for the investigative teams.' He pointed. 'What you can see here is the organisational structure of the Ustasha in Australia.

'It's not simple because they've had to learn to hide themselves. They've divided into splinter groups and cells to avoid detection, but as you can see, at the top of the pyramid is the HRB—the Croatian Revolutionary Brotherhood. The three key leaders of the Brotherhood, as you might expect, are Katich, Kraljevic and

Bilobrk. At the pointy end of the pyramid is Ivo Katich. He's the real leader. The other two are his key lieutenants. We believe that Katich signs off on every significant Ustasha action. He is our primary target.'

Sharp clicked to the next slide. 'Now, as you can see from this family tree, Ivo Katich has two sons.'

10.

January 1963

Marin Katich stared out the car window at the treeless, boulder-strewn plain of the Monaro. The sky above it rose to infinity. The boulders were marbles from a game abandoned by careless giants.

That was his father's story. Lewis had a different one. He claimed these granite spheres were rolled into place by the glacier that scythed away the surface of the earth as it moved towards the coast, slowly, inexorably, taking everything in its path and levelling the land. The first settlers found it like this, empty and flat with topsoil so thin that not even a gum tree could take root.

It was the summer of 1963, Marin was twelve years old, and they were driving south to Khandalah, close to the Victorian border. Ivo had bought this property soon after his first son was born. It was just a couple of shacks on a hill above a bend in the Towamba River, with a stretch of wild country on either bank. Every January they took the same long journey, Marin and Petar sitting up front on a salt-stiffened towel stretched across the hot vinyl seat.

As he drove, their father sang the *ojkanje*, taught to him by his own father when he was a boy. The old man, Ivo would tell his sons, had been a mystic. 'He told me that the *ojkanje* are wolf songs,'

Ivo whispered, as if imparting a great secret. 'In the old times, when men were closer to the earth and its creatures, we learned them from the wolves.'

The two brothers had heard the *ojkanje* many times, whenever their father had been in the mood to sing, but these songs were still strange to their ears. Long, breathless notes vibrated in Ivo's throat. Marin watched him anxiously, as he always did when Ivo was doing something unpredictable, which was often enough. From deep inside Ivo came an eerie, quavering sound, and you could hear in this, Marin was convinced, the howling beasts in the mountains.

Lost in his father's song, Marin stared out the window at the parched, empty grasslands, at the piles of boulders, at the vast blue sky and imagined they were on another planet.

When he was not singing, his father talked and talked. For the whole drive Ivo was rarely silent. He told them strange tales from the old country. He was at once captivating and disturbing. A psychiatrist might have diagnosed manic depression. When he was up, when he was in the manic phase, that was something to see. Marin imagined at those times that his father was all bright colours, and everything else was black and white.

At Khandalah, on one of the hottest days of summer, Ivo took Marin for a walk in the bush. It was full of noise. Bellbirds, currawongs, whip-poor-wills and many others—the usual sounds. But there was a constant background roar, because this was one of those years when the cicadas came out of the ground in swarms, like a great plague, and they were more deafening than ever. It was a cicada summer and the air throbbed with their song.

In summers like this Marin and Petar caught as many as they could—Green Grocers, Yellow Mondays, Floury Bakers, Redeyes,

TONY JONES

Cherrynoses. They kept them in shoeboxes. They dared each other to put them on their arms and let the claws dig into their skin. Marin felt the thrill of holding a live one in his fist, feeling it vibrate and struggle, the twitch of its wings and abdomen against his hand.

Ivo loved the cicadas as much as they did. They reminded him of his boyhood in Croatia. They were called *cvrčak* in the old language. That was what he still called them. Sometimes Marin saw tears in his eyes when he walked out in the sun and into the great racket they made. One time he saw Ivo standing outside, clamping his hands on his ears and then taking them away; then repeating this, over and over, tears streaming down his cheeks. That was something beautiful and terrible.

That day was special because he had asked Marin to walk with him, just the two of them. He'd never done that before.

'They are like me, these *cvrčak*. They love the heat,' Ivo told Marin as they followed the path beside the river.

Eventually he stopped in a grove of mountain gums and river peppermint.

'You hear that? When it gets hotter, their song becomes louder?'

Marin nodded. It seemed the noise was much louder in that place, as if a great swarm had massed there.

'They like it close to the river too,' Ivo explained.

The cicadas were hypnotically loud, yet it was hard to spot the individual insects. Then a butcherbird was in among the trees, and a lone cicada panicked and took flight. Its broken cry was cut off as the predator caught it mid-air.

Ivo clapped. 'Well done, bird. Well done. Perfect!' he called out, as if the butcherbird might stop and take a bow.

Then Ivo went quiet and made a show of listening, as the massed song of the cicadas grew louder again, pulsing in regular waves of sound.

'Do you hear that?' he asked.

Marin listened. 'What?'

'Do you hear what's different, Marin?'

'It's sort of up and down. Loud and quiet, loud and quiet.'

'That's right. That's right!' Ivo cried.

He put a fist in front of Marin's face, opening it and closing it in rhythm with the noise.

'It's called the pulsing phase. Old Lewis told me about it. Only one tribe makes this sound. It's their language and this is their place. This is where they come up out of the ground. These trees are their trees.' Lewis was their nearest neighbour. Years ago he had taken it on himself to teach the newcomers bush lore.

Ivo searched around, peering at the tree trunks.

'Here, see here,' he said, pointing at the empty shells still clinging to the trunks. Marin looked at the split and discarded exoskeletons, from which cicadas had emerged to spread their wings. He and Petar had been picking them off trees for years.

'I know all about these shells, Papa,' he said, wondering what his father was trying to tell him.

'Yes, yes. Of course you do, Marin. But not these exact ones.'

Ivo walked around under the trees, his eyes searching in the lower branches. Then he stopped and reached up.

'Here is one.'

His hand closed on a dark shape.

'Come close.' He opened his hand and took the creature between his thumb and forefinger, holding it firmly over the wing joints so it knew it could not fly away.

'You see him?' he said. 'Look close.'

The cicada was a shiny black creature. Its alien eyes had a glowing sheen.

'Some *cvrčak* we see every year. Not these ones. Not this tribe.

They're hidden deep underground for many years, longer than the others. Lewis says these come out maybe every fourteen years. Somehow they know when their time is, and then they burrow out of their deep holes. They start two metres down, or even further—and then they come all that way up into their trees. You know what he's called, Marin?'

The creature rattled in Ivo's fingers, struggling even though the effort was futile.

'Black Prince,' said Marin.

'Good boy. He's a Black Prince, this one.'

'He's a beauty. Can I keep him?'

'No,' said Ivo. 'He doesn't have long out in this world.'

Without warning he threw the creature into the air. It went up like an inanimate thing for a way and then, with a burst of energy, took flight and disappeared into the branches. The pulsing sound grew louder.

'Marin, I want you to think about this carefully.' Ivo paused and put his face close to his son's, holding him by the chin. 'You are like him, the Black Prince. Remember this. This life here in Australia is not real. You are deep underground. One day it will be time to come out.'

When Ivo moved the family to a house in Leichhardt he planted a little orchard of plum trees in the backyard and built a still. By the time the trees were bearing fruit, his wife had gone.

Every year the plums were picked and fermented, and Ivo fired up the still. He would feed the furnace with ironbark logs and turn the handle until the stench of *šljiva* cooking away in the copper boiler hung over the house and clung to everyone's clothes. It was like a sickly sweet cologne and Marin would always associate it with his father, in the same way that the smell of floor polish brought with it a wave of nausea and vivid memories of his mother.

Ivo and Branko Kraljevic would arrange time off work to tend to the still during the days of the distilling process. It was their annual tradition. They took turns at cranking the handle of the boiler and poured each other shots of last year's *rakija* from an old stone jar. They would drink steadily while the copper pipes groaned and squealed, as the vapours forced their way through to liquefy in the cooling tank. A pure, clear liquid dripped from a tap into a bucket.

Marin once caught Brutus licking drips from the tap. The drunken dog looked up guiltily before staggering in circles around the yard. Behind the shed Marin found his father and Branko lying unconscious on the grass, an empty stone jar beside them.

Marin had always been wary of Branko. He had fingers like sausages and there were many dark rumours about him, all of which he gleefully embraced. He had worked with explosives in the mines and spent time in prison; he had killed a man—well, many men, but they were all communists. He had fought alongside Ivo Katich in Stalingrad and they had both been in the bodyguard of the *Poglavnik*. Ivo never talked about Stalingrad, but he was happy to admit his closeness to the *Poglavnik*—that was his greatest pride.

Sometimes Branko was a friendly uncle, sometimes a thug. The *rakija* was the anaesthetic that put his better angels to sleep.

Walking home from school one day with Petar, Marin saw white puffs rising from the still's narrow chimney. The familiar stench carried on the wood smoke filled him with dread. As he opened the gate, he heard loud laughter coming from the backyard, and found his father and Branko Kraljevic slumped in folding chairs, playing cards.

'*Dobar dan*, boys!' Branko called as they came in. His voice slurred ominously. 'Come, lads. Come. We need help, some extra hands here.'

His purple-veined cheeks were flushed, his eyes were swimming.

The stone jar was nearly empty. Marin was instantly on edge. Their *rakija* was sixty per cent proof. It could strip the varnish off old furniture—and strip away a man's inhibitions even more thoroughly.

Ivo looked up from his cards. 'Go and wind the handle for us, Petar,' he said with an odd deliberation, trying and failing to give the appearance of sobriety. 'And Marin, throw some more wood into the oven.'

As Petar walked past Branko, the giant suddenly lurched up and grabbed his arms, squeezing the boy so hard that he winced.

'Look at this skinny thing,' Branko cried. 'Couldn't take the skin off a rice pudding! You need some meat on these bones, boy.'

Marin expected Ivo to jump up and separate them, or at least to tell his friend to leave Petar alone. Instead his father gave a bitter laugh. 'He's a mummy's boy, that one,' he said. 'A sensitive soul, like her.'

Petar's face crumpled; he was close to tears. Branko kept hold of him, staring into his eyes as if looking for evidence of the reviled Samira staring back out at him. Then he let the boy go, as though dropping something unclean.

'That's not good for you, Petar,' Branko growled, poking a sausage finger into his chest. 'You don't want to be like her. She left you. She walked out and left you without a word. You remember that. You must never forget it.'

Petar was sobbing now, but Branko was relentless. 'Your father is here for you. You must follow him and forget all about her.'

Marin watched Ivo sitting there mute.

Petar suddenly cried out, 'Mama!'

Branko reverted to the old language—'*Jebo ti pas mater!* May a dog fuck your mother!'—and grabbed Petar's arms again.

At this Marin yelled at him. 'Leave him alone!'

Branko shook the boy like a doll. Petar was weeping. But Ivo still hadn't moved.

A mist of anger rose in Marin. He grabbed a piece of firewood and in one swift movement smashed it into the back of Branko's head. Marin watched the man go down. A sack of shit. Freed from his grip, Petar scampered away.

Ivo rose unsteadily and bent over his groaning friend, registering after a moment that Branko was still alive. Then he came at Marin and tore the log from his hands. He grabbed his son by the throat.

The huge hands around his neck burned hot as an iron. Marin was lifted off the ground, his legs dangling in the air as he was carried into the house. Floating down the corridor, he kicked out like a hanged man until his father threw him on to his bed and thrashed him with the dog leash, raising welts on his legs, his arms and his face.

Marin yelled and yelled back at his father, ignoring the pain, daring Ivo to murder him. There was a perverse power in tipping his father over the edge. Marin was flirting with death, playing chicken on a highway, but he was not afraid. He welcomed the pain.

When Ivo's fury was finally spent, he slumped down beside his son, weeping. 'Marin, Marin,' he sobbed. 'This hurts me more than you.'

Ivo sat there, streaming tears, wiping snot from his nose. He was as regretful as a child trying to repair the favourite toy he had just smashed against the wall.

In the end, as always, Marin felt sorry for his father.

*

Soon after he turned fifteen Marin found himself backstage at the Sydney Town Hall, hiding behind the organ. Above him, thousands of pipes reached up into the darkness, silent and waiting. He peeked out at the crowd flooding in through the entrances, jostling to take their seats. He was nervous, silent as the organ pipes. He had to make a speech to these people.

His suit was buttoned up tight as a straitjacket. It was the first one he'd ever owned. Ivo had taken him and Petar all the way out to a factory in Granville, where a Bosnian friend gave them a special deal. He had never known his father to spend money on fancy clothes. For his confirmation he'd worn a hired suit stinking of mothballs.

That was how important this day was—more important than sealing the spiritual bond with Christ's flesh and blood. This was about the spiritual bond with the homeland. The suit was black, with sharp creases in the trousers and a three-button coat, underneath which was a starched white shirt and a thin black tie.

Petar said they looked like bodyguards to the president. The two of them emerged from their hiding place and drifted about in the crowd, pretending to talk into their sleeves, until Ivo caught them at it and clipped Marin so hard over the ear that his vision blurred with sudden tears.

'Don't be the goat!' he growled. 'Not tonight.'

Ivo was in the vestibule, greeting new arrivals like the host at a wedding. There was great excitement. Loud voices and laughter filled the big room right to its high ceilings. Some appraised the fittings like dealers at an auction, calculating the value of the crystal chandelier, the gold leaf, the ceramic tiles patterning the floor. The Town Hall had been built in the nineteenth century for the city's English gentry, but tonight it was being occupied by a horde of Balkan migrants in their Sunday best.

Marin felt they were—all of them—out of place and out of time. In a pocket of his jacket, folded over his heart, was the speech his father had helped him write. He had been made to recite it over and over again. Now Ivo looked at him, nodding as if to say: *You're up for this, aren't you?*

The crowd was large and boisterous, but he was mostly nervous about speaking in front of his father. The prospect of letting him down or, even worse, embarrassing him, was terrifying. For this was their national day—10 April 1941 was the sacred day on which the Independent State of Croatia, *Nezavisna Država Hrvatska*, was born. Today was the twenty-fifth anniversary of this great event.

Hard-looking men encircled Ivo Katich. As more arrived, they went into orbit around him. Ivo greeted them all with hugs and kisses, friends and supplicants alike. Waiting to greet him, they smoked like chimneys, before dropping their spent butts and grinding them into the tiles with their shiny shoes.

Branko Kraljevic was there too under the blue cloud, hugging the new arrivals and squeezing their shoulders with his sausage fingers. A huge man with a scarred face was nearby; Vlado Bilobrk was another of Ivo's wartime comrades. Marin stared at the man. His face had been torn apart by shrapnel and reconstructed into a Frankenstein monster with a permanent scowl. Katich, Kraljevic and Bilobrk were revered names in this company.

The younger ones paid their respects. They too were hard men, toughened by physical work, their weathered faces darkened by the sun. Decked out in polyester suits and wide-collared body shirts, they swaggered and postured. They passed a bottle of *rakija* from hand to hand. They laughed at their own crude jokes and whispered confidences, fixing Marin with suspicious stares until Ivo took him by the arm to introduce him to their leader, an intense fellow in his mid-twenties called Ambroz Andric.

'Marin is to make a speech tonight,' Ivo told him.

Andric shook his hand and Marin felt calluses in his hard, dry grip.

'What a privilege for you,' he said, eyes like probing searchlights. 'You're lucky to have a father such as this. Katich—that is a name to be proud of.'

Marin nodded, uneasy under the man's scrutiny and too embarrassed to respond.

When Ivo drifted off to greet someone else, Andric leaned in close to Marin. 'The ones who were there, like your father,' he said, almost in a whisper. 'Can you imagine it? To have seen the *Poglavnik*, to have stood as close to him as we are standing now. To have heard him speak, to have worn the uniform. What a time to live through! Does your father talk to you about those days?'

The eyes of Ambroz Andric were shining with something Marin couldn't quite grasp.

'He doesn't say much about that. Many things, but not that,' he told Andric, and the man gifted him with a reassuring smile.

'One day he will tell you everything. When you are ready.'

Marin wanted to ask him more, but at that moment they were called to take their seats. Petar was there already in the front row. Next to him was a woman with a beehive hairdo, Astrid Capan, who had been active in the movement for many years with her husband. Marin wondered where he was tonight. She was wearing a shimmery gown and lots of make-up.

Marin sat down next to his brother. Even from one seat away he caught wafts of Mrs Capan's perfume. Then his father came and took the spare seat next to her and Marin felt a frisson of something pass between them.

On stage the music was starting up, with a massed string band of young kids in national costume. The boys in white smocks with ballooning sleeves and waistcoats hand-sewn by their mothers, the girls in long white dresses embroidered with patterns of spring flowers. Marin didn't envy them. He knew what it was like to be dressed up as a village boy. The musicians were strumming their long-necked *tamburitza* and the wall of sound evoked in the crowd a joyous sentiment. Marin turned and saw that his father's eyes were moist.

Dancers sprang out on to the stage, their boots hitting the wooden floor in a hard rhythm, and Ivo started clapping along. His face was infused with the exuberance that surged through the crowd, until everyone was clapping and stamping their feet. Then there was a burst of activity at the back of the hall as, through the doorways on either side, came flag-bearers leading ranks of costumed youths down the aisles towards the stage. They held high the tricolour flag of the NDH, emblazoned with the red and white chequerboard. The sight of this beloved symbol broke the clapping rhythm and an ecstatic roar rose up.

Ivo jumped to his feet, clapping wildly, and soon Marin too felt compelled to stand. His father's face glistened with tears. Everyone was now on their feet as the flag-bearers, the tallest and best-looking young men and women, swept past them and up on to the stage. High above, stretching across the ornate fan of the grand organ's dormant pipes, was a banner proclaiming:

ZIVJELA HRVATSKA! ZIVIO! DESETI TRANANJ

LONG LIVE CROATIA! HURRAY! THE 10th OF APRIL

On one side of the banner was a large portrait of Queen Elizabeth II, and on the other a huge photograph of the *Poglavnik*, Ante Pavelic, founder of the Ustasha and NDH.

God save them! That was what Marin was told to say if anyone asked. *God save our gracious Queen. Long live our noble Queen.*

And God save our noble Poglavnik, *long to reign over us. God save them both!*

None of them—not Ivo Katich, nor his friends and followers, nor the special guest politicians from the Liberal Party, nor the young musicians and dancers, nor their cheering parents—thought for a moment that this juxtaposition of Queen and *Poglavnik* implied any disrespect. They all accepted, without question, that the allegations against Pavelic—the war crimes set out in the vicious, lying indictment of the Nuremberg Trials—were all built on evidence fabricated by the communists and on witnesses suborned by Tito's agents.

The celebration proceeded with performances and speeches. A small girl recited an *Ode to the Poglavnik*; another sang a song she had written herself to honour the great man.

Before he was ready, it was Marin's turn to speak. He walked stiff-legged to the lectern. It was draped with the chequerboard flag and behind it an image had been projected on to a large white screen. It was the *Poglavnik*, noble and resolute in his peaked hat, in the black uniform of the supreme commander of the Ustasha.

Marin spoke in English for the benefit of the visiting dignitaries. 'Ladies and gentlemen, boys and girls and special guests, it is a pleasure to see you all here on the twenty-fifth anniversary of the state we hold so dear. Although we love our adopted country Australia, the Croatian homeland lives always in our hearts.

'It was twenty-five years ago today, 1941 in Zagreb, that Archbishop Stepinac sent a special message to all his priests: "The times are such that it is no longer the tongue that speaks but the blood with its mysterious links to the country in which we have seen the light of God."

'The archbishop's words were read out in every church in the Independent State of Croatia. I am only a young man and I was born here in Australia, but even so I can understand what the arch-bishop meant because my own blood is still linked to Croatia. It is mysterious, but it is real.'

When Marin paused, a rumble of applause filled the silence. Then it stuttered and died as he started again.

'We all know the painful truth that Croatia is not free today. But we can still dream that day will come again just as Ante Pavelic dreamed it would come. He had the will to make it happen. The army he built to free Croatia he called the Ustasha. For those who don't know, you can translate it as "insurgent", or "revolutionary". And that is what they were—revolutionaries for independence, in the same way that George Washington, Thomas Jefferson and the founding fathers of the United States were revolutionaries. General Washington took up arms against an oppressive English king to fight for their independence. Ante Pavelic took up arms against an oppressive Serbian king to fight for ours.'

Here Marin paused again and the response of the crowd was like rolling thunder, with many shouts of support. He glanced behind him and saw that the projected image had changed to marching ranks of Croatian soldiers. He looked down from the stage at his father and saw he was smiling up at him. Not just smiling—Ivo was in tears again, unable to contain his emotions.

Marin drew his speech to a close. 'Clearly the Ustasha was not a fascist organisation. It was a revolutionary movement organised as a military force. The Ustasha's aim was military. The end of Serbian rule over Croatia, and the protection and preservation of the Croatian national state.'

Marin saw the nods of approval in the crowd for this line of thinking. With his speech finished, he proclaimed the famous cry: 'ZA DOM, SPREMNI!' FOR THE HOMELAND, READY!

Another great cheer came from the audience and a surge of

fearsome pride ran through Marin's body like an electric charge. Galvanised, he called out again: '*ZA DOM!*'

And there came from the crowd the longed-for response: '*SPREMNI!!*'

Men rose to their feet and Marin felt a delicious power that could move mountains.

'*ZA DOM!*' he called again.

'*SPREMNI!!*'

A few of the men flung up their right arms. Marin saw that Ambroz Andric was one of them, his stiff-armed salute mirroring the old newsreels. Marin was shocked to have produced this reaction, but then the arms dropped as quickly as they had come up.

Then those men still on their feet were clapping and singing what was immediately recognisable as the Ustasha fighting song. It was a rousing anthem about dying for the homeland, about blood and sacrifice. Soon everyone was on their feet—men, women and children, clapping and singing along.

And even the Liberal politicians in the front row, somewhat bewildered, rose and joined in.

11.

Anna Rosen woke to the usual traffic noise from Glebe Point Road. Her abhorrence of airless rooms meant she'd left the windows wide open and a strong breeze was blowing sheets of typed paper off the desk. She heard them fluttering up one by one and became fully awake.

'Shit!'

She jumped out of bed, ran to the desk, thumped a heavy bust of Trotsky on to the pile and then gathered up the loose sheets from the floor, sorting them back into order before also putting them under the commissar's weighty protection. The bust was a fine-featured bronze with rimmed oval specs, a neat, pointed beard, a mandarin collar, the wild hair swept back from a high, smooth forehead. It was a present from Pierre that Anna had always suspected had been liberated from the bourgeois home of a former believer. She had never asked after its provenance, but she knew that, if pressed, Pierre would explain away the theft as a justifiable act of redistribution.

Meeting Trotsky's implacable gaze, Anna was suddenly aware of her own nakedness. She turned him to face the bookcase, closed the window and sat in the captain's chair, feeling the coolness of the black leather against her flesh. When she spun slowly around to face the desk, the chair pitched and rolled on its springs as if she really were at sea.

There was a china cup half-full of cold coffee next to the typewriter. She rolled out the typed page still in the machine and read it, sipping the coffee and stopping from time to time to make corrections with a pencil. She was now working hard to turn her research on Ivo Katich's eventful life into a book, and it was starting to take shape.

Her radio documentary ten days ago had revealed his role in establishing a terrorist organisation in Australia, and in funding and orchestrating the Bosnian incursion. It had sketched out his wartime past in the Ustasha and implicated him in war crimes, alleging the complicity of various security services in facilitating his immigration to Australia.

Anna thought about the Sydney Harbour Bridge. It was where she had first learned of Ivo's existence. It deserved its own chapter, if she had the courage to put herself into the story.

From deep in the house a phone began to ring. Anna was about to throw on a robe and run to answer it when it stopped.

Pierre's voice boomed down the hallway. 'Anna,' he shouted. 'It's for you. Wake up!'

A few moments later he banged on her door.

'It's one of your spooky fwiends on the phone,' he began. But before she could respond, he pushed the door open and stuck his head in, just as she spun the chair around from facing the desk.

'Oh! *Whooops!*'

When Pierre started laughing, Anna jumped up and threw a cushion at him. 'Piss off, you perve!'

'Kinky!' he managed to say before ducking back behind the door. 'Christine Keeler, eat your heart out!' he cried.

Anna grabbed her kimono, wrapped herself in it and stomped into the corridor. 'How about knocking?' she said, pushing past Pierre.

'I did. I did.'

'And came straight in.'

Pierre tried to conjure a crestfallen look but quickly gave up. 'Sorry about that, but I will have that mental picture forever.'

Anna let it go. 'You can make me a coffee in return.'

In the living room Anna sat at the phone table and picked up the receiver.

'Hello. Sorry to keep you waiting.'

'Anna?'

'Yes.'

'It's Al Sharp, I got your message.'

'Al, thanks for calling back. Can you talk now?'

'Not on the phone,' Sharp said. 'That café we met at before. Can you be there in half an hour?'

'I can.'

'See you there,' he said and hung up.

Anna dressed quickly and cycled across town. She chained her bike outside the Piccolo, both front and back wheels. It was the Cross, after all. She was early, but Al Sharp was already there, stirring sugar into a cappuccino, his large body crammed into a corner table from which he could see anyone who came into the café.

Anna had known Sharp since his ASIO days, a strangely intimate connection born out of his surveillance of her. It was the secret intimacy of the peeping Tom or the stalker, but she forgave him for it. She was grateful he'd never attempted to translate that intimacy into something real; perhaps she had been saved from embarrassment by his natural reticence.

During the years she had known him, Sharp's physical shape had changed. He'd gone from athletic to corpulent, the result of a debilitating back injury. She knew him well enough to know when the pain was bothering him. It blunted his mordant wit.

Anna ordered coffee and sat opposite him. He gave her a curt nod.

'Your radio piece was good, very strong,' he said in a voice barely above a whisper. 'Definitely thrown a cat among the pigeons. The government is on the back foot, skittish as hell. Naturally there's an investigation into how you got hold of the internal memo and the report to the A-G by the Commonwealth Police. How did you get it, by the way? That was a surprise.'

'You're not my only source.'

'No, well . . . That's good, I suppose. It spreads the risk. I expected the leak investigation, of course, but it means we have to be extremely careful now.'

'Thanks, Al. They won't find out anything from me.'

'You destroyed any notes which might identify me?'

'Of course.' She nodded. 'Exactly as we agreed.'

Sharp gave her a searching look. 'Good,' he said finally. 'I won't stay long. Ask your questions.'

'How's your back?'

'It's fucked.' He winced. 'I'm on hydrocodone pills.'

'That's a narcotic.'

'Yeah, so I'm trying not to take them.'

'Give them to me if you don't want them.'

Sharp rolled his eyes. 'I really do know too much about you,' he said. 'Next question?'

'You're on the bombing investigation?'

'Yes.'

'Any leads?'

'Nothing yet. Watching the usual suspects.'

'Ivo Katich?'

'What do you think? He's had the press camped outside his house all week.'

'I've seen him on camera, lying through his teeth. I was wondering if you got more out of him.'

Sharp laughed at that. 'He's clammed up. Refusing to say a thing.'

Anna played the next card cautiously. 'Do you know where his sons are?'

'Marin, we suspect, is still out of the country.' Sharp paused to watch her reaction. 'We suspect he may have been part of the Bosnian incursion, but we've no proof. What about you? What have you heard?'

She shook her head. 'Nothing at all. If he was in Bosnia, would you get confirmation from the Yugoslavians?'

'Officially the Yugos aren't saying anything at all. But Marin is an Australian citizen. If they were holding him, they probably wouldn't tell us.'

'Would they tell you if he'd been killed?'

'They've passed on the names of eleven dead Australians. He's not on that list.'

Anna felt a wave of relief that made her legs go weak. She fought to control her face. Vittorio put an espresso in front of her and she was thankful for the distraction. She sipped at it, steadying herself before responding.

'How reliable was the intelligence that put him in Bosnia?'

'It came from the Germans,' Sharp said. 'But it wasn't definitive. We've asked for confirmation, but nothing so far.'

'What about his brother, Petar?'

Sharp shook his head. 'Damaged goods, that one,' he said ruefully. 'He definitely didn't go to Bosnia.' Sharp delivered a tight summary. 'Mental issues. Drugs and alcohol. Smack addict, the word is. We had a look at him for the Sydney bombings, but the strong feeling is he's too fucked up. That job required steady nerves.'

'You had a look at him?' Anna repeated. 'So where is he now?'

'Seems that old man Ivo sent him to the bush to dry out.' Sharp opened his notebook and flicked through it. 'South Coast, near Eden. Place called Khandalah. That's all I've got. We had a surveillance team down there for a while. Pulled out now. No phone there. Pretty basic.'

'Is he alone?'

'He was.'

'Isn't that odd?'

'Petar's not great company, by all accounts. He was interviewed, of course. By Ray Sullivan. Detective sergeant, one of our best. Incoherent, he reckons, a mumbling wreck. You thinking of going down there?'

'I might,' she admitted.

Sharp slowly drank his coffee. Tapping out a cigarette, he offered her one, but she declined. He lit up, considerately blowing smoke away from her.

'Well, he sounds like a fruitcake. You'll have to handle him with extreme care. I wouldn't go alone, if I were you. Listen, I've got to get going. Send me a message if you pick up anything, will you?'

'Sure,' she said. 'Anything else on this Khandalah place?'

'It's very remote, the property's on a river that comes out at Twofold Bay. That's really all I've got. I'm sure you'll find it if you need to. Good luck with that.'

Sharp nodded again, stood up gingerly and left without another word.

*

It took only a few calls for Anna to get a lead on Khandalah. A realtor in Eden knew the place and gave her detailed directions on how to get there. Its exotic name came from an Indian hill station south of Bombay, which struck her as a strange choice for a Croat hideaway.

Marin had talked about spending summers on the South Coast, but she had never imagined anything like a misty, green colonial hill station. He had always been vague, never named it. Of course she knew now that this was only one of his many secrets.

Anna called McHugh to tell him of this breakthrough and he agreed that Petar Katich was the best lead they had, if she could get him to talk. The travel office booked a room for her at the pretentiously named Hotel Australasia in Eden. When she rang the front desk, the manager—'Call me Dave'—told her that she should factor in seven or eight hours for the journey by car. He recommended she take the inland route via the Monaro Plains, along the foothills of the Snowy Mountains to Cooma, and then down Brown Mountain to the Coast. The restaurant would be closed by the time she got there, but he promised her a late supper.

'If you're up for some game fishing, the tuna are running now,' he offered.

'I'm afraid I'll be working, Dave.'

'ABC, eh?'

'That's right.'

Anna cursed herself for letting the travel office do the booking. So much for anonymity.

'Pretty quiet down here,' Dave said. 'We done something wrong?'

'No, I'm just coming down to interview someone. Nothing to do with Eden.'

'That's a relief, love. Make sure to bring your swimmers. Water's clear and perfect. They didn't call it Eden for nothin.'

Anna hung up.

They didn't call it Eden for nothin'. She fell into a brief reverie. Eden as the paradise you can visit but never leave—*Wake in Fright* by the sea.

In the end she did pack a swimsuit, her most modest one-piece. She dressed in a faded denim jacket, black T-shirt, old jeans, elastic-sided boots. Checking the outfit in the mirror, she reckoned she looked tough enough. She hid a little stash in her overnight bag, rolled a few joints and put four or five bennies in her change pocket, taking one straightaway for the road.

Along with her Nagra, she'd booked out a new Sony cassette recorder from the techs. She added a shoebox full of tapes dubbed from her record collection. With the speed buzz coming on, she loaded the back of the rented station wagon and put the Sony on the passenger seat, plugging in a cassette of the latest T. Rex album, *Electric Warrior*. Then at last she took off.

Her cash travelling allowance was in an envelope in her pocket; she was alone and on the road. She loved that feeling. Marc Bolan's rhythm guitar riffs started at high volume; in came the drums, the piano, the bass, the lead guitar and then his grungy, cool voice. He said she was dirty and sweet. He said he loved her.

'Love you too, Marc,' she said, outracing the slow-moving traffic.

Anna was high as a kite when she reached Eden. She had stopped on the coast road at sunset and smoked a joint, miscalculating the strength of the weed Pierre had sold her. For the remainder of the journey she had fought the sensation that the camber of the road would take her plunging off the edge.

Now the comforting ordinariness of the town stilled the paranoia. It was like reaching a fortified settlement after a long trek through hostile Indian country. In the last glimmer of dusk the streetlights flickered on enchantingly. The town's buildings, clustered on either side of a wide main street, were like an Edward Hopper painting.

The hotel was in the middle of the town, above the harbour. There was no way of missing it. She climbed out, stretched her back and looked up.

HOTEL AUSTRALASIA.

She stared at the building as if it were an epiphany. Someone had plonked a featureless white box on top of what must have once been a turn-of-the-century pub, built to service the prosperous whaling town. She saw that what would have been a wide colonial veranda on the second floor, along with all the original architectural detail, had been replaced by this plain, hard-edged structure. What were they thinking? All of it was done, she imagined, in the cause of modernism. The preposterous name was emblazoned right across the top storey in letters six feet high. So ... ugly pretty, or pretty ugly? Best appreciated when stoned.

Anna pulled from the back of the car the equipment case and her overnight bag, into which she stowed the cassette player. Because it was getting dark she took off her sunnies to consider the world for a moment in this new light. Then she put them back on and went inside.

Dave the manager was not at the front desk. In his absence, Anna found herself being scrutinised by a weather-worn and weary drudge of a woman with tobacco-stained fingers, who finally lit a cigarette and offered to show her the room.

It was at the back of the hotel. A pair of tall windows looked out over Twofold Bay. Floodlights around the fishing harbour reflected on the black water. Moonlight delineated the horizon and cast a beam over the ocean. One window was open and a sea breeze flowed in.

'Wanna keep the winda open?' the woman asked, tapping ash out of it. 'I was just airin' the place out.'

'Yep, I like fresh air.'

'Nice view in the daytime, anyways.' The woman brushed hair from her eyes. 'Kitchen's closed, but Dave said you'd be hungry.'

The sea and the clear pure air had a calming effect. Anna took off her sunglasses.

'He's right,' she said. 'It was a long drive. I'm starving.'

'I've put aside a plate of ham and salad. That do ya?'

'Thanks, that's fine.'

'Well, you go ahead and freshen up. Come down to the bar when you're ready.' The woman managed a smile. Not a drudge after all. 'Here's your key, love.'

Anna lay on the soft mattress and fell asleep.

She woke, her stomach griping with pangs of hunger. She sat up and checked her watch. Almost 10 pm. She'd slept for two hours.

Closing time, damn it! She jumped up, splashed cold water on her face and rushed downstairs. Far from emptying out, the public bar was loud and full. There was a fug of smoke, of stale beer, of inebriated men and their raging hormonal stench.

The noise bounced off the yellowish tiles, but it dropped when she walked into the room. Anna felt all eyes on her—an unexpected opportunity that had just presented itself to a roomful of boozy males. Then the sound levels rose again as if in embarrassment at their collective animal instincts.

She wove through the herd like a city girl in a cattle yard. The gauntlet of flannelette and sweaty T-shirts yielded a pathway to the crowded bar, where bodies shifted to make space for her.

The barman came over.

'I'm staying here tonight,' she told him. 'Is it too late to get something to eat?'

He grinned. 'Anna from Aunty ABC, right?'

'You're Dave?'

'Yep, kept yer dinner in the fridge.'

'I thought I'd be too late. Didn't realise this was a late-opener.'

Dave smiled. 'It's not. Doors are locked, but once you're in you're in. The "Snake Pit", Eden's best kept secret . . . But don't go puttin' that on your radio show.'

Anna made the connection: a roomful of Adams and a solitary Eve. At the end of the bar she noticed a uniformed police sergeant, tie askew, four sheets to the wind. That's how you get away with things in a small town—free beers for the constabulary.

'It's lively this time of the year,' Dave explained. 'Blokes down for the tuna. Boat crews who should know better, tree-cutters and farmers and what not. There'd be a riot if we shut the bar. I'll get your dinner. There're some empty tables out back. How about a drink?'

'I'll have a schooner of Resch's, thanks.'

Dave set a beer in front of her and started on orders from the backlog of drinkers.

'So, ABC is it, then?' asked the man squeezed in beside her at the bar. His thickly muscled arms pressed against her shoulder. It was like leaning against the flank of a racehorse, hard and twitchy.

She turned towards his weathered face; it was not unpleasant when he smiled, and he was smiling now.

'Yep, you heard right.'

'What you havin' for dinner then—alphabet soup?'

Anna took a sip of her drink. 'Good one.'

'Reporter, is it?'

'That's right.'

'That's a bloody novelty down 'ere.'

'That's how I've always thought of myself,' she said. 'A novelty item.'

'Wipe off the beer moustache, then, and I'll take you seriously.'

She quickly found the froth on her upper lip and brushed it off. They both laughed.

'Got me,' she said.

'Do you like fishin', ABC?'

'Not in the least. The tuna are running, right? I like eating it. Someone else can do the hard work. Is that what you do?'

'I've got a boat, yeah. Tell Dave if you change your mind, ask for Bob Johnson.'

'I don't have time for fishing, Bob. I've got work to do.'

'Pity. Where you headed?'

Anna pulled a face. Too many questions.

'I've got to meet someone.'

'Whereabouts?'

'Inland, up the Towamba River.'

'The Towamba, eh? That's hillbilly territory up there. Take care—a lot of odd folk on the river.'

Dave returned with her dinner tray. 'Here's your supper, love,' he said. 'Give her a bit of space, Bob.'

Anna loaded her beer on to the tray with the cling-wrapped plate, some cutlery in a paper serviette and a couple of bread rolls.

She found a table away from the bar. The meal was better than she expected: slices of leg ham, homemade potato salad, lettuce and tomatoes that tasted like they should. She ate fast, slapping chunks of hard butter on the bread rolls and washing it all down with beer.

She was so engrossed in eating that she didn't notice the man pull up a chair and sit down beside her.

'Hello, Anna.'

She looked up, startled. This was no fisherman or forestry worker. He might have walked off a sugar plantation in Jamaica. It was the crumpled linen suit that created that illusion. He was unshaven, with the narrow face and deep-set eyes of a serious drinker. Fading contusions gave one of those eyes a purplish-green shading.

'I'm sorry,' she said warily. 'Do I know you?'

The man raised his eyebrows apologetically, took a sip of his drink. Vodka, by the looks of it, a big one.

'N-No,' he stuttered. 'But I know you. And I know what you're really d-doing down here.'

'What are you talking about? Who are you?'

'That's not important.'

'Oh, I see.' Anna stared at him coldly. She'd been here before. They had something about them, these blokes, all of them. They carried the mark, like a brand on their foreheads. 'I should have guessed. I don't talk to strangers, especially not spooky ones.'

'You can c-call me T-Tom.'

'Did you follow me here . . . Tom?'

'No, Anna.' Tom's face radiated irony and secret knowledge, the currency of spies. He leaned in close, ready to confide something. 'It's the m-merest coincidence, actually. Happens I came here to see the same f-fellow you're looking for.'

'And how exactly do you know why I'm here?'

The man drained his drink, immediately looking around to see where the next one might be coming from. Anna saw that he would need a trip to the bar sooner rather than later.

'Don't worry, Tom,' she said with deep condescension. 'It's a while 'til last drinks.'

He winked his good eye. 'That's s-sweet of you. Clever thing. How do I know why you're here? I c-could say that we know every-thing ... But you've been around the block a few times, so no b-bullshit. Truth is, I recognised you when you came into the b-bar. Put two and t-two together.'

Anna's curiosity got the better of her. 'Recognised me? How?'

'In my world, let's just say you're a familiar f-f-face.'

'Are your people tapping my phone, Tom?'

'Most probably, I expect. But I'm n-not aware if they are.'

Anna finished the last of her beer and readied herself to get up. Tom put a hand out, fingers splayed.

'Hold on, Anna, I've been here for t-two days already. Saw our f-friend yesterday. How's that fit with your own t-timetable for getting here? I'm pretty good, but I'm not c-c-clairvoyant.'

'Well, Tom—if that really is your name—I've known men like you since I was a kid and I don't need to be a clairvoyant to predict nothing good can come of it.'

'Nicely put. You've got sp-spunk. Actually, you can even see that in the old s-surveillance photos, but they d-don't do you any j-justice ... Now, I need a sharpener. Can I b-buy you a drink?'

'You can't be serious ...'

'You might need something stronger before you go see our f-friend Petar. He's in poor shape, almost c-catatonic. I don't like your chances of getting anything out of him. But I would be inter-ested to know if you do.'

'Can you really imagine me reporting back to ASIO?'

'I'm a b-born optimist.'

'You're drunk is what you are.'

'No need to get p-personal. We have c-common interests here, Anna. I know a lot about the K-Katich family. We could help each other out.' He got to his feet unsteadily.

Anna paused. A deal with the devil was on the table. It felt like a cold wind had blown into the room. She shivered, looked up at the man and smiled thinly.

'You know, Tom, it's kind of appropriate to meet a snake here in Eden, but I'm definitely not tempted.'

Tom reached down and put a card on the table in front of her.

'You might change your m-mind one day,' he said and headed for the bar.

Anna looked at the card: *Thomas Moriarty, Security Consultant*. There was a Canberra number on it. She put it in her pocket and went back to her meal.

But it wasn't long before she was interrupted again. The culprit was a clean-cut young man with a blandly handsome face. Dressed in moleskins and a pale-blue stockman's shirt, he could have been a farmer's son. She had noticed him earlier, drinking with the police sergeant, and taken him for an off-duty cop.

He put two beers on the table and pulled up a chair.

'Got you a drink,' he said.

Anna pushed her empty plate aside and stared at him for a moment.

'I must look lonely,' she said.

'No, but your drink was finished.'

She picked up the offered beer. 'Cheers, then.'

'Name's Carl,' he said. 'Saw you brush off that pisshead. I didn't come over to try my luck.'

'Why then?'

'Thought you might be wanting something for the night.' Carl lowered his voice. 'Something special. I've got some top-grade hammer, just in from Sydney.'

Anna looked him over. To operate so brazenly, Carl was obviously kicking back to the police sergeant. So, a protected species—best not get him offside.

'Thanks for the thought, but I'm working tomorrow,' she said with a smile. 'Besides, that particular powder doesn't do much for me.'

'I can get you some crank if you want.' He went into full salesman mode. 'Pills, Buddha sticks, hash, acid? Name your poison.'

'Cocaine?'

Carl laughed out loud. 'Ohh! Not much call for that down here.'

'I'm just pulling your leg, Carl,' Anna said mildly. 'I don't want anything. Thanks for the beer, though.'

'No worries.' He shrugged and got up. 'Plenty of other customers. Thought I'd give you first dibs.'

Anna glanced at the policeman and realised that he'd been watching the exchange with Carl. Had that been a set-up? Still looking at her, the sergeant sculled the rest of his schooner.

There was some back-slapping with his drinking companions, then he levered himself off the bar stool and headed for the exit. The accommodating Dave reached the doors ahead of him, opened the locks and, after some more back-slapping, the sergeant staggered off into the night.

She noticed that Carl had already found another customer, a sinister-looking man sitting alone at the far end of the bar. This must be Carl's prime time, she thought as she watched the dealer negotiate his sale. His customer had the look of a gypsy, one who'd done hard prison time. He was a tall man, tough, wiry and tattooed, with long, greasy hair that he kept pushing away from his face. They were chalk and cheese, Carl and his customer.

The two men got up together and adjourned to the gents. When they emerged, the gypsy split away; with a foil of smack now burning a hole in his pocket, he hurried to the exit.

The Snake Pit was reaching peak drunk. Everyone seemed to be yelling now. Time to go.

Anna was about to move when Tom Moriarty, even drunker, came back and threw himself into the seat next to her. Too close.

'Quite the small-town scene, eh?' he said. 'The crooked c-cop, his pet dealer, stoned woodchoppers, a foreign j-junkie . . .'

'And a pissed ASIO pants man.'

'One for the road then?'

'No, thanks. I'm going to bed.'

Moriarty put a cold hand on her arm. 'I don't suppose I could come and t-tuck you in?'

'Take your fucking hand off me or I'll scream, and this mob will probably lynch you.'

Moriarty pulled his hand away as if he'd grasped a live wire.

12.

Anna woke to clear blue skies. It was an unseasonably hot early morning, heading for a stinker. She packed her gear, ate bacon and eggs in the next-door café and headed off in the station wagon. The directions soon took her out of town past a holiday camp and a caravan park. There was a causeway over a river and then for a long time nothing but bush on either side of the road.

As she was drawn into it, Anna had the familiar sense of dissonance. The green density of undifferentiated eucalypts as they crowded the narrow strip of road seemed threatening. She felt as though the vast sameness might swallow her up, erupt into flames and burn her existence away like an impurity in a forge.

She wondered if Marin Katich had felt that he belonged here, if he was torn between the land of his birth and the dream homeland his father had breathed into his imagination. She felt she was moving closer to him. She was anxious about the prospect of seeing Petar again, but there was a stirring of excitement. No matter how different they were, no matter how damaged Petar might be, Marin was his flesh and blood.

She came to the landmarks she was looking for, a second causeway over sandy tidal flats and a distant river on her left. Then the road twisted up a hill, and after a mile she found, at the first exit, the dirt road. She trundled along on the badly maintained dirt until she reached a fork and took the right arm on to an even narrower track.

Now she slowed to a crawl and bounced over the deeply rutted surface, pushing the station wagon towards the edge of the road to avoid the biggest holes, until she came at last around a tight bend and found herself high above the river, blue and calm against the framing of green.

She rolled down her window and heard bellbirds ringing through the trees. She had never heard so many in one place. She stopped the car and listened. The ringing had an intoxicating, almost magical quality. From time to time there came a whipbird's call.

The sun was gentler here, filtered through the trees. Occasional shafts of light picked out the pale, peeling trunks and variegated colours of different species. Now that she was deep inside it, the bush was no longer fearsome in its immensity. It had a close, intimate beauty, and she understood how someone could become attached to such a place.

As she drove on, she realised there was no sign of other people— no poles, no fences and no buildings. Only the road, until she finally came to a gate with a sign that brought her straight back to the world of men:

Khandalah. Private property.
Trespassers not welcome. Keep out.

Anna opened the gate, drove through and then closed it behind her. After a while the track descended sharply, becoming steeper and rougher until she realised that, if she went any further, she might not be able to turn the car around to get back out.

She pulled into a small clearing. She took the bag of notebooks and recording gear, and slung it on her back. She put the Nagra over her shoulder and set off downhill.

The shrill pulsing of cicadas was now the dominant sound. It grew louder and louder as she stumbled down the path.

Eventually she saw a second gate. It was open and there was a dwelling beyond it. She saw a movement on the other side of the gate and stopped. She was about to call out when a gunshot split the air. For a moment the cicadas and birds went quiet and the explosion of sound hung there in eerie silence before the insects regained their voices.

Anna called out, 'Hello! Is that you, Petar?'

There was no reply, so she called again. 'I'm coming down. Don't shoot.'

She began walking towards the dwelling. A man staggered from the bush. There was a rifle in his hands. The way he was moving she thought he was drunk or drugged, or both.

'Petar?' she called again.

'Stop! Go back,' the man yelled. 'Get off my land!'

'Petar? It's you, isn't it? I've met you before.'

'I already spoke to the police. Turn around and go away.' The man raised the rifle carelessly and pointed it in her direction.

'I'm not the police, Petar. I won't go, not until I talk to you.'

He jerked the rifle up and fired over her head. Again the bush sounds stopped before gradually returning.

'Petar,' Anna pleaded as she came nearer. 'Don't you remember me?'

'Remember you? Who are you?' He peered at her, squinting into the sun. 'No! Don't come any closer.'

Anna kept walking towards him, her hands away from her body, open and unthreatening.

'You've changed, Petar, but I still remember you. We've met before. I was with Marin.'

He became agitated. 'Liar!' he cried. 'That's a lie. A *lie*! Who sent you?'

She was close to him now, perhaps ten feet away. He was walking in circles, or rather stumbling, the rifle pinned to his chest.

'It was a long time ago, Petar. Nearly two years. My name is Anna. Do you remember? I was having dinner with Marin at that Lebanese place he liked to go to and you came to see him.'

'I don't,' he said, shrugging and shaking his head. 'I don't remember that.'

'You were pretty out of it.'

Petar now stopped his incessant movement and, to Anna's surprise, he sat down in the dirt with the rifle across his lap.

'That is possible, it's possible.' He let out an odd laugh. 'Fuck that for a joke. Why are you here? Who sent you? Are you another fucking spy? First the police, then the spies. All buzzing round like blowies on shit. Who the fuck are you, anyway?'

Anna sat down cross-legged in front of him before answering, putting the Nagra and her shoulder bag to one side. This close to him, she could smell the alcohol leaching from his pores. She fixed her gaze on his face, trying to get his eyes to stop darting about, to settle him.

'I'm trying to find Marin. He's my friend. I'm not a spy. I hate spies.'

'Everyone's trying to find Marin,' Petar said, his voice shifting from calm to fretful. 'The spies are trying to find him. I told them nothing. Nothing. Not a word from me.'

'I'm not a spy, Petar,' said Anna soothingly. 'You could ask Marin about me.'

Petar pointed at the Nagra, its dials and meters visible. 'What's that, then? If you're not a spy.'

'I'm a journalist. That's my tape recorder. I couldn't leave it in the car. I had to park way up the hill.'

'You try and turn that on, I'll put a bullet right through it.'

'I'd never turn it on without asking you.'

Petar's head dropped, and for a moment she thought he had passed out. Then she heard that he was sobbing, quietly at first, but after a while his shoulders began to heave.

'I don't remember you. No,' he cried out, raising his head to reveal tears streaking his dusty face. 'I don't remember anything much. I'm totally fucked up. Memory's gone to shit.'

Anna said nothing, waiting for him to say more.

But then his mood shifted again. 'You shouldn't be here! No, you should not . . . I shouldn't even be here. I'm not meant to be here. I should be with them.'

'Where's that?'

'What?'

'Where should you be, Petar?'

He waved his hand in a chopping motion, so violently that it nearly knocked him sideways.

'Don't worry about that! Forget it. It's none of your business.'

'You mean you should be with Marin? Where he is?'

Petar stared for a moment and then jabbed a finger at her. 'What did you say your name was again?'

'Anna.'

'Your other name . . .'

'Rosen.'

'Rosen? Rosen, is it? That's a Jew's name, isn't it? Don't think about it—just tell me.'

'Yes. I was born a Jew.'

'My father says I have to watch out for Jews.'

'Why's that, Petar?'

'The Jews want to hunt us down, because of the war.'

'What do you mean?'

'You know what I mean! Don't act dumb. We were on the German side. Now the Jews want to hunt us all down. Don't trust fucking Jews.'

'You weren't even born then, Petar.'

'Doesn't fucking matter. You hate us because of what we believe in.'

'Marin didn't think that. I was his girlfriend, Petar. I know he cared for you as best he could. He wanted to help you get well, your big brother. Didn't he?'

Petar's head dropped again, staring at the rifle, his shoulders still heaving. Without warning he snatched at the barrel and pulled it under his chin, fingers on the trigger.

'Don't do that, Petar.'

'I'm not strong like him. I'm the weak one.' He was weeping now with self-pity. 'The bad seed, that's what my father says. That's what he thinks of me.'

'Please put the gun down.'

'Marin thought it too. I know he did. He never said it in words, but I could always see it in his eyes. He's not good at hiding what he thinks. He couldn't do it. He felt sorry for me—' Petar broke off and threw the rifle aside, sobbing like a child. 'I never wanted his pity. It just leaves you shrivelled up and small.'

'Marin didn't think that at all. He loves you.'

'Love that comes from pity. He thought I was defective. Something not right. Something broken that he couldn't fix. So he stopped me doing things. But then I showed him what I could do. I showed them all!'

Anna desperately wanted to ask what he had done, but she sensed it would trigger his paranoia again. She would come back to it.

'Petar, the reason I've come here to see you is because I'm worried about Marin. I'm afraid he's in trouble. I've . . . been dreaming about him.'

Petar's expression changed, as if a sudden wind had washed the pain away. He wiped at his face.

'He's in your dreams?' he asked. 'What happens?'

'They're strange, like visions. I wake up with this fear that Marin might have been killed.'

'I have dreams, too.'

'About Marin?'

'I have dreams and fucking nightmares.' Petar jumped to his feet. Towering over Anna, he hit the side of his head with the heel of his hand. 'I want them out of my head. *Out!* I want to be left alone. It's fucking my head. My head!'

Petar's legs seemed to buckle under him. He stumbled to his knees and, before Anna could reach out to him, he toppled over. He lay there in the harsh sun, unconscious.

Anna slapped his face until his eyes rolled open. He mumbled in a delirium. Then she managed to pull him up and manoeuvre herself under one of his arms. In this fashion she helped him down the hill and into the largest of the two dwellings.

From a concealed position high above Khandalah, two men watched Anna struggling to support the weight of the semiconscious man as she made her way across a clearing of long grass. The men had one pair of powerful binoculars which they shared from time to time. From their position they could see the two buildings—both of them old, rundown wooden farmhouses with rusty tin roofs and brick chimney stacks. There were several ancient couches on the covered veranda of the main dwelling; they lost sight of Anna and her burden when she hauled the man on to its veranda and into the house.

To the right of the farmhouses the land dipped steeply to the river, while to the left was a wide section of pasture that was wild. No other dwelling was visible in any direction. Khandalah was isolated from the rest of the world. The men knew that isolation was the reason Ivo Katich had purchased it in the first place.

It had taken them a long time to find it. The woman was a problem they had not anticipated. Previously they had watched the drunken spy come and go. They had monitored his movements and were aware that he had left town first thing this morning. They could not afford a run-in with the Australian security services, so they had waited. Their brief was to be as inconspicuous as possible. No one must know they were here, or their purpose. The arrival of the woman was an inconvenience, but they would have to wait her out as well.

If Anna could have seen the men watching her, she would have recognised the taller of the two as the tattooed junkie who had purchased heroin at the Snake Pit.

The other man was older, thinner and appeared to be in charge. He swivelled the binoculars from the veranda back to the area near the gates where she had confronted Petar Katich. The rifle was still there on the ground and nearby were the two items she had been carrying. The man had been wondering if it would be worth the risk of snatching the weapon; but then Anna came out on her own, picked up her bags and the rifle, and went back into the house.

*

Anna came back inside with the Nagra, her bag and the rifle. She carried the gun as if it were about to go off. She sat down with it, trying to figure out how to remove the magazine; then she worked the bolt and ejected the round in the breech. She opened a kitchen drawer at random and dropped the cartridge and the magazine inside. Having made it safe, she propped the rifle against the wall.

When she put her head through the open bedroom doorway, she saw that Petar was sprawled unconscious across the bed. She looked around the sparsely furnished farmhouse. The place was dirty and dishevelled, but not the filthy junkie's lair she had imagined. In the living room was a couch and a couple of old sagging armchairs with blankets covering the worn upholstery. The fireplace was full of ash and charred logs, but there was dry timber beside it. A standard lamp was lying on the wooden floor, as if it had simply given up the ghost and toppled over. Scattered across the floor was a collection of empty stone jars; another jar, half-full of a clear viscous liquid, sat on the battered coffee table with a glass alongside it.

Anna picked up the jar and sniffed its contents—industrial-strength alcohol, some kind of homemade brandy, she guessed. She took a sip and it burned all the way to the pit of her stomach.

She decided to make a cup of tea and rummaged through the kitchen until she found what she needed. She spooned tea leaves into a pot, lit the gas stove and put the kettle on. She cleared away dirty cups and plates from the kitchen table and piles of old news-papers. Among the detritus she found an exercise book mostly filled with a tight scrawl written in pencil. She flicked through it, page after rambling page, and then she read the latest entry:

The same nightmare over and over. I'm in the pit. Slowly slowly
I claw my way out. A dead man come to life and crawling
over piles of stinking bodies. I wake up in breathless panic.

The stench of corpses on my skin. It's your fault, Jurjevic, you fucking Serb lover. How did you get my address? Of all the shit you sent me I can never get those fucking pictures out of my head. The old photos, you can't unsee them, you just can't.

They're propaganda, right? The old man's always told us that. The communists dressed up men in Ustasha uniforms and had them take off another man's head with a saw, or slit throat after throat until their faces and bare chests were so covered in blood they were drunk with it, laughing and proud. Or they made them hack heads off with an axe, or beat out men's brains with hammers, or stand in pits full of bodies to get their souvenir photos with the fuckers they just killed.

It could only be propaganda, right? My father wasn't like that. He wasn't a blood-sick monster, was he? Not him. Not such a good old fellow. He's crazy, but not that kind of crazy. Even so, it still takes all my strength to pull myself out of the pit he put me in.

Now Branko, he could have done all those things. I can see him with a curved knife strapped to his wrist cutting throat after throat, and throwing the bodies aside like a shearer tossing sheep. Then I think of the two of them, young men, mates together in the uniform, Ivo's arm over Branko's shoulder, Branko's over Ivo's, and then I remember the bodies lying on George Street. I think of those people a lot, bleeding and twitching on the pavement.

That's how the day starts. Every day. Then the mind starts to rev up and I can't stop it—it's like an engine without a governor. It just revs up and up and up until I can't stand it. The roaring in my head is unbearable. You can drink and drink, but the only thing that slows it down is the smack. Thank God for that, but it's only temporary, and then I come back down into the pit and I think of the line from the old Croatian poem my father once recited to me—'Weak children are born in joy but these offspring perish quickly.'

The whistle on the kettle screamed and Anna jerked back to the present. She jumped up and grabbed it off the flame.

The bodies lying on George Street . . . bleeding and twitching on the pavement.

Was that a confession, or an accusation? Whichever it was, Petar's journal was evidence. She had no choice but to hand this over to Sharp. The police would have to question Petar again.

She poured boiling water into the pot absentmindedly and the smell of brewing tea was good. It stilled her mind. But she had a strong sense of the sickness that clung to this house. Its presence emanated from the man in the bedroom: the sickness of guilt.

What else was in the journal? Of the many revelations contained in the one entry she had read, one of the strangest was the reference to Jurjevic. This could only be Marjan Jurjevic, her contact in Melbourne, the dissident Croat and enemy of the extremists in his own community. Jurjevic had been targeted for assassination by the Ustasha and yet here he was in contact with the leader's son.

She knew exactly the old photos Petar was referring to. Jurjevic had given her the same material. Black-and-white photos of unimaginable brutality, proudly taken during the worst excesses of the 1940s by the Ustasha perpetrators. It was a time when the written policy of Pavelic's government in Zagreb, with the direct assistance of a cohort of Catholic priests, was for them to convert one-third of Orthodox Christian Serbs—Jews were never given that option—expel another third, and then kill the final third.

Officers of Hitler's SS, who had been sent as military advisors to their new Croatian ally, wrote detailed accounts of the horrors they witnessed. Even the SS could not stomach the Ustasha's savagery. For Anna, those accounts—field reports from German military officers—were convincing evidence.

Anna poured herself a cup of strong tea and stirred sugar into it. She needed to settle her own mind. She knew that Jurjevic would have sent Petar those German SS accounts, along with the documentation put together by the War Crimes Tribunal at Nuremberg. These provided the necessary background information about those gruesome photos. But did Petar have copies of the documents that she had been able to source—the ones that detailed Ivo Katich's own direct involvement in these killings, when he was the commander of the Mobile Court Martial in Bosnia?

She opened the journal again and was about to start reading when noises from the bedroom interrupted her. Petar was awake. His door slammed shut and she heard him rumbling through drawers. Then silence.

She stood nervously outside the door. The man was disturbed and out of control. Who knew what he was capable of? She considered fetching the rifle and reloading it, but she knew she would never be able to shoot him if it came to that, and he might be strong enough to take it back and use it against her.

In the end, she knocked softly on the door.

'Petar, are you all right?'

'Leave me alone,' he called. The tone was plaintive and followed by a deep sob.

'I'm coming in.'

'No, stay out.'

She cracked the door open and caught a glimpse of his slumped figure in an old rocking chair by the bed, then a small flame. She opened it fully and saw him shaking like a leaf, cooking up a hit of heroin on a spoon. He glanced up at her, a tormented face.

She said nothing. She had seen people do this to themselves enough times for it not to disturb her. There was nothing she could do but hope he'd gotten the dose right.

Petar tied off his arm with a piece of rubber and hit up in front of her. He let go of the rubber, sighed at the drug's surge and rocked in the chair, nodding off, the fit still in his arm.

She went and knelt beside him, slapping his face until he came around dreamily, calm now, his eyes pinned.

'Where is Marin?' she whispered.

'I can't say, I can't.'

'Tell me where he is, Petar. I need to know.'

'Dead, for all I know, with the rest of them.'

'Did he go to Bosnia?'

'Leave me alone.' He closed his eyes.

She slapped him again, harder. 'Did he go to Bosnia?'

'Marin, the fucking hero—'course he did. Took my place. My place!'

'What do you mean?'

'I was ready. Done all the fuckin' training . . . Fuck it.'

Again his eyes drooped and closed. She slapped his face once more.

'Don't go away, Petar. What do you mean, he took your place?' There was an edge to her voice.

'He came here and took my place. "You're not taking Petar, no way! He's not going. I'll go instead of him." Fucking hero, my brother. Well, fuck him. Want to be a martyr? Go ahead. Fuck him. I hope he's dead.'

Petar nodded off again, deeper now, into oblivion. His breathing was steady. She felt his heartbeat and it was strong enough. His tolerance was obviously high. This wouldn't kill him, but he would be out for some time. Anna stood and looked down at him. She had the answer she had been seeking. The pity she had felt for him was gone. He was a loathsome creature.

She left him lolling in the rocking chair and began to search his room. She found a good deal of the historical material Jurjevic had sent him beside the bed. Some of it was scattered across the floor. The black-and-white photos were in his bedside drawer, like some sort of ghastly pornography. Snuff photos—which was what they were when the monsters took them back in 1941.

Among them she found something else: a creased tourist pamphlet for the city of Zagreb, capital of the state of Croatia in Yugoslavia. She leafed through the photos of street markets and trams, the chequerboard roof of the cathedral and the cartoon-ish statue of King Tomislav, forever riding into battle outside the railway station. Finally, she turned to the back page and found a printed sticker: *Adriatic Trade and Travel Centre, 668 George Street, Sydney 2001.*

It wasn't forensic evidence of a bombing, but it was enough for her. She stomped around the bed to the rocking chair.

Petar was unconscious. She tried slapping again—once, twice— but he barely stirred. She reached down in disgust and pulled the fit from his arm, then turned and jabbed it hard into the old plaster of the wall. It stuck there like a badly aimed dart. A trickle of his blood dripped down the wall.

She couldn't bear another moment in his presence. She closed the bedroom door, leaving behind the pamphlet and the documen-tary evidence of the dark inheritance his father had bequeathed him. From the kitchen she retrieved his journal, rationalising that he had forfeited any right to privacy. Gathering up her belongings, she left the farmhouse.

From the hide high above her, the older man watched through the binoculars as she left the house.

13.

Monday, 21 June 1972

It was after midnight when Marin Katich and his nineteen companions reached St Oswald, close to the border at a point high in the Austrian Alps. The persistent rain of the past few weeks had finally ceased and the town's chocolate-box houses were washed clean of remnant snow. The old bus stopped at a white church with a high, pointed steeple. All twenty of them were spirited through a walled courtyard into the chapel to receive the priest's blessing for the operation. Marin hated priests as a class, but this one was an especially smarmy prick, happy to send men off to die with God's name on their lips, a last communion and some mumbo jumbo about their sacred mission.

At 2 am they were taken as far as they could go in the bus. They tumbled out into a clear, dark night. Torches were forbidden. Starlight and a half moon lit their way. Old snow glimmered on the ground.

Marin squinted into the darkness ahead. There was no way of knowing if trip-wires or mines lay in front of them. Maybe they were there, or maybe they were a myth. However, the Brotherhood's intelligence on border patrols proved correct: twenty heavily burdened shadows passed into Yugoslavia unobserved.

Most of the men crossed the border in their *troikas*. That is to say, eighteen of them made the crossing in six groups, which left Juro Horvat and Marin to cross as a pair.

Marin was sure that Ambroz Andric had put the sinister little Tasmanian on his case. Horvat was Andric's lickspittle—a defective, acne-scarred creature; but not to be underestimated, despite his appearance. Marin knew the man's reputation. Horvat had been sent to Hobart to train recruits in bomb-making and to pass on his signature skill of killing with a knife, having gained expertise in both disciplines in Europe. Marin felt his skin crawl every time Horvat was behind him. God forbid he would ever have to trust his life to him. The man was built for betrayal, designed to fail under pressure like fuse wire.

During the crossing Horvat was hunched over, bent by the weight on his back. Each of them carried a heavy pack, stuffed with food and hundreds of rounds of ammunition. They were armed with an assortment of automatic weapons, rifles and Browning pistols, all of which had been provided to them by the Brotherhood in Salzburg and paid for by funds raised in Australia.

Marin couldn't complain about that side of things. They had given him a fine Austrian weapon, a Steyr SSG 69 sniper rifle, the military version with the long barrel. It had been modified in a secret workshop to fit a hand-tooled suppressor. They had made silencers for the automatic weapons too, but he suspected they would overheat and malfunction in a firefight.

Horvat was a thin man, stringy as a half-starved street dog, but strong. He managed to keep up with Marin, but he didn't like the cold, and every time they stopped his teeth began to chatter. The ground was spongy in patches, where the rain had melted the snow cap away, and Marin felt soft moss on the mountain rocks when he leaned against an outcrop to get his bearings.

Horvat slumped down beside him, uncomfortably close. His breathing was as ragged as an asthmatic's. On the slope ahead was a stretch of icy snow; when Marin peered down, looking for some sign of the others, he caught a shadow moving stealthily across the whiteness.

He grabbed Horvat's arm. 'Shhhh, stay quiet,' he whispered. 'There's something there.'

The shadow stopped, merging with a rock. Marin stared hard at the dark place on the snow. Had the movement been a trick of the mind? The concertina of the other man's breathing started up again.

'I don't see anything,' wheezed Horvat. 'Let's go.'

'No, wait.'

Marin slipped off his pack and crawled forward on to the icy ground. He felt the cold damp through his gloves and the knees of his fatigues as he crunched across the compacted snow until the dark smudge of the rock was about ten feet away. Then a shadow detached itself from the blackness and came towards him. As it got closer, he saw a creature with its head down under high withers. Its luminous green eyes gleamed in the moonlight.

An ancient instinct froze Marin to the spot. It was a wolf, a wolf by God! It stopped a few feet short of him, close enough for him to make out yellowish teeth etched into its dark muzzle. It was a big animal and in Marin's vulnerable position on all fours it stood taller than him. It smelled of soil and bracken and blood, fungal and moist.

A strange stillness enveloped the two beings, man and wolf. Contained within it, Marin was not afraid. The wildness in the creature's eyes was ineffable—neither alien, nor threatening.

As if bidden by the creature, the wolf song rose from deep in Marin's throat—the *ojkanje*, which his father had done his best to teach him. He sang it softly, aware of the silent mountains around them. In that moment he felt as if the wolf and he were together on this earth and that moment was all there was.

Still singing, he rose to his knees and the wolf took a step back, cautious but not fearful. Marin was about to reach out to it when, without warning, the wolf's eyes glowed red and for the first time he saw the whole of its grey heft illuminated—the upright ears, the width of its face, its rising hackles and flaring fangs. He turned to the source of the light, a torch.

'Get down!' Horvat yelled. The muzzle of his gun was pointed at Marin's chest.

'No!' Marin cried.

Then the wolf was gone. Vanished into the blackness.

Still pinned in the beam of light, Marin stumbled to his feet and ran clumsily through the snow back to Horvat.

'Turn it off!' he demanded in a harsh whisper, grabbing Horvat's arm and forcing the beam down. Then darkness returned and Marin was blinded, blinking to readjust his eyes. Vivid images of the wolf were imprinted there.

Horvat broke the spell. The bronchial rasp of his breathing punctuated his high voice. 'What . . . the fuck . . . was that . . . about?'

'Keep your voice down! It's bad enough you used the torch.'

'That thing would've torn your throat out.'

'Keep it down, I said. Have you forgotten where you are?' Marin tightened his grip on Horvat's wrist until the man winced. 'That light can be seen for miles. Come on, we've got to move.'

He let him go, shouldering his pack. Horvat didn't move.

'I saved you from that thing,' he said.

'Bullshit! Let's get out of here. Now!'

A few hundred metres further down, they stopped. Ahead of them, across a final stretch of icy snow, was the dark mass of the forest.

'Where are they?' Horvat's breathing was ragged again.

Marin took a frog-shaped tin toy from his pocket. He pressed it rapidly, making half a dozen clicks, and then waited. A moment later a barely perceptible echo of the noise came from the tree line. He tapped Horvat on the shoulder.

'Come on, this way.'

They moved quickly downhill towards the sound and found the others huddled together at the forest's edge. When Ambroz Andric saw them, the last two shadows, he pocketed his clicker. The D-day paratroopers carried the same things to identify each other in the dark. It had been Andric's one good idea.

'What took you so long?' he hissed. 'And what the fuck was that light?'

Marin peered at the outline of Andric's face, but it was too dark to read anything in it. 'We ran into a wolf.'

Horvat wheezed and then rasped. 'Katich decided to crawl up and sing to it.'

'You used a torch, Katich? Are you insane? You could get us all killed. I should put a bullet in your head right here before you do.'

'Don't be a fool. It wasn't me.'

Andric turned and grabbed Horvat by the shoulders. 'Is that true, Juro?'

'I saved his life. That's what I did. The fucking beast was big as a lion.'

'A wolf, you say, up here? It's hard to believe.'

'I wouldn't have believed it, either. But I saw it and Katich there kneeling in front of it singing, I tell you.'

The shadow crouching next to Ambroz Andric broke into laughter.

'Heh, heh, heh!'

Marin recognised the loud sneering laugh of Ambroz's brother Adolf, crackling like gunfire.

'What did I tell you? He's a fucking werewolf, this one! A *werewolf*. You know what the gypsies say? Never trust a man with green eyes. I knew there was something wrong with him.'

'No,' another voice chimed in. It was Pavlovic, the leader of the German youth wing. 'A wolf has welcomed us. That is a good omen, by God!' Pavlovic came over and grabbed Marin in a clumsy embrace. 'The wolf chose you, Katich. You're our good luck charm.'

'Keep it down, you damn fools!' another voice whispered urgently from the darkness. It was Paul Vegar, the one man apart from Marin who'd had actual military training. He had been in Vietnam too.

There was a faint glow from his position and Marin saw that Vegar was crouched under a blackout sheet using a torch to take a compass reading. The glow was extinguished and he whispered again. 'We need to get away from here as fast as we can.'

'You're right, Vegar,' said Ambroz Andric, standing up. 'Which way?'

Vegar's dark shape rose from the ground and moved swiftly ahead of them. 'Follow me,' he said.

As they started down the mountain, Marin watched the dark shapes of the Andric brothers. Until now they had been careful to keep their hostility under wraps, but the tension of being here had at last sharpened their nerves and loosened their tongues.

As Horvat fell in behind him, Marin felt his back tingling from the man's proximity. He sensed the others around him, knowing he would need to find allies in the group. He had joined them too late to know any of them well.

One thing Marin was sure of was that Ambroz Andric had had it in for him from the moment he pulled Petar out of the operation. Andric was both ambitious and possessed of an inflated sense of his own intelligence. Magnifying the threat was his brother, Adolf, a cruel psychopath who backed his every move. Ambroz was the schemer, Adolf his hammer.

Marin blamed his father for allowing such men to assume leadership positions. Ivo was blind to their faults. Ambroz had won Ivo over by flattery. He paid lip-service to Ivo's authority while hiding his true face. From time to time, the clouds parted and Marin saw the truth. For Ambroz, Ivo Katich was an old man whose time had passed. It had pleased Ambroz greatly to have Petar under his control, to order around like a pet dog—but Marin had robbed him of that pleasure. In doing so, he had undermined the man's tenuous grip on leadership, an unpardonable sin.

On the long descent of the mountain the sure-footed Vegar displayed the quiet confidence of a military professional, stopping from time to time to check his map and then calling for the others to follow his lead. It took them three hours to reach the base of the mountain.

As the terrain levelled out, the sky began to lighten and the men in the forest around Marin took form in their green camouflage. They wore the uniforms of US NATO troops, stripped of insignia. He had argued against that choice, for surely the territorial forces in Yugoslavia had that uniform keyed into their training manuals as 'enemy'.

'You're wrong,' Ambroz Andric had told him. 'They don't look to the West at all. They are conditioned only to expect a Soviet invasion. Anyway, by the time they realise we're in the country, we will have a much larger force of men bringing their own uniforms and weapons.'

It was useless to argue with him. Marin only hoped that they would stick to the plan of operating mostly at night. He had made sure to pack a set of civilian clothes in the bottom of his rucksack.

Now at first light at the foot of the Slovenian Alps, he wondered how long it would be before someone spotted this motley group of revolutionaries and ran to the local police. As the faces of his comrades clarified in the gloomy predawn it was clear that many were having the same doubts. He saw in those faces the fault lines of the operation—the men most likely to crack. After one night some were already haggard and looking around with anguished expressions, as if seeing each other for the first time and being astonished, as if roused from a dream, to find they were really here.

Marin knew little of the group chosen by the European leadership. There was Buntic, who called himself Rocco, creeping through the forest with wide fearful eyes. He had been sent by the leaders in Germany to join the group on a promise that he would be made interior minister in the revolutionary government.

Walking next to Buntic was a man whose whole body seemed to be writhing with anxiety. Ivan Prlic was another of the German Croats, born in a village south of Dubrovnik. He jumped at every sound. Marin watched him bond with Buntic as weak men sometimes do, in an alliance of cowards. Prlic was another liability.

There were other émigrés in the group recruited by the German leadership who might prove more useful. But who could say which man would meet the challenge and which would succumb when facing death?

The leadership vanguard was drawn from the Australian group, simply because that was where the operation had been planned and funded. Marin knew his own countrymen better than the others, but that was not to say he had more trust in them. There were strong bonds between the Andric brothers, Horvat and Paul Vegar. They were all part of the movement's Melbourne faction.

Their group also included the big thug Ilija Glavas, a headstrong man who now steamrollered a path through the undergrowth, heedless of the noise. Glavas demanded they refer to him as 'General'. He had paid for that right. It was an honorary rank, or rather an imaginary one, which no one took seriously, not even Ilija Lovric, the one man Glavas had personally recruited.

When he was a young man, Glavas had trained as a baker in Bosnia; but his qualifications were not recognised in Australia, so he had worked as a night watchman in a mortuary in Camberwell. Marin had learned these scant details from Lovric. Then one night in Salzburg, after a long drinking session, Lovric told Marin a bizarre tale.

When they were still training for the mission in Melbourne, Glavas had summoned Lovric at 2 am to a meeting at the mortuary. He arrived to find that Glavas had hauled three corpses out of the body fridges and propped them up against the wall. He was made to watch the general haranguing the corpses as if they were his troops, exhorting them to intensify their efforts to free the homeland and be prepared to sacrifice their lives to the cause.

'So what should I have done, Katich? What would you do?' Lovric asked him. 'I decide it is better to humour him. I say to him, "General, these ones have already given their lives." But he just shakes his finger in my face and tells me that I must get used to the dead. Get used to them, he says, for we will create such a clamour in Herzegovina that Croatian martyrs will surely rise from their graves to join us.'

Lovric laughed at the memory.

'I tell you, Katich, Glavas is completely insane. If I hadn't already sworn the oath, I would have walked away from the mission that very night; but I'm sure that Adolf would have sent Horvat to put a knife between my ribs. I have no doubt about that and I wouldn't be the first. You must be very careful with Horvat. You know that, yes?'

Eventually Vegar dropped into a crouch and put up a hand to stop them, and signalled they should conceal themselves in the darker parts of the forest. They waited. Some men pulled silenced weapons from their shoulders, a sign that at least a few were prepared to fight. Marin hoped that a hapless farmer didn't come stumbling across them. He would surely be cut down in a hail of bullets.

Then he heard a heavy vehicle coming their way. Vegar's senses had again proved reliable. They were near a road. The vehicle was climbing, roaring through gear changes to maintain its speed on the hill. It was a truck, a big one, and its straining engine was thunder-ous in the quiet of dawn. When it passed, everyone began speaking at once, like chattering birds.

Vili Ersek, one of the Europeans, was the first to bounce to his feet, his nerves clearly frayed. He walked in circles, swearing, clenching and unclenching his fists.

'Fuck, fuck, fuck,' he cried. 'If we stay here they will catch us.'

'Quiet, Ersek!' Ambroz commanded as Vegar moved towards him. 'You'll be the one who gives us away.'

Vegar reached Ersek from behind and kicked his legs out from under him. As the man tumbled to the ground Vegar was on him like a predator to prey. There was a knife at Ersek's throat before he could protest.

'Another sound and I will end you myself.' Vegar's whispered warning was heard by all of them. 'This is where we are meant to be,' he said, climbing off Ersek. 'That road is our first destination point. I have brought you here and we must stay here until it's dark again. Do you understand?'

Ersek nodded. Vegar stared down at him remorselessly.

'If you shout again, I will bury you right here.'

There was silence. No one had any doubt that Vegar would do it.

Marin nodded at Vegar. He had been right to make the threat. The men must fear something more than the Yugoslavs. He went down on one knee and touched the soft ground. It would be easy to put Ersek in a shallow grave here. At night the wolves would come for his body. Wolves were smart enough to hide in the daylight, and now that was what the men must do. They were wolves now.

They holed up for the day in a ditch hidden by thick undergrowth, just a short distance from the road. They ate cold rations and buried their waste. Cars and trucks occasionally droned past, waking them from fitful sleep.

Marin had dozed off only to wake soaked in sweat, disturbed by violent dreams. The wolf had been there, huge and green-eyed, slipping in and out of the trees, stalking him. Stumbling through a frozen wilderness, Marin had come across bodies: Horvat with his throat torn out; Adolf Andric almost unrecognisable; the dismembered parts of others, the snow soaking up their blood like blotting paper. It seemed to him now that the wolf was not a good omen at all but a warning of the violence to come. He stayed awake, disturbed by that thought.

Propped against his pack, Marin thought about the ill-defined plan his father had cooked up. He had little faith in it, and even less in the capacity of his comrades to carry it out.

Glavas, the former baker, was snoring next to him. He was a

huge man with a pale slab of a face like a lump of dough waiting for the oven. Marin imagined him in an apron, his thick forearms dusted in flour.

He first met Glavas in Melbourne, where he had the reputation of being a violent standover man. Reports had filtered back to Sydney that he had extorted large sums from Croatian businessmen, but Ivo wasn't too choosy: he was desperate for money for 'Operation Phoenix' and Glavas was an outstanding fundraiser.

So Ivo had ignored the rumours and sent Marin south to collect the cash. Glavas wanted to meet at the Croatian Club, where he spent most of his days drinking and playing cards. Marin knew the club was under surveillance and pressured him to meet in a non-descript café across town. He found Glavas there, bent morosely over an espresso.

'Fuck you bring me here for?' the big man grumbled by way of a greeting. 'Can't even get a brandy.'

'Marin Katich.' He offered Glavas a handshake, which was ignored.

'I know who the fuck you are. Thought your old man would want to meet me himself.'

'Ivo sends his apologies. The troubles in Melbourne have drawn a lot of heat.'

'We're in a fucking war here, you tell him that. We're not pussies down here.'

'I'll tell him, of course, but his message to you is that things need to quieten down.'

'Who the fuck . . .?'

'Hear me out, Glavas!'

'No, I won't! You upstart cunt. You blow in here and tell me what to do? This town is crawling with Tito's agents. That's where the trouble comes from.'

Marin hesitated so as to control his own anger. 'And each time one of them is found dead, there are more police banging on doors and tapping our phones,' he said. 'You get that, don't you? We know it was you who tried to blow up Marjan Jurjevic. Every one of us will be under 24-hour surveillance if this keeps going.'

'I am just saying the bosses in Sydney haven't got a clue what's going on here.'

'They do, Glavas, they do. But right now there's only one operation that counts. That's what you've been raising money for.'

'Fuck them! They should come here and see things for themselves!'

'I'm here.'

'You're not them. You're just a messenger boy. We should send your head back to them, like in the old days.'

Marin stiffened. He locked unblinking on the man's eyes.

'Are you threatening me?' he asked quietly, waiting until Glavas dropped his eyes.

'No, I just think they should see for themselves what is happening here.'

'They sent me here to do that. There's a chain of command. You know that. You'll get to see them soon enough. And if you talk to them like that? You'll be lucky to survive the meeting.'

'I don't think so.' Glavas reached down for the tattered sports bag at his feet and dropped it on the table. 'Cunts need me. Twenty thousand dollars in there.'

When Marin reached for the bag, Glavas pulled it back on to his lap. 'Not so fast,' he said, his stupid face full of slyness. 'I want something in return.'

'And what's that?'

'They have to make me a general.'

*

When it was dark, Vegar and the Andric brothers crept up to the roadside. Eventually Marin saw a high beam, lighting up the forest below. Then came the rumbling of a big motor and three shadows climbed up on to the road. When Ambroz Andric was lit up by the headlamps Marin saw he was wearing a peaked cap with some kind of insignia on it. The other two were behind him, weapons held across their bodies.

Andric waved the truck down. When it stopped, he drew his pistol and moved swiftly to the driver's door. The figure inside raised his arms and shuffled into the middle to let Ambroz behind the wheel. Vegar leapt on to the running board as Ambroz crunched the truck into gear and drove it into the cutting ahead.

Marin rose with the rest of them, and rushed through the undergrowth to meet the truck. When he reached the small clearing Adolf Andric had hauled the driver out of the cab and on to the ground. He had a gun on him and was dancing around the man, hooting like a child.

'Woo! Woo! Here's our ride, boys! Here's our ride!'

Ambroz kicked the driver's leg. 'Give me your papers,' he demanded.

The man was from Sarajevo. There was fear in his voice when he spoke. 'What kind of police are you?'

'You will hear more about us soon enough,' Ambroz told him. 'But we are not police. We are revolutionaries. You'll see what flag we follow. We are Ustasha and these men are the beginnings of a great Croatian army.'

Glavas took him by the arm and moved him away from the man. 'Save your speeches, Andric,' he said quietly. 'We should cut this one's throat and bury him in the forest.'

Marin tensed, ready to intervene.

'No,' said Andric. 'That would curse us from the beginning.'

He turned his back on Glavas and ordered the men to unload the truck. Marin saw the general's seething anger. They unloaded the truck, concealed the goods in a ditch and covered them with bracken. When the driver protested, Glavas knocked him unconscious with a rifle butt and threw him in the back of the truck.

The rest of them climbed in with their rucksacks and weapons. Marin made himself a place next to the driver and in the occasional flashes of torchlight saw that the man was conscious again, as wide-eyed as a trapped animal.

They drove south-east through the night, Glavas at the wheel because he insisted he knew the route. As he drove, sometimes with caution, sometimes recklessly, the general griped on and on to Adolf Andric about the mercy his brother had shown to the driver.

A little after 3 am they reached Gracanica, deep inside the state of Bosnia-Herzegovina and the last town before the wild forests at the base of Mt Radusa. Glavas drove slowly through the town, which was his place of birth, and then a few more kilometres on to a hidden place at the edge of the woods, where the men unloaded their packs and weapons.

Marin climbed out of the stifling truck box and stretched his limbs. In the darkness he checked the Steyr rifle—loaded, safety on, ready. The shadows of his comrades milled around him, anonymous shapes. No one was saying much, but he felt their nervous energy and, in some cases, their fear. Despite his own deep misgivings, he was elated at having come so far, to the estranged heart of the mother country, where the night would allow them to disappear like ghosts into the wilderness.

Like ghosts.

Most, if not all of them, would surely end up as ghosts before this was finished. Marin was under no illusions about the likely consequences of him taking his brother's place. His father liked to quote from *The Odes* of Horace: *Dulce et decorum est pro patria mori*—'It is sweet and right to die for your country.' It was an exhortation to the young warrior to brace himself under cold skies and plunge through a tide of blood.

A memory surfaced from his childhood. Ivo, the great dark shape that blocked the sun, his younger self clinging to him in the churning surf, body tight against his father's. The man he knew and didn't know.

The truck driver was now cowering on the ground, convinced his number was up. In the torchlight Marin saw Adolf Andric haul the man to his feet. Marin tensed as Horvat came up behind. There was the glint of a moving knife and then the blade was poised at the driver's throat, pressing against his carotid artery.

Holding the torch in the man's face, Ambroz spoke into the silence. 'Careful now,' he told the driver. 'Don't move, or God's work will be done for us.' He pulled the man's identity card from a pocket and read it in the torchlight. 'Habernik? You're a Catholic?'

The man gave a nod, his throat straining against the blade, a millimetre from extinction.

'A believer?'

A nod again.

'You have children? How many?'

'Three.'

'Their names?'

'Leon . . . Dora . . . Marta . . .'

'Your wife's name?'

'Marija.'

'Very well. Now, you realise that, for us to have come all the way here—armed and ready to start a revolution—we must have people everywhere. *Everywhere!* And such people would not hesitate to kill Leon and Dora and Marta if you were to betray us. And they would make your children's mother watch as they did it, and then they would kill her . . .'

Habernik nodded so vigorously that the knife drew blood.

'Don't cut your own throat, Josip. I intend to let you live. You will remain here until dawn. Don't even think of leaving—we will know. Then climb back in this old bomb and clear off home. Go and see your wife and your children, and remember that their lives now depend on your silence.'

The driver slumped to the ground, weeping as the twenty men slung on their knapsacks in the moonlight and walked towards the forest.

At dawn the peaks of Mt Radusa were ahead of them. They walked into a stretch of alpine grassland overlaid with buttercup. In the crevices of pale limestone karst outcrops, the protruding bones of the Dinaric range, there were patches of mountain violet.

Marin was set off kilter by the sudden rush of colour. The whimsical Pavlovic ran into the meadow, laughing as he picked a bunch of yellow and purple flowers, until Adolf Andric screamed at him to stop. Others, wary of exposure, started moving to the edge of the field. But the foothills of the mountain were ahead and there was no choice but to cross the wide space as quickly as possible.

Vegar took the lead and broke into a trot, submachine gun slung across his chest. The others shifted their burdens and fell in behind him, a single line snaking across the field, the sweet smell of crushed buttercups under their boots.

When they reached the other side, sheltered by a thick forest of black pine and tall stands of beech, Marin found himself next to Lovric.

'My parents brought me there when I was a child,' Lovric said. 'That field we crossed is Kupresko Polje. Do you know anything about it?'

'No, nothing.'

'There are many such *polje* in these mountains. They were created in a past age, when the caves and caverns collapsed and the land sunk down.'

'I didn't know you were a geologist.'

'Geology, my friend, is the only thing that'll save us in these mountains—they are riddled with limestone caves and tunnels. The partisans used them to hide from the Wehrmacht. But, of course, the local people know where they all are.'

Marin looked at Lovric and dropped his voice. 'You mean the people we're expecting to flock to our banner?'

Lovric clasped an arm over Marin's shoulder and whispered in his ear. 'Yes, the very ones who will lead the army to us. These fools are marching to their deaths. You and I need to think of an escape plan.'

Before Marin could answer, he noticed Horvat hovering nearby. Andric's spy was still on his case.

'Hey, Juro!' Marin called to him. 'Come give me a hug. That little arse of yours is looking better every day.'

Horvat's right hand moved so fast that Marin barely registered its purpose, until he saw the glinting menace of the knife.

'How about I cut your balls off, funny man?'

Marin didn't move.

'Put that away, Horvat,' said Lovric. 'Save it for the enemy. They'll be here soon enough.'

Horvat squinted at them and sheathed the knife with another rapid movement.

'I know this,' he hissed. 'The worst enemies are the ones within.'

With that the little man stepped back, turned and walked away.

*

After a short hike they came across an empty chapel in a clearing. Ambroz Andric called a halt and ordered them inside to say a prayer for the mission. The moment the prayer was done, Glavas stepped forward to address them.

'Now there is no going back,' he said, his voice unnaturally loud in the confines of the chapel. 'We should recommit ourselves, here in the sight of God.'

Glavas took the crucifix from around his neck, knelt down, put it to his lips and laid it on the stone floor. Then he placed his pistol next to it.

'Someone bring what we need,' he demanded.

Men came forward to place the sacred objects in a tableau. Crucifix, pistol, dagger, grenade—they all knew what was coming.

Glavas, still on his knees, stared at them. Then he stretched out his arms in a messianic gesture. Marin caught Lovric's eye and the single thought—*the man's insane*—passed between them. Glavas lowered his arms and several men sank to their knees, then a few more, until all twenty of them were kneeling on the ground.

'I swear by almighty God,' Glavas began, and waited for them to repeat the line. 'That I will uphold the principles of the Ustasha, and unconditionally execute all orders in the name of the *Poglavnik* . . .'

Marin had been sixteen when he took the oath. It had been done at night, illuminated by flaming torches in the bush at Khandalah. His father, Branko Kraljevic and Vlado Bilobrk were among the witnesses. Back then he had been moved by the ritual, but now, despite the imminence of peril, despite the closeness of death, he felt nothing save for his own insincerity as he mumbled the words.

I swear that I will fight in the ranks of the Ustasha for Croatian independence and to defend Croatian national freedom. I accept that the penalty is death if I violate this oath or reveal the secrets of the Ustasha to anyone. So help me God! Amen!'

'Amen,' Marin repeated, nodding to himself, for only God could help them now. His brief sense of elation had drained away. He knew that Lovric was right, and that it would not be sweet and right to die in this company.

They left the chapel and walked into the heavily forested hills. The sun was gone; the weather was closing in. Mt Radusa, ahead of them, was shrouded by low clouds. According to Lovric, the trail they were on was one of the old 'tobacco routes' used by smugglers to take tobacco from Herzegovina to the north.

Eventually the way grew steeper and the forest closed around them. Marin walked with Lovric, a sense of companionship forming between the two men. Lovric would stop from time to time to point out edible herbs or medicinal plants—winter savoury, thyme, nettle, leopard's bane and mountain tobacco. Marin found his knowledge oddly comforting. It reminded him of walking in the bush back home with Lewis. *Back home!* The thought came to him unbidden.

One time Lovric stopped and picked a handful of purplish fruit from a low plant. 'It's bearberry. You can eat it.' He ate a few himself and handed the rest to Marin. The purplish berries were sour but tasty.

During their first day on the mountain they made one recruit, a horse they found tied up in a field. It was a small, scraggly creature and became a hostage really, for no one could judge its will. They loaded the poor thing with supplies and ammunition.

The next morning it began raining, lightly at first, but it soon grew into a heavy downpour. They stopped to eat rations at the edge of a clearing, their American ponchos drenched and slick against their bodies. Hunkered down in the partial shelter of the black pines, the men reminded Marin of some exotic species of green tree fungus.

It was in this place that they met the first people since the truck driver. Two rangy peasants with shotguns walked without warning into the clearing. The two men squatted down with the group after Ambroz Andric bid them to stop and take some food. When he learned they were both Croats, Ambroz launched into a political lecture about the evils of Tito's regime and revealed to the incredulous strangers that this group of armed men was the beginning of an uprising.

But the men were perplexed.

'What are you—actors?' the older of them asked. 'Is this a performance, a joke?'

Ambroz hastened to reassure them that this was no joke but the beginning of a revolution that would free their families from the yoke of communism.

'Do we look like we are not free?' asked the man. 'We come and go in the forest. We can hunt. We live on our land. What would you free us from?'

'From Tito's oppression,' said Ambroz, explaining that the Ustasha had finally returned to set all Croats free.

The older man stood up at that and beckoned his friend to do so.

'The Ustasha are long gone,' he said. 'They are dead or gone.'

'Now we have returned,' said Ambroz.

The man took a cautious step back, a hand on his shotgun. He looked around at the band of men in the clearing. Sensing trouble, several of them reached for their weapons. Dropping his hand from the shotgun, the man reassured his friend with a touch and produced his friendliest smile.

'So, you've come from the past, have you?' he asked. 'Well, we wish you no harm. We will leave you in peace.'

Ambroz stood up. 'Wait!' he called.

But the men had turned back into the forest and vanished as suddenly as they had appeared. Horvat wanted to go after them and there was a heated debate about it.

In the end Ambroz won the argument with a point that even Glavas was forced to agree on: 'We're not here to kill our brothers. The moment we do that our cause is lost.'

'What if they come back to kill us?' asked Horvat and the question, which remained unanswered, exacerbated the dread that many of them were feeling. That no one wanted them here. That they would remain isolated and alone.

The unhappy band had no way of knowing it, but the driver had already screwed up enough courage to report his encounter with them to the police. His wife had warned him that an investigation would connect him to the plot if he remained silent. She was far less concerned about threats from strangers than the sure retribution of the secret police. So, after agonising for a day, he presented himself to the regional police station in Bugojno late in the evening.

When the sergeant on night duty was finally convinced the bizarre story was true, he summoned his commanding officer to the station. For the police in Bugojno it was the word *Ustasha* that transformed the driver's disturbing intelligence from a local criminal incident into a national crisis. Calls were swiftly made to the security services in Belgrade. For the men at the top of those services, this was a confirmation of long-held fears, confirmation of an infectious outbreak with potential to destroy national unity. So critical was it that the spymasters decided to wake the president late at night to brief him.

Tito, shaken from sleep, told them they were right to disturb him. He ordered the immediate formation of a crisis group of military and security generals to coordinate the manhunt. He demanded that the incursion be treated as a national emergency. An armed terrorist group had infiltrated their country and, according to the truck driver's testimony, they proudly called themselves Ustasha. *Ustasha*, for Christ's sake! The most reviled fascist group ever to emerge in the country's history. The terrorists must be found and destroyed; anyone who might have offered them support must be rooted out and interrogated.

Within hours thirty thousand members of the regional militia were mobilised under the direction of the army and the police. Their orders were to contain the threat; to surround the area; and to scour every town and village, every cave and crevice and crack in the mountain until every last terrorist was killed or captured.

Bugojno was designated as the headquarters for the operation, and from there a spearhead military force was swiftly raised and sent into the forest on foot. On the driver's evidence the terrorists had a 24-hour lead. And so the massive manhunt got under way.

Leading the advance force was Army Captain Milos Popovic. They had not gone far before his radio man received a transmission from Bugojno, where the police had received fresh intel that a horse had been stolen from a field near map reference Kota 1390.

Popovic drove his men hard through the remaining hours of darkness and reached the field in the morning. Following the trails beyond that point, the pursuers found footprints in the mud and the deep tracks of a burdened horse. They were closing in. Eventually his scouts reported sighting uniformed men with a horse up ahead, climbing across an open space towards the concealment of a thick forest.

Popovic had his soldiers throw off their packs and run ahead. He wanted to cut off the armed band before they made their way deeper into the mountain and its hidden networks of caves. Reaching the forward scout, Popovic saw the distant group and pulled out his binoculars. A jolt of adrenalin ran through him as he saw the faces of the men, the weapons they carried, and the heavily laden horse they were pulling uphill. Throughout his life he had heard stories of the Ustasha terror: the sadism, the mass killings of Serbs, the concentration camps. Now here they were, in human form, and it was his job to destroy them.

It was a poor strategic position from which to attack. Popovic conferred with his second-in-command. The enemy was on high ground and his men would have to cross a wide-open field to reach them. But it was agreed that, if he didn't act now, the Ustasha would escape into the mountain.

It was decided. Popovic signalled for his men to fan out into two groups; he ordered them to run up either side of the open hill, ready to stop and fire on his command.

It was Adolf Andric who spotted the attackers. He was the lowest man on the hill. Having stopped for a piss, he was stuck behind the horse. He shouted a warning, gesturing wildly. Marin was not much higher, and turned in time to see Adolf take a bullet in the centre of his face before a volley of gunfire scythed across the side of the hill. Two other men were falling, cut down by the raking fire. A round slapped into the horse's flank.

Marin unslung his rifle and dived for cover behind a lime-stone outcrop. The horse wheeled past him, panicked and in pain, hurtling downhill until it tumbled headfirst into the ground, sliding and kicking. Much of their party's ammunition and supplies had gone with it.

There was sporadic firing now from their own position, behind and beside him. Vegar was firing short bursts from behind another nearby rock. Ambroz Andric ran to his brother's body. Someone else was firing on full auto using a silencer—*blatblatblatblatblat*—and then it stopped, overheated.

He saw men running away from the fight uphill in slow motion to the cover of the forest above them. One took a bullet in the back.

Marin levered himself up, steadied the Steyr rifle and scanned the lower ground through his scope. The troops below were standing in the open, firing with no regard for their safety. Militia, not regular army—crazy-brave or ill-disciplined.

Marin picked a target, a young man who appeared to be firing directly at him. He put a round through his chest. He felt nothing, merely chambering the next round and swivelling the weapon, searching for officers.

A man with a radio. A tall man beside him standing upright, directing the fire—a captain's insignia on his beret. Marin squeezed the trigger, watched the beret fly off in a red mist. The man collapsed like a puppet whose strings had been cut.

Another man ran to the fallen officer. Marin shot him too and he slumped on to his comrade's body. Two officers down.

The radio man, staring wildly about, stripped the heavy transceiver from his back and dropped it as if it were radioactive before running off.

He was not alone. With their leaders gone, there was a general panic among the attackers. They stopped firing; some dived to the ground; some whirled about in disarray; others flew back to the woods.

Vegar called out to Marin, signalling a retreat. Ambroz Andric was trying to drag his brother's body up the steep hill and Vegar ran to help him. On his way up, Marin saw the body of Ivan Prlic. Like Adolf Andric, he had been killed in the first volley; Marin took his weapon and spare ammunition.

Lovric was bent over another body further up the hill that had been shot in the back.

'Dead,' he said. 'Fucking Glavas got out. He was the first to run. I'll bet his weapon hasn't been fired.'

Marin nodded grimly. 'They'll regroup soon.'

'I know. We've got to go. Fuck, fuck, fuck!' Lovric hit the ground with his fist. 'So much of the ammo was on that fucking horse.'

'It's gone. Nothing we can do.'

The two of them helped Andric and Vegar haul Adolf's body into the forest, where the others had taken cover behind trees. The rain started again. There was no time to bury his brother, so Ambroz covered him with a poncho and said a prayer over the body. No one waited for him to grieve. They were already scrambling up the mountain as fast as they could.

Marin assessed the situation. The first engagement had been inconclusive. The army had grabbed for the scorpion and been stung. The casualties they had taken would slow the pursuit, but not for long. To their motivations you could now add revenge.

The momentum of the escape prevented Marin dwelling on the men he had killed, but he couldn't avoid the flash-frame images: the disbelief on the young man's face, like someone hit by a car they hadn't seen; the officer's beret flying off with the contents of his skull; the third man as motionless as a sleeping lover, draped over his commander's body. Three more ghosts for him to haul up the mountain; three more to haunt him in his sleep.

They stopped, exhausted when the adrenalin ran out. They

needed to find a secure hiding place and lose themselves on the mountain. Lovric, who had previously hiked on Radusa, advised they should keep climbing to find the caves at higher altitudes. There was no time to lose.

They took a steep route through the forest, avoiding the main trails and sticking to areas densely covered by black pine and mountain ash. The rain subsided to a cold drizzle that barely touched them on the forest floor where in the darkest reaches snow beds lay year round.

After some hours Vegar called them to a halt and stood in silence, staring up through the treetops.

'Shut up,' he called when someone began chattering. Then they all heard what had stopped Vegar in his tracks—the deep grinding sound of heavy aircraft labouring against gravity to stay aloft. As the machines came closer, they discerned the rhythmic beat of rotor blades and the roar of large engines.

'Take cover!' cried Vegar.

Soon the fearful noise echoing in the high mountains was all they could hear. The foliage over them was thick, but Marin could see patches of sky, pale as the limestone. He pulled the poncho over his head and crouched behind a thick tree trunk.

The sound grew into an unbearable roar and he felt the downward crush of air shaking the treetops into madness. Moments later the undercarriages of two huge choppers crossed his vision. Then they were gone and he found himself shivering.

'They're Mi-8s,' said Vegar. 'Each of them can carry more than twenty men. If they're putting troops on the mountain ahead of us, we're in more trouble than we thought.'

Buntic spoke up with a quavering voice. 'Maybe we should split up now. We'll be easier to find as a large group.'

Marin looked over in surprise. The would-be interior minister of their imaginary government had been in a silent funk for days. No one replied.

'Does anyone have a plan?' Buntic asked.

'I won't stop you, Rocco, if you want to go off on your own,' said Ambroz Andric.

Buntic was shaking now, tears in his eyes, a man at the end of his tether.

'How do I know you won't shoot me in the back?' he whimpered.

Without warning Glavas barrelled over, put an elbow into his face and knocked him to the ground. Buntic sat there with blood pouring from his nose.

'Buntic is just crying because his bum-chum, Prlic, was killed,' said Glavas, glaring with disdain at the man on the ground. 'One coward could destroy us all. Does he want to put his underwear on a stick and surrender? How long before he'd give us all up?'

Andric stepped between them. 'Leave him, Glavas,' he said, before turning to address the group. 'You all know what will happen if they catch us. They'll put us on meat hooks. At least for now, you are masters of your own fate. Remember you swore an oath to the death. My brother died for that oath. I guarantee this: the people are with us. The army has turned them against us but, when they hear that twenty men stood against Tito's mighty army, they will come to join us in their hundreds. Until then we must run and hide and stay alive.'

There was silence as the diminished band of revolutionaries absorbed the idea that the only plan now was to play hide and seek.

Marin knew that there had never been any other plan. They were here to become martyrs. His father had sent them for that purpose.

Ivo would grieve for his death, because the wrong son had made the fatal pilgrimage, but he would still rejoice in his martyrdom. Until then, however, while blood flowed in their veins, they must find the deepest, darkest cave to crawl into.

It was Lovric who eventually found it, below Idovac, the highest peak of Mt Radusa.

14.

Just after dawn Al Sharp and his armed response team clambered into a flat-bottomed boat at the Eden wharf. He had hired a local fisherman, Bob Johnson, to ferry them upriver. Two teams would converge on the Khandalah farmhouses from different directions in a coordinated operation. Sharp's team by water, the other by road.

There was a low fog hanging over Twofold Bay as their boat slapped against the swell. Sharp winced each time they breached a wave and his three men braced themselves, cradling their armalite rifles to avoid bashing them on the aluminium hull.

'Hold on,' Johnson cried out as they hit rougher water. Sharp saw the fisherman wreathed in fog, grinning at his discomfort. He had never liked the open ocean, and the bay was exposed to its uncertain conditions.

'Maybe you should slow down a bit!' he cried out.

The fisherman ignored the advice and called over the whine of the motor and the thump of the hull: 'My grandfather used to hunt whales out here.'

Sharp shook his head. 'Rather him than me.'

'I can tell that.'

'I never liked boats.'

'We're nearly out of the chop.' Johnson peered through the fog. 'River mouth's comin' up.'

Soon the boat was through the swell and on to the river, its surface still and glassy. Sharp began to glimpse wild green banks through veils of thinning mist. Prehistoric was how it felt to him, strange and beautiful.

He glanced at the set faces of his men and sensed their minds were concentrated on the near future and the possibility of armed resistance. Anna Rosen's account had begun with gunshots, so they knew there was at least one rifle and an unstable suspect prepared to use it. They assumed Petar Katich was alone, but they had no way of knowing if there might be others. There were rumours the place had been used for military-type training for would-be guerrillas.

'It's a few miles upstream,' said Johnson. 'So what've the Katiches been up to, then?'

'You know them?' asked Sharp.

'The family's had that place a long time. Keep to themselves, pretty much. They do a bit of pig huntin', so I believe.'

'Anything strange about them?'

'Wild country up 'ere, mate. Nothin' much counts as strange.'

'No rumours, then?'

The fisherman thought for a moment. 'Groups of strangers turn up from time to time, all men. Like I said, they seem to like their pig huntin'.'

'Is that all?'

'Who knows. No one's gonna ask armed men too many questions, are they?'

'What do the neighbours think of them?'

'There was an old bloke called Lewis who had the property next to them on the river. Heard he was close to the Katich boys. The father's a bit of a ratbag, so they say—went off the rails after his wife left him. Lewis took the boys in hand when they were stayin' 'ere. Good bloke, Lewis. He passed away last year. His place's gone to wrack and ruin since then.'

It was the most revealing exchange Sharp had had with Bob Johnson and the fisherman suddenly seemed to regret it. He said little more, even when Sharp tried to coax him, and they motored up the river in silence as the fog rose to reveal a serene wilderness.

'We're here,' he eventually whispered, cutting the motor. They drifted through lingering fingers of mist and put the boat ashore on a low sandbank that jutted into the river.

'You just follow the path uphill,' said Bob to Sharp as the men nimbly disembarked and checked their weapons.

'You stay right here, Johnson,' Sharp told him. 'I don't want you approaching the farmhouses under any circumstances. If you hear gunfire, just stay put and keep out of sight.'

'You'll get no argument from me. I've got a thermos of tea. I'll sit 'ere and have a smoke.'

The armed police spread out and climbed through the bush until they sighted two rustic buildings on the hilltop. Sharp called them to a halt, took out his walkie-talkie and clicked the *Send* button three times to communicate that they were in place.

Detective Sergeant Ray Sullivan responded with three clicks, indicating he and the other three armed police were ready on the hill above the dwellings. Sullivan knew the layout better than Sharp, having been to the property previously to interview Petar Katich. It was his assessment of the man's deteriorating state of mind that Sharp had passed on to Anna before she drove down there.

*

Sharp had been surprised when Anna had contacted him on her way back to Sydney and asked for an urgent meeting after her confrontation with Petar. That was what he'd asked her to do, of course, but he knew plenty of journos who would have sat on the information she had uncovered.

'Honestly, I'm really worried about him, Al,' Anna confided when they met at the Kings Cross café. 'He's in such a bad way he's either going to kill himself or someone else.'

She had made him a copy of Petar Katich's journal. The closely written scrawl made him think of Gogol's *Diary of a Madman*, but without the talking dogs. He reluctantly agreed she could keep the original journal, on the proviso that if he found it contained actual evidence of criminality she would have to hand it over.

'I've been through it line by line,' said Anna. 'Mostly it's a long rant about historical injustice. It's pretty incoherent, but towards the end the tone changes. That's after he gets sent the documents and photos that I told you about—from Marjan Jurjevic in Melbourne.'

Sharp nodded. 'Have you spoken to Jurjevic about how he made contact with Petar?'

'Not yet, but I have a theory. It's important that Jurjevic is a Croat; I don't think Petar would have paid any attention otherwise. But here's another Croat telling him that his father's been lying about his wartime history since Petar was a kid.'

'Ivo Katich is a murderous old bastard,' said Sharp. 'I can't imagine he was a kindly father.'

'That's it exactly,' Anna agreed. 'Petar's full of resentment and old grievances. He's the younger son. He's small and fragile, and far less capable than his older brother. He's convinced that the old man thinks he's a worthless weakling. You can imagine what it's like growing up with a father like that. Then suddenly Petar gets evidence that Ivo's not only been a brute to him but was also a dyed-in-the-wool war criminal responsible for terrible savagery. I reckon this all rang true to Petar and that's when the guilt kicked in.'

Sharp considered this as he sipped his coffee.

'It's a bit of a cliché, isn't it?' he mused. 'Sins of the father and all that. But it would help explain the downward spiral he's in.'

Anna pulled out the copy of the diary; she pushed aside Sharp's half-full cappuccino and the ashtray and laid it on the table. She flicked through to the pages she'd marked.

'It's all in here,' she explained. 'Petar starts fantasising about what Ivo and his Ustasha brothers really did during the war—especially that demon, Branko Kraljevic. Then you get this section I've marked for you. Here, I'll read it out: "I think of the two of them, young men, mates together in the uniform, Ivo's arm over Branko's shoulder, Branko's over Ivo's, and then I remember the bodies lying on George Street. I think of those people a lot, bleeding and twitching on the pavement. That's how the day starts. Every day."' Anna stopped and looked up at Sharp.

'Christ on a crutch!' he spluttered. '*I remember the bodies lying on George Street*! It's almost a confession.'

'Almost, but not quite.'

Sharp considered this. 'Circumstantial, I suppose. He could say he was talking about newspaper photos. Is there anything else in there?'

'No.' Anna shook her head. 'There's nothing else like that, but he said something when I first got to him, after he fired the rifle over my head . . .'

'That was foolhardy by the way,' Sharp cut in to admonish her. 'I told you not to go alone.'

'He'd have never spoken to me otherwise. Your people got nothing out of him, did they?'

'No, that's true.'

'Anyway, when I got to him he was hysterical. Raving about how his father thinks he's a worthless nothing, and then he says: *But I showed him what I could do. I showed them all . . .*'

'Did you ask him what that was?'

'Never got the chance,' Anna replied. 'He passed out cold.'

'You think he was talking about the Sydney bombs?'

Anna shrugged and looked down at her hands. 'There's one last thing I haven't told you. I managed to drag him back into the house and got him on to a bed. He was pretty much comatose, so I searched his room.'

'You're more like a spy than a journalist.'

'I'm not proud of it, but this fellow had just shot at me, right?'

'Sorry, go on. What else did you find?'

'In the drawer of the bedside table there was a tourist brochure for the city of Zagreb.'

'Maybe he was planning a trip to the old country.'

'There was a sticker on the back of the brochure. It was from the *Adriatic Trade and Travel Centre*, on George Street.'

Sharp straightened his aching back. He grabbed his cigarettes, lit one and drew deeply.

'Agatha fucking Christie you are, saving the crucial piece of evidence to the last.'

'Still circumstantial, though.'

'What did you do with it?'

'I left it where I found it.'

'Good girl.'

'Don't call me a girl.'

Sharp's teams had now surrounded the farmhouses. Amid the morning birdsong, he heard the ringing bellbirds Anna had talked about. From somewhere nearby a rooster crowed. Nothing else. No sign of life from the houses.

The teams hit the buildings simultaneously. His men took the larger of the two where Petar Katich had his bedroom. Methodically entering room after room, the armed team called out: 'Clear! Clear! Clear!'

Sharp went out on to the veranda between the farmhouses. Ray Sullivan emerged from the doorway of the smaller house.

'Nothing,' he called. 'Not a sausage.'

'Fuck,' said Sharp. 'He's in the wind. Turn the place over, Ray. Every nook and cranny.'

'And here was I thinking we'd just have cheese on toast and go home.'

'Smart-arse.'

'Yeah.' Sullivan smiled. 'At least the *hup hup* boys didn't get a chance to ventilate the place with those fucking cannons they brought along. They were psyched up for it, ready for the Last Stand at Glenrowan.'

'Can't be too careful, Raymond.'

'Could've ended badly, is all. Get one of those jockstraps to make us a cuppa, will you? Kitchen here's empty. Actually, the whole place looks like it's been stripped clean.'

Stripped clean? This bothered Sharp. He went straight back into the bedroom he knew to be Petar's. The mattress was bare. There was an old rocking chair, a couple of bedside tables, an empty cupboard, and nothing else. Nothing on the floor. No sign someone had been living there.

He opened both the bedside tables. Empty. Anna had said she'd found the Zagreb brochure in one of them and left it there. It was gone. The photos and documents sent by Jurjevic. Gone. The piles of old newspapers she'd mentioned. Gone.

He flipped the mattress. On the underside he found a large, nasty-looking brown stain. Forensics would have to check it, but he knew dried blood when he saw it.

He told his men to search everywhere for the rifle and ammunition. They came up with nothing. There were no letters, not even a utility bill. No notes, nothing in writing at all—in fact there was nothing to even write on. No paper, no notepads. No bottles of Balkan hooch, full or empty. No remnants of drug-taking. No old syringes, no burnt spoons, no rubber strap, no cotton wool. The place was so blank, so empty, he could come to only one conclusion. It had been systematically cleaned of evidence. Everything was gone except the bloodstained mattress.

Petar Katich might be in the wind. He could just as well be in the ground.

No Name read a small sign above the Chapel Street doorway. Entering it, Anna Rosen climbed a narrow staircase to a big, overly lit room full of laminex tables. She spotted Peter McHugh across the room, pouring a drink from something that resembled a urine bottle for the bedridden.

She knew that the piss-coloured wine it contained would be no better than it looked, but McHugh didn't seem to mind. He professed to love this place, with its unchanging blackboard menu and Italian working-class ambience. It could have been a cafeteria in a regional Fiat factory.

His face was transformed by a wide grin when he saw her. Waving the dubious carafe, he cried, 'Anna! Sit, sit. Some wine?'

She saw that, mercifully, the piss bottle was at a low ebb.

'No, thanks. You finish that. I'll have some red.'

'Righto,' McHugh said and drank from his glass to make space for the last of the wine. In the unflattering light his cheeks glowed reddish pink.

Anna took it all in. Something was not right. 'You celebrating?' she asked him.

McHugh poured more wine and drained half the glass before answering.

'No, not at all. Well, lunch as an institution, I suppose. Lunch with you as a special treat. That kind of thing. I've hardly seen you outside of the office since . . . You know, since *that* night.'

Anna recognised the plaintive look and knew then that he'd been fortifying himself for the long avoided talk.

'It's been a crazy few weeks,' she said cautiously.

'I ordered pasta for both of us,' he said. The presumption was so typical of him that she smiled, glancing up at the blackboard to see what she might otherwise have chosen for herself.

He followed her eyes. 'It's just the entree,' he said defensively. 'You were a bit late, and I thought I should get in before the crowd.'

'I'm not late, Peter. You were early.'

'Maybe you're right. Making sure we got a good table.'

'And having a few drinks.'

'That too. That too. Settling the nerves. Who'd have thought it at my age.'

'Peter . . .'

'Don't say anything yet. Just hear me out, will you?'

'Okay.'

'I want to start over with you. I stuffed things up. That bad joke about you being the kind of girl Lionel Murphy would like—that was just stupid.'

'Forget about it. I told you what I thought when you said it. That's done.'

'You made me feel like a lecherous old fool.'

'Sorry for jumping down your throat.'

'So, is that the reason you don't want to see me again?' McHugh paused, looking around to see if anyone was listening. 'In that way?'

'You mean the reason I won't fuck you?'

'For Christ's sake, Anna!'

He would have gone on; but a waiter interrupted, sweeping in over his shoulder to lay a large plate of spaghetti bolognese in front of him, then swivelling to put a second one in front of Anna. Then the waiter plonked a bowl of grated parmesan on the table and turned to her.

'You like somethin' to drink?'

'*Una caraffa di vino rosso, per favore.*'

'*Va bene.*'

McHugh waited until the waiter was out of earshot, then he bent in so close she saw the burst blood vessels in his eyes.

'I can't get you out of my head.'

'I'm sorry, Peter. I really am. I just woke up the next morning and it all felt wrong. I can't help that. That shouldn't stop us being friends, or affect our work . . .'

'It's affecting everything.'

'Don't say that.'

'I just can't look at you across the room and pretend it didn't happen—'

Again the waiter interrupted him, reaching in to place two glasses on the table and then pouring the wine, while McHugh sat slumped, elbows on the table, hands covering his face. He didn't look up until the waiter had gone.

'I know, I know. I'm not a pretty sight. Behaving like a besotted teenager.'

Pity and contempt jostled as Anna's emotional response. She started to reach out a hand to him, but stopped herself and took up the wine glass instead.

'We should eat, you know,' she said, spooning parmesan on to her spaghetti. 'Pasta waits for no man.'

McHugh twirled spaghetti in a desultory fashion. He ate a few mouthfuls before dropping the fork. 'I don't want to feel like this, Anna. I thought we had something.'

Anna stopped eating, annoyed now, having discovered how hungry she was. She drank some wine and stared at him. 'Has no one ever said "no" to you?'

'Not like this,' he confessed. 'Normally I have time to get used to the idea.'

'It was one night, Peter.'

'I just keep wondering what went wrong. All I did was say that other men would find you sexy.'

'It's not about that. I gave you a rap over the knuckles because you sounded like an old chauvinist. I'd already told you it was wrong to fall into bed with you. I told you that the next morning.'

'At the risk of being pathetic, I need you to tell me why it was wrong.'

'Why can't you just leave it alone?'

'Because I can't.'

Anna took a deep breath. She felt cornered. 'There's someone else, Peter. There's someone I can't get out of *my* head. Honestly, I wish I could sometimes. That's the problem. I can't be with you because I want to be with him.'

'I've never seen you with anybody. You've never mentioned a boyfriend.'

'It's complicated.'

'Why?'

'He's not in the country.'

'Where is he? Is he coming back?'

'That's too many questions. I told you it's complicated. Look, is this going to be a problem?'

'No.'

'You want me to go and work somewhere else?'

'No, of course not. Fuck, I'm really sorry. I feel stupid.' He ran his hands absentmindedly through his hair and left it looking like an overgrown hedge.

'I'm being an idiot,' he said, and Anna nodded.

'A village idiot with your hair like that.'

'Oh shit,' he said, smoothing it down. 'Go on, eat your lunch. Have a drink. Look, we can talk about your story. Where are we at with the mad, fucking Katich family?'

Anna sat still, said nothing.

Oh, Peter, if only you knew.

Contempt rose in her throat like bile. She looked down at the plate of pasta, at the bowl of cheese, at the red-lipped wine glass, at the stained butcher's paper, at Peter's liver-spotted hands. Over his shoulder babbling diners sat laughing, clattering utensils and roaring in their complacency.

How to reconcile this avalanche of trivia with the disappearance of Marin Katich? Was he lying dead on a mountain in Bosnia? Was he rotting in a cell in Belgrade? Was he being tortured by Tito's secret police?

'Anna?'

McHugh interrupted her thoughts and she stared at him. There was no way she could talk to him about this. She knew that he'd use it against her. She foresaw all his arguments, foresaw that his rhetoric would be fuelled by the indignation of the spurned lover: she'd been dishonest; she'd kept critical information from him; her journalism was compromised; and this, in turn, had compromised him and his program and the ABC. On and on it would go, until he had had his revenge.

'Are you okay?' asked McHugh.

No, she wouldn't tell him.

Then she had an epiphany. There was only one man to whom she could talk about this. One man who might be able to answer her questions. Only one man with whom she could be honest. But, even if he agreed to see her, he would almost certainly lie. That was a perverse fact.

Anna pushed her chair back from the table. 'I have to go,' she said abruptly.

'Wait.'

'I can't, Peter. I just realised there's something I have to do.' She stood up and dropped her napkin on the table. 'Can you fix this up?'

'Sure, of course, but—'

'Sorry, there's no time to explain,' she said. 'I'll speak to you later.'

She left the restaurant. The one man who could answer her questions was the patriarch of that mad, fucking Katich family: Marin's father. It all started with Ivo, and it ended with him. He was at the very heart of it all.

Anna hailed a cab and gave a Dawes Point address. The taxi dropped her at the end of Lower Fort Street, close to the harbour's edge. Beneath the span of the bridge's southern approach she saw the naked Opera House sails, now denuded of the spindly cranes that had overshadowed them for as long as she could remember. She paid the driver and climbed out.

Above her was one of the massive granite-faced pylons that seemed to anchor the steel arch of the bridge as it vaulted the harbour to the city's north. The bridge's maintenance crews were based inside this, the south-west pylon, and she knew that all the men who crawled over the great structure twenty-four hours a day accessed their workplace through it. The pylon was fenced off by a high chain-link barrier, which also enclosed the workers' car park.

There was a sleepy guard at the gate. She talked her way through by explaining that she had an urgent message for one of the workers about a sick child. She was directed to the staff entrance, a human-sized door next to an arched wooden gateway locked and barred but big enough for a giant.

She entered a cavernous space filled with the sounds of industry. It was so gargantuan in its dimensions that she stopped and stared up into its heights. A steel stairway with suspended gantries rose nearly fifty metres up the interior stone wall into the dimly lit reaches. From the top, she counted twelve steep flights down to the vast and noisy maintenance area on the ground floor.

She was still transfixed when a man in blue overalls approached her.

'First time in here then?' he asked loudly, breaking the spell.

'Yes, it's—'

'Fucking humungous.'

'It really is.'

'And fucking noisy,' he shouted. 'Eric Briggs. I'm the operations manager.'

She shook his offered hand.

'Anna.'

'Come over to the office. We can talk there.'

Anna followed him into a demountable of the kind she'd seen on building sites. It was barely furnished—just a desk, filing cabinets and a kitchen space with an electric kettle. The desk was large and uncluttered, apart from four telephones. Briggs settled in behind it and gestured for her to take the seat opposite.

'Members of the public don't often wander in here, love,' he said, not unkindly. 'What can I do for you? I hear someone's got a sick kid.'

'I have to talk to a fellow who works here,' Anna said. 'Ivo Katich. Do you know him?'

'Steve Katich, we call him. Yeah, I know him. He's a foreman of the painting crews. He's got two sons, hasn't he?'

'Yes, I've got some bad news about Petar, the younger one. He's very ill.'

'You a relative?'

'No, I'm a friend of his son. It's really important I speak to him. It's a matter of life and death.'

'I suppose you know Steve's been in the newspapers recently. A lot of bullshit. He's a good bloke.'

'This is nothing to do with that.'

'You're not a journalist, are you?'

'Look, could you tell him it's about his son Petar? He's in a very bad way. My name is Anna Rosen. Will you tell him why I'm here? I'm sure he'll want to speak to me.'

'There are blokes from his team mixing paint down here on this level, but he's somewhere up on the bridge.'

'Can you find him?'

'Life and death, you reckon?'

'It's critical.'

'Tell you what, Anna,' said Briggs, picking up one of the phones. 'Why don't you go over there and make us a cuppa while I see if I can find him.'

Anna made a pot of tea while Briggs worked the phones. She poured a mug and took it over to him.

'Thanks, love,' Briggs said, spooning sugar into it. 'Steve says he'll meet you upstairs. There's a rec room inside the pylon, up above the roadway. A bit of a hike, I'm afraid.'

She was about to ask how to get there when there was a knock on the door and a younger man entered. He did a comical double take when he noticed Anna.

'Hello, Briggsy. Not interrupting anything, am I?'

'Come in, mate. This is Miss Rosen,' Briggs said, ignoring the innuendo. 'I want you to escort her up to the smoko room. Steve Katich is going to meet her there.'

'Lucky old Steve.' The young man winked. 'Win the lottery, did he?'

'Pull your head in, Hoges,' said Briggs sharply. 'One of Steve's sons is in a bad way. She's come to give him the news.'

'Oh jeez, righto.' The young man turned to Anna, a crestfallen expression on his handsome face. 'Sorry, Miss Rosen, I was just pulling his leg.'

'Anna.'

'Paul,' he said, shaking her hand vigorously. 'We'll get our skates on, then. It's a lot of stairs. Not a smoker, are you?'

'I am. Is that a problem?'

'Nah, I am too.' His eyes crinkled as he smiled. 'Might have to stop for one halfway. Give you a chance to catch your breath.'

Anna laughed.

'Let's go,' said Paul, leading her out the door by her elbow. 'See ya 'round like a rissole, boss.'

'Behave yourself, Hoges, or I'll cut your overtime.'

Outside the office Anna discreetly disengaged herself from the garrulous Paul, who obviously fancied himself as a ladies' man. He had blond, tanned good looks and the lean athletic build of a surfer. With all that came the whiff of arrogance that Anna had long associated with such men.

*

After they had climbed twelve flights of stairs they came to a landing with a doorway. Paul led her into a high-ceilinged room with a long narrow window. There was an old wooden table and chairs and half a dozen public service-issue green vinyl armchairs scattered around a battered coffee table that was littered with old copies of *Pix*, *Man*, the *Sun* and the *Mirror*. A series of topless centrefolds were taped to the wall and Anna had the same irksome feeling that assailed her every time she entered a men-only domain, as if the locker room stench of testosterone clung to the place.

Paul noticed her discomfort. 'It's the smoko room,' he said with a grin. 'Women's lib's not big around here. So, listen, I'll have to leave you. Steve'll be down in a minute. When you're finished, dial 9 on that wall phone and Briggsy'll send someone to fetch you back down.'

He turned to leave, then stopped at the doorway.

'If you want to meet up for a drink later, I'm headed for the Harbour View. Just up the road. What do you reckon?'

'Maybe. I'll see how I'm feeling.'

'Stiff drink, game of pool . . . Fix you right up.'

'We'll see.'

Anna sat at the table to wait. Five minutes later the door opened and its frame filled with a silhouette. A hulking figure in paint-spotted overalls came into the light and her eyes were drawn to a grim face with cold, dark eyes. He was clearly the progenitor of Marin Katich, but the depredations of time had thickened the body and coarsened the features of a once handsome man.

Anna stood, but made no move towards him. She found that her heart was pounding. 'Mr Katich?' Even to herself she sounded tentative.

'Yes,' he answered gruffly, moving to the other side of the table.

While she sat back down again, he remained standing.

'You say you have news about Petar. So, tell me.'

'Would you like to sit down?'

'No.'

He was even taller than Marin, broad across the shoulders and thick through the chest. He stared down at her with imperious contempt. Anna, as she guessed was his intention, was duly intimidated.

'I went to the South Coast to see Petar at your farm,' she said, her voice quavering. 'He was in a very bad way. He needs help. I think he needs psychiatric help.'

'You are a medical doctor, Miss Rosen? You have some qualification to say such things?'

'I know when someone is suffering. I think he's suicidal.'

'You don't know Petar. You know nothing of him. He was always the same after his mother ran off and left him, always suffering from his nerves. He's a troubled boy.'

You are the source of his troubles, she thought, staring up at the remorseless creature who seemed to bristle with barely contained rage.

Anger lent strength to her words.

'He's not a boy, Mr Katich. I can only tell you what I saw for myself. I watched him put a loaded gun to his head. His finger was on the trigger, but he was so drunk that he collapsed. I helped him to his bedroom to sleep it off and, when he came to, I caught him injecting heroin.'

'How dare you! A journalist! On my property—'

'Would you prefer I'd left Petar lying on the ground where he collapsed? You should be thanking me.'

'Oh yes—thank you, thank you very much, Miss Rosen ... Thank you for sneaking into my property to spy on my son. Did you go through the cupboards while you were there? A journalist! As God is my witness, your breed has no morals. You come up from the sewers. Rats gnawing away my guts. I've met many journalists. Not one I trust for a minute.'

'You're his father. I'm shocked that you care more about who's been on your property than for Petar's welfare.'

'I am his father, yes. I care for my son his whole life. I know him. And I know you. I know who is your father. The filth you spring from. We don't need help from your kind.'

'My kind?'

'Communists! The same people who destroy my country.'

'I don't much care what you think about me, Mr Katich, but I'm not a communist. I came here to talk to you about Petar.'

'Now we've talked. Good. Is finished.'

'Did you know that the police went to Khandalah this morning to arrest him?'

Katich lowered himself into a chair and leaned across the table. 'What! What are you saying?'

'Police went to the farm this morning at dawn, but Petar wasn't there. The whole place was cleaned of all his belongings, but there was no sign of him. They found blood on his mattress. Do you know anything about this?'

Katich raised two huge paint-stained hands to his face. His fingers kneaded at his temples for a time, until he lifted his head and stared back at her.

'I don't know what the hell you are talking about,' he said, quieter now.

'Do you know where he's gone?'

'No.'

'Was Petar involved in the Sydney bombings?'

'Are you crazy? To ask me such things!'

'He feels guilty about the people who were blown up on George Street.'

'What? You say Petar tells you this?'

'He's been keeping a journal. He wrote it in there.'

'Fuck!' Katich slammed both hands on the table and then pointed a finger at her. 'You have something private of my son's? So, is true. You search through his belongings. You trespass and you steal! It's you the police should be arresting.'

'Petar gave it to me, Mr Katich.'

Anna lied without compunction. She told herself she was lying to a liar so it didn't matter, it didn't count. She could live with it.

'He wanted me to have it. There is much in it about you.'

'Petar is not in his right mind. You tell me this yourself, and yet you take advantage of him. You make me sick.' Ivo Katich jumped back to his feet, towering over her again, his voice filled with menace. 'Get out of here! Get out of my sight! Or I won't be responsible for what happens.'

Anna had grown used to his tactics. She felt she was getting under his skin now and dared to taunt him further.

'What are you going to do? Throw me off the bridge?'

Katich moved towards her around the table. 'You think I wouldn't do that?'

There was such vehemence in him that Anna stood up and put the chair between them, as one might prepare to fend off a wild animal.

'You like to make threats, don't you,' she said. 'You bullied your sons, held them under your thumb. I won't be intimidated by you.'

Katich took a step closer and lowered his voice. 'I know what you are. How you get men to talk. Did you fuck Petar, too?'

'So you know about me and Marin?'

'I know all about women like you.' He jabbed his finger close to her face. 'Women who reek of sex.' He leaned forward, his face grotesque, contorted.

Anna reeled back. 'Get away from me.'

Katich moved closer. 'I know the smell that comes off you. Some women give off this smell, like animals. They wrap men around their fingers.'

'Marin would never forgive you for this.'

He threw his head back and laughed. 'Young men are weak.'

'Marin is not weak, and he's nothing like you.'

'You may have fucked him, but you don't know my son.'

Anna stepped backwards. She imagined him chasing her around the table, in some kind of dark farce. But the fear in her had now evaporated and, rather than fumbling for words, she became more articulate. 'You've really taken off your mask, haven't you? It's easy now to see the monster behind it. I think Petar saw it too. He saw you, didn't he? He knows what you really are, and it drove him mad.'

Katich suddenly put both hands on the table, as if he planned to scramble across it and strangle her. Then he screamed at her: 'Stay away from my sons, you Jewish whore!'

Anna was so shocked she lost all sense of caution. 'Now come the words you've been thinking all along,' she said mockingly.

'Stay away from my sons, or you'll regret it.'

'Stop pretending you care about either of them except as reflections of your own ego. You abandoned Petar. You left him alone to rot in the bush. You care nothing for him. He must remind you too much of his mother.'

Katich hit the table with such force she thought it might splinter. She flinched as he shouted at her, 'Shut your filthy whore mouth!'

'No, I won't.' She risked a last roll of the dice. 'You have nothing but contempt for Petar. That's obvious. But what about Marin? Your "real" son, as you must surely think of him. And yet you sent him to his death in Bosnia.'

'He's not dead!'

'They're all dead. You sent them all to their deaths.'

'Marin is not among them.'

'He escaped?'

Katich seemed to gather his wits and she imagined him realising that the clever little Jew had gotten under his skin.

'Get out!' he said with quiet intensity.

'Tell me.'

'No more talk. This was a mistake. Forget about Marin. You'll never see him again. Now get out.'

Anna reeled out of the room, slamming the door behind her. She heard a chair crash against it. She was shaken to her core, but there was one thought in her head: *He's alive! Marin is alive!*

15.

Monday, 28 June 1972

A bloodless dawn crept over Mt Radusa. Marin Katich lay, cold and stiff, hidden in a cleft of the mountain. He had volunteered to take the last watch rather than lie awake in the claustrophobic cave. As the alien wilderness below came slowly into focus through the mist, blackbirds were startled into flight. Thousands of them rose from its depths, smudging the sky with dark patterns. This should have been a beautiful thing, but their cries filled him with a premonition of terror.

Marin gripped his cold weapon. Vili Ersek was sleeping next to him like a puppy. He kicked him softly, until Ersek opened his eyes.

'Hey!'

'Shut up,' Marin whispered. 'Go wake the others.'

'What is it?'

'Something's moving down there. Be quick.'

They were above a cave and there was a hidden entrance that allowed Ersek to climb back inside it.

Blackbirds continued to swirl above Marin as he scanned the forest floor through his scope. He moved the rifle back and forth, adjusting for its different balance and weight with the suppressor screwed onto the barrel.

Ambroz Andric came scrambling up in a low crouch.

'What is it, Katich?'

'Something spooked the birds.'

Andric detached the scope from his own rifle and lay on the limestone ledge, searching the dark valley for movement. Ersek and Vegar crept up beside them.

'Don't let anyone else up here, for fuck's sake,' Marin whispered.

'I'm not stupid,' Vegar said. 'Lovric has taken two men to a position on the other side of the entrance. See anything?'

'Not yet.'

Marin was starting to think it had been a false alarm when Andric stiffened.

'My two o'clock,' he said.

Marin swung the Steyr to his right, caught movement in the scope and stopped. A figure in camouflage emerged from the forest cradling an automatic weapon. A big man. He was alone. A scout, perhaps.

'He's heading straight for the cave,' said Andric. 'Take him out, Katich.'

The man's face filled Marin's scope. He was older, with a big drooping moustache. Fifty or so. His father's age. Marin let his breath out, his finger on the trigger. Probably had a wife and children.

He hesitated.

'Katich!' Andric snapped.

Still he hesitated. But then there was a sound to his right—a sound like someone stapling a thick pile of papers, the sound of a suppressed subsonic round. The old soldier in his scope wheeled and went down. Vegar had shot him.

They waited. The man didn't move. Didn't call out. No one else came out of the woods.

It began to rain. Vegar slapped Ersek on the shoulder. 'Vili, here's your chance.'

Ersek looked up apprehensively. 'For what?'

'To prove your worth. To prove you're not a little coward.'

'What do you want?'

'Get down there and see if that Serb is really dead. And take his weapon and ammo and any food he's got in that pack. We're going to need it.'

'How do you know he's a Serb?'

'He's trying to kill us, isn't he?'

'I guess.'

'So he must be a Serb.' Vegar laughed. 'Who else would chase a bunch of Croats up a mountain?'

Ersek produced an edgy smile and looked over at Marin, who refused to meet his eyes.

'Get down there quick,' said Vegar. 'Or I'll wipe that shit-eating grin off your face.'

They watched Ersek scramble clumsily down the steep slope, slipping on the wet limestone as the rain grew heavier. Marin followed him through the scope. On the forest floor Ersek ran crouched, his submachine gun in two hands. He hopped over a log like a rabbit and ran the short distance to the body. He checked for a pulse, turned his face up to them and gave a thumbs up.

'Does that mean he's dead?' asked Andric.

Vegar shrugged. 'We forgot to agree on a signal.'

'That one's counterintuitive,' said Marin.

Vegar decided for them. 'I say thumbs up means he's dead.'

They watched Ersek strip the body of weapons, ammunition and a small pack. He looked up, wiped rain from his eyes and gave a second thumbs up. Then he rose to a crouch again and ran towards them.

As he hopped back over the log, a shot rang out from some-where in the forest. The back of Ersek's head exploded.

Marin flinched. Ersek's body pitched forward into the ground, a tangle of dead limbs.

Vegar cried out, but his voice was quickly drowned by a torrent of fire from hidden positions in the forest. It was concentrated on the cave mouth, but bullets whined over their heads. The three of them flattened behind cover.

Marin snatched a look and saw two groups of soldiers, running from either side of the forest. 'They're trying to outflank us!'

Infantrymen in the forest kept up cover fire on the cave. They still had not spotted the defensive position above it. Marin swung his rifle to the attackers on the right. Lovric would have to deal with the threat on his side. The rain had stopped, but it was unnaturally dark under the low cloud cover.

Marin concentrated on the assault group. In quick succession he shot the third and fourth man as they laboured uphill. Soldiers still coming up stopped to help the wounded.

The attack on the left had slowed, but Lovric and his men were still being hit by heavy fire from the forest. Andric called out that he was going down to help the defenders on that side. As he climbed back into the cave, Marin heard familiar percussive thumps from the forest.

'Get down!' he yelled at Vegar as mortar shells began exploding on the mountainside.

Again the mouth of the cave was being targeted, and Marin realised that the attackers knew exactly where they were. His ears rang from the multiple concussions. Limestone dust filled the air, stinging his eyes. There was a film of it on his face.

He turned to Vegar, who appeared to be wearing ghostly theatrical make-up. Marin laughed, for surely this was the last act of their tragedy.

Then a roaring noise came from below. A tongue of flame reached out, blossoming into a fireball that scorched the pale rocks at the cave entrance.

A flamethrower!

Marin had seen in Vietnam what these could do to a man. The enemy was pushing up on the left behind the surging flame. He heard screams and shouts inside the cave and swivelled the Steyr. Sighting into the flame, he felt its radiated heat on his face—*the devil's breath,* exhaled in bursts of fire. During the brief pause between when the flame bloomed and dissipated in the burning air, he saw the dark outline of a demon with fuel tanks on its back. He targeted the shape and squeezed the trigger as another fireball leapt from the weapon.

The line of flame suddenly twisted and bucked like an untended garden hose writhing on the ground, spurting its deadly stream in all directions. The demon with the flamethrower had gone down, with his hand locked on the trigger. Marin saw a nearby soldier, lit up like a torch, run screaming down the hill.

A last flame shot into the air and then the rain fell again with a new intensity. It poured down on the demon's body and extinguished the weapon's pilot light. The soldiers retreated to the forest under the downpour, dragging their dead and wounded through the mud.

The assault was over. Marin lay drenched on the ledge.

Vegar turned to him, shouting over the rain. 'They must have come in on the choppers to have gotten here so quickly.'

Vegar's face had been washed clean; his thin hair was plastered to his scalp and his eyes burned in sunken pits.

Marin saw the skull beneath the skin and imagined a dead man was talking to him.

'That's what I think,' he replied after a moment. 'They carried the mortar bombs on their backs. Limited supply, or they'd still be dropping them. So, maximum fifty men?'

'If we're right.'

'They took at least eight casualties. They won't try that again soon.'

'They'll wait now for the main force to get here. If the weather hadn't closed in, they'd have choppers up here strafing the shit out of us. But we're trapped like rats. Put a fucking rocket into the cave and we're all dead. Only thing keeping us alive right now is the fucking rain.'

Marin was astonished to find that, apart from Ersek, they had all survived the assault. But most of the men were still cowering at the back of the cave. The explosions had rattled them, but it had been the hellfire that poured into the cave entrance, seeking them out, sucking the breath from their lungs, that had left them paralysed. Some clutched their unfired weapons as if they were a talisman against evil.

While Vegar briefed the others, Marin found Lovric and took him aside. The man's nerves were stretched thin from the battle, his eyes moist with emotion.

'We were moments away from being overrun,' Lovric said. 'It's a miracle we're still alive.'

'It's only a matter of time now,' said Marin. 'Our only chance is to hope the storm keeps up and for us to try to escape after dark.'

'And to split up.'

'That's what Vegar is telling them.'

Marin nodded in the direction of the group huddled on the other side of the cave, now in loud argument.

'It makes sense for smaller groups to go in different directions and split the search,' he went on, grasping Lovric by the shoulders. 'I have an idea, but you're the only one I trust.'

'You already know my answer,' said Lovric.

Marin looked around to make sure no one was in earshot.

'You better hear me out. This will sound crazy,' he said quietly. 'When the others leave the cave we will go with them, but break away as soon as possible. None of them must know what we're doing. If they're caught, they will give us away.'

'What's your plan?'

'There's only one way for them to go. They will keep climbing and then head off in different directions. The best chance we have is to do the opposite. We'll go back down the mountain.'

'Straight into the arms of the enemy?' said Lovric. 'You *are* crazy.'

'No. In the rain, in the dark, we can pass through them. It's the last thing they will expect. Then we must find a secure place to hide during the day and let the main force pass. They'll be looking forward, not behind them.'

Lovric considered this, shaking his head.

'You really are a mad fucker.'

'That's been said before.'

Lovric clasped his arms around him and whispered in his ear. 'I'm with you, brother.'

The storm continued to worsen. The lookouts reported no movement at all from the forest, but regular shots rang out, the army snipers having resolved to keep them pinned in their cavernous trap. The opening was sheltered by rocky outcrops, which created a dog-leg at the entrance; but still the occasional round got through and ricocheted, sending sparks off the walls.

Some of the men were stoically calm, some were strung out

and some at the point of madness. Marin saw that many of them had reached the edge of endurance. They had seen how easily death had caught up with their companions and how patiently it waited for them. They had barely slept for days; they were wet and they were hungry.

Circling the cave, Kancijanic—a man so reticent that Marin had barely heard him utter a full sentence since they had crossed the border—came across Ambroz Andric and stopped in front of him, his face twisted with contempt. Andric was sitting on the floor, picking sardines out of a can with the point of his knife.

'What do you want, Viktor?' he sighed.

'This is your fault, you fucking madman!' Kancijanic shouted. 'You and your halfwit brother and your imbecilic plans.'

Andric threw aside the can. As he tried to scramble to his feet, Kancijanic pushed him in the chest with both hands and he fell back on his arse. Men began to shout. Someone yelled, 'Kill him!', but it was unclear who they meant. Andric made it to his feet and went for Kancijanic with the knife.

Marin stepped in, blocking him and seizing hold of the arm with the knife.

'No,' he shouted in Andric's face. 'We can't afford to fight each other.'

But Andric turned his anger on Marin. 'I should have let Adolf kill you, daddy's boy,' he hissed, pulling free of Marin's grip. 'I'll do it myself now.'

Vegar jumped to his feet behind Andric and wrapped his arms around his friend. 'No, Ambroz,' he spoke into his ear. 'No.'

Now other men who had never spoken out climbed to their feet to challenge Andric. They'd had enough of his leadership and his stubborn delusions. Even here, trapped in this fetid cave, he had continued to insist that the common folk would hear of their brave deeds and climb the mountain to join them. They would have one hundred new recruits within days—that was his mantra—but they had all grown weary of it and they now openly abused him. Men who had once been frightened of their own shadows told Andric his words were shit. As his power diminished, they lost their fear and derided him and his plans. For his part Andric denounced them as motherless cunts, and wished only that they would die soon and think of their shame as they took their last breaths.

Marin was not surprised that Vegar remained loyal to Andric, but only two others, Rocco Buntic and Mirko Vlasnovic, agreed to stay with him as the group disintegrated. The original *troikas* had become meaningless and new alliances formed in the cave as men calculated who was most likely to survive. Marin saw the treacherous Horvat finally turn on Andric, a dog biting his master's hand. Horvat announced he would abandon the group and try to escape. No one argued with him.

The rest of them, including Marin and Lovric, who of course had their own secret plan, agreed to follow Glavas. The demented general, despite everything, was ecstatic at finally having his own army. Marin listened to the pompous fool's plan to march them west and then south to cross the Cetina River into Dalmatia. Watching the man pace up and down, he was reminded of the story Lovric had told him of Glavas haranguing the group of frozen corpses. Marin glanced at the pale, strained faces of the men around him. They might as well be corpses. No Croatian martyrs had risen from their graves to join their holy war, but he felt sure these men would soon be sharing eternity with them in the darkness.

The long day came to a melancholy end. As night fell, men who now found themselves in different camps hugged and said their goodbyes.

Andric and Vegar went up first through the shaft that took them out above the cave. One by one the men followed, each of them clad in their wet ponchos. The thunderstorm had passed, but the heavy downpour continued and they crawled through a small waterfall all the way up to the opening.

Marin was the last to emerge, Lovric just ahead of him. As his eyes adjusted he made out the shapes of men climbing ahead of him low to the ground. Through the driving rain he heard explosions down below in the forest.

'Get down! Get down!' he yelled, and the call echoed up the chain of men. The sky above the cave was illuminated by two flares, blazing like green suns as they swayed down on small parachutes. More thumps came from below and mortar bombs exploded in a pattern near the mouth of the cave.

Marin knew the escapees had not been seen or the bombs would have fallen around them, exposed on the open mountain. They lay still until the flares dimmed, and then began the steep ascent once more.

Marin grabbed Lovric's shoulder. 'Let's go,' he whispered when there was enough space between them and the last men in the group, and slithered down and off to the right.

Lovric soon followed him. They made perhaps twenty metres before he heard the thump of the mortars once more. They slid through the mud to an outcrop as the illumination rounds again bathed the cave opening with green light. This time lines of tracers streamed up from positions in the forest as fire was poured into the cave.

Marin looked up and realised that the climbing men had gone beyond the range of the flares and were in shadow. Their own situation was much more perilous.

When the flares died, Marin and Lovric angled down across the mountain to get as far away from the cave as they could. The descent was much steeper on this path and in the darkness Marin began to fear that the rain would wash them into a crevasse or over a cliff edge. He dug his fingers into the cracks in the limestone and inched down metre by metre. It took them more than an hour, but somehow they found a path to the bottom.

The attacks continued at random intervals. Using the firing positions as his reference, Marin took a compass bearing under his poncho, then they set off into the forest, skirting the concentration of soldiers. They only felt safe when they heard the gunfire faintly behind them.

When the sky began to lighten, they knew that it was time to disappear. Lovric suggested traversing the slope until the woods thinned. He was looking for an area of bare karst, where they would be likely to find another cave.

As they worked their way across the forest, they found clumps of mushrooms, chanterelles and morels, which they picked and stuffed into their pockets. By the time they reached the first clearing the rain had eased with the dawn. They were exposed on the steep slope, but Lovric soon found a narrow opening in the karst. He took off his pack and edged inside, with Marin following.

The entrance was no more than five feet high, but it opened out to a larger space at the back which was miraculously dry. They laid their packs on the ground, shucked off their damp ponchos and emptied their pockets.

They ate the mushrooms, along with a few salted biscuits, and washed them down with rainwater from their canteens. Marin was almost delirious with fatigue. He lay with his head on his pack and fell into a deep slumber.

Anna Rosen came to him in his sleep, her breath on the side of his face, her voice whispering in his ear, urging him to come home.

Marin had forced thoughts of her from his conscious mind, locked them away, and yet here she was and he felt her loss like the deep throbbing pain of an amputated limb.

He woke, his heart thumping, startled by the noise of heavy choppers ascending from the valley. Two of them—the Mi-8s—which he presumed were returning, now that the weather had cleared, to drop reinforcements and ammunition, and to pick up the wounded and the dead. Then came two more, smaller machines: reconnaissance choppers, he was willing to wager.

Lovric was at the front of the cave, peering up from the shadows. When the aircraft passed over he came back and slumped down against his pack.

'They'll stop at nothing now,' he said. 'Every man in every village and town will be searching until all of us are hunted down.'

'How long were we asleep?'

'An hour, maybe less.'

'We'll need more than that.'

'You got any sleep pills? I'm full of adrenalin.'

Marin reached into his pack. 'No, but I've been saving this.' He threw Lovric a battered flask. 'My father made it.'

Lovric held it up. 'Here's to your father.' He took a long pull and handed the flask back. 'The stupid prick that put us here.'

'I'll drink to that,' Marin said.

Lovric lay back on his pack and closed his eyes. 'I don't blame him. I don't. I blame myself. I never told you this, but I left my son to come here. The boy is two years old. I ran from his mother and him. He was going to tie me down, you see, and put an end to the great adventure. That's how big a fuckwit I am. Fathers can be such cunts, am I right?'

'You are right.'

*

They slept fitfully, woken through the day by the comings and goings of helicopters and by distant gunfire. Before nightfall they checked their meagre supplies. They calculated that the food could be made to last three days, if they carefully rationed it. They shared a chocolate bar from a US ration pack. When it was completely dark, they resumed their climb down the mountain.

In the early hours of the morning they reached the foothills and a large open space which, by Marin's reckoning, was Kupresko Polje, the field of buttercups. He was about to step into it when he saw a light flicker and a red glow. Someone had lit a cigarette. A sentry? He held Lovric back, put a finger to his mouth.

Marin knelt and rubbed mud on his face and hands; Lovric did the same. Marin led them to the edge of the field, which they began to cross on their bellies. Part way across he realised that the strange shapes he'd been seeing in the field were not rocks but tents, dozens of them, tent after tent. They were crawling through a large encampment. They must have stumbled into the territorial army's forward operating base.

They had no choice but to keep going. If there were sentries at the far end, they didn't spot them. Marin avoided the pathways that he assumed were military supply lines and found a way back into the forest.

In this way, exposing themselves only at night and hiding out during the day, they moved steadily south. As their food supplies dwindled, they risked raiding isolated farmhouses.

After two nights' walking, they thought they had put the main search parties behind them. But in the tiny village of Zahum they almost walked into an ambush. At the edge of the village Lovric spotted a militia outpost. They were able to backtrack and circle around it. But the incident disturbed Marin. If a place that small had soldiers waiting for them, where would they be safe?

They hiked one night to Rama Lake and saw its famous blue waters—the mountain's eye—gleaming black in the moonlight. After avoiding houses by the water, they climbed down from the lake, heading south through thick forest until they came to a small hamlet at the base of the mountain. It was after 3 am and Lovric decided these farmhouses were ripe for the picking.

'It could be our last chance for a while,' he whispered. 'Since we'll soon be back into the mountains.'

'It's not worth the risk,' said Marin, still shaken by their close shave in Zahum. 'We have enough food to take us through the mountains.'

But Lovric was determined—the little white farmhouses were tempting, and they seemed so benign. He stripped off his pack, tucked a hessian bag into his belt and left his rifle. Taking out his Browning pistol, he crept into the back of the closest farmhouse.

After a brief search of the outbuildings, he found a wooden hut with salamis and dried corncobs hanging from beams. He cut down bunches of each and was shovelling these into the sack when the farm dog sensed his presence and started up a maniacal barking.

Marin, from about one hundred metres away, saw lights come on in several farmhouses; the dog's alarm rang through the close-knit hamlet as effectively as an air-raid warning. He cursed and pulled the Steyr from his shoulder, peering into the pools of light and darkness. A silhouette passed fast through the scope—a figure running through the fields with a gun?

Lovric cocked his pistol and sprinted into the courtyard, the booty in his other hand. The dog came at him out of the shadows, barking and snarling. When it bit his leg, he put a bullet in its brain.

The gunshot ended all doubt and all sleep. Lights came on right across the low hillside in dwellings even Marin had not seen. His own position was exposed now and he jumped up. Shouldering the two packs, he retreated a further fifty metres into the forest.

Through the Steyr's scope he saw Lovric running towards the woods. Then a blast came from the darkness. Shotgun pellets sprayed across Lovric's left shoulder, spinning him around. His left arm went limp; it hung by his side and he dropped the sack of food. Lovric was motionless, illuminated by a porch light at the back of the house, his left side a bloody mess. When he began to move a voice from the farmhouse called out to him to stop.

Marin watched Lovric turn towards a small figure, framed in the doorway by a kitchen light. The Browning was in his good right arm and he threw it up. The figure stepped into the light and the image resolved into a boy, perhaps thirteen years old, with pimples on his face, a mop of black hair, wide eyes full of terror. He had a hunting rifle at his shoulder trained on the thief in his yard. Lovric hesitated and Marin knew he would not shoot the boy.

Fathers can be such cunts.

When Lovric lowered the pistol the boy shot him in the forehead.

Lovric crumpled to the ground. A farmer with a shotgun jumped a fence, ran into the yard and shouted something at the boy. Then he put a round into Lovric's chest for good measure. Marin had the man in his sights. He held the target for a moment, but then he lowered the rifle, picked up the packs and withdrew into the deep darkness of the forest.

Working by torchlight under his poncho, Marin emptied Lovric's pack, taking from it the food, a few useful items and a wallet he found tucked away in a pocket. He buried the rest, including Lovric's rifle. The militia would come to collect his body and they would search the area forensically. Best they found nothing.

He took another compass bearing, got to his feet and headed south as fast as he could. There was no time to lose. No time to grieve.

He moved at double time for two hours, stopping only to check the compass. South, always south—go far enough and you'll hit the Adriatic.

Before dawn he found another hiding place in the narrow, concealed entrance to a small cave. The faint stench of some long-dead animal clung to its walls. Lying there on his back, he allowed himself to think of Lovric and for the first time he felt the despair, which he had held at bay for so long, come gnawing at his entrails.

There was security, but no comfort, in the darkness. He pulled out a torch; after all, he had two of them now. He could afford a little light. He dug around in the pack and found his father's brandy, and the wallet he'd retrieved from Lovric's pack. He flipped it open and, behind the plastic window, he saw the little boy, the son Lovric had left behind. The boy had a cheeky grin, which was to be expected, but he was destined to grow up with an unfulfilled longing. The loss of a father, a piece of his soul missing forever. Marin didn't even know the boy's name. He drank all the remaining brandy and fell asleep, overwhelmed, at last, by exhaustion.

Marin slept undisturbed for ten hours and woke with the inkling of a plan that centred on a single idea. Hungry and dehydrated, he drank half the water in his canteen, then ate two apples, a pear and a large chunk of the remaining salami. He pissed into a pannikin and put it where he wouldn't knock it over. Then he emptied his pack and peered at the contents in the dim light.

He set aside his military gear. He stripped down to his underwear and boots, and pushed the pile into the darkest corner.

He wiped the Steyr clean of fingerprints and laid it on top of the pile. He felt no reluctance leaving it behind—the weapon had killed enough people and he had no intention of staging a final shootout if the army tracked him down. He did the same with the Browning, his spare ammunition and every piece of equipment that might carry prints.

Moving awkwardly in the small space, he dressed himself in the jeans and T-shirt he'd stowed at the bottom of the pack and pulled on the jumper he'd brought for the cool mountain nights. He took the photograph of Lovric's son and slipped it into his passport. Then he wiped the wallet clean and threw it on to the pile.

He refilled the pack with the remaining food, the canteen, torches and spare batteries, a filthy sleeping bag, tin plate, utensils and the few books he'd brought with him. The pack looked like something a young Western tourist might have picked up in an army disposal store, but he decided he would ditch it at the first opportunity. In the pocket of his jeans was a roll of US dollars, to which he added the stash of Yugoslavian dinar he'd found in Lovric's pack.

That night Marin climbed high into the glacial valley between the peaks of the Cvrsnica and Vran mountains. Then, crossing the saddle, he began a slow descent, making it to the foothills before dawn. Here he crawled into a cave to see out the day.

When night fell he set out for Posusje, a large town straddling the main road to Mostar, which was a further fifty-odd kilometres to the south-east. His plan depended on reaching Mostar, but he had no idea how he could make such a long journey.

As he came closer, by his reckoning, to Posusje, the forested country gave way to cultivated farmlands. He entered a wide field of waist-high crops laid out in long neat lines. He stopped to pinch off some leaves, crushing them in his hands.

The sweet fragrance of a fresh pack of Drum.

He looked around at this vast crop, recalling what Lovric had told him about the tobacco routes through the mountains. For years the smugglers had made a killing. The rich tobacco of Herzegovina became so popular that Joseph Stalin used to crumble cigarettes from the region into his pipe. Lovric told the story with a punchline. 'A smooth, clean taste . . .' he had mugged, holding an imaginary pipe. 'Number one choice of dictators everywhere.'

On the edge of the tobacco fields Marin found a series of large wooden buildings. He scouted around for dogs. There were none, because no one lived here. Two of the buildings were tobacco barns with unlocked doors, racked from top to bottom with drying leaves. He concluded that none were ready to be smoked. He knew it was a foolish risk, but what better place to top up his tobacco pouch?

The third building was much larger; it appeared to be a store-house. It was locked, of course, but he was determined now. He took off his pack and used a drainpipe to climb up to the wooden slats of an air vent, where he was able to wriggle his way through. Once inside, he flicked on his torch. The walls were stacked high with neatly compressed, yellowed bundles of dried tobacco. In the open space in the middle was a truck.

Marin went around to the back of the vehicle. It was packed with identical bundles of tobacco. He immediately understood the implications. It wasn't here to unload: it was packed and ready to go.

A way out! A way out, by God! But where was the truck going? Maybe there were papers in the front? He shone the torch, revealing a sign, neatly painted in yellow letters edged with black on the green enamel, beneath the window. *Fabrika duhana Mostar d.d. Mostar*.

Mostar Tobacco Factory. Mostar! Marin could barely believe his luck. Lovric must have been sitting on his shoulder as an angel.

After considering his options, he scanned the walls and found a door, which he unlatched and propped open while he retrieved his pack.

It took him an hour by torchlight to unpack the truck and create a large enough space for him to crawl into backwards, leaving two bundles of dried tobacco to be pulled back in to reseal the hiding place. He had no idea what time the driver would come to make the return journey, so he pissed in a far corner. He drank a little water and climbed on to the back shelf of the truck.

He left just enough of a gap to allow a flow of air, but the sickly sweet smell of the tobacco was intense. He fell asleep wondering if he'd ever again enjoy rolling a cigarette.

He woke to the sound of a door slamming, followed by the whirr of the ignition until it caught with a roar. There followed a series of rapid growls as the driver pumped the accelerator and then let it idle. Marin heard the diesel's steady ticking before the truck was finally crunched into gear and driven out of the building.

The journey was uneventful. There were no roadblocks as far as he could discern. He was bumped around and tossed from side to side but, for the first part, he felt the elation of an escapee who has left mortal danger behind.

Then he began worrying about how to get out of the truck unnoticed at the other end. It would all fall apart if he were discovered. A simple phone call to the police and he would be a fugitive, trapped in a city with every eye on the lookout.

Eventually the truck slowed and jerked along in low gears, in what Marin assumed to be city traffic. After some time, the brakes squealed and the truck wheeled left, bumping into a driveway, then it turned right sharply and stopped. He heard the handbrake engage, the door open and slam shut, footsteps retreating ... and then nothing.

Marin pushed the loose bundles of tobacco aside and listened for the sound of men. The truck appeared to be in a warehouse loading dock. It was quiet, apart from passing traffic. He paused, straining to hear anything that he may have missed. He froze there for a moment, his limbs unwilling to move. Still he heard nothing.

He shuffled forward on his elbows and climbed carefully out of the hiding place, dragging his pack behind him. He lowered himself to the ground, paused again to look around once more, straining to hear any human activity. There was nothing. The driver had left the truck unattended.

He crept out of the covered dock into the sunshine. Beside the old factory building there was a line of fir trees in an unkempt garden, and he walked through it unchallenged and out the front gate into a busy street. At the first intersection he looked up at the street sign—*Marsala Tita.*

'You're fucking kidding,' he said, and laughed out loud. The absurdly simple final leg of his escape had spilled him out on to Marshal Tito Boulevard, or Avenue or Drive or whatever. Of course they'd name every main road after the murderous old tyrant. If Lovric was still on his shoulder, this was surely his last joke. He started laughing again.

A man on the street stared at him as if he was crazy. Maybe he was. Marin saw a middle-aged woman looking askance and he stopped. When he showed her his palm, as if to say 'no worries', he noticed a tremor in it. He dropped his shaking hand, made a fist of it and walked on, anxious not to draw a crowd. Further down the road he asked a passer-by in English where he could find Stari Most.

'You want bridge?'

Yes, the bridge. Of course, the bridge. The famous fucking bridge. He smiled the harmless smile of a foreign backpacker and nodded. How was the man to know he had recently transformed from terrorist to tourist?

Straight ahead, the fellow indicated: straight down this road, maybe two kilometres. You can't miss it.

So he continued on Marsala Tita. It was a long, wide street with old buildings on either side, three or four storeys high. There was a stream of one-way traffic heading in his direction. Ahead of him a green mountain dipped steeply into a gorge through which, he knew from the map, the Neretva River ran. Taking his bearings, he figured the river was to his left.

It was still early, but a hot summer's day was brewing. Marin took off his jumper and shoved it in the top of his pack. He stopped at an optometrist to buy a pair of sunglasses, replica Ray-Bans, and there he saw himself for the first time in a mirror. He'd washed in a riverbed a day ago, but the dirt seemed to be ingrained. With his ragged beard and red eyes, he looked like a hippy coming down from a mushroom trip. Further along he found a pharmacy and bought himself shaving gear, a tube of toothpaste, a toothbrush and a bottle of aspirin.

As he got closer to the old town, he started to see other foreigners. He heard a couple talking with American accents and approached them to ask if they knew a good place for breakfast. The young man was a TV version of a Yank, with a flat-top crew-cut, a freshly pressed shirt and chinos. He regarded Marin with alarm, as if Charles Manson had just tapped him on the shoulder. But his girlfriend was more than happy to give Marin directions to a 'really cool place' above the river. When she smiled at him, her boyfriend gave her a hard look. Best to wash and shave as soon as possible. The last thing he wanted was to draw attention.

But first he needed to eat. The smell of meat cooking somewhere on a grill was an irresistible lure. He had never been this hungry. He followed the girl's directions into a side street and down a set of stairs that led to a terrace café. And there he stopped.

As hungry as he was, Marin was nonetheless transfixed by the scene in front of him. He'd seen pictures, of course, but no two-dimensional photograph could possibly convey the sense he had of having walked into the medieval past, into a still thriving corner of the Ottoman Empire. The fine, high arch of Stari Most, the Old Bridge, rose nearly thirty metres above the blue-green river, flanked by stone towers and minarets. The bridge, the towers and the surrounding buildings seemed to flow up organically from their footings in the raw, rocky banks of the river, all rendered from the same pale limestone. Behind his sunglasses, tears welled up as Marin was assailed by a wave of unexpected emotion.

He allowed an imperturbable Bosnian waiter to lead him to a table by a low stone wall overlooking the gorge. He ordered Turkish coffee and *burek* which came quickly. The waiter poured the sweet, silted black drink from a beaten-copper pot. His father, despite his hatred of the Turks, still made coffee like this. And with his first taste of the *burek*, Marin's eyes moistened again as he remembered his mother in the kitchen, pressing spiced meats into a soft pastry, and the fragrance of them cooking in the oven. All around him in the bright sunshine young tourists chattered like songbirds. He had the strange feeling that he had stepped on to a stage set. He closed his eyes to blink away the tears and saw again, in the darkness, Lovric crumpling to the ground.

When Marin had finally devoured a long meal of many courses, the waiter, encouraged by a large tip, led him to a bathroom with a basin and a mirror. The steaming hot water seemed an incredible luxury and he stripped to the waist. He shaved off the ragged beard and washed away the accumulated sweat and grime, until the creature in the mirror more closely resembled the young Western wastrels en route to Istanbul, Tehran and Kabul on the hippy trail. It was a good enough impersonation. He cleaned up his mess and left the place.

Nearby he found a phone box with an intact local directory. He located the name he was looking for and an address on Ulica Gojka Vukovica. It was a short walk to the house and, by chance, there was a small café across the road from it. He took an outside table, pulled from his pack a battered copy of *Sevastopol Sketches* and settled down to wait.

Before midday the traffic dwindled to a few passing cars and then, echoing down the near empty street, came the call to prayer from a nearby mosque. The muezzin's song, though redolent of the supplanted Ottoman faith, was not jarring to him. It seemed natural enough in this anachronistic place, yet he still felt offended by the idea that God was peering down at his puny undertakings from high above the minaret.

Then the front door of the house opened and an old man, wearing a good suit and a crimson fez, stepped into the street, dutifully answering the call to prayer. The man passed close by: he was a handsome, well-made fellow with white hair and pale blue eyes.

Marin waited a short while before crossing the road and knocking on the door. It was opened by a middle-aged woman who looked at him with a puzzled expression until he said: 'Hello, Mother. It's Marin.'

16.

Three days before Christmas, on a warm, clear morning, George Negus walked to Parliament House. His route took him alongside the artificial body of water he derided as Canberra's Lake Geneva knock-off. Even its giant waterspout had been carefully calibrated to peak nearly thirty feet higher than the famous one in the Swiss city.

Negus felt irrationally pleased that antipodean engineers could throw water further into the air than their European counterparts, but his nationalist sentiments were still offended by the foreign trees that lined the lakeside pathways—the elm and oak, the claret ash and ornamental pear. Eucalypt forests still ringed the city, but here in the centre the natives had been lopped down to pretty up the place with interlopers. Why had the exotics been given pride of place?

Walking now in their pleasant shade, he found himself even more disturbed by the bucolic quiescence that had settled on the capital less than three weeks after 'the great event'. This was so at odds with his own surging emotions. As a Queenslander, he'd grown up with outlandish weather events, and now the Labor Party had made landfall on a somnolent nation with the very intensity of one of those tropical storms whipped up in the warm waters of the Pacific.

How could a single fucking leaf be left on these trees after the cyclone of Whitlam's victory? Everything should still be in the air—roofs torn off, multitudes of red tiles flying about like shrapnel, and people exposed to the open skies, clinging on for dear life to whatever was nailed down as their Holden cars were lifted into the roaring winds. The old certainties were gone, swirling about in the tempest.

The conservatives had been vanquished. Nothing would ever be the same, would it? And yet . . . And yet the lake was placid, the trees rustled, commuters commuted, public servants prevaricated, carols played in shopping centres and girls in miniskirts, as always, turned his mind to earthly things.

But in Lionel Murphy's office the storm still raged. His boss, the new attorney-general, was full of the animal spirits of revolution. Murphy was out to change the country, and nothing would alter his course. His momentum was unstoppable.

To Negus's surprise, Murphy had even managed to work his charms on the incumbent departmental secretary, the venerable Clarrie Harders. Everyone had expected Lionel to sack the old public servant who for many years had advised his hated predecessor, Senator Ivor Greenwood—aka Ivor the Terrible.

'How can you keep Harders on, Lionel?' Negus queried Murphy soon after the election. 'It's not just that he's a Greenwood man—he's a bloody anachronism.'

Murphy smiled indulgently at his upstart press secretary. 'He's a good fellow, George, you'll see.'

'They reckon he's in line for a knighthood. Aren't we supposed to be getting rid of them?'

'They're a dying breed,' said Murphy. 'But we're not going to cut them off at the knees—we'll phase them out. Knights and dames will have a natural death. But I need this one alive.'

He explained that Clarrie Harders was vital to the efficient functioning of the A-G's department—he'd keep the public servants in line and prevent foot-dragging.

Nonetheless, Negus had still been aggrieved by a conversation Harders had initiated with him ahead of Murphy's swearing in as attorney-general.

'So, let's talk about policy,' the old mandarin had said, coming swiftly to the point after the usual formalities. 'I know the attorney wants to make a lot of changes: no fault divorce, the trade practices act, freedom of information laws and broad law reform. This will be like working in an experimental wind tunnel. We really need to get a sense of what can sensibly be achieved, George. When are we going to sit down and talk about what he's planning?'

Negus had opened his top drawer, pulled out a document and dropped it in front of Harders.

'It's all here in the party manifesto,' he'd said. 'Senator Murphy wrote it. Why don't you just run off copies and give them out to everyone in the department? Just tell them, "Read this and get on with it."'

Negus jogged up the Parliament House stairs, hair bouncing on his shoulders, moustache bristling. At this time of the morning there were few people in the cavernous King's Hall. As his shoes slipped pleasingly on the highly polished parquet floor, he managed to resist the schoolboy urge to try a running slide.

Ahead of him the tall bronze statue of George V was lit on all sides by the lines of translucent windows high up near the ceiling.

As always, the simple inscription on the marble plinth—*Rex Imperator*—infuriated Negus. King *and* Emperor, for fuck's sake! The bloke must have had huge tickets on himself.

He glanced above the King's head to the clock on the wall. Ten to eight. He just had time to get to his office and listen to *AM*. Murphy wouldn't be in yet, so he bypassed the A-G's office and went straight to his own. The in-house monitor was set to ABC Radio. He flicked it on and plugged in the electric jug to make a cuppa.

The morning's newspapers were waiting on his desk and he sat to skim through them. The main headlines were all about Whitlam's letter of protest to President Nixon over his decision to resume the bombing of North Vietnam after the collapse of the Paris peace talks. Negus saw that no one had the prime minister's actual missive, but a 'senior source' in the PM's office—he translated that to mean Whitlam advisor Jim Spigelman—was quoted as saying that the letter expressed 'strong opposition to the US action'.

After the pips on the hour, *AM*'s strident theme cut in and the prime minister's 'up yours' letter to Nixon was their lead story, too. Negus opened his notepad when the coverage began with a live interview with a new cabinet minister. He soon heard the familiar, hectoring voice of Dr Jim Cairns, distorted on a crackly phone line: '*I say to the Nixon administration, stop your attacks on the Vietnamese people. Leave them alone. Take your armed forces home.*'

Three years ago Cairns had led one hundred thousand people in the Melbourne Moratorium March and become the key figurehead of the anti-war movement. He wasn't the type to back off just because he'd been elevated to the cabinet, but this was his first public outing as a minister and every word was steeped in his trademark moral outrage.

'*The bombing of North Vietnam is totally and completely unjustified,*' Cairns pronounced. '*It will not bring the end of the war any nearer. It is simply resulting in the purposeless killing of more and more people.'*

A woman's voice interrupted Negus's note-taking: 'This is really going to piss off the White House.'

He looked up and was surprised to see the journalist Anna Rosen standing in the doorway.

'As if Whitlam's letter wasn't enough to get them going,' she added as Cairns banged on in the same vein.

'Jim's off on a frolic of his own,' said Negus. 'That said, the septics are just going to have to get used to the fact that we're not their little lapdogs anymore.'

Anna put the rhyming slang together: *yanks = septic tanks = septics.* She laughed. 'That may be, George,' she said. 'But I think that little lapdog just pissed on the Oval Office carpet.'

'Yeah, maybe,' said Negus, pointing across the desk. 'Pull up a chair, I've got to listen to this.'

Anna sat down and held her tongue as Jim Cairns told the interviewer that President Nixon had never really been serious about the Paris peace talks. They were just part of a charade he'd created to pacify his critics during his election campaign and, now that Nixon had won his second term, all bets were off. He could bomb and kill to his heart's content. Anna didn't disagree with Cairns's argument, but she sensed that his recklessness would not go unpunished.

Negus continued to jot down points, glancing up at Anna from time to time. She was smart, intense and interesting. He'd always fancied her, but he was in a serious relationship right now—more's the pity.

When the Cairns interview ended, *AM* moved on to the election of the new leader of the Liberal Party. It had taken the Libs an age to finally get around to dumping the defeated prime minister, Billy McMahon. Perversely, they'd plugged for another Billy: Billy

Snedden this time—a sly Melburnian, almost as silly a Billy as his predecessor. Anyway, Snedden was already in strife with his Country Party partners over power-sharing. No need to worry about this, Negus thought. He stopped writing, lowered the volume and turned to Rosen.

'So, what are you doing in Parliament House, Anna?'

'I've just made the move down here to the press gallery,' she replied. 'I'm starting today with the *Herald*, national security round.'

'What?' He was surprised. 'You left the ABC? I thought you were number one with a bullet after breaking those yarns on the Croats.'

'I had a few unresolved issues at the ABC and they weren't going away any time soon,' she explained. 'The approach from the *Herald* came at the right time, an early Christmas present, really. So here I am.'

'Unresolved issues?'

'It's personal, George. Let's leave it at that.'

Negus nodded, imagining various scenarios. 'So here you are,' he said.

'Yep.'

'Well, what do you want—a medal?'

'No, a chat with Lionel Murphy will do.'

'Oh, is that all?'

'Yep.'

'On your first day? That's pressing your luck, isn't it?'

'Will you just ask him for me?'

'I'll ask him,' he agreed. 'No promises. He's pretty fucken busy.'

'And you're the gatekeeper, George, I get that. But those pesky Croats haven't gone away and I think he's going to want to talk to me.'

'We'll see.' Negus remembered that he'd just boiled water and stood up. 'I'm making a cuppa—you want one?'

'Sure, thanks. Black, no sugar.'

Negus quickly re-boiled the water and poured it over tea bags in two mugs. His he sugared and doused with milk. He plonked the black one in front of Anna with a teaspoon to fish out the tea bag.

'Anything else on your mind?' he asked as she debated what to do with the sodden thing on the teaspoon. In the end she placed it on the banner of *The Australian*, rather than risk staining the wooden desk.

'As a matter of fact, George, there is. I understand the attorney met with the director-general of ASIO last week.'

'You shouldn't believe everything you hear from gossipy journos.'

'I'm sorry?'

'Don't worry. I just can't imagine the spooks leaking to you of all people.'

'My sources are good. I'm told Murphy got stuck into Peter Barbour over the Croats and that he wants to ban ASIO's bugging operations, and that's just for starters. That is of tremendous public interest, don't you think?'

Anna paused to blow on her tea and take a sip.

'I'll tell you what,' said Negus. 'Even if you're right—and I'm not saying you are—it would be of tremendous *private* interest. We're not going to go around putting out press releases about our first conversation with the boss of ASIO.'

Anna frowned. 'So much for open government,' she said.

'We can't all shoot from the hip like Jim Cairns,' said Negus irritably.

'Shame. Anyway, I've got enough to run the story without the attorney, but he might want to get on the front foot and talk to me.'

'Look, Anna, I've got a lot to do.'

She stood up. 'Okay, thanks for the tea,' she said. 'Just let the boss know this will be on the front page tomorrow.'

Negus stared up at her. Rosen had him over a barrel. He decided to offer a deal.

'All right, maybe I can give you something else if you agree to hold off on the ASIO story for a couple of days and let us manage the issue so's the attorney doesn't end up at loggerheads with Peter Barbour.'

'What is it?'

'Do we have an agreement?'

'Not until you tell me what you've got.'

'You gonna turn this into a pissing contest?'

Anna Rosen winked at him. 'I've shown you mine. You show me yours.'

'For fuck's sake,' said Negus, giving up. 'Okay. Lionel's just hired a former Commonwealth copper to advise him on Croatian extremists. I could arrange for you to meet him for a briefing. Off the record of course.'

'Who is this person?'

'Kerry Milte, his name is. Ever come across him? Big red-headed bloke.'

'No.'

'Milte's a bit of a firebrand. Youngest ever police superintendent. He trained as a lawyer and wanted to shake things up at the Commonwealth Police. He took a bloody hard line on the Croats. Foot on the throat stuff . . .'

Negus paused to see if she'd taken the bait; but when she said nothing, he went on.

'Here's the other thing. He was also running an undercover investigation on police corruption in New South Wales, but he had a serious run-in with the top brass. It got so bad that he quit the force and went back to Melbourne to put up his shingle as a barrister.'

'That is interesting,' Anna acknowledged. 'When can I meet him?'

'I've got to talk to the attorney and clear it with him. Give me your number at the bureau and I'll call you once I've done that.'

She wrote it down and then straightened up and looked him in the eye. 'George, if I'm going to spike the ASIO story, I'll need this to happen very soon. And I still want to speak to Lionel Murphy.'

'I said I'll call you, Anna.'

As Negus watched her go, he caught himself staring at her bum and shook his head. Then he picked up the phone.

'Morning, Daphne. Is Lionel in yet?'

Anna made her way back up two flights of stairs to the cramped chicken coop that was the *Herald*'s newsroom. A corridor, lined with the bundled newspaper archives and named pigeonholes, took her past the empty telex room. The telex operators, all men from what she'd seen, would arrive in the afternoon, most from shifts at the Post Office. It seemed they all worked second jobs and earned more than she did.

A narrow doorway at the end opened into a room barely larger than the corridor itself. Half a dozen desks sat crowded together on a grubby black and white vinyl chequerboard floor. There were desks on either side of the room so that the reporters could sit back-to-back with a tiny space between them. On each desk was a fat Olivetti typewriter, reams of paper and a telephone. Like the telex room, the place was unoccupied at this time of the morning. Locked into late deadlines, her new colleagues were not expected to make an appearance for several hours.

Anna dropped her leather bag beside the typewriter on her allocated desk, just inside the doorway, and sat. She put both hands flat on the desktop, leaned back and closed her eyes. She got nothing, no redolence, save the stench of stale tobacco.

Harry Lang, the journalist she was replacing, had gone, like so many others, to join the new government as a press secretary, but he had been kind enough to ring her in Sydney to offer some advice.

'It's a young bureau, love. Now that I'm gone anyway,' he said with a chuckle. 'You may be the only sheila, but you'll have no problems with the blokes you'll be working with. They look like they've come off the cover of a Led Zeppelin album.'

Anna opened her eyes. She checked the desk drawers and found them all empty. Then she noticed the typewriter had a single page rolled into it. She unspooled it and saw that Lang had left her a note.

> The scribbler's fate's to write and write
> From dawn into the dead of night,
> to light your fags from end to end,
> hear endless crap but not offend
> the silly pricks the voters chose
> who then go on to primp and pose
> and lie and cheat and fulminate.
> It's time for me to beat this fate.
> It's time for YOU to write and write
> So stay and fight . . . but I choose flight!

Anna shook her head and smiled. She searched around, found some sticky tape, stuck the page above her desk and read it again.

'Thanks, Harry,' she said aloud. 'Who says you can't teach an old doggerel new tricks.'

Harry could not possibly have guessed how much she was regretting the scribbler's fate. She tried to write and write but she had hit the wall with her book. It had happened after the confrontation with Ivo Katich on the bridge, which had shaken her to the core. She had seen the old fascist through the eyes of his victims, and it had made her think of her mother's escape from the demons in Europe.

That was how she'd always thought of them—demons who rendered people into smoke—but she had learned that they were not. Yes, they were monsters, but they were not inhuman. Ivo Katich was living proof of that. They were flesh-and-blood men like him. At least that was all he was in the cold light of day: just a man. It was in her nightmares that his eyes flickered with the flames of the ovens.

Since that afternoon Anna had begun to worry if she could write objectively about such a man, if she was capable of explaining his existence with mere words.

She had gone to see her father, to ask for his advice. Frank Rosen had listened to her silently, then he'd excused himself and gone into his study. When he returned, he handed her a piece of paper with one name and a phone number in Vienna.

'This is the man you must speak to,' said Frank. 'He'll give you better advice than I could hope to. Make sure to give him my best wishes.'

The name on the note was *Simon Wiesenthal*. The Nazi hunter. Anna couldn't believe it.

'You know him, Dad? How come you never told me?'

'I'm telling you now.'

'I've been working on this for a long time.'

'Anna, it's all tied up with what happened to your mother's family. She didn't want you to bear her burden. She wanted your life to be untainted by this horror. That's what she said, and I respected it. But I think now you need his advice.'

'How do you know him?'

'I met Wiesenthal in Vienna many years ago. I was there on Party business. He wasn't famous back then. He ran a place called the Jewish Documentation Centre with a handful of volunteers. I'd read that he'd survived Mauthausen Concentration Camp. That's where they murdered your Uncle Samuel, so I went to see him to find out if he could tell me what had happened to him. It turned out that in the last days the Nazis destroyed most of the records at Mauthausen, but Wiesenthal went through the transcribed testimony of other inmates, many of whom he'd interviewed himself. He discovered that Samuel had died in the stone quarry. He was half-starved, but they used to make the prisoners carry huge blocks of stone up incredibly steep stairs and whip them if they faltered. It was like some ghastly perversion of Sisyphus. Samuel was made to do it over and over until it killed him.'

'Does Mum know all of this?'

'Yes, and she asked me not to tell you or the boys. As for me, I was so very grateful to finally hear the truth it made me cry. That hasn't happened often in my life, Anna. Simon Wiesenthal is a good man; he took pity on me when he saw this and agreed to help me find out what happened to the rest of your mother's family.'

'I've always thought that Mum just didn't know any of the details. That it was lost in the chaos and confusion or something.'

'That was true for her. You know the story without the details. Your mother and her two sisters were taken to Ravensbrück. Your grandmother was sent there with them, but she was too old and frail, so she was no use in the slave factories and she was soon taken from them.'

'The only thing I know is that Grandma died in Auschwitz.'

'Yes, that's what we found out from Simon Wiesenthal. Your grandmother was marked for transportation to the gas chambers. Your mother and her sisters stayed together in Ravensbrück, but eventually Hanna and Julie became very sick—we think it was probably typhus—and they were moved to the sub-camp called Uckermark. Your mother was told they were going to a hospital, but she never saw them again. Simon discovered their names on the Mittverda list and he told me that this word *Mittverda* was a code for the gas chamber.'

Anna felt a physical shock at the revelation. She bent forward, brought her hands up to her face. Eventually she wiped the tears away and stared at her father, shaking her head. 'Oh Dad! Dad,' she stammered. 'We should have been told about this. Why weren't we? This is our history.'

Frank was silent for a time.

'I understand why you feel that,' he said. 'You mustn't be upset with your mother. She was there; she lived through this horror. Eva is alive and they are not. She didn't want her children to live under this dark cloud.'

'It found me, anyway.'

'Yes, it did, and now you must speak to Simon Wiesenthal. Few men have his wisdom.'

By the time she spoke to her father, Anna's career in the ABC was on unstable ground. The shifting sands of her relationship with Peter McHugh had eroded to the point where she knew they could not work together for much longer. She felt his simmering resentment when he demanded she put aside her 'obsession' with the Croats to work on other stories.

So she continued her investigations after hours. Late one night she stole into the phone-recording booth and rang the number in

Vienna. One of Wiesenthal's assistants put the call through to him and Anna explained who she was.

'I remember your father,' said Wiesenthal. His accent was a sweet blend of Central Europe and further East, somewhere in the Pale of Settlement. 'How is Frank?'

'He is very well, Mr Wiesenthal. I'm surprised you remember him. That was a long time ago.'

'I have good memory. Anyway, Frank is hard to forget. He was first Australian I ever met. A Jew from "down under", *ja*, and a communist! Of course, if he'd been a Stalinist I would not speak to him.'

Anna smiled at that. 'He's still fighting against the Stalinists.'

'And your mother, how is she?'

'She's still fighting against her memories.'

Wiesenthal said nothing. She heard his laboured breathing down the phone line. 'Like so many others,' he said quietly. 'And what about you, Anna—you're a journalist?'

'Yes, I am. This is why I'm calling you. In my work I have found Nazis who came to Australia after the war.'

'I see.'

'People who should not have been allowed to come here. War criminals.'

'Anna, you should know that we have here in Vienna files—open files, on two thousand cases. But this is just a small number, tip of iceberg. We believe that more than one hundred and fifty thousand Nazis have done war crimes in the Holocaust. Only forty thousand have been put on trial so far. The others live peacefully among us, as if nothing happened. And many escape to other countries—to South America, to the US, to Britain, Canada. And, yes, is true, to Australia.'

'Mr Wiesenthal, can I interrupt you there? I have a tape recorder here. Do you mind if I record our conversation?'

'No, of course not. People must hear this.'

Anna had adjusted the levels while Wiesenthal had been talking. Now she set the machine to record.

'Mr Wiesenthal, can I start by asking for your advice? I am writing about one of these men who came to Australia. He was in the Ustasha, in Bosnia. He was close to the Ustasha leader, Ante Pavelic. He's a terrible man and I want to expose him. I know some of what he did and I know what he is, but he will just deny everything and it's such a long time ago. What can I do?'

'Pavelic was their führer—they call him *Poglavnik*, you know this?'

'Yes.'

'Perhaps you know too that Pavelic was indicted at the Nuremberg Trials for war crimes. They made many documentations during the trials about what happens in Croatia during the war. You can find everything of this in Washington now. All the Nuremberg documents are there in a great vault in the national archives. That can be a starting point.'

'They let journalists access those documents?'

'Sure, why not. You have problem, I write letter for you. Also there are documents in Yugoslavia. In the archives in Zagreb and Sarajevo. The Ustasha had its own newspapers. They publish in them their racial decrees. In all things they follow the Nazis. Pavelic enacted racial laws in the first weeks after Hitler kindly permitted him to set up his puppet state. Yellow stars for Jews, blue armbands for Serbs. Mixed marriages were banned, non-Aryans were forbidden to work in Aryan houses. All these new laws they publish in their own newspapers. And they publish lists of those they execute. Why do they do this? It sounds crazy, *ja*? *Meshuggah*. But at that time they are simply arrogant, proud of these acts.'

'The man I'm writing about, his name is Ivo Katich. He came from Sarajevo.'

'Ah, then you must go there. If he was with the Ustasha in Sarajevo in the summer of 1941 then he must have been part of the pogrom there. After the Nazi occupation, they let the Ustasha do their dirty work. And Pavelic set up his own extermination camp. I'm sure you've heard of Jasenovac? You will find records of all of this in the Nuremberg files in Washington. You should remember, Anna, with documents you can build a case, but you need also to find living witnesses. Discovering witnesses is just as important as catching criminals, and you will have to go to Yugoslavia to do that.'

Anna knew he was right, and she also knew how Ivo Katich and his cohort would defend themselves. 'They will call the witnesses liars, Mr Wiesenthal. They will say the communists forged the documents.'

The old man sighed down the phone line. 'Yes, they will do that. I know this better than anyone. You must make a case that you could take to court. It must be . . . What is word in English? *Watertight*. One mistake and they will try to destroy you. We owe it to the dead to get this right. The new generation has to hear what the older generation refuses to tell it. I have said many times that the history of man is the history of crimes, and history can repeat. So information is defence. Through this we can build, and we must build, a case against this repetition. There is no denying that the monsters are alive today. They are waiting for us to forget. Forgetting is what makes possible their resurrection.'

After this conversation, Anna had thought about Wiesenthal's advice. She decided to put the Katich book aside, but in the meantime she wrote letters to the National Archives in Washington, and to the archives in Zagreb and Sarajevo, and put a visa request to the Yugoslavian Embassy. She began planning a trip to the US and Yugoslavia for July 1973, during the northern summer.

When she'd accepted the *Herald*'s offer to go to Canberra, she insisted they agree to her taking a month off at that time. Steven Boyce, the editor, had pressured her to reconsider the trip and only gave in with a show of reluctance.

'You owe me one, Anna,' he had told her. 'Don't make me regret it.'

Daphne Newman swore that, even from behind the closed door, she could tell when Lionel Murphy was coming halfway down the corridor. She imagined a force field—some form of radiated energy—pushing ahead of him, like the air driven down a tunnel by an underground train. People talked about force of personality, about different-coloured auras, but she'd never heard of one that got there before the actual person. That was a Lionel thing.

Maybe she was imagining it; perhaps it was just his distinctive heavy tread that she heard or felt without realising it. Regardless of the cause, she was expecting the door to fly open and it did. And there he was, beaming at her like she was the best friend he hadn't seen for years.

'Daphne, good morning, what a beautiful day,' Murphy exclaimed with unfeigned enthusiasm, as if he hadn't been dictating letters to her at 10.30 the night before—or polished off half a bottle of whisky while doing so.

Not that she minded. Lionel had repaid her, a thousand-fold, with his loyalty when ASIO had come after her over her meetings with that Russian lothario, Ivan Stenin. If only she hadn't left her bloody briefcase in the man's car. That was done and dusted now, thanks to Murphy.

'You're a little late,' she told him.

'It's never too late to change the world, Daphne,' said Murphy, handing her a stem he'd plucked from the Senate rose garden.

She looked at the crimson flower and was mollified; she got up to find a vase.

Maureen Barron came out from the kitchenette holding the electric jug. 'You missed your meeting this morning with Clarrie Harders,' she said sternly. 'I tried ringing you, but it was constantly engaged.'

Murphy nodded at the jug. 'Careful, Maureen, that would be assault with a deadly weapon.'

'Don't tempt me.'

'I'm sorry I missed Clarrie. Will you ring and apologise? I had to take a call from Peter Wilenski. Gough's going to announce the decision to establish diplomatic relations with China later today.'

'Really?' Maureen was intrigued. 'That's a lot earlier than we thought, isn't it?'

'Yes, it is.' Murphy nodded. 'We'll also be recognising East Germany. You could call this a red-letter day.'

'An early Christmas present for the atheist commies?'

'It'll keep the Americans on their toes anyway, and perhaps push Jim Cairns off the front pages. Oh, before I forget, don't mention this to George, will you? Wilenski doesn't want the whole gallery to know about it before the announcement.'

'George wouldn't like being singled out like that.'

Murphy shrugged. 'They think he's a blabbermouth, Maureen, and, to be honest, he does like a chat.'

'Oh dear.' Maureen sighed. 'Don't worry. I won't say anything to him.'

Daphne walked past them and settled the vase on her desk. 'George has already rung in,' she said. 'He wants to see you as soon as possible. He didn't say why.'

Murphy turned to his private secretary. 'What else have I got on, Maureen?'

'You've got a meeting in half an hour with the Family Law reform working group. Harry Messel's keen to sit in on that. I suspect Clarrie Harders wanted to talk to you about who'll be drafting the legislation.'

'Half an hour? All right.' Murphy turned back to Daphne. 'Ask George to come in now, will you?'

'Since I can't brain you with this jug,' said Maureen, 'do you want a cup of tea?'

'Does the pope shit in the woods?' asked the attorney-general, and gave her a wink before disappearing into his office.

Negus knocked and walked straight into the attorney's office. Murphy was on the phone. He'd swung his chair around to look out into the gardens beyond the French windows. He hung up the phone and looked at his press secretary.

'Daphne said you needed to see me urgently. What is it?'

'I had a visit this morning from Anna Rosen,' Negus said. 'She's quit the ABC and joined the press gallery with the *Herald*.'

'Really? She's smart as a whip that one, but that's a turn-up. Why'd she leave the ABC?'

'She wouldn't say. Sounds like personal issues. But, more to the point, someone has leaked to her the details of your meeting with Peter Barbour last week. At the very least she's got you calling for an end to ASIO bugging operations and getting stuck into him about lack of action over Croat terrorism.'

Murphy hit the table with an open hand. 'Bloody hell, that's the last thing we need!' he thundered. 'Three weeks in government and the outfit's leaking like a sieve.'

'Look, we don't know where she got this from.'

Murphy fixed Negus with a steely look. 'It wasn't you, was it, George?'

Negus stared back, his face flushing not with embarrassment but a deep sense of injustice. Did they have a trust issue? 'For fuck's sake, Lionel,' he said angrily. 'I'm here trying to shut this down.'

Murphy paused before speaking. Perhaps he'd been too rash in assuming the worst. 'I'm sorry, George. Go on.'

'Rosen reckons she's got enough to publish an account of the ASIO meeting. I thought that would probably hurt relations with the director-general, so I offered her a deal if she agrees to hold off for a few days until we can prepare the ground, maybe put out a joint statement with ASIO.'

'What sort of deal?'

'I told her you'd hired Kerry Milte and that we could organise a briefing with him.'

'Is that it?'

'She also wants an interview with you.'

Murphy weighed up the idea. 'Is that wise? With what she knows?'

'We'd have to put out the ASIO statement first, to get ahead of it,' said Negus. 'But, look, the last interview you did with her worked out pretty well. I think we should give her this. With what she knows about the Croats, we should keep her in the camp. But she obviously wants to start off in Canberra with a bang.'

Murphy looked at his young charge shrewdly, then surprised him with a wink. 'I'm sure you'd like to oblige her in that, George.'

Negus was confused. 'What?' he asked. Then: 'Oh, get your hand off it, Lionel.'

'You're both healthy young animals,' said Murphy. 'It would only be natural. Anyway, you can go ahead and set it up in the interest of damage control. And you better get moving on the ASIO statement.'

*

Anna was back at her desk when the phone rang. She snatched it up. It was Negus.

'You've got your meeting with Milte,' he said.

'Thanks, George. When can I see him?'

'He'll be free at lunchtime. I'll give you his number.'

She wrote it down. 'What about the interview with Murphy?'

'Look, he'll do it. But it's Saturday tomorrow. Christmas is on Monday, and everyone needs a holiday. Let's do it after the New Year—there's not much happening now anyway.'

Anna was sceptical about the timing. 'The ASIO story won't wait until then,' she said.

'We'll put out a short statement after Christmas. I'll make sure you get it first.'

'If I know about the ASIO meeting, someone else will.'

'Lionel won't speak about it,' said Negus. 'No one will get anything but the statement.'

'I'll have to go with what I know if someone else breaks the story.'

'Look, Anna, I'm doing you a favour here.' Negus sounded impatient. 'Just go see Milte, will you? I've set it up for you. I can't do any more than that.'

17.

Anna was on the phone to Kerry Milte when the other journalists started arriving at the office. One of them bumped hard against the back of her chair.

'*Ooops*, sorry!' he said as Anna lurched forward.

'Kerry, it's starting to get a bit crowded in here,' she said. 'Let's meet in King's Hall at 12.30 and we can head off from there? I've got a car ... Yep, you won't miss me. I'll be the woman with the notepad.'

She hung up and stood to greet the two young men who'd just arrived with varying degrees of clumsiness. Harry Lang had been right about Led Zeppelin. If you overlooked the cheap suits, they both had the dissolute rock star image—sallow complexions, shoulder-length hair and deep-sunken eyes. But perhaps that was just a consequence of working in the gallery.

'I'm Anna Rosen,' she said, shaking their hands.

'I almost didn't recognise you without your notepad,' said the taller of the two. 'I'm Dave Olney.'

'Bruce McKillop,' said the other, holding her hand a few beats too long. 'You on to something already, are you, Anna?'

She released herself from McKillop's damp grip and shook her head. 'Just trying to find a story.'

'It's pretty cutthroat around here, Anna,' said Olney. 'Keep your cards close to your chest, if I were you.'

'Or just keep me there if you like,' said McKillop.

Anna turned and sized up Bruce McKillop: the shaving rash, the watery red eyes, his skin's greenish hue, the stench of tobacco and stale booze that clung to his crumpled suit.

'Up late, working on that line, were you, Bruce?' she asked, and got a glimpse of his incisors as he tried not to snarl.

'Oh, don't worry about Bruce,' said Olney. 'He's only half a wit when he's hungover.'

'Fuck off, Olney, you try and keep up with that bloody Walsh.'

McKillop shrugged off his jacket and hung it over the back of his chair before slumping into it. He put his head into his hands.

'That's Eric Walsh he's talking about,' Olney explained. 'You know him?'

'Whitlam's press secretary?'

'That's him. He'll feed you stories if he likes you, but you have to follow him around half the drinking holes in Canberra.'

McKillop groaned, then retraced his day like an amnesiac trying to pick up lost clues. 'I was at the Non-Members' Bar from 11, then lunch at The Lobby—must have gone through a case of wine. Back to the Non-Members'. I might have even filed a story in there some-where, fucked if I can remember. Then I ended up with the PM's staffers at The Lotus for a Chinese meal. There was a mob from DeeFA there, too. All I can remember is at the end of the night they were all doing toasts to Chairman Mao.'

Anna became alert. 'Bloody hell,' she said. 'Maybe they're about to announce the recognition of China.'

'What's that?' a voice boomed from the doorway.

A tall, thin, dapper man in his thirties walked in and stopped in front of Anna.

'Who are you?'

When Anna introduced herself he shook her hand.

'Peter Tennant,' he said and she recognised the by-line of the bureau's chief political correspondent. 'So, what's this about China?'

'I was just speculating about a strange incident that Bruce told us about.'

'Bruce got on the ran-tan with Eric Walsh last night,' Olney chipped in. 'Whitlam's staff were out late at The Lotus with a bunch of foreign affairs bods and they were all doing toasts to Chairman Mao.'

'You saw this, Bruce?' Tennant asked.

'I might have been hallucinating,' said McKillop.

'Mate, that's a fucken story. Anna here's right, sounds like they've sewed up the China deal and they were out celebrating. This might well be today's story. I'm gonna go see Walsh right now. See if I can shake something out of him. Tell Barton where I've gone, will you?' Tennant turned back to Anna. 'Well done, new girl,' he said.

Anna held her tongue and watched him leave.

'Yeah, thanks a lot, "new girl",' said McKillop.

Anna refused to let him off the hook.

'Don't call me a girl, Bruce.'

King's Hall was crowded as a busy railway station even though parliament was in recess. Freshly sworn-in ministers patrolled the space with their staff like schools of fish in a new tank. Favoured journalists interrupted their progress from time to time to ask questions. It brought to Anna's mind descriptions of the Forum in ancient Rome. White-haired senators milled around in the public space, having forgone their robes for sober suits, while the MPs, the people's representatives, mostly younger and consciously in tune with the times, joined the lunchtime *passeggiata*.

Anna recognised the immigration minister, Al Grassby, when he entered the hall with a brace of staff. Indeed, he was impossible to miss—a short man in a blue-and-white seersucker suit, with a black shirt and the widest, most colourful tie she had ever seen. Grassby had ink-black hair and a matching thin moustache and, when he stopped in a bank of sunlight to put on dark wrap-around sunglasses, it completed the picture of a Neapolitan gangster.

Anna watched a young woman of serious intent, with thick framed glasses and a sensible dress, make a beeline for him. The minister gave her a dazzling smile and made to leave with some excuse, but the young woman had somehow managed to position herself between the man and his destination. Up came her notepad like a shield and he was pinned to the spot, still smiling, for a brief, intense cross-examination.

Anna deduced the interlocutor must be the Melbourne *Age*'s Michelle Grattan, one of the two, now three, women in the press gallery. The other one's name was Noel Pratt and she wondered if, like George Elliot, Pratt had adopted a male-gendered *nom de plume*.

When he appeared in the hall Kerry Milte was also unmistakable. Negus had called him a 'big red-headed bloke', but his hair was closer to titian, and his tall, burly figure made a striking impression as he bustled past the Rex Imperator, his eyes scanning the room.

Milte stopped momentarily, a few yards away from the odd tableau of Grattan and Grassby, evidently puzzling as to whether or not this was the right combination of woman and notepad. He was about to step in and ask when Anna reached him.

'Kerry Milte?'

He turned, raised his eyebrows and gave her a pleasant smile.

'It's an easy mistake,' she said as she moved him away. 'I should have said, "Woman in denim jacket".'

'I have to admit, it crossed my mind for a moment there that Frank Rosen's daughter might well be a serious insect with Coke-bottle glasses.'

'I love my father, but I didn't follow his calling,' said Anna. 'Shall we go?'

They made their way out through the bustling hall and into the bright summer sun. Anna stopped to put on sunglasses and Milte squinted at her, pushing back his hair when it flopped over his eyes.

'You must have studied Marx, though,' he said.

She paused and considered her answer. 'Not with the passion of a believer.'

'What else did you study?'

'History mainly, and politics, English literature, social anthropology . . .'

'With a major in public protest?'

Anna felt off balance. Milte had the copper's knack of making simple questions sound like allegations. She was not at all sure where he was coming from.

'I thought I was meant to ask the questions,' she said.

'I don't mean to pry,' he said. 'But I do like to know who I'm talking to. It's a matter of trust, don't you think?'

At the car park she located the Holden ute she had bought in Sydney from a government car auction Pierre had taken her to. It was a blunt-ended machine, but she had found its wide chromium grin appealing.

'Hop in,' she said. 'It's not locked.'

'There's a hint right there,' said Milte, deadpan. 'A Marxist disregard for the protection of private property.'

Anna laughed. 'Actually, my dad told me to make sure I got insurance.'

She started the ute. The engine coughed, then rumbled pleasantly, and she gunned it fast out of the car park.

'Why the interest in Marxism?' she asked.

'I studied arts and law at Melbourne Uni,' Milte said. 'They were rather rigorous in requiring us to understand social constructs in the context of their history, philosophical and social theory. How can one consider crime without Marx and Durkheim, or the bureaucratic theory of Max Weber in the organisation of police and security apparatus? You can't just look at, say, ASIO, without putting it in the context of the social evolution of the construct of "control", from the Sumerians to the present.'

Anna was quiet, contemplating all this as she navigated her way to their destination. Soon she pulled into the circular driveway of The Wellington Hotel and parked in front of its colonnaded entrance.

As they walked up the front stairs, she turned to Milte.

'I love the idea of measuring ASIO against the ancient Sumerians,' she said.

'ASIO is a priestly class, perhaps better measured against the Aztecs. I was talking about the evolution of social control. The Sumerians were the first to invent a written law, the Code of Hammurabi.'

Anna led him through the foyer, past the famous bar. 'Didn't the Code of Hammurabi include some weird provisions, like throwing alleged criminals into the river?' she asked.

'That's right,' said Milte. 'If he drowned in the river, his accuser could take his house. But if he didn't drown, it was the accuser who was put to death.'

Anna poked his arm. 'So, if you were a criminal, you'd just learn to swim, wouldn't you?'

Milte returned her mischievous grin with a smile that softened his tough Irish face. 'You know, I never studied swimming in ancient Sumer. There's probably a PhD in that.'

They reached the near-empty restaurant and Anna told the waiter she had a booking. They scanned the menu and both ordered steak and chips and a bottle of house red.

'I can't believe you were a policeman,' said Anna.

'Why not?'

'Too erudite.'

'I was meant to be part of the new breed in the Commonwealth Police. Youngest ever superintendent third class,' he said proudly. 'The commissioner has a law degree, too. He took a liking and put me in charge of the Central Bureau of Intelligence.'

'So what happened? That doesn't sound like something you'd give up lightly.'

'Lightly? No, not lightly.' He gave a sardonic laugh. 'That's a story for another day, but I will tell you this: that Grassby fellow that the other notebook girl was talking to, well, he's from Griffith, one of the great Mafia strongholds in the country. That's the last thing I was investigating, the links between the Mafia and certain corrupt police, before they shut me down. Keep that in the back of your mind ... But you really want to talk about ASIO and the Croats, don't you?'

'Is that what Lionel Murphy wants you to advise him on?'

Anna pulled out her notepad and laid it beside her on the table. Milte took a sip of his wine.

'I'll give you the background, but you can't quote me on any of this,' he said. 'Some of it you may get from other sources. I'm happy to talk to you because I listened to your radio documentaries, so I know I don't have to explain everything to you from first principles. You got closer to the truth than anyone.'

'Do you have anything concrete on the links between ASIO and Croats involved in terrorism?'

'That's the key question, isn't it? That's what Murphy wants to know. Has ASIO been protecting these bastards while they've been blowing things up and sending armed groups into Yugoslavia to bring down the government there?'

'So, do you have proof that they have?'

'First of all . . .' Milte held up the index finger of his left hand and grasped it with his right. 'I left the Commonwealth Police in 1970, so that's more than two years before the latest Bosnian incursion, back in June, and those two big bombs near the Town Hall. But don't forget there were plenty of bombings before that and at least one other Australian-organised incursion into Yugoslavia, in '63. There's a long history to all this stuff. But Billy Wentworth and Senator George Hannan have exerted real influence inside ASIO.'

'What about the Croats?'

'I had two run-ins you should know about. The first was in '69 when we were investigating the Croatian Revolutionary Brotherhood. Have you heard of the Franciscan priest, the Reverend Father Josip Kasic, in Melbourne?'

'No.'

'He's the spiritual leader of the Brotherhood, a very turbulent priest indeed. Like one of those IRA fellows with the detachable collars. We had a good deal of evidence he was inciting violence, so I went to see him. I was with my deputy commissioner, who's also a devout Catholic as it happens, and when he realised I was planning to arrest Kasic the blood drained from his face. He said he couldn't be part of arresting a priest, so I told him to stay in the car. Anyway, I went into the church and told Kasic: "Reverend Father, I'm afraid I'm going to have to arrest you for inciting crimes against the Commonwealth."

'Well, he came straight back at me: "Call ASIO," he said, and I said, "Nup, they won't help you." And then he said: "Call Senator Hannan." And I said: "Nup, he's not going to help you either. You're coming with me." So I got out the handcuffs and he said: "Can we talk? Come, sit down."

'He took me out to the presbytery, pulled out a bottle of *slivovic* and some Dalmatian ham, and we sat there drinking and eating like two old friends. I told him: "Look, the simple thing is *no more bombs*. Otherwise I'll come back and take you away." And he said: "There will not be bombs."

'When I eventually staggered back to the car, the deputy commissioner asked: "What took you so long?" and I told him: "Oh, I was taking confession." And he says: "Well, one thing's for sure, you're not driving."'

Anna laughed, imagining Milte telling this story to a receptive audience in Murphy's office. Little wonder the attorney had hired him. When the food arrived, she spoke to give Milte the chance to start his meal.

'*Call ASIO*,' she said, chewing thoughtfully on a piece of overdone steak. 'I suppose the whole thing could be in his imagination. You can easily imagine Kasic being close to an old conservative hardliner like Senator Hannan, but ASIO? What use could he possibly be to them?'

'It'll be buried in the files at St Kilda Road,' said Milte. 'I'm sure they regarded him as a protected species, most likely an informant.'

'Did the bombs stop?'

'For a period. We had a window of peace and Kasic even became a useful source of information. But soon enough Ivo Katich and the Brotherhood were making trouble again. We got serious intelligence that they were amassing a stockpile of weapons. Then a large quantity of cyanide was stolen from the Ford plant at Broadmeadows; certain information pointed to the same Croats.

'So in early 1970 I hauled Katich in for a formal interview. He just sat there, arms folded, gave me the mad eyes and refused to say anything. Then, just like the priest, he says: "You should phone ASIO first before you talk to me." '

'Did you ask him who to call?'

'Of course.' Milte drained his wine glass and nodded when she offered to refill it. 'He kept shtum on that and, understand, I'm no pussycat in the interview room. But it was like playing five hundred against someone who's holding the bird, the left and right bowers, and all the aces.'

'So do you think that ASIO gave protection and clearance to war criminals like Ivo Katich to migrate here because they were anti-communists with networks behind the Iron Curtain?'

Milte toyed with his food. 'I'd love to know the answer to that,' he said. 'There's a logic to it and it would certainly help explain ASIO's inaction, but we never had the resources to do that kind of historical research. I think it's your job to get to the bottom of that.'

'It seems that way,' said Anna. 'I'm planning a research trip next year.'

'Well, you'll have to go to Yugoslavia. They'll probably want to help you, but you'll have to be careful to keep them at arm's length. Their secret police—the infamous UDBA—are very dangerous.'

'I know UDBA's been after the old Ustasha leadership for decades. They got to Ante Pavelic in Buenos Aires in '58. Ten years later they assassinated Maks Luburic at his villa in Spain. In March this year, the Australian Josip Senic was murdered in Germany and all signs point to a UDBA hit.'

'That's right,' said Milte. 'They play for keeps, those blokes. But their killings have left a vacuum at the top of the Ustasha and it seems that Ivo Katich is in with a chance to become their global leader.'

Anna looked up from her notes. 'Really? Katich has that kind of ambition?'

'I've got an intelligence report that was done after I left the police,' said Milte. 'In November 1970 he did a big overseas trip, a kind of global tour of the Ustasha in exile: South America, Canada, the US, Spain and Germany. The conclusion was that he's gathering support to take over as the international president of the Croatian National Resistance movement. The current leadership is regarded as too old and inactive. Katich is seen as intelligent, energetic and a powerful personality. If that happened, then Australia would effectively be the headquarters of the global Ustasha movement. Now, there's a headline for you.'

'It's not a headline without that intelligence report, Kerry,' said Anna carefully. 'Could you get it for me?'

'Not without running it past the attorney,' he said. 'He may think it's a good idea to put it out there. He's going to be tabling it in the Senate at some point. It's part of the brief I'm putting together for him.'

'Do you know if this was raised in Murphy's big ASIO meeting last week?'

'You know he met with Peter Barbour?'

'I do,' said Anna. 'And much of what they discussed.'

'Are you planning to put that in the paper?'

'Not yet. I told George I'd hold off, in return for this meeting.'

Milte looked relieved. 'Good,' he said. 'That's a shit fight we don't need yet. Anyway, if you're looking for an ASIO story right now, you should be talking to the prime minister's office.'

'What do you mean?'

'Whitlam's got his own battle with ASIO. Straight after the election he had a meeting with the public service heads and introduced them to his staff—Hall, Spigelman, Walsh, White and Freudenberg—and then he says: "These appointments are not subject to the security check. These men are not to be harassed by ASIO." I mean, you've got to admire his loyalty; but since I've been back in Canberra I've been running into security types all over town who are up in arms over this. They're not going to stand for it.'

'Thanks for the tip-off.'

'That's just something I picked up from the gossip mill. You'll have to find your own sources.'

He looked at his watch and she realised they were nearly out of time.

'Kerry, one final thing before we go.'

She pulled from her jacket the card she had been given at Eden's Hotel Australasia and handed it to him.

'Ever heard of this man?'

Milte scrutinised it for a moment and handed it back with a laugh. 'T-Tom M-Moriarty,' he said. '*Security Consultant*? That's a new one. He usually tells the ladies he sells Victa lawnmowers.'

'I presume he's ASIO?'

'That's a reasonable assumption.'

'Do you know him well?'

'I was in crime intelligence, he's a spy—our interests coincided from time to time. Moriarty likes to keep close contacts in law enforcement. You might find this odd, but a few of us used to get together on Thursday nights to watch *Callan*.'

'Really?'

'I think Tom identified with the character.'

'That's disturbing.'

'I'm not saying he went around assassinating people,' said Milte, as if to clarify that he would not have condoned a trail of bodies across the capital.

Anna sighed. 'As you can imagine, thanks to my father's rank in the Party, I've met quite a few ASIO agents over the years. They don't kill people outright. Their go is to assassinate people's reputations.'

'Look, Moriarty's no angel, but he's not entirely what he appears to be, either. Definitely not an ASIO hardliner. Do you want to know the strangest thing about him?'

'Don't tease me, Kerry, of course I do.'

'His real name is Timur Moroshev. He was born in Shanghai; his parents were White Russians.'

Anna stared at Milte in disbelief. 'ASIO employs Russians? You must be joking.'

'White Russian, I said—refugees from communism. All of them on Stalin's death lists. Moriarty's father worked for the British police in Shanghai. My bet is that he was a Sherlock Holmes fan.'

'Moriarty?'

'Yeah, weird choice of name, don't you think? Anyway, they were caught there by the Japanese invasion. The whole family was interned by the Japs during the war.'

'He approached me and I brushed him off. Was that a mistake?'

'If Tom Moriarty wants to bring you into his orbit, you'll find it very interesting as a journalist. Of course, he may have ulterior motives.'

'You mean he's a pants man?'

'Your words, not mine.'

'In the brief conversation we had, I already found that much out.'

'He does work fast.'

'He's subtle as a ton of bricks.'

'He was pissed then?'

'He could barely stay upright.'

'That's his fatal flaw, the booze.'

'I imagine he has others.'

'Well, he's a spy after all.'

'You mean a born liar?'

Milte grinned. 'You wouldn't want to trust his word on anything. He's spent too long in the wilderness of mirrors. But he's good company, I can vouch for that.'

Anna returned to Parliament House and was puzzled to find the *Herald*'s offices empty until she recalled that the bureau chief, Paul Barton, had invited her to join the team for Christmas drinks at the Non-Members' Bar. It was early afternoon when she got there and, despite the hour, a tumultuous clamour greeted her.

The overcrowded bar was three-deep in thwarted drinkers. As she neared it, a man in a Santa hat suddenly pushed past her. His shabby red jacket had stained white trim like dirty snow, but somehow the intrinsic magic of the costume caused people to step away without rancour. When the rogue Santa reached the bar, he swept aside empty glasses and scrambled on to the beer-slick counter. A coterie of elves arrived in his wake and drew together as their Santa began to sing: 'Deck King's Hall with boughs of holly.'

The elves roared out the chorus: 'Fa la la . . . la la . . . la la la la . . .'

A short, stout man with a black bow tie stopped pouring beer and yelled: 'Get your fucken cunthooks off my bar!'

'Now It's Time for Whitlam's folly, Fa la la . . . la la . . . la la la la . .'

'Get stuck into him, Dick!' cried one thirsty customer and Dick,

268

sufficiently encouraged, took a run at Santa and stiff-armed him so hard that he toppled off the bar into the arms of three elves. A cheer went up as the elves skittered backwards under the weight of their fallen comrade. Tables tipped, drinks spilled, offended patrons pushed back against the burdened elves.

Anna took advantage of the confusion to push her way through to the bar, where she found herself next to a tall, lanky fellow with a long, straggly beard. She recognised him from Leunig's frequent drawings of him in the *Nation Review* as the man everyone knew simply as Mungo.

Anna bent close to him and yelled over the hubbub. 'Did I just have an acid flashback?'

'It's definitely worth checking with other eyewitnesses, unreliable as they are, but I'm reasonably confident that it really happened.'

Mungo MacCallum's familiar drawl lingered over the final syllables of key words, stretching them out, savouring the very sound of them. It had the pleasing quality of slowing things down, as if to give proper consideration to each thought. Mungo's voice had so often featured in radio commentary during the election campaign that Anna felt she knew him.

'You're a reliable enough witness for me,' she said.

'Incidentally,' he said, 'I think you'll find that was the Parliamentary Librarians' Glee Club.'

When Dick the barman finally worked his way over to Anna she bought Mungo a beer. 'My shout,' she said. 'Anna Rosen. I'm at the *Herald*. It's my first day.'

Mungo raised his glass. 'It's rare these days to meet a gallery virgin.'

Before Anna could even think of taking offence, Mungo punctuated his witticism with a smile that crinkled his eyes and raised his arched eyebrows, while his mouth, framed as it was by the bushy beard, opened wide to reveal long tobacco-stained teeth and a line of pink gum.

'I saw the *Herald* mob here earlier by the way,' he continued. 'And I observed another Christmas miracle—Paul Barton was buying the drinks.'

'I have to find them,' said Anna, looking around the packed room. She noticed other familiar faces in the crowd. George Negus was breasting the bar, while the legendary correspondent Laurie Oakes, thick-rimmed glasses the shape of two small TV screens, pursed his sensuous lips as he bent in to listen to a man she believed to be the prime minister's press secretary, Eric Walsh.

'I didn't expect such a scene,' she said.

Mungo leaned back on the bar, shook out a smoke from a soft pack and lit up.

'It does seem a bit more feral than usual,' he agreed, pausing to suck the life out of the cigarette, his thin frame working like a bellows. 'Remember, none of the journos have had a break since the election was called. Same for the pollies. This is like one of those Christmas truces on the Western Front. An unspoken agreement that everyone should get shitfaced for a week before they crawl back into their trenches and resume hostilities.'

'So it's compulsory to get pissed?'

Mungo smiled at her indulgently. 'Let's just say it's recommended you go along with tradition.'

'Anna! There you are!'

She turned, surprised to see Bruce McKillop elbowing his way through the crowd towards her. 'Barton sent me to look for you. Oh, hello, Mungo.'

The bearded journalist raised his eyebrows with comic effect.

'Bruce, still on your feet after last night? The miracles just keep coming.'

McKillop unconsciously straightened his drooping shoulders, pushed long strands of hair back behind his ears and fixed his interrogator with bloodshot eyes.

'Don't worry about me, mate, I'm piss fit.'

'I'll head off, Mungo,' said Anna. 'See you again, I hope.'

'You know where to find me.'

She followed McKillop through the boisterous, jostling crowd, keeping her beer in his narrow wake to prevent spillage. He led her outside where she saw that the *Herald* team and a number of strangers had occupied a table under a huge maple tree. She was about to make her way over when McKillop grabbed her arm.

'Anna, we got off on the wrong foot this morning. I wanted to apologise.'

'Barton put you up to this?'

'No, nothing like that.'

Anna caught McKillop's eyes and noticed his pupils.

'You're stoned, aren't you?'

'No, no . . .' he began. 'Well, yes, a bit.'

'Doing smack in Parliament House? You must be crazy.'

'No, I'm not.'

'Your eyes are pinned, mate.'

'Oh shit.' He fumbled to put on his sunglasses. 'I just smoked a bit. Don't say anything.'

'Don't worry, Bruce. I'm not going to dob you in.'

'I've got some speed too,' he said abruptly. 'You want some?'

He put a couple of pills in her hand before she had a chance to reply, and she slipped them into her pocket. As McKillop stumbled down the stairs to join the others, Anna wondered what the little dopehead saw in her. She couldn't imagine him slipping ampheta-mines into Michelle Grattan's handbag.

When she reached the table Paul Barton jumped up and asked her what she would have, even though she was nursing an almost-full schooner. She decided to go with the flow.

'Vodka and ice, thanks, Paul.'

Before Barton could set off, orders for a fresh round came from others around the table.

'Got to get in quickly when Paul's buying,' Dave Olney explained as Barton made for the bar. 'They'll be closing here soon, then it's off to The Wello. As soon as we leave campus, his pockets'll get deep again.'

It was going to be a long night. Anna surreptitiously reached into her pocket for the pills and swallowed one down with a swig of beer.

Eventually last rounds were called at the Non-Members' and someone yelled, 'On to The Wello!'

As the only one even remotely sober enough to drive, Anna offered to transport as many of the party as could fit into the Smiling Ute. Some of them squeezed into the front while the others pulled off the tarp and clambered into the back, weighing down the suspension so much that she crawled through the empty streets, ignoring the drunken passengers whipping the side of the ute as if it were a slow nag on a racetrack.

When she delivered her rowdy cargo into the forecourt of The Wellington, its stately precincts had been taken over by an increas-ingly wild party. There was a dull roar from the bar. Her colleagues climbed from the ute and stumbled towards it. Bruce McKillop had latched onto a straitlaced Liberal staffer and twirled her in a slow dance in the car park. She looked so out of it that Anna thought to intervene until the young woman reared up, slapped McKillop hard and stormed off.

Anna noticed the silhouettes of randy couples groping in the darkened gardens and others pressed against the sides of parked cars. Argumentative drunks sat about on the front stairs and, as she was drawn up into the melee, a white-faced man in crumpled pinstripes rushed down past her and threw up in the garden.

Anna found herself separated from her companions as she entered the uproarious bar, the heart of the debauch. An aromatic admixture of tobacco and marijuana smoke hung in the air, and she also caught, she was sure, the resinous hints of burning hashish. There was an infectious quality to the exhaled drugs, and the high volumes of alcohol added to an edgy recklessness. Her own perceptions had been lent an icy clarity by the speed. Everywhere she looked, people seemed to be on the verge of passionate embrace or sudden violence. She would not have been surprised to see men taking bets on downing bottles of rum, or Pierre Bezukhov dancing with a bear.

'Anna R-Rosen! Fancy m-m-meeting you here.'

Anna was startled to find Tom Moriarty standing in front of her with a beer in each hand. She couldn't stop a burst of laughter.

'Something wr-wrong?'

'No, not at all. I was just thinking of a different Russian. Is that for me?' she asked, accepting the drink. 'You got my message, then.'

If Moriarty was taken aback by the Russian reference, he concealed it well. His face was unreadable as he scrutinised her. A handsome face, she realised now. He had been too drunk when she met him in Eden for her to see past his dissolution. It was a narrow face with well-proportioned features and defined cheekbones—a bequest, she imagined, of his Slavic genes. His dark hair was cut short, with tiny ringlets fringing his high forehead. He reminded her of Brando as Mark Antony, though his long sideburns located him in the present.

'Way too n-noisy to talk here,' he said at last. 'There's a c-courtyard out back that no one uses. Shall we?'

She followed him to where the crowd thinned out, and he pushed through a pair of glass doors into a dimly lit alcove with a small garden and a single table. He was wrong about no one using it. They interrupted a couple in the middle of a passionate argument. The woman's eyes were moist. The man looked up resentfully.

Moriarty turned to Anna. 'Wait here,' he said.

He walked over and whispered something in the man's ear. The man froze; an expression of frustrated anger crossed his face before he took the woman firmly by the hand and pulled her back into the hotel. Moriarty sat down at the vacated table and lit a cigarette.

Anna sat. 'What did you say to him?'

'I told him to p-piss off or I'd ring his wife.'

'You know his wife.'

'No, of course not.'

Anna nodded, took one of his cigarettes and lit it herself. 'So, are you selling lawnmowers tonight, or security advice?'

'I'd be happy to c-come around and c-cut your grass anytime.'

'And I was just starting to like you.'

Moriarty's eyes seemed to sharpen; his face tightened, changing subtly as if he'd removed a mask. 'You've been speaking to Kerry M-Milte,' he said. 'He's usually m-more discreet.'

'You mean the Russian reference?'

'*The Spy was a R-Russian*—that's not a headline the organisation would w-welcome.'

'Milte trusts me not to do that. You can trust me too.'

'Do you think there's p-power in the knowledge of s-secrets?'

Anna shook her head. 'I was talking about trust,' she said. 'Not power.'

Moriarty left his cigarette burning in the ashtray, cupped his palms over his nose as if he were praying and closed his eyes. After a moment he opened them and moved on.

'I heard on the grapevine that you got something out of Petar K-Katich, but then the little b-blighter disappeared off the f-face of the earth.'

'The grapevine?'

'Everything's put into written reports.'

'Do you know what happened to Petar?'

'He's either done a r-runner or UDBA got to him. If it's them, he'll probably be hauled out of the ocean in a f-fishing net. But you're much more interested in his big b-brother, aren't you?'

'What makes you say that?'

'Oh, come on.'

'No, seriously. You know nothing about me.'

'Your files, Anna. You must have known that, with your f-father's pedigree, there'd be agents all over you when you joined the anti-war m-movement. Suddenly you start t-turning up everywhere with Marin K-Katich . . . F-Fucking the enemy. That really threw them for a loop.'

'Why would anyone care about who I'm sleeping with?'

Moriarty produced a crooked grin, took up the burning stub of his cigarette, sucked it down to the filter and crushed it brutally into the ashtray.

'Don't be dim, Anna,' he said. 'Your f-father, his father, our enemy and our f-friend. All of a sudden there's a Romeo and J-Juliet plotline going on with their ch-children. That certainly p-piqued their interest, I can tell you.'

'You people are despicable.'

'How were they to know your father wasn't r-running you in some operation?'

'That's insane, like something out of Kafka. Did they get to Marin? Warn him off me? Is that what happened?'

'You'll have to ask his f-father.'

'I did ask him. Ivo Katich is a fucking monster and, now I know for sure, he's your monster.'

'It's not like that. He's out of anyone's c-c-control, a loose c-cannon.'

'Milte says your people have been running him for years.'

'He's extrapolating from sc-scraps of information. Look, it's true the organisation is full of Ch-Chinese walls. Ivo Katich may be r-reporting to someone and I wouldn't know . . . But the thing is, Anna, you and I should not be enemies. We can w-work together. It's vital we find M-Marin. You want that too, don't you?'

'Was he in Bosnia or not?'

'I believe he was. Intelligence d-does indicate it. I know he wasn't on the l-list of the dead or of those c-captured.'

'Maybe he was there, maybe he wasn't there at all,' Anna said. 'In any event those men trained under your noses, they raised the money here, they travelled to Europe on Australian passports and no one stopped them. No one in your useless "organisation" even raised an eyebrow. What's so vital about finding him now? Why do you care where he is?'

'Anna, you talked about t-trust. I have something to t-tell you, something that will inform your r-reporting, but you c-can't put it in the papers. Not yet, anyway. Do you agree?'

'Yes.'

'In two months the p-p-prime minister of Yugoslavia is due to visit Australia. His name's Dzemal Bijedic . . . *Bee-yed-ich* . . .

After Tito he's the biggest t-target for assassination in Yugoslavia. I'm t-telling you this because your boyfriend is the man most capable of k-killing him.'

'What? Oh. Come on! I don't believe you.'

'Really, what do you think he's been doing in B-Bosnia? P-P-Picking grapes? That little team of insurgents killed d-dozens of Yugoslav police and soldiers in firefights before they were run to ground. One of their snipers managed to k-kill the two officers leading the manhunt to track them down. If M-Marin was the only survivor of a mission like that, what does that tell you?'

'I don't know anything about his role, and neither do you. We don't even know that he was there.'

'You go away and think about it, Anna. I know you've been p-putting the jigsaw together. I'm b-betting that you learned something from P-Petar Katich before he disappeared. You're an intelligent woman. It must be obvious to you, at the very least, that M-Marin was leading a double life when you were with him. Believe me, I know all about d-double lives. He would have put you in one c-c-compartment and locked the door to it. His father, his brother, his nationalist beliefs, his training, the blood oath to the c-cause—they were locked away from you in different ones. I don't know you that well, but I'm p-pretty sure you're trying to prise open those boxes.'

'Like Kerry Milte, I've picked up scraps of information, but I'm a journalist, not a policeman and certainly not a spy!' Anna felt her voice catch on a spike of emotion. She'd been so careful to remain composed but this man was strangely perceptive. Her eyes were hot, on the verge of tears, but she refused to give him that little victory. 'There's no way I'm going to help you put Marin in prison.'

'I don't want to put him in p-prison, Anna. I want to s-save him.'

'Why?'

'I'm not ready to t-tell you that yet—you'll have to t-trust me on that. If M-Marin really did survive the B-Bosnian mission, I believe he will c-come home sometime soon. Ivo K-Katich doesn't care less about the lives of the men he s-sacrificed. It doesn't matter to him that it f-failed. The dead are m-martyrs now. He's b-brimming with self-importance. He's a m-murderer—you know that b-better than anyone. There's intelligence that he was behind the assassination of Ambassador R-Rolovic in Stockholm. Now B-Bijedic. Can you imagine it, Anna? The assassination of a Yugoslavian p-p-prime minister would be Ivo Katich's c-crowning glory. You know him well enough to know that he wouldn't hesitate to t-turn his son into an assassin.'

'Do you have ASIO's authority to approach me like this?'

'No, they have n-no idea about this.'

'So, who the hell are you working for?'

'I have my own r-reasons, Anna. Listen to me . . . If you m-made the same impression on M-Marin that he did on you, I think he will try to make c-contact with you when he comes home.'

Again it seemed as if Moriarty somehow had the ability to rummage around in her subconscious. She felt exposed, violated. Above all she yearned to see Marin again, if only to finally answer her questions, to explain why he had vanished. She took a moment to calm herself and stared at the spy, choking back revulsion.

'And what do you expect me to do if he does?' she asked.

'It'll be up to you and me to st-stop him.'

18.
20 February 1973

When Marin Katich returned to consciousness, he found himself slumped in the bow of his own tinny as it motored upstream. It was a still afternoon, no breeze at all. On the dark-green mirror of the river an inverted forest was cloaked in shadows. The little boat cut a neat wedge in the surface. The wake spread from shore to shore, rippling on the sandbanks. Rising out of the bush the parched white antlers of dead mountain gums bristled among the mass of ironbark on the ridge above the steep shoreline.

Marin saw this through the slits of his swollen eyes. His face was battered and blood dripped into his lap from the tip of his nose. His hands were tightly bound.

Above the birdsong, which filled the air, he heard the old outboard motor straining under the weight of three men. Through his muddled thoughts Marin perceived order in the cacophony of the birds. He picked out individual calls and cries, conducting the avian orchestra. With a nod and a jerk he queued bellbirds and whipbirds, then the magpies, a pair of pied currawongs, the golden whistlers and treecreepers, the starlings, wattlebirds and butcher-birds, the fantails and wagtails. He heard them all—the sorrows, the whistlers, the waverers, the peepers, the carollers, the cacklers and the criers.

He sensed his captors were unsettled, in unfamiliar territory. They muttered to each other in harsh Slavonic tones. They jumped at a sudden screech.

Gang-gang cockatoo, you stupid fuckers!

It was Lewis who had taught him how to identify birds. What he wouldn't give for the old fellow to arrive on the riverbank right now, the 12-bore across his arm. But if he did appear he would only be another ghost.

As Marin stirred, the man with the rifle snarled and his lip curled over teeth as stained as an old toilet bowl.

'He's awake,' he said.

This was the one who had done the beating when they strung him up like a *piñata* in the Khandalah farmhouse. Now he jabbed Marin hard in the stomach with the rifle's long barrel.

When Marin cried out in pain, the man made an obscene wink.

'Squeal like pig, boy,' he said and jabbed him again. 'Squeal!'

Lank strands of black hair fell across the man's face, a cage for his eyes. Through the unwashed tangle Marin saw madness. Charles Manson eyes. Marin weighed up his opponent. The man was lean as a boxer, prison-hard, arms all veined up, but he fidgeted and scratched like a junkie.

A real fruitcake, aren't you, Manson? he thought.

The other man, sitting behind Manson and driving the boat, was the boss. When he barked out orders, Manson obeyed automatically. So, a command hierarchy.

It was the boss who had interrogated him. He'd begun in the Serbian dialect but, when Marin made out that he couldn't understand, switched to heavily accented English. The way this man carried himself—his manner, the nature of his questions—all pointed to him being a professional operative. UDBA, most likely, and much more worrying for that. Marin knew the communists had agents in Australia and they were certainly capable of dispatching assassins from Belgrade to the other side of the world. He was less certain about Manson. Most likely a local sleeper.

Fully conscious now, Marin felt pain across his body and deep internal bruising. He pulled carefully at his bound wrists to loosen them. He was trying to piece this together.

His father had warned him often enough about security, but these blokes had come out of thin air. They were on him before he had a chance to react. They knew the approaches. They knew the layout of the property. Marin had come down to find his brother and these two animals had found him instead. The implications for Petar's safety made him sick with fear.

Neither man referred to the other by name. They were disciplined and gave the impression of having worked together before. The boss was a small man, also thin, with the deeply lined face of a heavy drinker. His dark, wavy hair was styled in a bouffant. His thick eyebrows jumped about when he talked; when he stopped to think, his eyes rolled up unnaturally, as if he were looking for answers written inside his eyelids.

That's it! Bob Hawke's doppelgänger.

Marin stifled a laugh at the thought and Bob glared at him. The struggling outboard jumped into a different pitch, roaring louder as Manson muttered to Bob. Marin strained to hear them, but he picked up only one phrase. *Vuko jebina*—the place where wolves fuck.

Manson was talking about the river. A place so remote, so removed from humanity, that wolves would comfortably copulate there. He couldn't argue with that. There was no one here, no one within cooee of the place. No witnesses. No one would be coming to help him.

He felt the boat shift its line as Bob angled into the shore, throttling back the outboard. On the sandbank a kangaroo straightened up, cocked its head. It was a big one, calm and swaying slightly as it stretched its spine, leaning back on a powerful tail. There were perhaps a dozen others higher up the bank. Bob tapped Manson on the shoulder, pointing like a tourist at the mob congregated on the riverbanks.

When the boat nudged the shore, the big roo took a couple of languid bounces across the sandbank, floating camouflaged into the grey-green undergrowth. Then Bob jumped on to the bank and the animal took off, powering up the slope on a hidden track.

A fresh wave of pain left Marin dizzy. He closed his eyes, feeling faint; he went to catch himself, but forgot his hands were bound and bashed his elbow on the metal rim of the boat. His eyes flew open.

There was a flash of silver on the water. A big mullet jumped out of the river and flopped back in.

'See thad?' he slurred. 'Shoo'be fuggen fishing.'

'You want to go fishing,' Bob said in his quiet, deliberate voice, '*nema problema* ... You answer my questions and we leave you alone. I let you go back to jerking off in your filthy little shack.'

'Y'already beat the shid owd o' me,' said Marin. 'Doan you thing I'd've tole you whadya wanna know?'

Bob leaned in close. 'Come now, Marin,' he whispered. 'We know who you are and I'm sure you know who we are.' He smiled serenely, tipped his head to one side. 'You thought you'd got away from us. You were wrong to think you were safe. We were always going to find you. The others are dead. You understand? All of them, dead.

We tracked them down in the mountains. One *budala* tried to hide in a hayloft. A farmer killed him while he slept.'

Manson giggled. 'The red smile,' he said, slicing a finger across his throat. 'The people loved you so much they killed you like pigs.'

'We captured six of your men,' said Bob. 'They told us everything. They always do—you know that. Why do you think we know so much about you? You're the last one. Marin: brother of Petar, son of Ivo. The apple never falls far from the tree.'

'I don't fuggen know whad you're tawging about!' Marin yelled. 'I tole you that already.'

The effort left him panting. Bob leaned in close again. Marin, smelling stale liquor on his breath, turned away. Bob pulled his chin around and Marin saw the man's black eyes roll up, searching for the next line.

'Do you want to know what happened to Petar?'

Marin's body spasmed, as if from a physical blow. Somewhere deep inside him he knew what was coming.

'He is in the ground, Marin,' said Bob, almost whispering now. 'I put him there.'

Marin's muscles went slack. He could barely hold himself up. Petar had been missing for months. He had come back to Khandalah to find him, or to pick up his trace. Blood sung in his ears as Bob droned on.

'We know he did the bombing in Sydney. Did you really think we would let him get away with that? Maiming and terrorising people? And for what? Because they do business with Belgrade. Your brother was a crazy man. He had to be crazy to think he could get away with that. I interrogate for a long time. In the end he loses control of everything. He shit his pants like child. That is truth. He's *kukavica*—a coward. He has no honour. And all the time he calls your name. *Ma-rin! Ma-rin!* Over and over he calls. *Ma-rin! Mar-in! MARIN!'*

Bob shouted the name so loud on the final repetition that it came straight back from Echo Rock.

Manson was gleeful. 'Hear that?' he cried into his captive's face. 'He's still calling you . . . from hell.'

Tears squeezed out of Marin's swollen eyes. Bob reached over and wiped them away with his thumb.

'It is your own fault, Marin—you let your brother die. You know that, don't you? The bullet was a mercy for him.'

Marin was sobbing now. 'No, he did nothing. Nothing . . .'

Bob shrugged and patted Marin on his damp cheeks like a kindly uncle.

'You can lie to me. You can't lie to yourself. Petar told the truth. Sitting there. He must have felt the shadow behind him, but no one ever looks around. They don't. You know that? They can feel it. They can smell it. But they don't want to see what's coming.'

Bob pulled a stubby handgun from his waistband, a Makarov, semiautomatic. He moved behind Marin and touched the back of his head with the steel barrel.

'This was last thing Petar felt. The barrel knocking against his skull. You are close to him now. Never closer. Do you feel it? You see what I mean? These last seconds last forever. You wonder. Why are they waiting? Maybe just to scare me. Maybe they won't do it . . . Then . . . *BANG!'*

Marin jerked up, his legs straightening as if on springs. Manson moved in quickly, grabbed him by the collar and pulled him off his feet, out of the unstable boat. Marin went sprawling on to the sand.

A few metres away, a dead wallaby was slumped on the tidal sandbank, a pair of eagles tearing at the carcass. Startled, the huge birds rose up from their feast, flapping ungainly into the air.

Marin saw the wallaby's head, stripped of fur and flesh. The eyes were gone, the head a bloody skull. He reeled away from it.

Manson kicked him hard in the ribs. 'Up. Up. You dog! On your knees!'

Bob crouched down in front of him, fingering the cold pistol.

'You know I'm telling you the truth. Don't you?'

Marin stared at him blankly.

'Petar is gone. The nineteen in Bosnia are all dead. Ustasha murderers, all of them. Which just leaves you. Marin Katich, the Twentieth Man.'

'The Twentieth Man.' Manson giggled. 'Ha ha hah!'

'You don't want to end up like your brother, do you?' Bob asked with an indulgent smile. 'I can put an end to you right now. That's in my power. Or I can forgive you. That is also in my power to do. Wouldn't that be better?'

The wet sand had soaked Marin's trousers. His body throbbed with agony, but it barely registered. Tears streamed down his face. He let them come.

'Just answer my questions, Marin, and you can live.'

Bob worked the slide on the Makarov. Took the safety off.

Marin was shivering now, his teeth rattling with it.

'How does your father plan to kill Bijedic?'

'I really doan know . . . whad you're tawging about.'

'Who did he send to Canberra? How many of you did he send?'

'I have no idea . . . what you're on abowd.'

'Their names?'

'I . . . doan . . . know.'

'He didn't tell you?'

'Nothing . . . to . . . tell.'

'Just give me one name?'

'I doan have any names. You're fuggen . . . crazy!'

Bob moved behind him again. With the gun barrel pressed hard against his skull, Marin's teeth chattered and his body shook.

'Stop moving! The safety's off this time.'

'I c-c-c-carn . . . stop.'

'Then give me a name before you bump my hand—'

'N-n-no . . . n-n-names.'

'—and blow a big hole through your head.'

'Ask my . . . f-f-fuggen father! I don't even speak to the b-bastard anymore!'

An explosion roared in Marin's left ear and sand kicked up in front of him. He screamed. He felt a terrible pain in his ear, deaf now on that side. He fell to his elbows, sobbing.

'No need for thith,' he said, whimpering. 'You've god the wrong bloke . . .'

Through the tears he saw Manson's contempt. At some signal from Bob, Manson dragged him up by the hair.

'You fucking woman! Go, go, move!' Manson spat out the words and shoved him into the kangaroo track. '*Govno yedno!* You piece of shit!'

Marin stumbled. Manson hit him hard with the rifle butt, pushing him along now, driving him deeper into the bush.

'Why the fugg are you doing this?'

Manson pushed him harder, into a broken trot. Marin knew it was getting to the end. They wanted it over.

'No, no, no!' Marin repeated as Manson drove him forward with blows. He lost coordination as he staggered on, careening off trees, bowed over. Bushes whipped his face. Long strands of sputum hung from his nose. His face was wet with tears, scratched and bleeding.

Deep in the bush they entered a clearing and stopped. Marin looked around, turning to face them, a pathetic creature, lacking all dignity. He saw that, to Manson, he was no longer a man—he was no better than a screaming pig ready for slaughter.

'On your knees!' Manson yelled. The rifle, waist-high, held firmly, pointed at his stomach. Bob was next to him, breathing heavily.

'No, don't!' Marin cried out, staring wildly.

He turned to Bob, begging him with bound hands. He was crying, his eyes and nose streaming. 'The lub of God! Don't do thith.'

'Get it over with,' Bob said, walking away.

'*Nooo!*' Marin bellowed. A terrible inhuman noise came loose from his throat. He let go of his bladder, soaking his trousers.

Manson's face contorted with disgust.

Marin reeled at him wild-eyed and yelled: '*Idi u picku materinu! Crawl back into your mother's cunt!*'

At this Manson struck out in a rage, knocking Marin down with his rifle butt. The assailant pivoted, drawing back his boot and preparing to deliver a savage kick. But as he did so, Marin twisted up from the ground. He was carrying the heavy branch he had fallen on, and, though his hands were still bound, he had enough leverage to swing it two-handed like an axe. A tree feller's blow hit the side of Manson's left knee.

The branch disintegrated in a cloud of splinters and dust. Marin heard bones crushing as Manson's smashed knee shifted radically to the right and crumpled. The man screamed as he fell, still clutching his weapon.

Then Marin was on him, pinning the rifle across his chest. Manson screamed again from the searing pain in his destroyed knee. Marin forced the barrel around and under Manson's chin, groping for the trigger.

At such close quarters the explosion roared in Marin's ears. The flash burned his face. The back of Manson's head had been blown off, spraying the undergrowth with its contents.

Marin rolled off the dead thing, clutching the rifle in his bound hands. He looked up to see that Bob had returned and was pulling the Makarov from his waistband. Now only a few feet away, Bob swung his weapon up. His hand was shaking. He squeezed the trigger.

Nothing. Safety still on.

Marin rolled away, dodged into the trees, clumsily working the bolt on the rifle.

Bob fired. Missed. Fired again. A chunk flew off a tree.

Marin couldn't aim the rifle with his hands bound.

Bob fired again wildly. Two shots. Both missed.

Marin swung the rifle up and pulled the trigger. The recoil knocked him sideways. He staggered back behind a tree for cover. Waiting for the next shot. Nothing.

Where was Bob?

Gone.

Then he heard him, trying to make his escape, crashing through the undergrowth.

Marin slumped beside Manson's body and, taking the knife from the dead man's belt, cut the bonds on his wrists.

He heard Bob down at the river, pulling frantically at the outboard's starter. In his haste Bob choked the old motor.

Marin was on his feet with the rifle when the motor finally roared into life. He moved fast through the bush in a loping run. High above the river he saw Bob midstream, motoring fast. Bob was close enough to hear the shot, but he never heard the answering report from Echo Rock. By then he was dead.

His body slumped sideways. The tinny veered off and kicked into a sandbank. The outboard leapt up, roaring at full throttle.

Marin swam across the river and shut it down. Then, on the bank, he stripped off his fetid clothes and waded back out. He sank under the warm, velvety water and held his breath for a long time, safe in the womb of his country. Slowly he came back up. The Twentieth Man, still alive.

He stood, as immobile as an ironbark tree rooted into the bank. Then real tears began to flow. He dropped his head and brought his hands up to his face, crippled by the intensity of his grief. They had killed his brother. Petar was gone.

19.

24 February 1973

Every morning for the last five months it had been part of Nigel Daltrey's daily routine to collect the tapes recorded from the phone tap and the bug he'd planted in the upstairs room of the Hrvatska Restoran. Twice during that time, he'd had to break back into the place in the middle of the night to replace the batteries in the listening device hidden in a television set. It had not been possible to leave the surveillance van in place for such a long time—it was needed for other operations—so he had installed mini Nagra recorders, voice-activated and wired to a radio receiver, in the boot of an old clunker and parked it in the lane behind the restaurant.

Daltrey liked to say that an ill wind blows no good, but he'd had to admit that fat bastard Al Sharp had been as good as his word. It annoyed Daltrey that it had taken a Commonwealth copper to somehow convince the commissioner to cough up the funds for them to buy new top-shelf equipment.

The old car in the lane had solved their surveillance problems, but at least once a week some fuckwitted Brown Bomber gave it a parking ticket. It didn't matter how many times the memo went out, instructing the council parking authority to leave the vehicle alone, it just kept happening. Daltrey became convinced it was a single culprit, most likely some disgruntled Mediterranean type, pissed off that the police had rejected him for a job.

'I'm going to get the bastard one day,' he told Bob McCafferty. 'The prick has stolen hours of my life on all that fucking paperwork to overturn the fines.'

'Maybe you should stake out the car,' his partner responded. 'I'll get Armed Hold Up to lend you a gun.'

'Don't tempt me, Bob.'

'Just remember how much paperwork you'll be up for if you shoot him.'

'I'll give the tickets to you next time, smart-arse, see how you like it.'

This Monday morning, Daltrey collected the tapes from the old clunker as usual and returned to the old hat factory that housed the CIB. Climbing to the third floor and the metal door of the Electronics Unit, he fed in the access code.

There wasn't much else on the floor so the Electronics Unit, with its half a dozen members and a few casuals, sprawled out across most of it. The Unit's premises comprised a locked tape archive; a large equipment room with a workshop for modifying and repairing listening devices; playback machines on desks along one wall, set up with headphones for transcription typists and translators; and two offices for the bosses to maintain the semblance of strict hierarchy. Or rather, as Daltrey theorised, maintain the myth that managers actually worked behind their closed doors.

When Daltrey entered that morning the only person in the big open space was the formidable-looking woman who sat in front of one of the tape machines. Dusanka Andric was silhouetted against the tall windows that had once cast light on lines of hat blockers. In profile, she reminded Daltrey of an emperor's wife on a Roman coin—until she ruined that illusion by placing a cigarette in her lips.

'*Dobra yoo-tro*, Dusanka,' said Daltrey.

The woman turned to him, revealing the large brown mole beside her nose, a flaw that he found perplexingly attractive. From the earliest days of her employment as a Yugoslav translator on the Croat operation, he remembered her name with the formulation: *Doo-shanka* is beautiful . . . *And-Rich*. He had kept it up even when he found out that she was struggling for a quid just like the rest of them.

'Good morning, Roger,' Dusanka replied, using his nickname, in her usual phlegmatic tone.

She was drinking the impossibly sweet, black Turkish mud that she made on the stove every morning in a beaten copper pot.

'I've got the tapes from the Hrvatska,' he said.

'*Dobra*,' she said. 'Shall we find out what the fascists are up to now?'

'I'll leave you to it,' he said, placing the boxes on her desk. 'Have you seen Bob?'

'Bob is in with boss. He called him into his office for a chat. He says "chat", but I think is more than chat. Mr Heffernon was a little . . . *argitated*, yes, I think it is *argitated*.'

Dusanka shucked one of the boxes and fitted the tape on to the right hand of the machine, threading the tape backwards to an empty spool. Daltrey left her rewinding it. He looked at the closed office door, then he went over and knocked.

Inside he found the ursine Bob McCafferty crammed into a chair opposite the Unit's chief, Detective Sergeant Tim Heffernon.

'G'day, Roger,' said Heffernon. 'I was just telling Bob: Jim Kelly came in early this morning to warn me that the top brass are getting really antsy. The federal government's sticking its nose into the Croat investigation. Attorney-General Murphy has got a former Commonwealth copper working as an advisor and he's starting to ask some tricky questions.'

Daltrey ran his hands through his hair and groaned. 'Oh, fucken hell. What sort of questions?'

'He wants to assess our product.'

'What do you mean?' Daltrey demanded angrily. 'He wants transcripts?'

'Murphy obviously doesn't know about the operation at the restaurant—he'd go off his dial if he did. He's supposed to authorise all warrants for intercepts and bugs.'

McCafferty cut in. 'Jim Kelly knows we never had a warrant. He signed off on this himself. You know we had that Commonwealth copper in charge of the op. Al Sharp.'

'Of course I know that,' said Heffernon. 'He hasn't spilled the beans.'

Daltrey gave a malicious laugh. 'He'll be fucked if he does,' he said. 'Anyway, we've got fuck-all from it in all these months. Except for a few new names. They're just too cautious.'

'I was just saying to Bob,' said Heffernon tentatively, 'the restaurant's the last one. Maybe it's time to quietly pull the bugs out and shut it down.'

McCafferty shrugged. 'Like I said, I'll let you break that news to Dusanka.'

Daltrey said nothing.

'What do you think, Roger?' Heffernon asked.

For a man who prided himself on being a no-nonsense bloke, Daltrey had a superstitious streak. When a knock came on the door he had a strange sense of predestination.

'Come in,' called Heffernon.

In came Dusanka Andric. She had her notepad in her hand and there was an expression on her face that Daltrey hadn't seen before. Something had penetrated her usual stoicism.

'What is it?' he asked.

'You must come and listen, all of you,' she said urgently. 'We have something. We finally have something.'

20.

14 March 1973

Inspector Harry Harper was in his Canberra office reading a memo from the Foreign Affairs officer whose job it was to liaise with the Yugoslavian Embassy. The Yugoslavian prime minister, Dzemal Bijedic, was due to visit the country in ten days' time, and his advance team had just flown in from Belgrade. No sooner had they hit the ground than they were demanding answers to a long list of questions. The questions were remarkably specific, revealing a detailed knowledge of Croat nationalist organisations in Australia and of individuals who could pose a threat to their prime minister. Harper was impressed. If he didn't know better, he'd suspect they'd been riffling through his intelligence files.

However, he wasn't especially surprised. The Yugoslavs ran their own agents in Australia and had succeeded, to Harper's sure knowledge, in infiltrating some of the extremist groups, which was a damn sight more than ASIO had managed. So, good on them—and full marks for being clever dicks. But now they wanted assurances that all the people on their list of suspects were under strict surveillance. It was a punishingly long list. He'd have to set up a meeting with the annoying buggers and bring Wal Price along to reassure them.

The most disturbing aspect was that the memo had come from out of the blue. The Yugos had been talking to his team about security arrangements for their PM for a long time and, until now, he'd thought they were satisfied. What had suddenly gotten their knickers in a knot?

Harper was pondering this when his senior research officer, Al Sharp, came rushing through the door looking unusually stern. He was carrying a bundle of papers. He closed the door behind him and lowered himself into the chair on the other side of the desk.

'What's up?' asked Harper.

Sharp took a deep breath. 'I've just been given evidence of a plot to assassinate Prime Minister Bijedic.'

'Sweet Jesus! What are we talking about? Where's it come from?'

'I got a call from Sydney this morning—Jim Kelly.'

Harper knew Kelly well. He was still in command of the NSW Special Breaking Squad, which had still not found the Town Hall Bomber. Ordinarily Kelly would not be passing on intelligence directly to an officer at Sharp's level, but Harper had sent Sharp to Sydney to work with Kelly on the bombings. They had a special connection.

'All right, I trust Jim,' said Harper. 'What's he got?'

'Well, I should tell you first that he's in a bit of a lather about giving this to us; he's sticking his neck out.' Sharp sounded anxious. 'I need to tell you that what he's got, what he's given us, comes from an illegal surveillance operation. Jim's our only source for this product. He wants a guarantee we'll treat it as confidential.'

'I'll be the judge of that,' said Harper bluntly. 'But Jim's a good copper. I've got no interest in burning him.'

Sharp nodded. 'Fair enough.'

'So get to the point, Al.'

'Right. Well, you know the pressure the Breaking Squad was under to get quick results after the Sydney bombs. Their tactic was to lift up every rock and stamp on whatever crawled out. There are blokes in that squad who'd happily fit up the first Croat who looked at them sideways. Kelly reined them in and put a major surveillance operation in place. They used my stuff. I gave them lists and contacts and meeting places for every key figure in the old Croatian Revolutionary Brotherhood. They didn't bother with warrants. Laughed at me when I questioned it. Just went straight at it. Wiretaps, bugs, the lot.'

Harper was not surprised. 'I warned you they operate on the edge. Those blokes don't fuck around.'

'You were spot on there, boss. To be honest, it was quite exhilarating.'

'I'm sure that's how the KGB feels when they're listening to you fart in bed.'

Sharp bit his lip. 'I know. I feel bad. I should have given you a full debriefing on this. Kelly turned me from virgin to whore in a couple of days. We were desperate to get the bombers. But the product we got was mostly rubbish. The targets aren't stupid. They know not to say anything on phones.'

Harper was growing impatient with the backstory. 'So spit it out. What's Kelly given us?'

'I'm getting to that, but I reckon you need to know the background. The upshot of it all was that I had solid intel that the core Croat leaders have a secret meeting place in a restaurant in the middle of the city, the Hrvatska, in Elizabeth Street. The informant told me the food's so bad you'd never eat there. The meeting room's upstairs, noisy as hell and hard to wire up, but the technical team did a hell of a job. They managed to get a device inside a television set. Since then they've been listening in on every suspicious gathering.

'That's where this comes from. After all this time they've finally come up trumps. Three baddies were in the room, key people. Kelly says there's a lot of background noise, but the TV was off at least. They've got these blokes on tape plotting to assassinate Prime Minister Bijedic when he comes here. And even worse, there's threatening talk about Whitlam.'

'Holy shit!' said Harper. 'Where's the transcript?'

Sharp held up a curling sheet of paper he had ripped off the telex and passed it over.

'Kelly has just sent us the key section. It's not long.'

Harper flattened it out on his desk and read it.

Top Secret/ To Compol Intel.
Eyes Only: Sharp, A. Harper, H.
'Hrvatska Restoran' meeting. Targets 'T', 'B' and 'A'
Recording Date: 23.2.73.
Time: 21.35
Translated transcript segment follows:

T: What about Bijedic?
B: We're putting people in place now. We can't let this opportunity pass.
A: Agreed.
B: The Bosniak cunt ... (inaudible) ... with Tito from the beginning. He's a fucking traitor to his people and to his religion.
A: Bijedic is an atheist. He has no religion.
B: He was born a Muslim. He's from Mostar ... (inaudible) ... recruited him at Belgrade University.

A: That nest of red vipers.

B: They should all be exterminated, every fucking graduate.

T: Bijedic is doing us a favour by coming here ... (inaudible).

B: That's right. That's right ... his big mistake. Our friends in Europe got Rolovic. They're looking to us now.

T: This will be our moment in history ... (inaudible).

A: Don't measure a wolf's tail until he is dead. First, we must agree on the method ... (inaudible) ... Whitlam will be next to him.

T: There's another socialist cunt. I know people who would give us a medal.

A: Don't be a fool.

T: Who are you calling a fool? Whitlam deserves what he (inaudible) ...

A: (inaudible) ... it has to be clean.

B: We need to look ... (inaudible) ... one man at distance ... (inaudible).

A: God willing, we will show the world how it's done.

B: No details here, understood.

T: You'll need our help, the network ...

B: I told you. No details! Even here.

T: (inaudible section).

NB: One word was identified here. The translator believes it to be *cvrčak*, which would translate as 'cicada' or 'the cicada'.

B: No fucking names! We can't talk about this. Anyway, we are not ... (inaudible) down only one track.

A: You'll keep us informed.

B: I will.

Harper felt a nervous griping in his belly as he read, already calculating the series of moves he would have to make. 'Is that all there is?' he asked, both hands holding the telex down, as if it might fly off his desk.

'That's the key part. Kelly has sent a copy of the full transcript to Compol in Sydney. They're sending it in a secure bag this afternoon.'

Harper stared at the top of the page, ran a hand through his hair in agitation. 'Look at the date! This was recorded on 23 February. That's more than two fucking weeks ago.'

'I don't know exactly what happened, but it seems that the boss of the Electronics Unit sat on it,' said Sharp. 'He was terrified about being prosecuted by Murphy. I told you they were doing illegal operations all over the city. This only reached Kelly's desk late yesterday. I think the translator got wind of what was happening and sent it directly to him.'

'Fuck, I just can't believe it!' Harper exclaimed. 'They've had a three-week head start on us. Who knows how far they've got with this.'

Sharp stayed silent. He understood Harper's exasperation.

'First things first,' said Harper, returning to his usual methodical style. 'Who are these bastards? Who's talking?'

Sharp consulted his notes. 'Okay. *B*, the one who seems to be the main organiser, is Vlado Bilobrk. He was another wartime Ustasha. Came here in '51 and became 2IC to Ivo Katich in the Croatian Revolutionary Brotherhood. We had him under surveillance last year.'

Sharp passed Harper a photograph of a large man coming out of a car-repair shop, late middle age but built hard, like an old rugby league player, his scarred face set in a scowl.

'Ugly bastard,' observed Harper.

'We know he's still close to Katich. Very close, but they never meet in public anymore. Haven't been seen together since the Brotherhood was broken up.'

'So, you reckon Katich is behind this?'

'I don't have any doubt about that. In Mafia terms, Bilobrk would be his *consigliore*. Something as big as this can only have been authorised by Katich. That reference to "our friends in Europe"— that's the global Ustasha leadership. Katich is the one who talks to them.'

'Who're the others?'

'*T* is Tomic, Darko Tomic, that is. He's younger but a fanatic, an organiser of HM—which is the Croatian Youth movement. No pictures of him yet. Kelly will send some. The third man, *A*, is Viktor Artukovic; he's HM too, but he's no "youth", that's for sure. Like Bilobrk, he's an older bloke.'

Sharp handed Harper another photo. It was of a lean, white-haired man, whose heavily lined face had a querulous expression that made him look like someone's favourite uncle.

'Artukovic was absorbed into HM when we broke up the Brotherhood. These connections confirm our intelligence. The Brotherhood is still running the show, using different organisations as fronts and recruiting a new generation. We suspected all along that they'd maintained some form of central control.'

Harper shook his head. 'The way they speak, it's so matter-of-fact. What do you make of this mention of Rolovic?' He looked back down at the transcript and pointed it out to Sharp. 'Here, look: "Our friends in Europe got Rolovic." '

'Well, that's the name of the Yugoslav ambassador to Sweden who was assassinated in his own embassy, isn't it?'

'I know that much.'

Harper was well aware of the details. In 1971, a two-man Ustasha team smuggled weapons into the Yugoslavian Embassy in Stockholm. Ambassador Vladimir Rolovic was their target; as a former head of UDBA, he'd been responsible for actions against Croat nationalists. After putting a gun in his mouth and shooting him at the end of a long siege at the embassy, the Ustasha team surrendered to police.

'There was also a hijacking of a Scandinavian Airlines jet in September,' continued Harper. 'Ultimately the Swedes caved in to the terrorists' demands and released Rolovic's killers.'

'That happened just before the Sydney bombings, didn't it?' asked Sharp.

Harper nodded. 'That's right. At the time we thought the attacks were probably coordinated. A bloke from Swedish intelligence contacted me back then to see if we could help them. That was when you were in Sydney with the Breaking Squad. Sven Schustrum was his name, the head of their national intelligence service. Looks like there's some kind of link between our little group of plotters and the people who killed Rolovic. This Bilobrk fellow might just be a big-noter, but we have to assume the worst.'

Sharp jotted down Schustrum's name, then turned back to the transcript.

'What do you make of this reference to "the cicada"?' he asked. 'Ring any bells?'

Harper shook his head. 'None at all. Obviously in that context it looks like a codename.'

'The assassin? Could we have our own Jackal here?'

'It's not conclusive, but look at the way Bilobrk shuts him down. It's sensitive. He really doesn't want anyone talking about it, even in their safe meeting place. It's extremely worrying. We need to get hold of the original recording and get our technical people on to it. See if they can get more out of it.'

'That's going to be difficult, Harry. You should speak to Jim Kelly yourself. He might respond to rank.'

'I'll do that,' Harper said, making another note on a list that was quickly getting longer.

Sharp watched the inspector gather his thoughts. He respected this about Harper. There was no bluster. He took his time to sum up the complex problems, and then responded decisively.

'Instinctively, I want to haul these three bastards in and sweat them,' said Harper. 'We may have to do that at some point, but we've got two problems. Without warrants, the fucking tape is inadmissible and, even if it was, they've been careful enough to make sure that their comments are ambiguous. That's the legal position. But as a piece of pure intelligence, it's clear to me that this is not just a group of lunatics frothing at the mouth. These men are sitting in a quiet room talking cold-bloodedly about assassinating a visiting prime minister. They seem to have concrete plans. The mention of Whitlam suggests the threat could extend to him.'

'I agree,' said Sharp. 'And the most worrying thing is that they've had weeks to develop those plans.'

'So we have to move fast,' said Harper, reeling off the orders he'd been compiling. 'The first job is yours, Al. I want you to work up a new threat assessment on the Bijedic visit. Pull in Wally Price and whoever else you need from the team.

'I want whatever you can pull together on the three plotters. I want them all under strict 24-hour surveillance as of now. Run this codename "cicada" past everyone. See if it rings any bells.

'And Al, I need all this done in the next few hours. That's all the time I can give you. When the threat assessment is done, I'll take it directly to the commissioner. It'll be up to him to alert the government. We've either got to get on top of this now or stop Bijedic from coming here.'

Sharp hesitated. 'I can do that, boss, but how do we describe the source of this intelligence? Kelly almost had a rebellion when he told his team he was giving us the transcript. Some of them were ready to sit on this, just to protect their arses. I got to know Jim pretty well. He's trusting me.'

'They're worried about the attorney-general?'

'In a nutshell. Kelly says that under no circumstances are we to let Lionel Murphy know that this came from a listening device. They know Murphy's got a big stick up his arse about that. He'll demand to know who approved the warrants, and we know that no one did.'

'Kelly's right to be worried,' said Harper thoughtfully. 'Murphy sees the state police forces as the enemy. They've been wiretapping him and his mates for decades, and he knows it. So . . . yes, it's tricky.'

'How do you want me to play this?' Sharp asked.

'This is all going to end up on Murphy's desk,' said Harper. 'Best you don't go into the legal question in the Threat Assessment. Anyway, bugging a room is not the same as an illegal wiretap. Tainted or not, we've got credible intelligence of an assassination plot. It'd be criminal not to act on it.'

'What will you tell the commissioner?'

'Everything. He needs to know.'

'He's a mate of Murphy's, isn't he?'

'They studied law together a thousand years ago. I don't believe he's in Murphy's pocket. Anyway, we need his backing. This is going to be a huge operation.'

21.
14 March 1973

Marin Katich sat, stripped to the waist, on a delicate little bench in front of a dressing table, an incongruous figure even to his own eyes. A line of high-wattage globes above the mirror, as one might find in an actor's dressing-room, illuminated the landscape of his torso, coloured in fading shades of green, blue, purple and mauve, as variegated as live coral. Three weeks after the beating he'd taken at Khandalah, he was now slowly healing.

He surveyed his arms and upper body, which had been covered in multiple contusions, welts, lacerations and scratches. He probed at the two fractured ribs, wincing at the sharp pain. They were, miraculously, the only broken bones; he would strap them back up before he left the house. All that damage he could cover up with clothes.

The real problem was his face. At least the swelling had subsided. He consulted the written instructions that had been left for him before applying foundation cream to conceal the discolouration. As he stared into the mirror he had the odd sense of sitting in front of a stranger, and he scowled, bearing his teeth, to make sure the reflection followed suit.

He picked up a powder puff and examined the delicate object with a grim smile, turning it over and over in his fingers, before applying a layer of powder to his face. Each time he closed his eyes his mind threw up flash frames, a gruesome slideshow of the explosion of violence on the river.

Faint with pain and exhaustion in its aftermath, he had wanted to sink into the warm sand on the riverbank and sleep, but he knew he had to stay on his feet. The Yugoslavs would inevitably send others to find out what had happened to their team. It was no longer an option to remain at Khandalah.

He dragged Bob's body across the sand and hid it in thick brush. Then he rinsed his filthy clothes, put them on wet and motored back upstream. At the main house he used a razorblade to make incisions in the lumps around his eyes and drained blood away to reduce the swelling. He washed his wounds and poured iodine into them, clenching his teeth at the acid burn. He took codeine for the pain and benzedrine to keep himself going.

It was dark when he returned to the river, but he managed to locate the two bodies. He wrapped the corpses in old tarps, weighted them with rocks and tied them into tight packages with rope and steel chains. He hauled his burdens into the tinny and motored downstream in the moonlight to Twofold Bay.

The bay was calm. He pushed on out as far as he dared into the steady swell of the ocean and then rolled the bodies over the side without ceremony.

Marin heard a noise outside. He moved stiffly to the window and pulled down a slat in the venetian blinds. Outside was a neat patch of lawn, a well-tended garden with a few shade trees. Beyond the trees was a typically quiet suburban Canberra street. It was a sunny morning, a few scattered clouds in a blue sky. A dog was barking. Birds twittered politely.

He let go of the blinds and backed away from the window. He went into the pink-tiled ensuite bathroom, emptied his bladder and bent to scrutinise the bowl. He had passed blood from his bruised kidneys for weeks, but his urine was clear now.

He went to the kitchen and made himself a bowl of Rice Bubbles. He poured milk from a bottle so cold it sweated with condensation. As he began to eat, the cereal box sat in front of him like a frozen TV screen. He stared at the clownish elves—Snap, Crackle and Pop—until a rush of memories stopped his spoon mid-air:

Petar in his school uniform, ear to the bowl, listening for the promised sounds . . . Their mother moving towards Marin with the milk bottle, straight from the fridge as he always demanded . . . There was a dark smudge around one of her eyes . . . The shadow of his father behind her . . .

Marin pushed the bowl aside and brushed tears from his cheeks. He busied himself making a pot of coffee and set it above a low flame on the stove. While the water heated, he walked into the dining room. His rifle and cleaning gear sat on the long table. He had spread out an old newspaper beneath it to protect the lacquered surface. He had kept the paper's front page separate; he now picked it up and reread the main story, with its startling headline and equally surprising by-line.

Friday March 2 1973, the *Herald*
Ustasha's World HQ in Australia
<u>Murphy to tell Senate</u>
From **ANNA ROSEN**, our Security Correspondent.
Canberra – Australia is the world headquarters of Croatian terrorism, according to the Attorney-General, Senator Murphy. Senator Murphy

will table documents seized by Commonwealth Police revealing evidence of Croatian extremists training in Australia before being sent to Yugoslavia as guerrilla fighters. The documents are part of a statement on Croatian terrorism the attorney-general is planning to make in the Senate next week. He will also claim that the extremists have been engaged in intimidation, terrorism and other acts of violence against other Yugoslavs in Australia . . .

Anna was here in Canberra—perhaps only a few miles away! Security correspondent? How strange.

Marin knew that Murphy had targeted his father. So had Anna, for that matter. What did she know? Had she been drawn here to witness his final act? Perhaps she was here to talk to his conscience, to remind him of what he was and what he might have been. He had often thought about how he would explain himself to her. Anna was bound into his fate in ways she would never know.

As Marin had come to understand it, fate existed beyond individual will. It was remorseless and it was random. It allowed some lucky people just to pass by; but others were seized by its talons and never let loose. He was sure now—absolutely sure—that his own choices were dictated by forces beyond his control. He had once thought himself free as a bird, but, as the meanest Croatian peasant could tell you, there is a hawk above every bird.

Marin took his coffee into the backyard, sat at the round wrought-iron table and smoked a cigarette. The hot sun felt good on his bare chest. He took out a map of the city and looked again at the locations he had marked. There was one, in particular, that he was keen to visit. If he was right, it was a potential firing platform fifty metres high. He calculated it was about nine hundred metres from the target; beyond the safe range, they would imagine.

He leaned back and closed his eyes. The sun's burning disc was imprinted on his eyelids. He thought of days on the beach with Petar, when the only thing you'd had to think about was how hot you had to be before you ran down and threw yourself back into the waves. He dozed off for a moment and, when he opened his eyes, Petar was gone.

He went inside, bound up his fractured ribs and got dressed. He put on sunglasses and a floppy hat and checked himself in the mirror. He went back to the dining room and covered the rifle with a blanket. He picked up the car keys, pocketed the small camera and a handful of cottonwool balls, took the binoculars in their brown leather case and left the house, closing the door quietly.

22.

Daphne Newman looked up at the sepulchral figures of the two spy-masters sitting across from her as they waited for Lionel Murphy.

The older one had angular spectacles, and wavy Brylcreemed hair swept up from a razor-sharp parting. She thought he had the guileful face of a private school headmaster who took secret pleasure in corporal punishment. He was Peter Barbour, director-general of ASIO, and he was preoccupied with reading a sheaf of documents in his lap. Perhaps they were surveillance reports on all the Soviet agents of influence who now occupied prominent roles in the Federal Cabinet. That would certainly explain the waves of hostility that radiated from him, even as he was doing something as innocuous as reading.

The other was a tall, thin, balding fellow, who she imagined as a master at the same school, perhaps an Ancient History teacher or a disgruntled chaplain too fond of the boys. He was in fact John C. Elliott, assistant director-general 'B'. Daphne wanted to ask him what the 'B' stood for, but she suspected it might have been a state secret. She had caught Elliott staring at her when she was typing and intuited that he was reminding himself of the details of her connection to Ivan Stenin. Such a pity Ivan turned out to be KGB, but there was never anything creepy about him. Not like these fellows.

She looked at the clock on her desk. Oh dear, Murphy was already five minutes late. Elliott looked at his watch and whispered something to the director-general. Barbour glanced up and caught her eye. His look gave away nothing. Then he went back to reading.

She felt like blurting out to them that Ivan Sergeevich had been a funny, decent man, not the type to go around assassinating Soviet defectors. She remembered the pain she'd felt when Murphy had gently explained to her that ASIO believed Stenin had been tasked with finding where they'd hidden away the Petrovs.

Why was Lionel always late? She wondered if she should offer again to make them a cup of tea.

The attorney-general had in fact been delayed at a state luncheon hosted by the prime minister in honour of His Royal Highness The Prince Philip, who was on a brief visit to the country. By the time Negus managed to extract his boss from this slightly bizarre event, Murphy was fifteen minutes late for the ASIO meeting and somewhat over the legal limit.

Having rushed him back to the office, Negus was gratified to find the two spies were still waiting. But he did feel a metaphorical chill coming off them, as frosty as the Cold War. Lionel Murphy, completely unabashed and seemingly unaware of their discomfort, greeted them both warmly.

'Director, good to see you again.' He pumped Barbour's hand, nodded to Elliott and led them to his office. 'I'm so glad you waited. Come in. Can we get you a cup of tea? My apologies for being so late. I blame the royal prerogative. The lunch for Prince Philip dragged on and on, and I'm told that it's bad form to walk out on a Royal Highness, even if he is a mere consort. George, please join us. What about that tea, Peter?'

'No, thank you, Attorney,' said the director-general. 'We're fine.'

Murphy dropped heavily into the seat behind his big cedar desk.

'Sit, sit,' he told his guests. 'George, you'll take notes, will you, since Maureen is not here? So, gentlemen, are you confident we can guarantee the safety of Prime Minister Bijedic during his visit?'

Peter Barbour nodded. 'Since we met a week ago, the twelve phone intercepts you agreed to on key Croatian targets are now active. Translators are going through the large volume of product as quickly as they can. There's nothing significant to report yet. Meanwhile, I have tasked the deputy director-general, Jack Behm, to coordinate with the Commonwealth Police and draw up an agreed plan for Bijedic's protection. I've also instructed him that, if the security authorities don't believe he can be adequately protected, we will advise the government to call off the visit.'

Murphy groaned at the last statement. 'That would be an extraordinary admission of incompetence, would it not? Can you imagine telling the Yugoslavs we are not capable of protecting their prime minister?'

Barbour straightened his glasses and glared at Murphy. 'I did stress to you at our last meeting that there is a high degree of risk attached to the visit.'

'And yet, Director, this "high degree of risk" is coming from a source whose existence the former attorney-general at various times denied or simply ignored. It makes me wonder what advice you were giving him about this threat for all those years.'

Barbour's indignation was evident on his face and in his every movement. Murphy's truculent tone had taken him by surprise.

He began to wonder if the man was a little drunk. He decided to placate him. 'I can, of course, provide you with that advice, Attorney.'

Murphy looked over to Negus, as if to confirm that he had noted this undertaking in his minutes. When he turned back to Barbour, the director saw that the last vestiges of the man's bonhomie had evaporated.

'Indeed you will,' said Murphy. 'In fact I direct you to do so and I want to see all the information ASIO has gathered on Croatian terrorist organisations in this country. I have promised to make a complete statement to the Senate on this issue and I want no stone left unturned.'

'I have brought Mr Elliott here to meet you for that purpose,' said Barbour, with a gesture to his balding companion. 'He is assistant director-general for research and analysis. His Branch "B" holds most of the relevant material and he will be tasked with putting it together for you.'

Murphy turned to the unprepossessing man next to Barbour.

'Very well,' he said. 'Mr Elliott, when you are gathering this material, I want you to include everything you have on ASIO's own association with these Croatian extremists.'

Elliott looked puzzled. 'Could you elucidate further on what you mean by "association"?'

'My meaning is perfectly clear, Mr Elliott. I want to see any documents that relate to ASIO's association with individual Croatian extremists. Is that enough elucidation for you?'

'Yes, sir, I believe so.'

Murphy turned back to the ASIO boss. 'As we are now perilously close to what you agree is a perilous visit by Prime Minister Bijedic, I require this material to be ready by this weekend. Is that clear?'

'That is quite clear,' said Barbour. Even as he spoke, loud bells began to ring through the hallway, indicating a division in the Senate. 'The material will be made ready for you this Friday afternoon.'

Lionel Murphy stood and came around from behind his desk.

'I am required in the Senate, as you can hear,' he said. 'Thank you, gentlemen. There are other problems to discuss, but they will have to wait for another time.'

Negus stood and opened the door for the visitors. Barbour went first, but as Elliott made to leave Murphy took his arm.

'Mr Elliott,' he said. 'You should think long and hard about giving me a nil return.'

'A nil return on what, Senator?'

'On the documents relating to ASIO's association with Croatians.'

23.

The high tower of the carillon, perched on the edge of Lake Burley Griffin, seemed to Marin like a modernist minaret. He looked at his watch as he climbed out of the car. It was almost midday. He sat on the bonnet and waited for the second hand to sweep around to 12. Moments later the automatic mechanism, fifty metres up in the bell chamber, played the Westminster chimes before the hour-strike hammer was activated to hit the bourdon bell twelve times in imitation of Big Ben.

Marin had spent the morning at the National Library, learning everything he could about the carillon. That had been easy enough, since no one had ever considered the structure as anything more than a remarkable musical instrument, built into one of the country's finest examples of late twentieth-century Brutalist Architecture.

Marin had smiled grimly when he read the description. No doubt, if his mission succeeded, most people would consider him to be an example of a late twentieth-century brute. Not fine, of course, but capable of looking at this structure as no one else ever had, or so he assumed—through the eyes of a sniper.

It was a matter of national pride that every aspect of the carillon's design should be freely available to the public. After all, a West Australian firm, Cameron, Chisholm & Nicol, had beaten off more fancied British architects to win the international design competition to build it. From their blueprints, he had been able to make copies of the detailed architectural plans. They showed, in multiple cross-sections, every access door and lift shaft, every emergency stairwell, and every nook and cranny in the structure. Moreover, the National Capital Development Commission had published management plans for the carillon, which included everything from the design philosophy to the maintenance routines.

At 12.30 pm he would join a tour group and enter the structure to gauge for himself its utility as a shooting platform. He left the car and began a reconnaissance of its exterior. The carillon was on Aspen Island, the largest of three artificial islands at the southeast corner of the central basin of the lake and located within a triangular zone known as the Parliament House Vista. It was the vista looking back at Parliament House that interested Marin.

Close to where he left the car in Kings Park was a curved pedestrian bridge to the island. As he walked the arced path on the bridge, he took particular notice of the lighting. He would be especially exposed crossing the bridge at night. But that was the only way on and off the island—unless he came by water, an unlikely option. There was cover on the island from alder and aspen trees planted some distance from the carillon and from the weeping willows close to the lake, but he knew he would have to wait for the floodlights to be killed at 1 am.

At its base, he stared up at the tower, a giant 55-metre-high tripod. Its legs supported the three-level carillon, which contained the Clavier Chamber, the Bell Chamber and a smaller viewing room at the top known as 'Chimes'. The legs formed a cluster of columns of different heights with sharply angled roofs. Each of the columns was hollow with central shafts, which were used to access all levels of the carillon. The highest shaft housed a passenger lift, the next a steel staircase, while the lowest shaft contained a service lift. Marin wouldn't trust the lifts. He would have to access the structure by the staircase.

Tourists were now gathering under the carillon, near the stainless-steel doors of the passenger lift. He walked to the second column and examined the door to the stairs. Like both the lifts, it was stainless steel and fitted with a complex security lock, of a type he was unfamiliar with. He would need a set of keys to this door, and likely to other doors throughout the structure.

'Ladies and gentlemen,' announced a loud voice. 'The tour is about to begin.'

Marin turned to see a tall, willowy woman with a fine-boned face and the abnormally cheerful expression of someone whose faith was rarely challenged.

'I'm Barbara,' she said. 'I'm a volunteer here at the carillon. We're about to go inside one of the world's biggest musical instruments.'

Marin joined the group, which consisted of two retired couples and the parents of a young family still trying to wrangle their three small daughters, who'd been racing around the island chasing swans.

'Right,' Barbara continued. 'Gather around. As you may know the carillon was a gift from Britain to celebrate the fiftieth anniversary of the national capital . . .'

Marin tuned out as Barbara repeated information he'd already learned.

'We're very lucky to have fifty-five bells, which makes it the biggest carillon in Australia. The bells are connected to a clavier, which is a kind of keyboard with wooden batons that we use to play the bells. That's our first stop, so if you all come into the lift, I'll take you there.'

Barbara used a key to unlock the lift and pressed the button to the first floor. As the doors closed she looked down at the girls.

'My father trained soldiers in Brisbane during the war and one day they sent him a group of New Guinea natives who'd never seen a lift before. They thought the lift was a magic box. You step inside the box and wait . . . and then it opens up to another world.'

As she said this, the lift stopped and the doors opened with a *ding* to the clavier chamber.

'You see,' said Barbara, holding the lift open to allow them all to step into the triangular room with the strange keyboard machine in the middle. 'Magic!'

'Can you play it?' the tallest of the girls asked after they had been led into the clavier.

'Actually, I usually play a church organ, but I'm training to play this,' said Barbara. 'I'm really not supposed to on tours but—do you know what?—I don't think anyone will mind if I show you how it works.'

When Barbara slid into the chair, Marin moved across to the windows to look at the view over the lake. There it was on the other side: the low white façade of Parliament House. The angle from here was not perfect. Marin knew he'd have to go higher. As Barbara began playing, he drifted around to the door on the other side of the room. It was open and he slipped out into the stairwell shaft and ran up two steep flights.

Behind the door on the next level he heard the clamour of the bells. It was unlocked and he stepped inside. The ringing bells were deafening at such close quarters; just noise with no discernible tune. He quickly stuffed cottonwool balls into his ears and surveyed the room.

The bell chamber was a huge triangular space. The largest of the bells, including the seven-tonne bourbon, were directly in front of him. They hung off a wide steel girder. Graduated by size, the other bells hung in ranks, with the smallest going up into the high ceiling. Each of the three sides of the chamber was open to the air, with the high slit windows covered by steel mesh to stop birds flying in.

Marin went first to the opening over the lake and pressed his hands against the mesh, testing its strength. He would need wire-cutters. He assessed again the angle to Parliament House. Still too low.

Despite the cottonwool, he felt the pressure on his ears from the incessant pealing of the bells. He climbed the steel ladder to the level of the first of the steel girders and walked along the maintenance gantry to the opening over the lake. This was closer but still not perfect, so he climbed to the next level, which was about five metres up from the chamber floor.

He hurried along the gantry to the mesh screen and looked out. Much better.

He took out the binoculars and focused on the front steps of the parliament. The angle was good and the flag fluttering above the entrance would give him windage. He lay down full length on the serrated grating of the gantry floor, and checked again with the binoculars. No doubt now—it was a potential firing position.

The frenzied ringing of the bells continued. He imagined Barbara was showing off. He got to his feet, pulled the small camera from his pocket. It was loaded with high-speed film. He took a series of photos of the position he'd chosen and of the mesh. After that he climbed down and took a second series of shots from the floor of the chamber. Then the bells stopped.

Marin was standing on the lowest level, behind the bourdon bell, looking at the city through the binoculars when the lift dinged.

'There he is!' cried the youngest girl, and Marin turned to see the tour group emerge.

Barbara marched over to confront him. 'Sir! You're not meant to be up here.'

Marin took the cotton buds from his ears. 'I'm sorry?'

'You're not meant to be up here on your own.'

'You didn't mention that,' he said mildly. 'I just wanted to see the bells while you were playing.'

'You're not allowed to do that—it could damage your hearing.'

'Like I said, you didn't mention that. But I had these in.' He held up the balls. 'So you needn't worry.'

He had her snookered and Barbara knew it. Today her faith was being tested.

'Please don't tell anyone,' she whispered.

'Don't worry,' he reassured her. 'I definitely won't be doing that.'

24.

It was a surprisingly cool night when the audience spilled out of the last session of *Cabaret*. Anna Rosen did up the buttons of her coat as she left the cinema. When Bruce McKillop went to take her arm, she neatly pirouetted away from him.

'We're not on a date, Bruce.'

'Oh, sorry, Miss Frosty,' said McKillop. 'I forgot myself. I was treating you like a friend. Not a date.'

'Jury's still out on the friendship thing.'

'Come on, you don't go to the movies with someone you don't like.'

'You might if you were trying to make up your mind.'

'Well, if watching a movie together in the dark didn't work, we should go have a drink.'

Parliament was still sitting that evening, but there didn't seem to be much happening. Anna had filed her story early and thought she deserved a break. Despite his insecurities, his occasional vindictiveness and his dalliance with heroin, Bruce McKillop could still be an entertaining companion.

'I could use a drink,' she said. 'The bar at The Lakeside's probably the closest.'

After they climbed into her car, McKillop pulled out a fat joint and lit up, his elbow out the window.

'Christ, Bruce,' Anna said. 'At least roll up the window. We'll be pulled over by the first cop with a sense of smell.'

McKillop frowned at her, but reluctantly complied. 'Don't be so paranoid. They couldn't care less. Here, have some of this and relax.'

She took a long toke and handed the joint back. They were high by the time they reached the hotel's car park.

The Lakeside had a sweeping spiral staircase that flowed into a foyer strewn with nests of primary-coloured modular chairs and, behind it, dark modernist bars with recessed lighting. They found places on tall, leather-topped stools in the crowded Bobby McGee's and ordered gin martinis.

After the second round, Anna announced that she needed to go for a pee. She pushed her way through to the restrooms, trying to maintain her equilibrium. On her way back a hand grabbed her elbow.

'Who's the b-boyfriend?'

She turned to the handsome, mocking face of Tom Moriarty.

'You've got to stop appearing out of thin air,' she said, sobering fast. 'And he's not my boyfriend. He's just a work colleague.'

'Smoke joints in the c-car park with all your w-work colleagues, do you?'

'What? Are you following me now? This is getting creepy.'

'No, Anna, something's happened. We need to t-talk.'

Moriarty led her to a table at the back with a window overlooking the dark lake. As soon as they sat down Anna turned to him angrily. 'How the hell did you find me?'

'I found out you'd gone to the m-movies. I just waited for you to c-come out.'

'What's so important that you've got to tailgate me around Canberra?'

'You need to speak to M-Milte as soon as you can. The C-Commonwealth Police have p-passed on solid intelligence to him about a plot to assassinate P-Prime Minister Bijedic when he's here in Australia.'

'Bloody hell! Do you know where it's come from?'

'They're not t-telling me anything. Lionel M-Murphy's convinced the Organisation is holding back what they know about the C-Croats. Seems to think we're behind the whole sh-show.'

'Maybe you are. It's a reasonable assumption, isn't it? I don't see why anyone would trust ASIO on this.'

'I told you before, it's c-complex, but I'll t-tell you another thing: n-no one in the Organisation has a c-clue about any assassination plot.'

Anna looked at her watch. It was less than two hours before the final deadline for the late edition. This was a significant tip-off. Moriarty had done her a huge favour. But why? She had to go. 'You say Milte knows about this? Anyone else?'

'He's still at w-work. You might reach other c-contacts, but he's your b-best shot.'

'What's in this for you? Why do you want it in the papers?'

'We have to hope M-Marin reads it and tries to c-contact you.'

'That just sounds crazy.'

'I know you think that, but t-trust me . . .'

'Trust you? Yeah, right . . .'

'I know what he's c-c-capable of, Anna.'

*

323

Anna went straight to the bank of phones in the foyer and shut herself in a cabinet. Tennant had told her she should always carry a bunch of coins for phone calls. She was grateful for that advice now as she tipped a bunch out of her pocket, pulled out a notepad and dialled Milte's number. He answered straight away.

She made two more calls and within fifteen minutes she had her story. She hung up and rang Paul Barton at home, telling him what she had.

'That's front page,' he said without a second thought. 'I'm not sure who's putting the paper to bed tonight, but I'll ring Boyce directly and let him know what's coming. You need to get this to the copytakers as soon as possible.'

'I can dictate it from here.'

'Well done, Anna. Good job.'

By the time she'd gotten the story away and returned to the bar, Bruce McKillop had gone. She imagined he'd left a trail, like the spoor of a wounded animal, but she decided not to follow it.

She went back to her room at The Wellington, still processing what she'd found out as she brushed her teeth. An assassin with the codename Cicada ... in *Canberra*, for fuck's sake! She shook her head, spat and rinsed her mouth out. She fell asleep thinking of Marin Katich, while the thrumming song of multitudinous insects rang in her head.

25.

Lionel Murphy threw the newspaper on to his desk. The *Herald*'s headline was bad enough:

Thursday March 15, 1973
Nationwide Manhunt for Croat Assassin
Codename: 'Cicada'

He felt like shouting, but in the end he spoke quietly. 'Fuck me dead, Kerry.'

'It's tempting when you put it that way,' said Milte.

Murphy let the moment settle, stroking sleep's residue from the corner of his eye with his little finger.

'Everyone's a comedian,' he said. 'You and Negus should be on stage together.'

Milte doubted there'd be any chemistry in that duo. He got up from the couch and picked up the paper. Anna Rosen had sourced the whole story anonymously, but where on earth had she got the detail about the codename?

'I don't see this story as a problem,' he said. 'If anything, it will ramp up the pressure on ASIO to start telling the truth.'

'Perhaps that's right,' said Murphy. 'Speaking of Negus, I wonder if I should call him back from Sydney to deal with this?'

Milte put the paper down, shaking his head. 'No need to do that, you shouldn't get involved at all. Don't give it oxygen. Let the Commonwealth Police respond. They'll refuse to confirm any of the details and make some bland statement about the task force they've put together to ensure the safety of Prime Minister Bijedic.'

'What if it comes up in Question Time?'

'Shut it down,' said Milte. 'You don't comment on operational matters.'

Murphy tapped his fingers on the newspaper. 'Anna Rosen again. Have we let her get too close?'

'I don't think so. This is her special subject. She has plenty of sources outside the government. As I said, this story is useful for us. It's a kick in the pants for ASIO.'

'Well, they have been next to useless,' said Murphy. 'We've heard nothing from them about threats to Bijedic. It's all come from the police.'

'Senator, I don't want to state this too highly, but I believe I know why that is. I'm chasing down a document right now that will prove, beyond doubt, that ASIO has been acting, covertly, behind the scenes, to prevent action being taken against the Croats.'

Murphy was tired. He hadn't been sleeping well. His wife, Ingrid, was in the final stage of her first pregnancy and waking at all hours. He was worried that his own crises were affecting his young wife, but Milte's last statement hit him like a shot of adrenalin. His head jerked up.

'What are you talking about, Kerry? What document?'

'I don't want to speculate any more on this until I have it in my hands,' said Milte. 'I've been told that the document exists and

I hope to have it late today. If what I've been told is true, it's a game changer.'

'Whatever it is, I want that document the moment you have it.'

'You'll be the first to know, Senator.'

In the late afternoon Milte took a taxi to the Belconnen Bowling Club. The place was full of superannuated public servants in the creamy uniforms of lawn bowlers. Balls clinked as the last ends of the day were played, but most of the old codgers had retired to the bar. That was where he found Tom Moriarty: at the quiet end with an empty whisky glass and a half-finished beer chaser.

'Your shout,' said Moriarty.

Milte shelled out for another whisky and a beer for Moriarty, plus a beer for himself. After the barman had set up the drinks, Milte asked in a quiet voice: 'So, did you manage to get it?'

'Sorry, they keep these d-documents locked away in the archive and I couldn't get in to w-winkle it out.'

'Which archive is that?'

'The West P-Portal. Colin Brown runs a t-tight ship.'

'Shit.'

The West Portal was ASIO's Canberra HQ in the Russell Complex, which also housed the Defence Department. Milte had puzzled over Moriarty's willingness to stir up trouble for his ASIO bosses. Was it a subtle power play against the Old Guard of the Organisation who were so on the nose with the new government? Moriarty was hard to read, but it had to be something like that.

'It's not a d-document I can go in and r-r-request. Not if you're g-going to make a scandal out of it.'

'No, I wouldn't want to turn you into a spy.'

'F-Funny man,' said Moriarty, nipping at the whisky. 'You do know that, as attorney-general, M-Murphy would be within his rights to go there and demand a c-copy.'

Milte knew for sure now that Moriarty was playing for keeps. He watched him chase the liquor down with half a glass of beer. 'That would be a dramatic move,' he said.

'It would.'

'I'd have to know exactly what we're looking for.'

'What do you know n-now?'

'All I know is that without the knowledge of the attorney, or myself, an interdepartmental meeting was called on the second of March, chaired by your colleague Ron Hunt with at least one other ASIO man in attendance.'

'You mean P-Penny?'

'Yeah, that's right and there were bureaucrats from the attorney-general's, Foreign Affairs, and so on, and they were led to the conclusion that Lionel Murphy should say nothing about Croatian extremism which would contradict statements by the previous government.'

'I wasn't there. I wasn't invited along, but that's a p-pretty accurate summary.'

'Tom, you're obviously aware that Murphy's position is diametrically opposed to what the previous government said. Ivor Greenwood was in such a state of denial about Croat terrorists that Murphy called him a liar.'

'Everyone knows that.'

'So, what the fuck is going on?'

'Certain people are trying to protect their r-r-reputations here, Kerry. They're d-d-delusional, of course.'

'You mean the ASIO geniuses who advised Greenwood that Croatian terrorists were a figment?'

'That's a r-reasonable conclusion.'

'What do you know about this secret meeting that I don't?'

'The committee was ostensibly called together to consider a C-Commonwealth Police report that another Croatian incursion into Yugoslavia was being p-planned for later this year. A group of seven were set to go from M-Melbourne. Still, Ron Hunt convinced the c-committee to advise M-Murphy not to deviate from the previous government's position. Then he wrote up the notes and his own c-c-conclusions into a m-memo for the Organisation. That's the document you're looking for.'

'The smoking gun memo.'

'It depends what you're sm-sm-sm-smoking.'

Milte smiled as Moriarty downed his whisky. He enjoyed the man's wit and the accommodation he'd come to with his stutter, using it to make you wait for a punchline. It was all about timing.

Milte waited impatiently in the attorney-general's suite for the Senate to rise for the dinner break. He had sent a note into the chamber, advising Murphy he needed to speak to him urgently.

Murphy came rushing in before 6 pm.

'I'm sorry that I couldn't get away earlier,' he said. 'Reg Withers is demanding a debate tonight on the Matrimonial Causes Rules.'

'Sorry?'

'The regulations I enacted to make divorce quicker and cheaper. The conservatives are trying to overturn them.'

'A busy night, then.'

There was a knock on the door.

'Come in, come in,' cried Murphy.

Daphne Newman cracked the door open and leaned into the room. 'Would you like some dinner sent in?'

'Yes, please,' said Murphy. 'Something simple. Two roast dinners?'

Murphy gestured to Milte to take the couch, then he pulled a bottle of red wine from a cupboard and uncorked it expertly.

'So, what have you got for me?' he said, pouring two generous glasses. He passed one to Milte and settled himself into a leather armchair.

'It's a long story,' said Milte.

'We've got ten minutes.'

As Milte briefed him on the mysterious interdepartmental meeting and ASIO's role in it, Murphy became agitated, frequently interrupting with angry ejaculations. Milte concluded by explaining that he'd so far been unable to get a copy of Ron Hunt's memo. Locked away in a safe in the Organisation's Canberra Headquarters, the memo was, he argued, confirmation in writing that ASIO was seeking to undermine his position on Croat terrorism.

'That's treachery,' said Murphy. He spat it out.

'That's a strong word, Senator.'

'There's no other word for it. It's treachery, pure and simple. The security service is bound to the will of the elected government and the evidence is, *a fortiori*, they are attempting to subvert it.'

'My source tells me that Hunt was trying to gather support in writing for the advice ASIO gave to the previous government.'

'It's simply unconscionable! They are maintaining their own fiction exactly as we're facing a plot to assassinate a visiting prime minister, an associated threat to the Australian prime minister and threats to two cabinet ministers.'

'What's that about cabinet ministers?'

'I learned today that death threats have been received in the mail at the offices of Al Grassby and Jim Cairns.'

Both ministers, Milte knew, had made strong public statements against the Croatian extremists. 'I'm sorry I couldn't get the Hunt memo,' he said. 'Given the heat around this issue, I suspect they've deliberately hidden it away.'

Murphy abruptly put his wine glass down and jumped to his feet, prompted by a sudden thought. 'Kerry, I don't want to appear paranoid. I'm just not sure what we're dealing with here. Is it possible they've bugged my office?'

'Nothing's impossible,' said Milte. 'I could request a sweep of your rooms.'

There was a knock on the door and Daphne Newman stuck her head in again. 'It's Senator Withers calling.'

'Thanks, Daphne, put him through,' said Murphy. 'Wait for me outside, Kerry. I'm going to tell Withers I'm cancelling the Senate debate. Then you and I should go for a walk.'

Anna Rosen was bent over the typewriter in her corner of the cramped *Herald* bureau, completing a boring follow-up to her exclusive on the manhunt for the assassin, codename 'Cicada'. The Commonwealth Police had called a press conference late in the day and used it to douse the flames of her story. While not actually denying it, they had refused to confirm any of the details.

She'd tried ringing Al Sharp and been told that he was out at a buck's night, which seemed to her a depressing indication that the manhunt wasn't quite as urgent as she'd been led to believe.

Writing the follow-up to her still unconfirmed story felt like a penance. She was about to pass it on to the telex operators, just after 8 pm, when Dave Olney stomped back into the bureau and threw his notepad on the desk.

'There goes my fucken story.'

'What happened?' Anna asked.

'Murphy's divorce rules were up for debate tonight,' he explained. 'Looked like the Senate was about to reject them, which would've thrown the cat among the pigeons. Then Reg Withers gets up, looking like a deflated balloon, and says the attorney-general's postponed the debate. Murphy gave them some weird excuse you really need to check out.'

'You've got my attention now.'

Olney picked up his notepad and read from his shorthand notes: '*The attorney-general, Senator Murphy, the author of the rules, has informed us that he is preoccupied today with two national security questions requiring his decision.*'

'Bloody hell,' said Anna. 'Any explanation from the government?'

'No.'

'I better get down there.'

Anna stopped at the telex room and dropped off her completed story, before running down the stairs. When she found Negus's office empty, she headed to the attorney-general's suite. Behind the frosted glass door was the elegant but equally frosty Daphne Newman.

'I'm sorry to bother you,' Anna ventured politely, offering her hand. 'Anna Rosen from the *Herald*. I'm trying to find George.'

'He's on leave, Miss Rosen,' said Daphne. 'He'll be back next Monday.'

'Is Kerry Milte around, by any chance?'

'He's not here, either. He's out with the attorney.'

Anna noticed a tray with two covered dinner plates sitting outside Murphy's office.

'Are they coming back for dinner?' she said, nodding at the tray.

'I really couldn't tell you.'

'Could I wait here for him?'

'No, Miss Rosen,' said Daphne firmly. 'That would not be

appropriate. They could be gone for some time. As I said, George Negus deals with the press.'

'Could I leave a note for you to pass on to Kerry Milte?'

'Yes, but I can't say when he'll get a chance to respond. He's very busy.'

'Do you know what's up? The attorney cancelled tonight's debate because of big national security issues, apparently.'

'Miss Rosen, if I did know, I'd hardly be likely to discuss it with a journalist. If that's all, you can leave your note.'

Anna went back to the office. There was nothing else for it. She rang Tom Moriarty.

Lionel Murphy switched on the in-house monitor in his office and turned up the volume. The voice speaking from the Senate floor was as anachronistic as a twenty-year-old Cinesound newsreel: '*You have abolished National Service and left the Australian Army in chaos.*'

'It's dear old Frank McManus,' said Murphy, beckoning Milte to come closer. 'It seems I've given the DLP a platform tonight by cancelling the divorce debate. Do you know what this debate's about, Kerry?'

'No, I haven't followed it.'

'We're pulling eight hundred troops out of Singapore ... Eight hundred, that's it. The Americans are pulling half a million out of Vietnam, but if you listen to the DLP the withdrawal of our little Commonwealth contingent will lead to the second fall of Singapore. To the commies this time. It's the domino theory.'

'If you put that to McManus,' said Milte, 'he'd tell you that the last domino fell when Whitlam came to power.'

Murphy smiled and nodded. 'They think it's the end of days.

But forget about McManus. I'm worried that the hardliners in ASIO have the same view.'

He folded a note, put it in an envelope and handed it to Milte. 'Here, go ask Daphne to get this in to John Wheeldon in the chamber. I've asked him to round up Jim and Arthur after the division and have them meet me outside on the Parliament House steps. And tell Maureen we're going to need her late in the evening as a note-taker. No need to go into any details.'

The three senators gathered on the steps of Parliament House. Jim McClelland was bemused. He thought they must look like a group of Renaissance conspirators in Florence. Not that the parliament bore any similarity to the Pitti Palace, nor did the dark lake shimmering in the distance remind one of the Arno River, but his colleagues certainly struck a pose.

John Wheeldon, brilliant and sardonic, was a natural conspirator. Come the revolution, Arthur Gietzelt would be the one pulling the rope on the guillotine. As for McClelland himself, he wondered how the others saw him.

'Do you know what this is about, John?' he asked. 'Why the cloak-and-dagger stuff?'

'I don't have the faintest idea,' said Wheeldon, shivering. 'But I could use a cloak.'

Murphy came through the glass doors and down the stairs in a rush.

'Sorry to make you wait out here, comrades. I have important news and I have reason to believe my office may be bugged.'

The musketeers were dumbstruck, but only for a moment.

'ASIO,' said Gietzelt.

'Yes,' said Murphy. 'ASIO.'

'Have you found a device?' McClelland asked.

'The office will be swept by police tomorrow. The reason we're out here is because they can't know what I'm planning to do.'

'What's that?' asked Wheeldon.

'Certain information has come to me about ASIO's activities that has to be acted on immediately. Evidence of a conspiracy against the government. There's an attempt on to assassinate the prime minister of Yugoslavia and these bastards are keeping vital intelligence from me. I want you fellows to know that I'm going to go down and get to the bottom of it.'

'Go down?' asked Wheeldon. 'You mean to Melbourne.'

'Yes, they have been working against us. There's proof of that now, and I'm planning a surprise visit to ASIO Headquarters to root it out once and for all.'

'Go for it, Lionel,' cried Gietzelt, ever the good soldier. 'We'll back you all the way.'

But McClelland still had questions. 'What do you mean by "proof"?'

'There's a document, an ASIO memo, which proves what I'm saying.'

'And you have it?'

'No,' said Murphy. 'But I know of its existence. I know who wrote it and when, and I'm going to demand they open their files and cough it up.'

'How can you be sure?'

'It's important that you know I'm not going off half-cocked, so I'm going to tell you something that must remain strictly between us. I have a mole inside ASIO. A young fellow who knows exactly what's happening inside Barbour's citadel of secrets. He knows the extent of the anti-Labor feeling in the Organisation and who's behind it. The life of a visiting prime minister is at stake. Bijedic is coming next week. I have to nip this in the bud now.'

26.

It was now 2.20 am on Friday, 16 March 1973, a cold autumn night in the capital. Inspector Harry Harper shivered and pulled his thin coat tight before stepping into a phone box. He fumbled a coin into the slot and dialled up headquarters. Outside, Al Sharp got out of the car and lit a cigarette, stretched his back and stamped his feet, rubbing his hands together.

Harper pressed the receiver hard to his ear. There was a panic on—death threats made against the attorney-general. This on top of the Bijedic nightmare. He shook his head in disbelief.

On the other end of the line was the duty officer Sergeant John Bennett, a competent copper. Murphy's security advisor Kerry Milte had called in the threat against Murphy.

'I logged Mr Milte's call at 1.50 am,' explained Bennett. 'He asked for you first, and when I couldn't get on to you he asked for Deputy Commissioner Jessop's home number.'

'Have you heard from Mr Jessop?' Harper asked.

'Yes, sir. He called me a short time ago. Says Milte wants a plain-clothes protection detail at Senator Murphy's house right away.

I only had Senior Constable Stockwell on duty, so I dispatched him. He's on the way.'

Harper clenched his jaw. *So Milte's pulling our strings now, is he?* He had known the man well when he was a copper, but now he was in politics.

'Where is Mr Milte? Did he say?'

'He's at Senator Murphy's residence, sir.'

'Okay. Give me that address.'

Harper wrote it down in a small notebook. 'Mr Sharp and I will go straight there,' he told the sergeant. 'Get on the radio and warn Stockwell we're coming. Then call around and wake up the interstate blokes from the intelligence team. They're all staying at the Kingston Hotel—Sergeant Price and the others. Call them in. I don't care how late it is, I want all hands on deck. I'll call you again when we find out exactly what's going on.'

Sharp had listened to Harper's string of orders with concern. He was dog-tired. His suit was dishevelled, his tie loosened, his hair rumpled. Irritably, he stamped out his half-smoked cigarette. Harper's call to headquarters had been in order to clock off; the two of them had been about to turn in. They had been going since 6 am on the Bijedic thing, so that was . . . what? More than twenty hours already.

Harper burst out of the phone box and announced: 'All hell's broken loose.'

'What fresh hell is this?' asked Sharp.

The inspector raised an eyebrow. 'Dorothy Parker? Really?'

'Sorry, boss,' said Sharp. 'A bit delirious. What's up?'

'Someone's threatening to kill Lionel Murphy.'

'Christ! They should join the queue.'

'Anyway, it's fallen into our laps.'

'On top of Bijedic, Grassby and Cairns. This is becoming an epidemic. Where's the threat come from?'

'Don't know yet. Fuck, it's cold out here. Come on. Get the car started.'

Harper climbed into the passenger seat, shivering. Sharp keyed the ignition, put the heater on full and turned to the inspector. 'This has got to be connected to the whole Bijedic thing, hasn't it?'

Harper put his hands up to the vent as warm air started to flood in. 'That's a reasonable deduction,' he said. 'Kerry Milte called it in. His brief is to advise on the Croats. So . . . yes, that would make sense.'

Sharp made the connections. 'Milte, eh? He's never far from trouble.'

Harper nodded. Kerry Milte was a known shit stirrer. The rumours about why he'd quit had swept through the force like a wildfire. Story was that he'd been running a secret operation and got close to nailing the NSW police commissioner on bribery charges.

'He's at Murphy's house right now.'

Sharp was curious; something didn't add up. 'Middle of the night and he calls in a threat to the attorney. That's weird. If that was picked up by the Sydney surveillance teams, we'd have heard about it before Milte did.'

'I figured that too. So it's come from somewhere else and we need to get to the bottom of it. Murphy and Milte are still up. We're going to go see them.'

As Harper read out the address, Sharp tightened his tie and ran a comb through his hair. 'Forrest, eh? That's a posh neighbourhood for a Labor man, isn't it?'

'He's a former QC,' said Harper. 'Must have made a squillion doing union cases.'

Sharp accelerated from the kerb. Alert now. Hands tight on the wheel, ten to two. He drove fast, eyes on the road. 'He's new to all this, Lionel Murphy. How's he handling the pressure?'

'A bit foam-flecked and wild-eyed, I imagine,' said Harper. 'Someone told Bennett that Murphy wants us to provide him with a pistol. Sounds like the rumour mill's spinning fast.'

Sharp rolled his eyes. 'Jesus wept. What if it's true? Imagine the headlines. *Whitlam's Wild West.*'

'It was always going to be a bit like that,' Harper proffered. 'What you'd expect after decades out of power. Maybe they'll improve with time.'

Along the way, they passed the squat Russell Complex, which housed the defence and intelligence establishments. In the early hours the complex was dark, except for one section. Harper peered at it through the smudged windscreen. 'The West Portal's lit up,' he said. 'We're not the only night owls. I wonder what's keeping the spooks awake?'

Sharp swung left on to the Kings Avenue Bridge and over the dark lake. 'Eternal vigilance, boss. The price of freedom.'

Harper gave a tired nod of appreciation. Sharp was one of the few coppers he knew who could quote Thomas Jefferson with any confidence. Harper yawned and rubbed his face. He leaned back in his seat and stared out the window until his breath fogged it, blurring the government buildings rolling past.

He wiped his hand across the glass and turned his tired mind to the implications of a death threat to Lionel Murphy. Of course, it could be a hoax—some crank trying to put the wind up the new attorney—but they couldn't take that chance, not with everything else that was going on.

Harper had already pulled out all the stops to deal with a serious assassination threat. In four days' time the Yugoslavian prime minister, Dzemal Bijedic, would arrive in Australia for his state visit and there was credible intelligence of a plot to kill him. Harper's teams had been working around the clock to contain the danger and secure the capital. A clock was winding down in Harper's head. It now had less than a hundred hours on it.

Yesterday his men had intercepted a driver on the Hume Highway en route to Canberra. The Holden Monaro with NSW plates had been driven by a giant, slab-faced fellow. His travel plans had been picked up on wiretaps that linked him to the Croatian Revolutionary Brotherhood. In the car boot they found a box of sweating gelignite.

Christ, was that only yesterday? The man was in custody, refusing to talk. Harper's men were sealing off the city as quickly as they could, but they didn't know who or what was already inside the security perimeter.

'We got lucky on Bijedic, didn't we?' he said to Sharp.

'We did, boss.'

The deputy director-general of ASIO was used to being woken in the middle of the night. When the phone rang at his Melbourne home, he sat up straight, swung his legs off the bed and checked the clock beside the phone. *2.30 am*. He picked up the receiver and said one word.

'Behm.'

He listened for a while before interrupting. 'I'll call you straight back.'

As he hung up his wife stirred next to him, and he leaned over and kissed her on the forehead. 'Nothing to worry about,' he said. 'Go back to sleep. I'll be back before you wake up.'

Jack Behm threw on some clothes, took his glasses and eye drops from the bedside table, glanced up at the darkened crucifix on the wall—an automatic reflex—and left the bedroom, closing the door quietly. He sat at his desk in the study, absorbing what he'd just been told.

Lionel Murphy was on a rampage. The man was a dangerous radical, a bigger loose cannon than Whitlam, but no one had expected this. Behm's eyes were smarting—*keratitis sicca*—most likely damaged, said the medicos, from the phosphorous smoke in anti-tank shells. He tipped his head back and administered the drops, wondering how Murphy and his peacenik mates would have gone against the Japs. He dialled the STD number in Canberra and heard, after the pips, the familiar voice of the Organisation's regional director, Colin Brown.

'Brown.'

'Talk, Colin,' said Behm. 'From the beginning.'

'Murphy rang me at home after midnight and demanded I come in to meet him in person at the West Portal.'

'And you agreed to do that?'

'He's the attorney-general, Jack.'

'What reason did he give?'

'He claimed to have new intelligence on a threat to assassinate Prime Minister Bijedic.'

Behm snorted angrily. 'Bite-ya-dick again!' he exclaimed. 'I'm sick of hearing about this fellow and his cursed visit. If they're so worried about his safety, they should cancel it. The man's a hardline communist. He's one of Tito's best mates. Brezhnev and Mao like to greet him with hugs, and we're going to roll out the red carpet for him? No wonder the bloody Croats are up in arms.'

'To be fair, Jack, it was the Liberal government who invited him. Anyway, Murphy said he wanted to go over his security arrangements ahead of a meeting with the president of the Senate tomorrow. So I went to the office, and he arrived with Kerry Milte and brought along his secretary, Maureen Barron, to take notes.'

'You let him do that?'

'For part of the meeting, yes, when we were talking about Bijedic's security. But it soon became obvious that wasn't Murphy's real agenda.'

'Right. So how do we get to the point where this mad bastard is planning a surprise visit to St Kilda Road?'

'This is why I'm calling. As far as I can make out, the real reason he came here was to find a memo that Ron Hunt wrote after an interdepartmental meeting on 2 March dealing with concerns raised by the Yugoslavs.'

'I think I know that memo.'

'Indeed, Hunt got the committee to agree that the new government shouldn't reverse Ivor Greenwood's longstanding advice that there's no Croat terrorist organisation that poses a serious threat. Murphy thinks this is proof positive the Organisation is secretly working against the elected government.'

'Did you give it to him?'

'No, I told him it's in Melbourne.'

'Hence his rush to get down here?'

'That's right.'

Having issued Colin Brown with a series of instructions, Behm grabbed his keys, threw two empty cricket bags into the boot of his car, backed out of the garage and headed for the city. It took him less than thirty minutes to get to ASIO Headquarters in St Kilda Road.

Once there, he was buzzed through by security into the underground parking area and he carried the bags up into the foyer. Security didn't question him. He was Jack Behm, after all. He took the lift to his floor, went straight to his office, opened his safe and quickly unloaded its contents into the two bags.

Behm knew he was breaking every rule under the sun. The material in the safe was all highest-classification Top Secret, not the sort of stuff you're allowed to haul around in cricket bags.

As deputy director-general, Jack Behm was in charge of operations. The way he saw it, his boss, D-G Peter Barbour, was nothing more than an administrator who didn't have a clue what it was like to get his hands dirty. Nearly three years after Barbour's elevation, Behm was still buggered if he knew what had possessed Charlie Spry to anoint this mild-mannered academic type as his successor. Barbour's war experience had been behind the lines as a Japanese interpreter; he had an arts degree from Melbourne Uni; he was a Trinity College toff. There was bloody persistent gossip that he'd done his thesis on *The Satyricon*, so in all likelihood he was a secret sexual deviant to boot.

At the time Behm had appeared to take the blow on the chin; but he told his acolytes that what it actually meant was that he, Jack Behm, would effectively be in the pilot's seat, flying the Organisation, while Barbour sat back with the passengers—first class, of course.

When the safe was empty Behm hoisted up the two bags and balanced the weight of them on either side of his large frame. There was plenty in these bags you wouldn't ever want a socialist radical like Lionel Murphy getting his hands on.

Just on the Croats, if Murphy knew the fellows they had on their books, he would go ballistic. There was Operation Amber. There was the Melbourne bomb-maker—they reckoned they'd managed to turn him, but the bomb was still out there somewhere. There were the Andric brothers, Adolf and Ambroz, both dead now. And then there were the many others whose identities had to be protected for their own safety. Whatever else you thought about them, they were, one and all, committed enemies of communism.

Behm took the lift back down to the basement car park, threw his bags full of secrets into the boot and headed for home.

He thought about Lionel Murphy as he drove through the empty city streets. This fellow showed every sign of being as mad as that other historical lunatic Labor attorney-general, Doc Evatt—but Murphy might prove to be even more dangerous.

There were many reasons why Behm regarded Murphy as a serious worry. First, he'd chosen two wives from behind the Iron Curtain—or had they chosen him? Then he had close confederates who were, undoubtedly, secret communists. And, finally, Behm had developed an enormous interest in Murphy's origins. Surely, by the look of him, the man had Jewish antecedents.

27.

Inspector Harper was feeling groggy. The interior of the Falcon was overheated. Warm air was pumping out of the vents, mingling with the sickly chemical smell of new carpet.

'Can you turn off that blasted heater?'

Sharp did so, turning left on to State Circle, the outermost of the concentric ring roads around Capital Hill, then swung down fast on the long curve and turned left again into the sleeping suburb of Forrest.

Harper regretted snapping at Sharp. He was edgy and he knew his colleague was uneasy too. The news of the threat to Lionel Murphy simply added to the sense that events were spinning out of control. Some of that was down to the chaotic transition to a new government bent on radical change.

Harper's police colleagues assumed he was politically conservative. In truth, he'd been as happy as Larry when Labor swept into power three months ago. Most of his mates in the force disagreed passionately, but Harper thought it was time to chuck a rock into the stagnant pond the country had become.

Unfortunately, Murphy wasn't prepared to ease his way in. From his first days in office the new attorney-general had put the wind up the police and security services. He was like one of those American do-gooders pushing a civil rights agenda, which most coppers interpreted as protecting the rights of criminals. Trying to get a handle on the new man, Harper had watched one of Murphy's first interviews on *This Day Tonight*. The reporter had asked for his reaction to news that police were still bugging phones.

'Well, it's the reaction of anyone,' said Murphy in the nasal voice of a man whose large nose had been broken and badly set. 'That means they are breaking the law, and it will not be permitted. It doesn't matter who does it—whether it's a policeman or anyone else—it's contrary to law.'

Within days the attorney had been threatening to open police and ASIO surveillance files to the public as part of his freedom of information push. Harper remembered the panic in his own organisation. He was tasked with going down into 'The Indices' to expunge all the Compol files on Labor politicians. He took a team in and they pulled out the alphabetical green index cards: M for Murphy; C for Cairns; W for Whitlam, and so on. They took all the documentation—including the surveillance files, photos and transcripts—and made a bonfire of them.

Sharp interrupted his boss's reverie. 'Wakey, wakey. Nearly there.'

'Not asleep,' said Harper. 'Just thinking.' He groaned loudly.

Sharp glanced at him. 'What is it?'

'Who's gonna save us from the true-believers, son?'

'Just the Labor ones—or all of them?' asked Sharp.

'Every blinking one,' said Harper emphatically.

Sharp let out a sardonic laugh. 'That'll be down to us, then.'

'That's what I'm worried about.'

They eventually found the attorney-general's house hidden behind an exotic hedge burdened with green fruit that resembled avocados. Beyond tall iron gates was an expansive garden, with shadowy trees and darkened shrubs that all looked to Harper like crouching assassins. As the Falcon crunched over the gravel driveway, its headlights swept the façade of the house and the beam picked up a dark-suited man, his face bleached white in the headlights.

'Stockwell's here already,' said Sharp, pulling up next to the man. Harper climbed out of the car.

'Evening, Inspector,' said the young senior constable, and Harper shook his proffered hand briskly.

'G'day, Bob, have you let them know you're here?'

'Yes, sir. I heard you were on your way so I told them I'd wait out here.'

At this, the front door of the attorney's house was flung open. A tall, heavy-set man with flaming red hair was backlit in the frame.

'Mr Milte!' Harper called, walking towards him. 'Good morning.'

'Harper.' Kerry Milte looked surprised. 'They said reinforcements were coming. I didn't know it'd be you.'

'We were still up. Got your news from headquarters. You know Al Sharp, I think. And Senior Constable Bob Stockwell, you've met.'

Milte nodded curtly to the two men.

'We're up to our necks in the Bijedic operation,' Harper told him. 'Now we hear there's a threat to the attorney-general. I decided to come straight over.'

Milte gazed at them. 'Righto,' he said after a moment.

'So the Murphy threat,' said Harper. 'Where's it come from?'

'The attorney will want to brief you himself. He's on the phone right now.' Milte's tone was conspiratorial. 'But he wants his house secured first. He's particularly concerned for his wife. She's a bit shaken. You probably know she's close to having their first child. She can't sleep for worry.'

So Ingrid's up at this hour, thought Harper. He understood why Murphy was fretting. A lovely young creature, that one.

He remembered when she was doing that game show on TV. He'd often wondered how she ended up with Murphy. He'd heard that the beloved Labor hero could charm ladies out of the trees and, if you believed the rumours, he was always searching through the foliage for new conquests.

Kerry Milte took Harper's arm and moved him away from his subordinates. 'Harry, can you see to it the grounds are checked thoroughly?' He made it sound annoyingly like an order. 'There are too many ways in around the perimeter and plenty of cover with all these trees. What do you think about putting in floodlights? Lionel thought that might be best.'

So, first name terms with the boss, was it? Harper looked around. Large trees loomed over the house, and there were numerous shrubs throughout the gardens and considerable growth in the garden beds immediately beside the house. The highest branches of the shrubbery partially obscured some of the windows.

'We'd have to put floodlights front and back and at the sides of the building. That's a big job,' said Harper. 'It's not something we could attempt at this time of night. The best I can do now is to put a protection detail in place. Post men front and back.'

'Well, he says he wants floodlights.'

'That's not going to happen tonight, Kerry. We'll have a look around now, and I've called the rest of my team in. We're taking this seriously—these are the blokes on the Bijedic detail. You can reassure Senator Murphy on that score.'

Milte let the issue drop. 'I'll tell the attorney what you've said. I'm sure he'll want to talk to you as soon as possible. It's all getting a bit urgent.'

'What's urgent, exactly?'

'Best you hear from him.'

'Kerry.' Harper lowered his voice. 'A word before you go.'

'What is it?'

'Is it true Murphy wanted us to get him a handgun?'

'What!' cried Milte. 'No, that's complete bullshit. I did ask what the procedure would be for me to get one. I am still licensed.'

'Can't see that happening, mate.'

'Well, we'll see. You're here now, in any event.'

The rest of the team began to arrive. Wally Price got there first. The detective sergeant was in charge of close security for Prime Minister Bijedic. A good man, but he always managed to look like he'd been dragged backwards through a hedge. Up close, he smelled like a damp beer mat.

Price stared at Harper through bloodshot eyes as he rolled a ragged smoke in his trembling fingers. Scraggly bits of tobacco stuck out the end and half of it burnt away when he lit up. He had a laconic drawl that drifted between charm and derision.

'What do you reckon, Harry? Have you ever wondered if this is hell and we're all dead?'

'You look like death warmed up, Wal, so maybe it is.'

'It's a bullshit time for an all-nighter. I'm full tilt on Bijedic.'

'And half-pissed, by the look of you.'

'The other half is working twice as hard.'

As more of Harper's men arrived, the Murphy house began to resemble a crime scene. All the entrances were secured and guarded. The dog team he'd called for now spilled out of their van, the beasts straining at their leashes.

Milte stuck his head out the front door and called Harper:

'The attorney's ready to see you, Harry. Could you bring Mr Sharp as well? We're in the living room.'

Once inside, Harper saw the two former barristers, Milte and Murphy, sitting face-to-face across a low table. Lionel Murphy was on the phone, listening intently as he conducted a fast-paced interrogation. There were pouches under his eyes and his large nose was drooping with fatigue. Strands of grey hair spilled over his face.

Harper checked his watch. 3.15 am. Who the hell was he talking to at this hour?

Milte looked up at the two detectives and gestured for them to come and sit down. Murphy terminated the call and dashed the receiver back into its cradle.

'Bastards!' he roared at the phone. 'Treacherous fucking bastards!'

Harper and Sharp glanced at each other. Milte said nothing.

Murphy gathered himself and sat up straight, immediately magisterial. He pulled down on the lapels of his rumpled suit and ran fingers back through both sides of his long, thinning hair, smoothing it down. Then he looked up at the two policemen as if suddenly aware of their presence.

'Sorry about the expletives, gentlemen. Take a seat.'

It was the attorney-general voice, the one he used for TV interviews. It was calm enough, but Harper noticed that there was cold rage in the man's hooded eyes, which were usually twinkling with mirth. It occurred to him that you wouldn't want Murphy coming after you.

'Go on then, Lionel.' Kerry Milte leaned in and urged Murphy to continue. 'What'd he say?'

Murphy stared at his advisor, gathering his thoughts. 'Turns out they've got the damn memo here in Canberra,' he declared. 'They lied to us. Had it all along. The fellow you mentioned has been ordered to take it down to Melbourne on the first flight. Straight to St Kilda Road. Don't pass go. Don't collect $200.'

'Jesus-fucking-Christ,' Milte exclaimed, his face almost as red as his mop of hair.

He's got his Irish up, thought Harper. For his own part, he was starting to lose patience with this mysterious by-play.

'Excuse me, gentlemen,' he interrupted. 'What exactly is going on here?'

The attorney-general looked at him and softened his voice. 'Sorry, Harry. You must be thinking I've got a screw loose.'

Murphy leaned over to the bottle of red on the table. He refilled his own glass and held the bottle out to the new arrivals.

'Not for me.' Harper shook his head. 'Bit late in the day.'

'Nor me thanks, sir,' said Sharp.

'Call me Lionel, Al,' said Murphy, taking a drink.

'Yes, sir . . . Senator.'

Murphy turned back to Harper. 'It's ASIO, Harry. This business with the Croats has taken a rather disturbing turn. We have evidence that ASIO is acting against the interests of the government. They're as bad as Reg Withers. They seem to think the election of a Labor government was an aberration.'

The attorney paused, a look of outrage clouding his pleasant face.

'While you and your team are doing everything you can to stop Croat terrorists assassinating Prime Minister Bijedic on our soil, our own security service continues to insist there is no real threat from that quarter. It's the same lie they've been peddling through Ivor Greenwood for a decade, as you well know. Now they've gone behind my back and put that conclusion in a memo they propose to pass on to the Yugoslavian government, as if they'd buy such a fiction. ASIO is acting as if the government hasn't changed, Harry!'

It's insupportable. They have either forgotten their duty as public officials or they've allowed it to be perverted. This is the last straw. I won't let ASIO set its own boundaries anymore. They're not a law unto themselves—they're an arm of government and it's time they understood that.'

Murphy paused, as if to judge whether the mystified policemen had fully comprehended his meaning. Then he continued.

'So, Inspector Harper, the first thing I need to know from you is exactly how ASIO responded when you asked them for intelligence briefings on the persons of concern in the Croatian community. I assume, of course, that you have asked?'

'Yes, sir. We have.'

'And?'

Harper had no brief for ASIO. The animosity between the Organisation and the Commonwealth Police was legendary, but this was high-stakes politics. He was extremely wary, but he answered directly. 'Well, it's never easy dealing with ASIO. It's like pulling teeth, to be honest. They do like to keep their secrets.'

'Good God, Harry!' Murphy thundered. 'Have they given you anything at all?'

'Frankly, no,' said Harper. 'Al Sharp's my research officer. As you may know, he spent some years working in ASIO. He's been dealing with them directly.'

Murphy turned to Sharp. 'So what do you think's going on, Al?'

'It's as the inspector says. We've asked them for whatever relevant information they may have on the Croatian extremists on our radar, and any others they know or who should be . . . Whatever they have in their files, really.'

'Do you know what they've got in their files? Have you seen the material yourself?' Murphy pressed him.

'No, sir. I didn't work in that area. They do have a Balkan Desk, which keeps track of all Yugoslavian communists resident in Australia. As to the other side—the opponents of Tito's regime? Well, I couldn't tell you. There's a lot of speculation about that, even within the service. At best, it's a low priority.'

Kerry Milte interrupted him. 'It's not speculation,' he said. 'They've been running Croatian Nazis as agents against the communists. The fucking Ustasha is under their protection. That's what they're hiding from you.'

'You may be right, Mr Milte,' said Sharp calmly. 'But I have no direct knowledge of it.'

'It's a fact,' said Milte.

'I'm sure you know more than I do. In addition, I've asked for ASIO's threat assessment on Bijedic's visit. They keep putting me off. If you want my opinion, I don't think they've done one.'

Murphy couldn't restrain himself. 'That's a pretty picture. Are you pressing them, Inspector Harper? Are you pressing them for answers?'

Harper didn't want to say anything likely to raise the already high temperature. 'We've been extremely busy,' he said. 'Running down our own intelligence leads, sir. ASIO appears to have clammed up on us.'

'Clammed up?' cried Milte. 'That's putting it mildly. They are actively withholding vital intelligence when we've got threats to a foreign head of state, the prime minister and three members of his cabinet.'

'I've seen no proof of them actually withholding anything,' said Harper.

'Well, now we've got the proof,' said Milte. 'This secret memo is damning—'

The attorney-general cut off his aide. 'Let's take this one step at a time,' said Murphy. 'I'd like to keep you fellows here while we get organised. Gentlemen, I'm afraid we're all in for a long night. There's another phone in the hallway if you'd like to ring your wives and tell them you won't be home for some time, but no other calls, please. This must be contained for the time being. I don't want anyone getting wind of what we're up to.'

'And what might that be, Senator?' asked Harper.

'I'll let you know soon enough, Harry. Suffice to say, we're going to be rattling some cages,' said Murphy with a wink. 'Now, if you'll excuse us. I have a few more calls to make.'

Harper caught Al Sharp's eye. The man's face had gone blank and Harper knew why. Politics and police work are not a good mix. It can make your career or fuck your career. Best avoided.

Harper stepped outside and saw that Ray Sullivan had arrived and was chatting to Wally Price. Detective Sergeant Sullivan had been seconded from the Commonwealth Police in Sydney for the Bijedic operation. He was an old hand who had been working on the Croats since they first came on the radar screen in the mid-1960s.

Harper greeted him warmly. 'Good to see you, Ray.'

'G'day, sir. Sergeant Price here reckons he doesn't know a lot about what's going on. What are they telling you?'

Harper addressed them both, carefully picking through what he'd just heard.

'It's still unclear, but one thing's for sure: Murphy seems to be gearing up for some kind of confrontation with ASIO. He's incensed about some document they kept from him. God knows who's telling him about it. Putting two and two together, it seems to be an ASIO memo about the level of Croat threat.'

'A confrontation with ASIO?' said Sullivan. 'That chimes in with something I picked up on the way here. One of the drivers reckons he had a job to take Murphy and Milte, along with Murphy's secretary, to ASIO's Canberra office around midnight. The three of them were in there for more than an hour. Came out all energised and tense, jabbering about a conspiracy.'

'That's not good,' said Price, folding his arms, a ubiquitous fag smoking in his fingers.

Harper mulled over this new intelligence. 'That's funny,' he said. 'On our way over here we saw the ASIO offices in the West Portal all lit up. I thought it was odd. The only flap on at the moment is to do with the threat to Bijedic. This could all be about this mysterious document, memo or whatever it is. Looks to me like Murphy's getting fed information from someone on the inside.'

'But why are we here, Harry?' muttered Price. 'What does he want from us?'

'That's the strange thing,' said Harper. 'They keep avoiding the question about this supposed death threat to Murphy. That's why I'm here, and that's why I brought you here. But it's starting to sound like an excuse for something else.'

Price stamped on the remains of his cigarette. 'Fucking politicians. I don't like this one bit.'

'Me neither,' said Sullivan.

'Nor do I,' Harper agreed. 'But Murphy's ordered us to stay put and keep shtum. Whatever he's up to, he's worried about it leaking out. So keep this under your hats. Looks like we're here for the duration of whatever this is. Al Sharp's inside calling up his wife to say he won't be home anytime soon. You fellas can do the same. But no details. Complete cone of silence.'

Harper stalked off to send the dog team home. His mind was turning over what Ray Sullivan had just told him. What the hell was Murphy doing at the ASIO office this evening and why hadn't he mentioned it? *We're going to be rattling some cages.* That was how Murphy had described it. Harry Harper was putting a scenario together in his head and, like Wal Price, he didn't like it.

TONY JONES

*

Milte came for Harper again just after 4 am. 'Harry, can you come back in? The attorney wants a word.'

'Is he going to tell us about this death threat?'

'Well, the protection's in place. He thinks it's time to go on the front foot.'

Harper showed his irritation. 'This is not Sheffield Shield cricket, Kerry. I'm not opening the batting. I just need to know what's going on . . .'

Harper had been rehearsing his protest, but Milte cut him off.

'There's not much time, Harry. The attorney will explain, I'm sure.'

As he hustled Harper back into the house, Milte spotted Sharp chatting to Wally Price. 'Come and join us again, will you, Al!' he called.

They found the attorney-general pacing around on the thick pile carpet in the living room. Harper was exhausted. In the well-lit room he saw the strain on Sharp's face, particularly in his red-rimmed eyes. He assumed that he'd look just as bad if he could see himself in a mirror.

Milte was a particularly robust character, but even he was showing signs of fatigue. Only Lionel Murphy's vitality seemed completely unaffected by the hour. Harper had seen this with other such men. As well as being an aphrodisiac, power seemed to keep them plugged into the mains.

'Harry, Al. Sit down. Sit down. How about a cup of coffee? Ingrid!' Murphy called out, waving away Harper's objections. 'She's up anyway, poor thing. Can't sleep with all the commotion. Just made a fresh pot.'

Ingrid Murphy appeared in the kitchen doorway, pale and beautiful. Harper stood up and she smiled at him. He saw that her face had been softened by the pregnancy.

'What is it, Lionel?' she asked.

'Ah, there you are, my dear,' he said fondly. 'Do you think we could manage coffee for these gentlemen? They've had a long night.'

'Of course,' she said and returned to the kitchen.

'I promised we'd be rattling some cages, and that's exactly what we're going to do,' explained Murphy. 'We're going to Melbourne this morning on the first flight. I plan to make an unscheduled visit to ASIO Headquarters. I want you and your team to accompany me.'

Harper glanced at Milte, who raised an eyebrow. *Wait for it*, the eyebrow seemed to signal.

'We won't make it down there before office hours begin,' Murphy continued. 'So I will need the Commonwealth Police in Melbourne to go to St Kilda Road ahead of us to secure the building and lock the place down. All the files, all the safes, everything. I want to see the material they've got on the Croats and this damned memo. I don't want to take any chances that they'll shuffle it away into some dark corner. With the threat to Prime Minister Bijedic, we need everyone working together. And God help them if they have been lying, or concealing anything which could have helped to protect his life.'

Harper was incredulous. 'You're planning to raid ASIO Headquarters?'

'Let's call it a ministerial visit, shall we?' said Murphy.

'After sending in the Commonwealth Police to lock the place down? That's not what the press will call it.'

'Let me worry about them, Inspector ... Ah, thank you, Ingrid.'

Murphy stood up as his wife placed a tray on the table between them.

'As to myself, or any Commonwealth Police, going to Melbourne,'

Harper continued, 'or locking down St Kilda Road, or whatever else you might want us to do—the orders for that would need to come directly from the commissioner.'

Murphy furrowed his brow and the fierce intensity returned to his eyes. 'Are you saying my authority's not enough?'

'Of course not, Senator,' said Harper. 'But we are a disciplined service, and orders for something like this would have to come from the top. I need instructions from the commissioner.'

When Murphy started to object, Milte broke in. 'No, he's right. He's quite right,' he told the flustered politician. 'You need to speak to the commissioner yourself and clear this with him.'

Milte brought the phone over and placed a call to Jack Davis. He apologised to the commissioner for waking him, before passing the phone to Murphy.

'Morning, Jack,' said Murphy. 'I've got a crisis and I need your help . . .'

Milte took Harper by the arm and signalled to Sharp, leading them both out of the room. 'Let's give him some privacy,' he said in a low voice.

In the corridor Harper confronted Milte again. 'What am I supposed to tell the commissioner about these threats to the attorney-general? That's the reason we're here, after all—not for some witch-hunt inside ASIO.'

'It's not a witch-hunt,' said Milte. 'You said yourself, ASIO is not cooperating. The attorney has every right to get to the bottom of this. And they need to know who's in charge.'

'The threats, Kerry. The threats.'

'Just tell him that the attorney-general is in receipt of information and reports which indicate that his safety and that of his family are in jeopardy.'

'And when will I see that information?' Harper demanded. 'I do run the Bureau of Criminal Intelligence. You'd think the attorney-general might trust us with that.'

At that moment Lionel Murphy called from the living room: 'Inspector Harper! Can you come back in?'

'Let's go,' said Milte, opening the door, and Harper allowed himself to be shepherded back in.

'All right. He's here with me now, Jack.' Murphy was on his feet again, pacing out the full length of a long phone cord. 'Ha, ha. That's right, Jack. Absolutely.' He put his hand over the receiver. 'Harry,' he said, 'the commissioner has approved my requests and put you and your team under my authority. Do you need to speak to him?'

'No, Senator. That's not necessary.'

Murphy put the receiver back to his own ear. 'All right, Jack, that's all understood at this end. We'll keep you briefed during the day. Thank you.' Murphy hung up and looked at Harper. 'Right,' he said, rubbing his hands together. 'Let's get down to some detailed planning.'

28.

From that moment things moved very quickly. Murphy instructed Harper to make permanent arrangements for the security of his wife and his house. The men working on the Bijedic detail would be relieved as soon as practically possible and replaced by a team from the Protective Services. Harper organised for a security survey of the house and grounds to be conducted first thing in the morning.

It was agreed that Harper and Sharp, along with Detective Sergeants Price and Sullivan, would accompany the attorney-general and Kerry Milte to Melbourne.

During the next frantic hour, Murphy and Milte were constantly on the two phones. Harper heard a call to Peter Wilenski, the prime minister's chief of staff, in a failed attempt to secure the use of the government's RAAF jet. There were calls to staffers charged with organising flights and transport for those joining the Melbourne odyssey. There were also calls to unnamed factional allies in the Labor caucus. When he thought about it later, Harper was not certain if Murphy had directly informed the PM himself. Keeping Whitlam in the dark would be hugely problematic for all of them.

At 5 am Murphy met again with Harper and Sharp to explain the specific orders to be relayed to the Commonwealth Police in Melbourne. He tasked the two men with drafting the telex.

'We've got to get the commissioner to approve every word and comma in the orders,' said Harper. 'They'll be in his name.'

'Do what you have to do. But do it quickly.'

Once Commissioner Davis had approved the wording, Sharp dictated the orders over the phone to Sergeant Bennett, still on shift at Compol's Canberra headquarters. Bennett typed the message into the telex machine himself, fumbling over the keys, aware of his own small part in something momentous.

ON ATTORNEY-GENERAL'S DIRECT INSTRUCTIONS, THE OFFICER IN CHARGE OF VICTORIA DISTRICT IS TO IMMEDIATELY PROCEED TO HEADQUARTERS OF THE A.S.I. WITH SUCH MEN AS HE CONSIDERS NECESSARY AND SEAL WITH COMMONWEALTH POLICE SEALS ALL SAFES, CABINETS AND ANY CONTAINERS FOUND IN THAT BUILDING.

A COMMISSIONED OFFICER IS TO REMAIN ON THE PREMISES UNTIL RELIEVED ON THE ATTORNEY-GENERAL'S INSTRUCTIONS.

NO PERSON IS TO OPEN ANY CONTAINERS IN THAT BUILDING.

ALL CRIME INTELLIGENCE PERSONELL TO REPORT IMMEDIATELY TO THE MELBOURNE TTOMMMMMM-MMMMMMMMMMMEEE MELBOURNE OFFICE.

COMPOL AA62001*
COMPOL AA31796

At 6.20 am, as the men readied themselves to leave for the airport, a call came in on the attorney's second line. Harper answered it, and there was a pause before the caller spoke. 'Is Kerry M-M-Milte there?' The stutterer was a male.

'Yes. Who's calling?'

'Tell him it's T-Tom.'

Harper signalled to Milte. 'For you.'

'Who is it?'

'Bloke called Tom.'

'Oh, Christ.' Milte rushed over and grabbed the phone. 'Tom. What is it? Okay. Hang on . . . This is a private call, Harry,' he said, shooing Harper away.

As he pulled the door closed behind him, Harper saw Milte crouched over the table, muttering quietly into the receiver. A few minutes later Milte came out and led the attorney to a corner of the living room. Harper watched them huddled together—the whispering advisor and the senator. He had the epiphany that politics had always been done like this, and he wondered how much they were keeping from him.

Harper walked outside and found Wally Price sitting on a garden bench, hunched into an overcoat and smoking his umpteenth cigarette. Harper sat next to him. 'We ready?'

'We need two cars,' said Price. 'Sharp can drive yours. Sullie's organising another one to come 'round to the front door.'

'Good.'

'You trust these blokes, boss?'

'It's not a question of trust. We're under orders.'

'Make sure you put it all in writing, will you? Cover all our arses. They feel a bit bare right now.'

Harper looked at Price for a moment, then at his watch.

'Time to go,' he said.

*

Two cars sped to the airport. Sharp drove fast, reversing the route he'd taken four hours earlier. Harper sat in the front of the official car; Milte and Lionel Murphy were in the back.

'You say you spoke to an Englishman at St Kilda Road,' said Murphy.

'The night officer,' said Milte. 'Harold Magnay ... A decent enough bloke, by the sound of him. An MI5 officer on second-ment to ASIO—just his hapless luck to be the duty officer. I explained to him the orders in the telex. Told him to cooperate with the Commonwealth Police. A complete lockdown. No files to be touched. If he was shocked, he covered it well.'

Lionel Murphy smiled for the first time since he'd climbed, grim-faced, into the car. 'He'll have a good yarn to tell them when he gets back to London.'

'I'd have given anything to be a fly on the wall when he rang Peter Barbour. "My dear chap, sorry to wake you. I've just had the oddest call from those Labor fellows . . ." ' Milte had a talent for mimicry.

Murphy snorted. 'A wake-up call is exactly what Barbour needs! He's no Charles Spry, that's obvious. So, what is he exactly?'

'It's a classic Weberian second-generation crisis,' said Milte. 'Colonel Spry dominated ASIO as a military leader with charis-matic authority. I feel sorry for Barbour having to take over from someone like that.'

Murphy arched his eyebrows, impressed. 'They really drummed this into you at Melbourne Uni,' he said.

'Max Weber never goes out of fashion.'

Harper was following their conversation closely. He was hyper-vigilant, absorbing any intelligence that built on his emerging picture of what was really going on. One thing he knew for sure: if you were setting out to make enemies, the director-general of ASIO would be a formidable choice. It was clear the attorney-general was planning to confront Peter Barbour. There was no doubt that Barbour would be seriously humiliated, and that was something no one in a position of power ever forgot—or forgave.

Harper turned and leaned over the seat to address Murphy. 'Senator, I heard you visited the West Portal last night. What were you looking for?'

'The memo, Harry. As I said earlier, it's the evidence that ASIO is still covering up the Croat threat.'

'And they denied the existence of this memo, did they?'

'They said they didn't have a copy of it. Claimed it was at headquarters in Melbourne. Colin Brown, the regional director, said that. But that's arrant nonsense. They keep copies of everything.'

Milte broke in. 'Brown's deputy, Ron Hunt, was there too. The attorney grilled both of them about the memo and about Bijedic's security. He even asked if they'd vetted the Parliament House cooks, who might poison his soup. They hadn't. Had they vetted the security staff? No answer. It was seriously embarrassing.'

'There'll be a Royal Commission into this one day,' said Murphy. 'The incompetence is breathtaking.'

'You may be right, Senator,' said Harper, contemplating his own potential evidence.

He turned to face the front and saw that they were close to the airport. He recalled Wal Price's advice and started composing his own memo. He would make sure there were plenty of copies.

Anna Rosen had received a phone call in her room at The Wellington at around 5 am. She brushed off all sleepiness when she heard the caller's unmistakable voice.

'I got your m-m-message.'

'What's happening, Tom? Murphy cancelled a big debate in the Senate last night. He said it was because of national security issues. Then he and Milte went completely off the radar.'

'When they come b-back on the radar, they'll be landing in M-M-Melbourne.'

'That's a bit cryptic. Why Melbourne?'

'What f-famous organisation has its headquarters in St K-Kilda Road?'

'That'll be ASIO,' she said. 'Should I take the money or the box?'

'You should t-t-take the fucking aeroplane, at 8 am.'

'What are they planning to do down there?'

'This will be the b-biggest security story since the P-P-Petrov Affair, you better not miss it.'

'Look, I do appreciate your call,' Anna said. 'But can you just tell me what's going on?'

'I've t-told you enough already. I'm giving you this because I want you to t-t-trust me. By the way, if you s-see me at the airport, you don't n-n-know me and I don't know you.'

Anna raced to Canberra Airport and got there at 6.45 am. She had bought the last seat on the 8 am Ansett flight to Melbourne. She had no way of knowing which airline the attorney-general was travelling on, but TAA's 8 am flight was fully booked.

Now, as she paced up and down the airport forecourt, watching each car pull up to disgorge its passengers, she suddenly felt foolish. She imagined calling up Paul Barton at the bureau later in the morning to explain that she was in Melbourne. He would, of course, demand to know what the hell she was doing there. Truth being her only defence, Anna would have to explain that she'd had a pre-dawn tip-off from a man with a drinking problem, whose job it was to lie for a living . . . A trusted source.

But don't worry, Paul, he did say it would be the biggest story since the Petrov Affair. You ask me what the story is? That's a reasonable question, but I can't tell you that yet. Sometimes you just have to go with your instincts. Just trust me, okay?

She stared at her watch, pacing up and down like a manic bellhop. People gave her curious looks as they climbed from taxis or pulled their luggage from the boots of cars.

At 7.10, a black Ford pulled into the kerb and out climbed a tall man in a dark suit, carrying a brown briefcase. Tom Moriarty walked straight past her, hurrying into the airport without even a glance in her direction. At least that part of his strange narrative stacked up; it calmed her nerves. She stopped pacing, found a discreet position with good sightlines and rolled a cigarette.

At 7.20, two late-model sedans came fast into the forecourt. Both stopped with a squeal of brakes and out spilled six men in suits. Anna ditched the smoke, immediately recognising one of them: Al Sharp. His dishevelled suit and tired, puffy face suggested a sleepless night. The two men with him—plain-clothes police, she deduced—looked no better.

Kerry Milte climbed from the back of the second car, while a lean, stern-faced fellow with military bearing got out of the front. The last man out, from the back door on the far side, was the attorney-general.

While the others all looked careworn, as if they'd slept in their uniform dark suits, Murphy was dressed in a well-pressed suit of dazzling iridescent blue, with a clean white shirt and a wide-patterned tie. He paused to run his fingers through his longish grey hair, pushing it back behind his ears, then he reached into the car for his briefcase and handed it to Milte.

Murphy led the phalanx into the departure area of Canberra Airport. It reminded Anna of a scene from *The Untouchables*, or possibly *Get Smart*, if she was to be brutally honest about it. Something told her to hang back, so she followed them in from a distance and watched as the attorney's party of six made its way to the TAA side of the terminal. If they really were on their way to ASIO Headquarters, something big was up.

She looked for an opportunity to discreetly talk to either Milte or Sharp, but the men were clustered together, intense and unapproachable. Her own flight would be boarding soon. At least she'd get to Melbourne ahead of them. She looked for Tom Moriarty and spotted him standing off to one side near the TAA gate. The brown briefcase was under his arm.

Milte touched the attorney's elbow and drew his attention to a man standing on his own. Harper felt a current of surprise when he recognised the man as one of ASIO's Canberra officers.

'There he is,' said Milte.

'Let's go,' said Murphy, heading towards the ASIO man.

Perturbed by this odd occurrence, Harper followed them over.

'Hello, Tom,' said Milte. 'The attorney would like a word.'

Tom.

Harper's ears pricked up as Murphy introduced himself to the fellow.

'Of course I n-n-know who you are, S-Senator. Tom Moriarty. Good to finally m-meet you.'

So this was the stutterer. Harper's suspicion was confirmed.

Murphy pointed to the briefcase. 'I know what you have in there, Tom. What are you proposing to do with it?'

'My orders are to take it to M-M-Melbourne.'

TONY JONES

Despite the stutter, Harper saw that Moriarty was cool as a cucumber. That was one benefit of a career in ASIO: the power to rummage through the secrets of others gave you a high degree of self-confidence. This was the man who had phoned Milte early this morning. It seemed obvious now that Moriarty was Murphy's mole in ASIO.

'You've got the memo in there,' said Murphy. It was not a question.

'I c-can't say that, Senator. My orders are to give this to my b-boss.'

'Who is your boss, Mr Moriarty?' Murphy pressed.

'The director-general, Mr Barbour.'

'I'm sure you know the actual chain of command.'

'You mean beyond the Organisation?'

'ASIO is subordinate to the elected government. So I ask again: who is your boss?'

Moriarty considered that before answering. 'You are ... str-strictly speaking.'

'So give me the briefcase, please.'

'I c-c-can't do that, sir.'

'I'm not giving you a choice,' said Murphy. 'That's an order.'

Moriarty handed over the briefcase with a display of reluctance, but Harper's impression was that the man was play-acting. He may not have expected the attorney to actually take possession of the briefcase, but it seemed he had informed him in advance of its contents. Harper wondered what else he had told Milte and Murphy. And what were his motives? His superiors would regard his handing over of the briefcase as an act of betrayal.

He was surprised when Murphy turned directly to him. 'Can you come with me, Harry?'

Milte lingered back with Moriarty as Murphy led the inspector to a quiet corner of the lounge. Harper had the uncomfortable feeling of being moved around like a chess piece. Perhaps not a pawn; more like a knight who, though valued, could still be sacrificed at any time to gain an advantage. As he sat next to the attorney-general, he concluded the whole scene had been a set-up. The attorney wanted an independent witness and a Commonwealth Police inspector was as good as you could get.

Murphy pulled a manila folder from the briefcase, flipped it open and scanned the document inside.

'This is it,' he said and passed it to the policeman.

'You want me to read it?' Harper asked cautiously.

'I need you to verify what it is.'

Harper could hardly refuse, but he was curious now in any case. The document was the *casus belli*, the proof that Lionel Murphy had sufficient reason to take on ASIO. Evidently the spies themselves had gone to ridiculous lengths to keep it from him. It was the reason Murphy's posse was headed to Melbourne and the reason teams of Commonwealth Police were marshalling at this very moment to descend on ASIO's St Kilda Road headquarters.

Harper scrutinised the offending article. It was a carbon copy of the minutes of an interdepartmental meeting on Friday, 2 March. As recorded, the minutes had been taken by Ron Hunt, the second-in-charge of ASIO's Canberra bureau.

According to the memo, the meeting was attended by senior bureaucrats from the Departments of Foreign Affairs and Immigration, and the Attorney-General's Department.

What? He read it again. Murphy's own people—surely not? That didn't make sense.

Then he saw that the representative of the Attorney-General's Department was none other than the assistant secretary, Lindsay Curtis. He knew Curtis. He'd recently seen the man in his cups at dinner at the Swedish Embassy, complaining bitterly that

Murphy was out to get him. This document was surely his death warrant.

The memo concluded that information provided to Yugoslavia on the threat from Croatian terrorists 'should not be at variance' with the position of the previous conservative government. Harper immediately understood the implications. His own view was that previous governments' responses to Yugoslavia had been nothing short of lies. The decision of this high-level meeting was clear: we should keep lying to avoid embarrassment.

Harper paused. No doubt the memo was scandalous, but was its mere existence sufficient justification for a raid on ASIO? It raised other disturbing questions. Why had Murphy had to go to these lengths to get his hands on the memo when his own department had been present at the meeting? Who were the other senior bureaucrats from other departments and what role did they play in the decision? Why was ASIO being held to account and not the others?

It was a can of worms. Harper handed the memo back to the attorney without a word.

'Well,' said Murphy, 'what do you think?'

'I think a lot of senior people in different departments have their fingerprints on this.'

'ASIO's the driving force, Harry. The others have merely ticked off on their lies and we won't forget the part they played. But at the heart of this is ASIO. They must be made to answer for this.'

'But your own people were in the meeting.'

Murphy smiled, the familiar twinkle back in his eyes.

'No, not my people, Harry. That's precisely the point. Ivor Greenwood himself recruited the fellows who were at that meeting. They're still his people. They're still slavishly following the same old line on the Croats, as if nothing has changed. They seem to have missed the fact we've had an election. Fifth columnists. But we've smoked 'em now. We've smoked 'em.' The attorney shook his head as if saddened by the sheer bastardry of it all. 'It'll be time to clean house when this is done. Mark my words.' Murphy flipped open the briefcase, pointing to a red number sewn inside the top of it. 'By the way, Harry, did you notice this?'

'What is it?'

'This briefcase is Commonwealth-issued equipment. They're all numbered. This one was issued to the ASIO boss in Canberra. It's Colin Brown's personal briefcase. He lied to us, and then sent us the evidence of that with his own calling card.'

When Murphy's party boarded their plane, the attorney directed Wally Price to sit with him, intending to quiz him about plans for Bijedic's protection. Price looked over at Harper and rolled his eyes towards heaven, his meaning clear: *Stuck next to the attorney-general in a metal tube at twelve thousand feet without a parachute. Not good, Harry, not good.*

Harper placed the briefcase into the overhead locker, handling it as if it contained a ticking bomb. He sat next to Sharp, who bunched his jacket up as a pillow and promptly fell asleep. Kerry Milte managed to convince a businessman to swap seats and sat next to Tom Moriarty. The pair were just in front of Harper and, as he closed his own eyes, he heard them talking.

'So w-what do you think's going to happen?'

'ASIO'S fucked,' said Milte. 'They're overdue for a shake-up.'

'What about m-me?'

'You're like that bloke in *Callan*.'

'What do you m-mean?'

'Lonely.'

'I won't be fucking lonely; I'll be d-dead if you don't help me,' said Moriarty, without a trace of flippancy. 'You need to get M-Murphy to put me on staff.'

'Don't worry, I'll speak to him again,' said Milte. 'He knows the risk you're taking.'

Harper woke with a start as the undercarriage thumped hard on the runway at Tullamarine. Lionel Murphy led the raiding party through the airport at a fast clip, as if it was up to him to create an unstoppable momentum.

29.

Anna saw them coming. She had already spotted the two uniformed Commonwealth Police drivers waiting in the forecourt next to a pair of long-bonneted black and chrome limos. She'd found a willing taxi driver and paid him to wait nearby, ready to move.

Lionel Murphy, in his electric-blue suit, was a swatch of colour in front of the ruck of his entourage. Tom Moriarty, denuded of his briefcase, spotted her and looked away. She caught Milte's eye; he returned her gaze with a startled look before the attorney stopped abruptly.

'Christ, that's discreet,' said Murphy, drawing his hands back through his hair. 'We'll be arriving in police vehicles.'

'Well, we can hardly hail a cab,' said Milte, directing him to the first car. The driver ushered the attorney-general into the back seat.

Milte turned to see Anna Rosen climbing into a cab. How the hell did she get here? He looked over at Tom Moriarty, but when the spy shrugged Milte shook his head and climbed into the front seat.

Harper was standing on the footpath, still holding the ASIO briefcase. He thrust the thing into Moriarty's arms. 'You better take this back,' he said.

Relieved of his burden, Harper climbed into the rear of the car with the attorney.

'Might have been wise to keep hold of that,' said Murphy.

'That's not my judgement,' said Harper, too tired for politeness. 'This is your show, but I didn't feel right lugging an ASIO briefcase around.'

Before Murphy could respond, Milte turned from the front. 'He's right,' he said. 'Better that Moriarty arrives with it. We all know what's in it, anyway.'

The rogue spy, clutching the briefcase to his chest, was wedged into the back of the second vehicle between the two sergeants. Doors slammed and the small convoy took off from the kerb.

Anna turned quickly to her driver, but he beat her to it.

'Follow that car?' he asked, accelerating in the wake of the fast-departing limos. He shook his head in annoyance as he wove through the slow-moving airport traffic and kept the police vehicles in sight. 'Bugger it,' he said. 'I've been waiting for this moment for ten years, and then I go and say it myself.'

'Want me to say it again?'

'Nah, it wouldn't be the same.'

'Don't lose them,' said Anna.

'Bewdy.' The driver smiled. 'That was properly in character.'

'I mean it.'

'Yeah, I know. It's just'—a terminal bus pulled in front of them and he hit the anchors, burning rubber as he jerked the wheel to narrowly avoid a collision—'it's normally a pretty boring job.'

*

Harper glanced over at the attorney-general. He was surprised to see the man's eyes closed and his lips moving, as if rehearsing lines backstage before a live performance.

When they hit the freeway and slowed in the peak-hour traffic, Murphy tapped the driver's shoulder. 'Can we put the siren on and go faster?'

Kerry Milte swung around. 'That's a really bad—' he began, before he was drowned out by the sudden high-pitched wail, and then a second as the other driver switched his siren on too. 'Fuck me dead!' Milte exclaimed in frustration as the two cars began yawing at high speed through the traffic.

Ahead of them, cars braked and pulled aside to let them pass.

Milte began flicking at switches on the dashboard. 'If the press gets hold of this . . .' he shouted. He reached under the dash and pulled out a bunch of wires. The driver glanced at him nervously as the siren sputtered out.

'Right, you're right,' said Murphy. 'Maybe we should've brought Negus in on this, after all.'

'I don't think so,' said Milte. 'We've got enough loose cannons on the deck.'

Harper smiled at this exchange. He'd been wondering where the press flack was. George Negus always looked more like an extra from *Zabriskie Point* than a spokesman for the attorney-general. Harper imagined him storming the ASIO stairs like the vanguard of the October Revolution.

The thought cheered him up, until Murphy interrupted his reverie. 'Harry, stay by my side when we get there? I imagine you'll be the ranking officer.'

Harper was puzzled. 'Apart from the director-general of ASIO and his top brass?'

Murphy held his gaze. 'I mean the ranking officer on our side,' he said evenly.

'I'm under your authority.'

'Just so, Harry. Just so.'

Harper watched the attorney-general bouncing around in the back seat as the cars plunged on dangerously towards their destination. Even after the second driver cut his siren neither car had slowed down. Through the window traffic zipped past.

Soon the two cars turned into St Kilda Road, barrelling down the wide thoroughfare.

Sitting up front, Milte was the first to see what appeared to be a blockade ahead of them. 'What the hell . . .?'

As they got closer, he saw a bank of cameras sprawled across the road, filming their approach. Soon little sunbursts came, flashes of light blossoming from the pack. Milte's face reddened with anger at this latest betrayal.

'Oh, fuck. Someone tipped them off.'

'No time to worry about that,' said Murphy. 'Just ignore them.'

Harper saw the attorney compose his face into a mask of resolution, his political instincts kicking in. On their right was the white-colonnaded façade of ASIO Headquarters. The modern concrete structure was featureless at ground level. The cars of its lower-level workers were lined up with their fronts to the kerb. There was a grass nature strip, a functional hedge and, above that, hundreds of dark windows. He saw no faces at them.

'Mind what you do now, Harry,' said Murphy. 'Your mug'll be all over the news tonight.'

'I wasn't planning to smile and wave,' said Harper. But, as they neared the bank of cameras, he felt like slumping down below the window ledge. Politics and police work, he reminded himself—a bad mix.

Then it all seemed to slip into slow motion. He saw blue-uniformed Commonwealth Police holding back the horde of journalists. There were multiple sunbursts now, bouncing off the long, shiny bonnet. A policeman directed the car to turn right. As it did so, Harper found himself staring into the black hole of a TV camera. He imagined Wal Price, in the car behind, giving them the finger, but he resisted the urge to turn around.

Microphones were waved at them and he heard muffled questions. Their car headed for a dark entrance, which opened in the wall as a large steel door rolled up. Harper watched a photographer slip the cordon and run in front of their car, targeting Lionel Murphy, who was now on the other side, hidden from the press pack.

Murphy lifted his chin. *Flash, flash, flash.* A policeman grabbed the man and the two of them whirled off together, like dance partners.

Murphy's vehicles entered a high-ceilinged garage and a policeman appeared from the gloom to direct them over to the pool of light spilling from an open doorway. As the cars pulled up, three men emerged from the doorway, their faces pale under the fluorescent lights.

At the head of the welcoming party was a man in the uniform of a chief inspector. Harper felt instant relief: this must be Charlie Jones, the boss of Melbourne's Commonwealth Police. Happily, he was now outranked. And besides, Chief Inspector Jones, in his immaculately pressed blues, gave the incursion a sense of authority.

Lionel Murphy obviously thought so, too. He bounded out of the car and headed straight for the commanding heights, hand outstretched, his red-headed advisor at his heels.

As Jones briefed the attorney-general, Harper took note of the big man standing just behind the chief inspector, an ominous presence drawing furiously on a cigarette.

The third member of the greeting party, a man in a plain dark suit, was standing well apart from this awkward tableau. Harper suddenly recalled who he was and walked over.

'Inspector Whitton, isn't it?'

'That's right, Harry, Lawrie Whitton.'

They shook hands. Whitton was a compact, well-made fellow with the weathered face of a sailor. 'We met in Canberra, a couple of years ago,' he reminded Harper. 'Seminar on terrorism.'

'That's right.'

Whitton looked over at the attorney-general and the chief inspector.

'Best let the top brass deal with this, mate,' he said. 'It's a bad business.'

'What's up?' asked Harper.

Whitton tipped his head in the direction of the furious smoker. 'You know that bloke?'

'No, I don't.'

Harper looked again at the man. The big fellow was staring hard at Murphy with barely concealed contempt.

'It's Jack Behm, ASIO's deputy director-general,' whispered Whitton. 'He's in a fucking rage. Incandescent. Ready to pop his cork at any moment.'

Harper saw the intensity in Behm's eyes.

'Thanks for the tip, Lawrie. I better go.'

'Wait,' said Whitton. 'One more thing. Before Murphy does anything else, he needs to speak to the ASIO staff. We couldn't let them go to their offices, so we had to herd them into a lecture theatre. It's getting ugly in there. Women crying. Men angry. Some of them think this is a coup. They're talking about being taken out and shot against a wall—and they're only half-joking.'

Harper was shocked. 'That's madness.'

'This mob is a bit mad; it goes with the territory. Murphy needs to go in and reassure them before something bad happens.'

'I'll let him know.'

As Harper moved to gather up his own team, he glanced over at Tom Moriarty, whose cool demeanour seemed to have finally abandoned him.

'You blokes come with me,' said Harper to Sharp and his sergeants. He took them to flank the attorney-general and made the introductions. 'Inspector Harper, sir,' he said, addressing the chief inspector. 'Bureau of Criminal Intelligence. With me are Sergeants Price and Sullivan, and my intelligence officer, Al Sharp.'

'Ah. Good morning, Inspector,' said Jones. 'I was just explaining to the attorney that all the offices, safes and containers are now sealed. We have twenty-seven officers here and I've stationed men on every floor. As they've come in, we've directed the ASIO staff to gather in the auditorium on the third floor.'

An audible groan now came from the Organisation's deputy director-general. Hearing the facts recited for a second time, the man couldn't contain himself.

'This is an absolute outrage!' said Jack Behm. 'What's happening here is tantamount to treason. You're holding hostage most of the security apparatus of this country, under who-knows-what authority!'

'Mr Behm,' Lionel Murphy cut him off, 'that is totally unwarranted. Please control yourself and lower your voice.'

'Senator Murphy,' said Behm, managing to make the title sound like an insult. 'This has already done untold damage. Can you imagine what our American friends will make of this?

A wet-behind-the-ears, socialist government rummaging through our safes . . . How do you suppose that'll go down at the intelligence-sharing briefings?'

'Stop right there, Mr Behm,' said Murphy, turning up the dial a few notches. 'Do you have any idea who you're talking to? I am the elected civilian official to whom you are answerable. I say *elected*! Do you hear me, Mr Behm? Do you take my meaning? I need to confirm that you understand there has been a legitimate change of power in this country. You are aware of that, aren't you?'

Behm said nothing. His jaw was clamped shut. His lips quivered with rage.

'I asked you a question!' Murphy roared. Even Harper was impressed by the effect.

'Yes,' said Behm, spitting the word out like rancid phlegm.

'Ivor Greenwood is no longer here to do your bidding. I am the attorney-general. And everything that has happened here, and will happen here today, is under my direct authority. Do you understand that simple fact?'

Behm nodded.

'I didn't hear you, Mr Behm. Do you understand that this is being done under the lawful authority of an elected attorney-general?'

'Yes,' said Behm.

Harper saw some of the steam come out of the man and wondered how long it had been since anyone had spoken to Jack Behm in this manner. Murphy was momentarily on top, but he was sure it wouldn't end there.

'Please listen carefully, Mr Behm,' Murphy continued. 'There is a matter of national security at stake here. The life of a foreign leader, soon to visit this country, is under threat. I have asked ASIO for information about the nature of that threat, and I have been bamboozled and I have been misled. To make matters worse, I was lied to by senior ASIO officers. The proof of that is here with us.'

Murphy turned and pointed to Tom Moriarty, who was still standing next to the big black car he'd come in, clutching the briefcase containing the proof of infamy. It seemed to Harper that Moriarty was fighting an urge to leap into the driver's seat and make a high-speed getaway.

'The evidence,' Murphy paused for effect, 'is in that very briefcase.'

Jack Behm stared at Moriarty. There was no hiding the naked hatred in his eyes.

'As to your employees in the theatre,' Murphy continued. 'They are not being held hostage. That is absurd. They will be free to go back to their offices as soon as I have had some answers. And I will be demanding them from the director-general himself. Is that all clear to you?'

'Yes, perfectly clear,' said Behm.

'Then our conversation is over. I would like to see Mr Barbour immediately.'

The man was mad! There was no question about it in Jack Behm's mind. Murphy was both mad and dangerous. Behm walked away from their confrontation convinced that he was dealing with an existential threat.

He barrelled up the stairs and burst into the headquarters foyer like a rugby player who's suddenly found himself in the clear. He ignored the startled looks of the uniformed police milling around. Just let them try and stop him! He'd knock them over like nine pins. More police were standing guard on the closed doors to the theatre, behind which his colleagues were being held hostage. Outside of tin-pot dictatorships, there wasn't a security agency in the world that had been subjected to this kind of intrusion, not to mention the sheer indignity of it.

The Five Eyes partners would be incredulous. In one fell swoop Murphy and his keystone cops had destabilised the most important intelligence relationships the country had ever had. Behm dreaded the telephone call coming across the Pacific from James Jesus Angleton. How could he ever explain this inexplicable outrage to the CIA? It would be a miracle if the US trusted them with a single paltry secret during the life of the Whitlam government.

The director-general's office was on the seventh floor. Behm jabbed repeatedly at the *Up* button on the lift panel. A young Commonwealth policeman made a move towards him, as if to challenge his right to move freely around the building, but Behm held him back with a glare so withering it stripped the fellow of all willpower. That was what was required today: the sheer will to confront this madness. Behm had no confidence that Peter Barbour had it in him to do so.

Murphy's dawn invasion had knocked the stuffing out of Barbour. For that reason, Behm had not informed his boss about his own pre-dawn raid to rescue the operational files in his safe. Behm knew now that this had been the right move. No one had expected this police takeover, but his own deepest instincts had been engaged when he read the short memo from John Elliott, the assistant director-general 'B' Branch, setting out the confrontation he and Barbour had had with Murphy two days ago in the attorney-general's office. Murphy had demanded to see 'all documents' regarding ASIO's association with Croat extremists. He clearly wanted to know which Croats were paid informants, the names of those used in operations, those who operated effectively as agents, the nature and length of those relationships, and so on. Such disclosure would put lives at risk. It could not be allowed. Yet Murphy had warned Elliott to think long and hard about giving him a 'nil return'.

It seemed to Behm that there was much between the lines in Elliott's memo. When he extracted the man from his cloistered enclave and chivvied him, Elliott had confided his belief that Murphy was drunk during the encounter. A high-functioning drunk, but drunk nonetheless. How could one trust such a man with the lives of others? Behm knew that some secrets had to remain sacrosanct from politicians. That was the nature of their business. So he had taken the sensible precaution of emptying his safe.

Before returning to St Kilda Road that morning, Jack Behm had stopped off at the City and Overseas Club. He had booked a room there and in it secured the two cricket bags full of secrets, locking them in a cupboard. He had privately confided this to his closest confederates, men who agreed with him that Barbour's insipid weakness was a threat to the Organisation. He told them that he was prepared to effectively run the Organisation from the club for the duration of the crisis.

Behm knew that by doing this he had established a shadow leadership. Barbour, if he found out, would consider it mutiny. But it was, Behm was convinced, a necessary measure to protect the integrity of their calling. He would also confide in Father William and Father John at the Institute of Social Order, men whose wisdom and discretion he could trust. He might even have to confess his actions to James Jesus himself, although that course would not be free of risk.

The lift disgorged Jack Behm on the seventh floor and he bustled past the uniformed policeman stationed there, aware that his movements would be monitored on security cameras by the police controlling the front desk. He went straight into the director-general's office without knocking and found Peter Barbour gazing out the window as if contemplating the drop and the 'honourable' option of *seppuku*.

Barbour's reverence for the ways of the Japs was yet another thing Behm held against him. That was what happened when your job was to speak to the bastards behind the lines, conducting soft interrogations, where you try to create a bond. It was a different kettle of fish when you actually had to fight them.

'Director,' he said.

Barbour turned, blinking with surprise. 'Jack?'

'Murphy's here with his party. He wants to see you now.'

'All right,' said Barbour, straightening his hexagonal, black-framed glasses, touching his hair.

Behm saw that the filing cabinets and safe in Barbour's office were sealed with yellow tape.

'I see they don't even trust you,' he said.

'No,' said Barbour. 'Trust is something we're going to have to work at with this government.'

'There's something you should know before you go down,' said Behm.

'What's that?'

'We've got a turncoat, a traitor in our midst.' Behm paused for effect. 'It's Tom Moriarty. He's with them. The memo that Colin Brown requested Moriarty to hand-deliver down here—he's given it to Murphy.'

Barbour's reaction was not what Behm expected. 'I ordered Moriarty to get close to Murphy,' he said. 'We need someone on the inside. In the attorney's inner circle.'

'You told him to give the memo to Lionel Murphy?'

'No.'

'Well, Murphy knows what's in that briefcase,' said Behm. 'He says it's proof that our people have lied to him and misled him.

Moriarty clearly gave him that—the proof he was looking for—or gave him access to it. He's betrayed the Organisation.'

Barbour shook his head. 'Tom Moriarty is one of our best operators. I prefer to think that he acted on his own initiative. What better way to establish trust with Murphy?'

'That's what he's told you he was doing?'

'He's acting on my orders.'

'With all due respect, that's a crock of shit. What better cover for a traitor than to have the blessing of the director-general?'

'Leave Moriarty to me, Jack. Shall we go down?'

From the phone box on St Kilda Road, Anna Rosen had rung the *Herald*'s bureau chief at home. To his credit, Paul Barton took her sudden relocation to Melbourne in his stride and she felt a small surge of gratitude. He really did trust her judgement.

Once she had explained the circumstances, he even congratulated her. 'Mind you,' he said, 'had you woken me up to explain, I'd have organised a cameraman to be waiting with you at Melbourne Airport.'

'That did cross my mind, Paul, but until Murphy and his entourage arrived at Canberra Airport I didn't know if this was for real.'

'I get that,' he agreed. 'Really, I'm just thankful to have you there. This will be huge. Commonwealth coppers all over the place, you say? That's a police raid, there's no getting around it. What is Murphy thinking?'

'I still don't know the answer to that. All my best contacts are locked away inside ASIO. As soon as we're done, I'm going to call Arthur Geitzelt. He's one of Murphy's closest confederates and he's an old mate of my dad's. Maybe he'll tell me something.'

'Good idea,' said Barton. 'I'll get Peter Tennant onto it as well. And . . . Bloody hell!'

'What is it?'

'I've just remembered: Gough's heading in your direction to do the Melbourne Press Club lunch.'

'What?' cried Anna. 'So Murphy didn't tell the prime minister? They wouldn't deliberately fly Whitlam into a press ambush.'

'You wouldn't think so. He's in the air now. They took the small VIP, the Mystere. Bruce McKillop's on board. I wrangled a seat for him just to get him off my back. He's supposed to call me when they land. I'll brief him when he does. Blimey, what a shower—Gough'll hit the roof when he finds out about this.'

When Murphy's party entered the foyer, Harper pulled Kerry Milte to one side, explaining in short, terse sentences what he had just learned about the fear and loathing in the lecture theatre.

'Right. Wait on,' said Milte. 'Murphy needs to hear this now.'

As Milte rushed over to brief the attorney, Harper looked around the modest foyer. It was the first time he'd been in ASIO Headquarters and it hardly resembled the seat of the nation's covert power. Before the spies acquired it, the building had housed the offices of the old Gas and Fuel Company; even now, the only indication that anything more interesting happened here was the security desk with its banks of TV monitors.

He watched as late-arriving ASIO employees were buzzed in through the secure zone behind the glass doors. They were already flustered, having run the gauntlet of the press.

One of the foyer lifts pinged open to reveal a man in a dark suit. It was the director-general of ASIO, robbed by circumstances of the mystique that normally came with his office.

Peter Barbour took a few steps and stopped some distance from Murphy and his entourage. He stood very still for a moment before adjusting the spectacles on the bridge of his long, straight nose. His hair was swept back neatly from an owlish face. He was meticulously dressed in a starched white shirt and handmade suit. His shoes gleamed.

Harper tagged him straightaway as a patrician type—Adelaide gentry. The hoi polloi may have invaded his inner sanctum, but he wasn't about to let anyone see that it bothered him in the slightest. Looming over Barbour's shoulder, his deputy, Jack Behm was, by contrast, the very picture of smouldering resentment.

Lionel Murphy didn't wait. He walked briskly over to the pair of ASIO men. 'Good morning, Director.'

'Senator,' said Peter Barbour without the offer of a handshake. 'The last time we met was by appointment, as I recall.'

It was a mild provocation, but Murphy paused before answering. 'I intend to explain to you why that was not possible on this occasion,' he said.

'That will be fascinating.'

'It was necessary, Peter. There are difficult times ahead with the Bijedic visit.'

'I do hope,' said Barbour, 'we're not doomed to have an unorthodox relationship. That would be most unproductive.'

Murphy refused to go down that path. 'Before we do anything else,' he said, 'I'd like to speak to your staff, to reassure them.'

'It would certainly be wise not to keep them confined any longer. Shall we go?'

Two lifts ferried the ASIO men and Murphy's party to the third floor, where it was possible to access the top storey of the annex built on to the front of the building. Murphy followed Peter Barbour out of the lifts and up a few stairs, entering a large anteroom.

'We hold receptions here from time to time,' said Barbour, as if conducting a guided tour. 'It has a kitchen, as you can see, for that purpose. The lecture theatre is through there.' He pointed to a pair of large doors, closed and guarded by several uniformed policemen. 'That's where my people are being held. We can go in. With your permission, of course.'

'There's no need for irony, Peter,' said Murphy. The attorney-general strode ahead and pushed through the doorway, the ASIO director and Kerry Milte hastening in his wake. Harper signalled for his team to wait outside before himself walking past the police guards and through the heavy entrance doors.

There was a loud hubbub in the auditorium and he sensed a hysterical edge to the tension. Several women were weeping; some of the men had pale, drawn faces, while others were angry and animated.

Murphy appeared surprised and leaned over to whisper to Milte, 'Some of them are crying. What do I say?'

'Make them feel good,' said Milte. 'Give them a morale booster. Cheer them up.'

There was a surge of noise as people at the front recognised the man in the electric-blue suit. Like a single nervous system registering a shock, the realisation spread rapidly through the crowd that the enemy was among them. Shouts came from different parts of the room and some jeered, as if a pantomime villain had just leapt on stage.

Harper saw doubt in Murphy's eyes for the first time. The senator was well used to addressing crowded rooms. In recent times, he had mostly fronted packed halls full of passionate supporters, there to catch a glimpse of the great man. But this was different; this was a room full of doubt, fear and anger. When Murphy hesitated, Peter Barbour stepped to the front and the noise began to subside.

'Quiet now, Quiet please,' said the director-general. 'You're all aware that Senator Murphy has chosen to pay us a visit today. He has asked to address you while he is here. Please give him your full attention.' Barbour paused to scan the room, as if to snuff out any remaining dissent. Then he turned to Murphy. 'Senator . . .'

Murphy walked to the front of the stage. 'Thank you, Director. Ladies and gentlemen.' His voice boomed in the room's fine acoustics. 'My name is Lionel Murphy and I am the attorney-general of Australia.'

'We know who you are!' someone shouted.

'Just let us out of here!' cried another interjector.

'Please be patient,' Murphy responded. 'There is no need for any of you to be concerned. No reason at all. I am here to meet Director-General Barbour. When I've finished speaking to you, you'll all be able to go back to your offices.'

More yelling was punctuated by another question, 'Why the storm troopers?', which prompted a howl of assent.

Murphy paused until the room was quiet again. 'The Commonwealth Police are here at my request to secure file rooms and information relating to a threat to the life of a foreign head of government. I don't intend to go into any more detail about that now.'

Murphy ignored scattered cries of disbelief.

'I've come in here to speak to you this morning because some of you have questioned whether my visit is lawful, and because there have been misapprehensions and wild rumours about my intentions. I am not blind; I can see the anxiety on your faces. Let me lay that anxiety to rest.'

The angriest voices were stilled, waiting.

TONY JONES

'Many of you will know that, at its last federal conference, the Australian Labor Party had a serious debate about the future of ASIO. That's no secret. It was a public debate, as such debates should be. Some in the party wanted us to get rid of ASIO altogether if we won government. I argued strongly against that. I told my colleagues—including those who had been subjected to intrusive surveillance because of their political beliefs—I told them that the Organisation would be subject to the lawful authority of an elected government, but that Australia still needs ASIO. All of you here are vital for protecting our national interest.'

Murphy paused and ran his eyes over the crowd for a moment before he picked up the thread again.

'My argument won the day. Yet you should understand this: I also agreed with your critics that abuses of state power would no longer be tolerated and that reforms were necessary to ensure that. But you don't need to burn down the house to roast a chicken. ASIO is a vital part of our government's apparatus and, like any part of the government, must be subject to the law. Whatever you may think, the very fact that I am able to visit you here today, without notice, is proof of that.

'Through the Office of the Attorney-General, ASIO is accountable to the government and thus to the people. Make no mistake, the Labor government has very different priorities to our predecessors. We intend to enact new laws to protect the privacy of individuals, and laws to create the openness necessary for a free society to function well. I will not exclude you from this process. On the contrary, we must work together. That is for the future. As for this morning, I thank you for your patience. Good day.'

In the brief silence that followed, Lionel Murphy turned and left the auditorium.

When Peter Barbour joined him a few moments later in the anteroom, Murphy addressed him coolly.

'Director, it's time for us to talk. You've suggested the seventh floor. I presume the meeting room is large enough for my team?'

'It is, Senator.'

'I would like Mr Moriarty to join us too.'

'Of course.'

'Along with his briefcase.'

Seated at the conference table, Harry Harper had the sense of two opposing football teams facing each other across a veneered mahogany pitch. A line of ashtrays marked halfway. Murphy and Milte were on his right; his own police team was arrayed to the left of him, all of them waiting for the kick-off. Jugs of water and glasses were set up for half-time.

The attorney-general glanced at his watch every few moments, staring across the desk at the empty chair with an intercom sitting in front of it. That place was reserved for the director-general of ASIO. They were assured that Peter Barbour would be there soon. He had a matter to attend to first.

While they were waiting, Wally Price lit up a smoke. Jack Behm followed suit, as did Tom Moriarty. Then Sharp got Moriarty's attention, touching two fingers to his mouth, and the spy slid his pack over the table, at which point Harper thought, *what the hell*, and took one too. When the director-general entered the room, a smokescreen had been laid between lines, the very fog of war.

Peter Barbour slid into the empty chair and met Murphy's gaze. 'I would say welcome to ASIO, Senator, but that seems rather redundant.'

Murphy was in no mood for flippancy. 'Mr Behm did greet us in the car park, but I don't recall the word "welcome".'

Harper saw Behm stab his cigarette hard into an ashtray as Murphy continued. 'There's no point beating around the bush. We are running out of time. Prime Minister Bijedic is due here in three days and there is a credible threat to assassinate him on Australian soil. The threat comes from Croatian extremists. As I made clear at our last meeting, Director, I want you to provide the files you have on those terrorists and, as I indicated to Mr Elliott'—Murphy nodded across the table to the 'B' Branch head—'I want to see for myself exactly what relationship ASIO has had with them.'

'We are preparing the final document for you and you will have it by 4 pm today,' said John Elliott. 'We have information in draft form—'

Murphy put up a hand and interrupted him. 'We will come to that, Mr Elliott,' he said. 'But before we go any further, a document was brought here this morning from Canberra. Mr Moriarty has it in his briefcase. Can I have it, please?'

Tom Moriarty lifted the briefcase from under the table, took out a manila folder and passed it over to Sharp, who handed it on to Murphy. The attorney scrutinised the contents briefly before sliding the folder across the table to the director-general.

'Director, as you see, this is a memo summarising decisions taken at an interdepartmental meeting, just over two weeks ago on 2 March,' said Murphy. 'At his headquarters in Canberra last night, your regional director Colin Brown assured me that the only copy of this memo was here at St Kilda Road. As we can see, he then placed copies of the non-existent memo in his briefcase and dispatched it to Melbourne in the care of Mr Moriarty. That is deception, plain and simple.'

At that moment Jack Behm leaned forward to stare at Tom Moriarty, who was busily lighting another cigarette.

'We'll find out who's deceiving who soon enough,' said Behm.

But the director cut in quickly. 'There's been no deception here, only confusion,' said Barbour, holding up the manila folder. 'Mr Brown sent this to Melbourne on my orders. You see, Senator, Brown stayed in the office when you left last night and, after a thorough search, he found the memo. Before joining you here just now, I telephoned Mr Brown to go back over exactly what happened.'

Barbour consulted the handwritten notes in front of him before continuing his narrative. 'Mr Milte called Colin Brown at home and woke him at 5.15 am with instructions that he formally notify me of your intention to visit ASIO Headquarters this morning. When Brown called me soon after that, he told me about the memo and your interest in it, so I instructed him to send two copies of it on the first flight. One for me and one for you, Senator. It's as simple as that.'

Murphy was silent and Harper turned to see how he'd respond. It seemed to him that ASIO had slid out from under the first charge: that of deliberate deception.

'Very well,' said Murphy. 'I will leave to one side what I was told by both Mr Brown and Mr Hunt last night, and their miraculous discovery of the memo subsequently. Now I would like to see the original, which I'm informed is held in your files here.'

'That may take some time.'

'I direct you to find it.'

'Very well,' said Barbour. He pressed a button on the intercom. 'Can you please send in Mr Fraser.'

Harper watched the confrontation with growing unease. Murphy was playing with fire. He recalled a senior spy once confiding to him that ASIO's chiefs considered themselves to be a reserve power, ready to step in and take control of the country in certain circumstances. He suspected such men as Jack Behm might consider today's events as falling into the category of 'certain circumstances'.

A mousey-looking fellow came into the conference room—Mr Fraser, evidently. He was a clerical type, unused to being called into the presence of power and painfully aware of the tension in the room. It was his job to escort the attorney-general into the seventh-floor file room.

Murphy and Milte stood up.

'Come with us, will you, Harry?' said Murphy.

Harper told his team to wait while he followed the small group down the corridor. A policeman stood aside, allowing them to enter a large room full of sealed filing cabinets, the yellow police tape still crisscrossing the locks. Fraser led them to a large, four-drawer steel cabinet.

'With your permission I'll remove the tape, Senator,' said Fraser.

'Go ahead,' said Murphy.

As he stripped it away, Fraser gave a running commentary.

'This is safe No. 16. It's a Class B container.' He held up a large key. 'It's a very secure cabinet. It would take eight hours to drill through this lock, even with a diamond tip.'

The document was not in it.

Fraser consulted the file numbers again and took them to safe No. 85. As he attempted to open the cabinet, the attorney-general loomed over his shoulder. Harper became aware of Milte's annoyance as the man fumbled with the locks and began an agitated search through the drawers.

'Are you deliberately stalling?' said Milte.

Then Murphy leaned over and pulled a green manila folder part way out of the top drawer.

'I think this is it,' he said.

Fraser pulled out the folder, scrutinised it, and handed it to Murphy, who took out the memo and signalled for Milte to look at it. 'This is it? The original?'

'Yup,' said Milte. 'It's initialled by everyone who's read it. Including, guess who?'

'Jack Behm.'

Murphy turned to Fraser. 'Right, let's go back.'

When they reconvened in the conference room, the two teams resumed their places on either side of the table. Murphy sat down, placed the recovered memo in front of him and began a cross-examination of Peter Barbour.

'How was ASIO represented at the interdepartmental meeting which took place in Canberra on 2 March 1973?'

'By the assistant regional director in the ACT, Mr Ron Hunt.'

'What instructions were given to Mr Hunt concerning this meeting and how did it come about?'

'None at all. I understand it is a standing group which meets ad hoc. Hunt is the ASIO representative in that group.'

'Mr Hunt's memo was logged here on 5 March 1973. You saw me in person after that date. Why was I not told of such a meeting taking place and of any decision taken at that meeting?'

'Well, the meeting was of a group that meets on an ad hoc basis for the purpose of coordinating intelligence reports on matters involving terrorism and political violence.'

'That is not an answer.'

'It is usual for each representative of such committees to consult his minister. If this is not understood, I will make it so.'

'I will deal with the representatives from my own department.

I am questioning your judgement now and I am very disturbed, Mr Barbour, that you didn't make me aware of this memo. It states here that the attorney-general should not be at variance with the previous attorney-general. That is to say that there is no evidence of Croat terrorist activity in Australia. That was Ivor Greenwood's position. Now I find that a document was being prepared for me that was completely different to every statement made by me on this subject. It also troubles me that it is at variance with the opinions you have stated and with what the police have reported.'

'You mean the memo?'

'Of course! This goes further than neglect. It is quite serious when such a decision is made behind my back. Especially when the government's position is so well known. I should instead have been getting material which quite clearly showed the existence of terrorism.'

'We are preparing such a document for you, as Mr Elliott said, and you will have it at 4 pm today. I have had relevant files brought in, which you can read for yourself, if you wish.'

'Do you accept that there has been strong recent evidence concerning people with a tendency to go overseas to engage in unlawful terrorism activities? Has it ever been taken into account?'

'There is a lot of evidence. It should have been taken into account.'

'But it was not taken into account *in this memo*. The evidence was ignored and I am not interested in the opinions of the previous government, who showed tolerance. My desire is to produce the evidence of terrorism and I wish to show it to the Senate. The previous attorney-general said there was no evidence of organised terrorism, but I have seen up to a hundred documents refuting this assertion. I must not be put in a position where I receive reports that smother this proof. There is so much evidence that I am astonished by it. Has somebody put together a document saying that there is an organisation of Croats and referencing the evidence supporting it?'

'Senator, I can only repeat, that is what we are doing and we will have that document for you later this afternoon.'

'That only begs the question as to what ASIO has been doing about this threat until now.'

As Murphy relentlessly pursued this line of questioning the director seemed to be drawing on his meagre cricketing skills, playing a dead bat to every ball. It would be typical of the silly fool, thought Behm, to imagine himself putting in a gritty innings for the team.

Jack Behm didn't bother with metaphors. Barbour was quite simply a coward who had quailed under Murphy's bullying. His predecessor, Colonel Spry, would have sent Murphy packing and demanded an audience with the prime minister. Spry would have barred the doors to the Commonwealth Police in the first place. He would never have allowed it to get to this point.

Inspector Harry Harper, for his part, sank deeper and deeper into his chair, not only from exhaustion but also from embarrassment for his own disciplined force. It had become clear to him that this whole mad odyssey had misfired.

The smoking gun memo had turned out to be a fizzer, a damp cracker. The charge of deception had been thrown out. The memo was essentially the work of one relatively junior officer, rather than a direction from the top; in fact, it seemed unlikely the director himself had even seen it before today. If ASIO had been protecting Croatian terrorists or running them as agents, the evidence of that would now have been buried so deep that it would never resurface.

In pursuit of phantasms, Murphy had alienated his own security service. When details of the raid became more widely known, he would almost certainly have made enemies at the highest levels of US intelligence. And for what? The clock ticking down in Harper's head told him he had eighty-four hours before Prime Minister Bijedic touched down in Canberra—and they were no closer to finding the would-be assassin.

Harper was going through this depressing checklist when Price passed him a note from Al Sharp. He unfolded it surreptitiously and read:

Get us out of here, boss!!

30.

Marin Katich followed strict procedure and rang his father at the agreed time from the designated phone box in the rotation. He knew the home phone was intermittently tapped—Ivo was usually tipped off when that was the case—but the practice in recent years was to assume that the tap was always in. Secure communication was critical, so Marin had a schedule of times and phone boxes that his father had the numbers for. The first call in the rotation was at 8 am from the designated box, the second at 11 am from a different phone, the third at 1 pm. This was the third time he had rung, so his father would be waiting by his phone for fifteen minutes every day from 1 pm. It was shortly after that time now. Marin let the line ring three times and hung up.

He stood in the phone box with the receiver to his ear and his finger on the disconnect button. Anyone wishing to use the phone would assume he was on a long call. It would take some time for his father to get to one of his designated boxes. Marin's jaw was clenched hard and he felt the familiar griping, nervous tension in his stomach that reminded him of sitting in the changing room moments before running out on to the football pitch.

He had no desire to speak to his father and, if it were not for the fact that he needed the Brotherhood's network, he would not be doing this. If anything, his feelings about Ivo had hardened. They had festered in his solitude as he dwelled on his father's past lies and manipulations, slowly working back through time. In Bosnia, his mother had finally been able to give him, one by one, the missing pieces of the jigsaw. But none of this altered his determination to avenge Petar's death. His brother's murderers must pay in blood and he intended to ensure they paid dearly. Bijedic would have to satisfy the butchers' bill.

This was now Marin Katich's single obsession. Fate had led him to an inflection point: the hawk was above him.

The phone rang and he lifted his finger to take the call.

'Marin?'

'Yes.'

'What is it?'

'I need the locksmith here tonight.'

'I can make it happen. What is mission?'

'I need to break into a house and find a set of keys, and he will need to make copies of those keys so that I can return them.'

'What are keys for?'

'You don't need to know that. Send the locksmith to the meeting place. I will be waiting for him from 11 pm.'

'He will be there.'

'One other thing.'

'Tell me.'

'The newspapers are saying there will be a big demonstration against Bijedic outside Parliament House on Tuesday. If that is so the police will take him around to the Senate entrance on the other side and all this will be for nothing.'

'I thought of this already. I was about to tell you we are moving demonstration, bringing forward to Sunday. This, the police have requested. So we are being good citizen.'

'Good,' said Marin. 'You must make sure that any stray demonstrators who come on Tuesday morning go to the Senate entrance. Then they will be forced to bring Bijedic to the front door.'

'I will organise small protest outside Senate.'

'Good. Unless there's an emergency the next contact will be an 8 am call.'

'Yes . . . Marin?'

'What?'

'My son . . .'

'I have nothing more to say to you.'

Marin Katich hung up. He left the phone box, put his hands on his knees and threw up on the nature strip.

Anna Rosen got to Tullamarine Airport well ahead of her flight. During the long wait in St Kilda Road she had roughed out a story narrative from what she knew, along with the little she learned from her call to Arthur Gietzelt. The senator had been cagey at first, but he finally gave her some strong quotes, backing Murphy's ministerial authority to visit ASIO and holding the Organisation to account for withholding from him—or distorting—vital intelligence.

Shortly before 1 pm Murphy and his team had left ASIO Headquarters, departing from the underground car park in two vehicles. They didn't stop to make a statement of any kind, nor did anyone from ASIO.

Anna picked up her boarding pass and headed to the bar, where she found Bruce McKillop nursing a beer. The prime minister, he explained, had gone on to an event at Geelong, where he intended to stay the night. Like her, McKillop had been called back to Canberra to work on tomorrow's coverage of the Murphy raid.

He was annoyed at the decision. 'I've got fuck-all to add to this,' he said morosely. 'Maybe I could have got something out of Whitlam tonight.'

'What happened at the Press Club?'

'Gough made a perfectly boring stump speech. Labor had a mandate to change the country. This is what they'd done, this is what they planned to do. *Blah, blah, blah*. He must have thought it was a receptive audience because the place was absolutely packed. Then he asked for questions and ninety people jumped up. "What was Murphy doing in St Kilda Road?" Whitlam said, "I've got no idea what you're talking about." I saw him look across at Eric Walsh, and Walsh just shrugged his shoulders.'

'Christ,' said Anna. 'So, it's true, Murphy did this without warning the PM.'

McKillop threw up two hands in a gesture of amazement. 'Gough's a good actor, but no one's that good. He didn't have a clue. After the event I overheard Walsh saying that he was being sent back to Canberra to shut this down.'

'I spoke to Arthur Gietzelt this morning,' said Anna. 'He didn't tell me much, but one thing's for sure: he certainly knew about this in advance.'

'So Murphy told his mates in the left, but he didn't bother telling Whitlam. That's a fucking joke.'

'What's Whitlam doing in Geelong?'

McKillop laughed. 'That's another joke. He's got a dinner at the Geelong footy club. They're making him the Number One ticket holder.'

'He's got a political crisis breaking and he's doing that?'

'No crisis is bigger than footy.'

'That won't be true by tomorrow.'

'I did get one quote from Eric Walsh, but I think it was off the record. He said: "Gough wouldn't even know what sort of racquet to hit a football with."'

Anna was still laughing when she saw Al Sharp enter the bar with the three plain-clothes policemen she recognised from this morning's raiding party. Sharp saw her at once and gave an almost imperceptible shake of his head. *Not now, we don't know each other*, it said. They found a table away from the bar, and the straight-backed, hard-faced fellow she took to be their senior officer went to the bar and bought a round of drinks.

Inspector Harper carried four beers back on a tray. He plonked the tray on the table, spilling the overfilled glasses.

'Most ungracious waiter I've ever seen,' said Sharp.

'That's what beer mats are for,' Harper replied, flipping one over to Sharp.

'And that's exactly what we are,' grumbled Price cryptically.

'The hell you on about, Wal?' said Ray Sullivan.

'Murphy's beer mats, we are,' said Price. 'Soaking up his fucken mess.'

Sharp laughed and raised his glass. 'To the mighty beer mats!' he said, and they clinked glasses.

'You keep that notebook of yours safe, Wally,' Sharp continued. 'That's contemporaneous history, that is.'

'Yep,' said Sullivan. 'None of the ASIO blokes were taking notes.'

'That conference room was probably miked up to the yin yang,' said Price. 'They'll be transcribing it right now, to send on to Langley.'

'Shut it down, boys,' said Harper. 'That's enough loose talk. We're going to be carrying this day around like an albatross for the rest of our lives. Every crazy thing we say will end up as part of the mythology. Al's right about those notes, Wal. That's the true history of this. But first we worry about Bijedic. Then we write up a full report for the higher-ups. And then we shut up about this.'

Price couldn't suppress a derisive laugh. 'Try that in front of a Senate Committee,' he said.

'We write it up and it'll be the commissioner who fronts any committee,' said Harper. 'That's how it works. You got more to say about this? Say it to me. Because, if we all start telling tales about what happened in there today, we'll never hear the end of it. You got me?'

Price blinked, took a drink of beer and started rolling a cigarette. He turned to Ray Sullivan. 'Who do you like in the pre-season?'

'Manly and Saints, I reckon.'

Anna watched the policemen do their toast. She would have given her right arm for a seat at that table—or even for a place within earshot.

She tuned out when McKillop moved on to his usual list of grievances against Paul Barton. The bureau chief, he was certain, had no respect for him. She decided to go for a walk and wandered along the line of storefronts until she found a chemist, where she was buying a packet of Disprin when a familiar voice came from over her shoulder: 'The b-b-boyfriend giving you a headache?'

She spun around to face Tom Moriarty.

'You really need to get some squeaky shoes or something,' she said. 'You'll give me a heart attack.'

'Come over here a m-minute, will you? I n-n-need some advice on hair products.'

Moriarty led her to the back of the chemist, behind the high shelves.

'What the hell happened in there today?' Anna demanded. 'I can't get anyone to talk.'

'Our flight's b-boarding in a few m-minutes,' said Moriarty, handing her a slip of paper. 'Call me on this n-number later. I've joined M-M-Murphy's staff.'

'What? Has ASIO sacked you?'

'No, n-nothing like that. It's a k-kind of s-s-secondment.'

'What was that thing with your briefcase this morning? Handing it over to Murphy?'

'Look, that's why I c-c-came to f-find you now. You c-can't write about that. Okay?'

'That was one of the strangest things I've seen—why wouldn't I write about it?'

Moriarty's eyes narrowed; he took her by the shoulders and leaned in close. 'Because it'll f-f-fuck everything up if you d-do, and I'll n-never talk to you again.'

'Hands off,' she said, and he dropped them to his sides.

'C-Call me and I'll give you p-p-plenty to write about tonight,' he said. 'Just not that.'

George Negus stood beside the white Commonwealth car on the tarmac at Sydney Airport, waiting for Lionel Murphy's flight to land. He was pissed off with Murphy for leaving him out of this. That is to say he was publicly ropeable, but privately relieved he wouldn't have to wear the consequences. At least he was off the hook with the media.

He could honestly say he didn't know what had gone on at St Kilda Road. Had he been asked for his advice ahead of the event, he would have told Lionel: *Don't do it, you mad bastard!* Sure, that was 20/20 hindsight, but you didn't have to be a political brain surgeon to see there was no proverbial light at the end of this tunnel.

Negus had been in Sydney for a long weekend, but there were plenty of journos who had his Balmain number, and calls had started coming through by mid-morning. That was how he'd first heard of the ASIO escapade.

Then came a call from Daphne Newman at the office. She sounded uncharacteristically rattled. 'George, I can't find the attorney-general,' she said. 'I don't know where he is.'

'Can't help you there, Daphne. But when you find him, tell him to give me a call.'

A few hours later the phone had rung and it was Lionel, all breezy and ironic. 'Where were you, George? You missed all the fun.'

That's rich, thought Negus. 'Well, you might have warned me.'

'Things got their own momentum last night,' said Murphy. 'I don't have much time. I'm flying up to Sydney, on the TAA flight at 3 pm. Can you be there? There'll be a Comcar and a police escort to take me to Ingrid.'

Negus had been surprised. He'd thought Ingrid was bunkered down in Canberra for the last weeks of her pregnancy.

'I'll be there,' he said. 'Ingrid got herself to Sydney, did she?'

'Protective services brought her to Darling Point. She's under police protection . . .'

'What?'

'We've had some death threats, George. I'll explain when I get there. Maureen's coordinating transport; you should give her a call.'

Negus had sat in his kitchen and made a series of calls. First to the office, where Maureen gave him the news that Murphy had taken her along on a midnight visit to ASIO's Canberra offices in the West Portal. By her account Lionel had cross-examined the local ASIO boss, Colin Brown, as if he were a defendant on criminal charges.

That meant that first, the gloves were off, and second, there'd been two ASIO raids. At least the press hadn't got on to the first one yet.

A few more calls and he'd learned that the prime minister was down in Melbourne too. That Whitlam was there on the same day as the raid meant he'd obviously known nothing about it. Not good. Apparently Gough had sent Eric Walsh back to Canberra to staunch the blood. Walsh was still en route, so who on Whitlam's staff was doing damage control in the meantime? Negus soon found out it was the PM's political advisor, Jim Spigelman, but it wasn't until the afternoon that he'd been able to get a call through to Speegers and the news wasn't good.

The public servants had their knickers in a knot. Murphy's own department head, Clarrie Harders, had first heard of the raid when journalists started calling him in the morning. A meeting of police and security men was split down the middle as to whether to cancel the Bijedic tour, with the pessimists arguing Murphy had damaged security for the visit.

To top it off, Bob Ellicott, the solicitor-general, was now looking into whether the raid was illegal and what offences Murphy might have committed. Bloody Ellicott! The man was a diehard Liberal and the cousin of another diehard Liberal, the chief justice of the High Court, Garfield Frigging Barwick. That was all they needed—entrenched conservatives destabilising them from the inside.

When he saw the plane touch down, Negus climbed out of the car. He was anxious about the meeting, worried about the bond of trust between himself and Murphy. He still couldn't get over the fact that both the boss and Milte had kept him in the dark. He was going to have to deal with that sooner rather than later.

A single policeman held back a large jostling media pack, bristling with cameras and microphones behind the terminal gates. They were anxious because there was still time to feed footage into the evening news bulletins. Negus knew this was just a taste of what was to come.

The raid on ASIO had been the most radical move so far by the new government and there was no question there'd be political damage. Murphy had overturned the chessboard when the government was in a dominant position. He'd scattered pieces all over the place and now it was time to put them back. The trouble was that no one would ever agree on how the board was set before he'd done it. All the careful plays they'd made had been lost. They'd have to go back and start the game again.

When the plane finally came to a stop, stairs were rolled up to it. Lionel Murphy was out first. The two cars moved to the foot of the stairs. Negus looked over to the media pack and saw two photographers push through the barrier.

'We've got to move, Senator!' he called.

With the first two snappers already sprinting across the tarmac, there was a mass breakout of TV crews and reporters. Murphy was quickly hustled into the back of the car as the first of them arrived but Negus was caught outside the vehicle.

'The attorney-general will not be making a statement at this time,' he said to the phalanx of cameras. As he climbed into the car he noticed Ian Leslie from Channel 0 News.

'Senator Murphy, why'd you raid ASIO?' the reporter called.

Negus slammed the door shut, but he realised he'd forgotten to wind up the window.

When Leslie stuck a microphone through the opening as the car began to move, Negus yelled at him: 'Ian, I'll wind the window up on your hand if you do that!'

As he withdrew his hand from the rapidly closing window, Leslie let go of the microphone and left it dangling inside, tapping on the glass. Ahead of them the police driver hit his siren and the pack scattered. As the Comcar accelerated into the gap, Negus saw that the microphone was still attached by a long cord to a cameraman who was now running alongside, screaming at them.

'Stop!' called Negus as the cameraman fell back. The fellow was either going to have to let go of his precious equipment or get dragged along like a man tied behind a horse in an old Western. At the last second the driver hit the brakes. Negus unwound the window and threw out the microphone, and the car took off, illuminated by the multiple camera flashes.

Lionel Murphy watched through the back window as the media pack receded into the distance, before turning back to Negus. 'I thought that went very well,' he said, pushing his ruffled hair behind his ears. 'It's good to have you back, George.'

It was 11 pm when the locksmith parked his van, as directed by Marin Katich, across the road from a plain house in a quiet street in Yarralumla. Marin had followed Barbara Dunning here to her home one afternoon after she had shown a group through the carillon. She lived in a modest three-bedroom cottage with a well-tended garden in one of the suburb's less fashionable streets.

Over three days he had followed her from a distance. At the island, he'd observed her through his binoculars as she locked up the carillon's entrances and then dropped the bunch of keys into her handbag. While watching her house he had gauged her habits and got a read on her life. He stole some of her mail, steamed it open and discovered that she was a widow. Her husband had worked in the Treasury Department. She had no mortgage and lived modestly on the spousal pension she inherited when he died. It appeared that Barbara was childless. She had a Persian cat she lavished affection on, but mercifully no dogs or lovers. She got four pints of milk delivered each week and he assumed the cat drank most of that. There had been no visitors to her home over those three nights, and Marin had watched all the lights go out in the half-hour period between 9.45 and 10.15 pm. Each morning at 6.30 am she took a walk to the lake.

Her social life revolved around St John's Church in the nearby parish, and she seemed to be close to the vicar and his wife. She played the organ there on Sunday and practised twice a week. And, of course, there was her volunteer work at the carillon two days a week, which must have seemed wildly exotic when she first began learning to play the bells.

He had no reason to think that she would change her habits on a Friday night, and so he had met the locksmith at the agreed location and driven to Yarralumla in the man's covered van. The locksmith's name was Ante Jurjevic. He was no relation to the merchant seaman Marjan Jurjevic in Melbourne, the devoted enemy of Marin's father.

'I have everything we need to make a new set of keys,' Jurjevic told him. 'I only need the originals for a short time to make duplicates.'

When they arrived, Marin saw that he had been wrong to make assumptions about Barbara Dunning. A car was parked in her driveway. The lights were still on in her living room and he heard faint music through the closed windows. He told the locksmith to stay put, pulled on a balaclava and crept into the front yard. He crawled through the garden bed to a large hibiscus below the window and peered inside.

The blinds were drawn, but through a gap at the bottom he saw two figures gently writhing on the couch. Barbara's skirt was hiked up to her waist. A pair of hands moved inside her knickers, gripping her arse. There was a bottle of whisky and two glasses on the coffee table. The cat was stretched out on the back of the red couch, licking its paws. A soprano sang in German. A Bach cantata, he wasn't sure which one. As the two figures shifted position, pulling apart for a moment to look at each other, Marin recognised the vicar's wife.

Some time elapsed before the music stopped and he heard the arm on the turntable retract. Barbara stood up from the couch, bending to kiss her lover. She went to the sideboard, flipped the record and set it going again. Marin noticed her black handbag on the sideboard.

Barbara pulled the vicar's wife gently to her feet and embraced her. Pulling apart to murmur something in her lover's ear, she took her by the hand and led her from the room. The cat followed them a moment later.

Marin moved in the shadows to the back of the house, where he found the door unlocked. Once inside, he heard the sounds of love-making and moved quickly to the living room. The carillon keys were in the black handbag.

He left the house swiftly, pulled off the balaclava and found the locksmith dozing in the van. He opened the door and shook the man's shoulder.

'I have them,' he said.

They climbed into the back of the van and Jurjevic tugged a dark curtain across the driver's compartment before switching on a small working light. He worked fast, carefully matching each key to one of his large stock of brass blanks and applying his skill to filing perfect duplicates.

'The lights are still on,' Jurjevic said as he worked. 'Can you get these back safely?'

'They will be busy for some time.'

Jurjevic paused, a sly expression distorting his plain face.

'I should have brought the camera,' he said. 'We could make a little money on the side.'

Marin stared at the man but gave nothing away. Of course it

made sense that the locksmith would have a side business in black-mail. He suppressed the impulse to throttle the rodent.

Jurjevic bent to his work without another word; it took him twenty minutes. He threaded the duplicates on to a ring and handed them over.

'Wait here,' said Marin.

He was back in the kitchen when he heard the bedroom door open and bare feet pad into it. He moved silently into the living room as the kitchen light went on. The vicar's wife, her back to him, naked and vulnerable, poured a glass of water at the sink.

'Bring the whisky, darling!' Barbara called from the bedroom.

Marin heard the light get switched off in the kitchen. He crept ahead of the woman, sliding past the partly open door to the main bedroom and into the kitchen where he heard the woman padding down the corridor behind him, the bottle and glasses clinking in her hands.

'Come back to bed,' said Barbara, as the woman entered the bedroom and pushed the door shut with her foot.

Marin's heart was thumping. He moved fast, replaced the keys and left the house.

Anna filed her story on the raid for the first edition well ahead of the 11 pm deadline. Barton read the copy and congratulated her. It was a first-hand account, crisply written and full of material he hadn't seen anywhere else.

Tom Moriarty had come through for her in the end, with vivid detail of the events inside ASIO Headquarters. She was still upset at the compromise she'd been forced to make, though, which meant she left out the story of how he had handed over his brief-case to Murphy. She would definitely come back to that. There were secrets within this story that she was determined to get to the bottom of.

'Great work, Anna. This will be front page for sure,' said Barton. 'Did you see those late pictures of Murphy dodging the press at Sydney Airport?'

'I did. George Negus was with him, but he wasn't in Melbourne.'

'I know, that's really strange,' said Barton. 'Why did Murphy go to Sydney?'

'His wife Ingrid was moved down there this morning and put under police protection.'

'That's not in your story.'

'She's heavily pregnant. Due to give birth any time now. I thought it was enough to say they'd received death threats. Why tell the enemy where she is?'

'Just put in a par near the end saying that his pregnant wife is under police protection at an undisclosed location.'

'If you insist, Paul, but—'

'It's part of the story, Anna. Nothing like this has ever happened before.'

She went back to her desk, rolled a cigarette and smoked it as she added the extra par.

Olney had already gone on to Friday drinks. McKillop and Tennant were finishing a joint story on the political fallout from the raid.

'You coming for a beer?' McKillop asked her.

'I'm pretty buggered, Bruce,' she said. 'I was up at 5.30. I've got to get some sleep.'

Anna headed back to her room at The Wellington. As she climbed between the fresh sheets and pulled up the covers, she recalled the saying about falling asleep as soon as your head hits the pillow. It was her last conscious thought before it happened to her.

31.

Marin Katich approached The Wellington Hotel from the unlit gardens to its south-east. It was close to 2 am and the place was quiet; there was no activity in the forecourt. He scaled the single-storey annexe and paused to get his bearings in the moonlight. Then he crept around the concrete edges to avoid the loose gravel laid on its roof.

At the main building, he climbed into one of the front-facing balconies. He moved stealthily to the other side of it, climbed around into the next one and then repeated the action until he was in the dark landing of the last balcony. He went to the pair of doors and found they were open.

He crept over to the bed in the centre of the room and looked down at the sleeping figure. He bent over the bed and whispered, 'Anna.'

She stirred and he spoke again, a little louder. 'Anna, wake up.'

She was startled awake by a blinding light, red then white as the bedside lamp came on. She felt herself clamped to the bed, her head pushed back into the pillow by a hand pressed over her mouth. Her heart was thumping. Over the top of the hand, she saw him with a finger pressed to his lips.

'Don't shout,' he said.

Anna's eyes widened, full of disbelief. Could it really be him? She must be dreaming.

'It's me,' said Marin. 'It is. I'm so sorry to have scared you. It was the only way. I'm going to take my hand away now, okay?'

Anna nodded.

The moment he released her, she sat up with a flurry of movement. She punched him as hard as she could in the side of the face. He reeled back as she struck again and again. Then she was up on her knees in such a fury that she knocked him backwards on to the bed.

He didn't resist her as he lay there, except to block the worst of the blows aimed at his face, his chest and arms. He covered his face with his forearms until her blows began to subside. Then she pulled his arms apart and cried into his face. 'How dare you! How fucking *dare* you!'

'I'm sorry, Anna. I'm so sorry.'

She was kneeling over him, both hands on his ribs. He flinched in pain as she pressed down on the fractures, but she didn't notice. Her own body was heaving as tears spilled out and ran down her cheeks, dripping on to his chest.

Finally she slumped against him, quietly weeping, her head buried in his neck. She could feel the drumbeat of his pulse against her cheek. After a while he wrapped his arms around her and they lay there, clinging to each other.

Then her hips began moving in a slow rhythm, and he responded.

'This won't work. I can't lie here with you, Marin,' said Anna, removing herself from his embrace. 'We have to talk, and we can't do it in bed.'

TONY JONES

She threw off the sheet and got up. Suddenly conscious of her nakedness, she pulled on jeans and a T-shirt. Marin climbed out the other side, retrieved his clothes from the floor and dressed himself without a word.

Anna sat on a chair, pulled her legs up to her chest and held on to them. Marin took the chair opposite her and she began.

'Why did you leave me?'

'I had no choice.'

'Don't tell me that.'

'It's the truth, Anna.'

'Not one word from you in two and a half years. That's a choice.'

'I had to let you get on with your life. I couldn't be with you anymore. I was given no choice. That was taken away from me.'

'And from me!'

'From both of us.'

'Except that you know why and I don't have a clue. I woke up in hospital and you were gone. Disappeared without a word. Do you know what that feels like? You talk about truth. You owe me the truth, Marin.'

'I did something that day that put me in their debt.'

'What did you do?'

'I can't tell you. They had me by the throat—'

'Who are you talking about?'

'—They still do.'

'Who are they?'

'The sort of people that you can't talk about . . .'

'Fucking spies?'

'I can't say any more.'

'Then why the hell are you here? Why did you come?'

'You know why.'

'One last fuck—'

'Don't!'

'—before you go and destroy your life forever?'

'Anna, it's not like that. There's not a single day—'

'What? Not a day you don't think of me?' She laughed derisively. 'Do you really expect me to believe that, Marin? Is that meant to be some sort of consolation?'

Marin dropped his head, bringing both hands up to his face. 'It's all the things I never got the chance to tell you,' he said quietly. 'I go over and over it in my head. And now I'm here, I can barely come up with the words.'

'You can make love, but you can't talk?'

'You felt the connection the same as I did. It's still there.'

'So what? It's just a fantasy, Marin—there won't be any connection at all if you go ahead with whatever crazy plan you've come up with.'

Marin stared at her for a time before answering. 'They murdered my brother, Anna.'

'What?'

'They killed Petar. They kidnapped him and they killed him.'

She stared at him in disbelief, but a shiver of fear ran through her.

'Who are you talking about?' she asked quietly.

'UDBA murderers. On orders from Belgrade.'

'I met up with Petar at your place near Eden. He was a heroin addict and an alcoholic. I saw him almost kill himself, Marin. He had the rifle under his chin. How do you know he didn't go ahead and do it?'

Marin shook his head. She saw it then in his eyes.

'Petar was tortured, Anna. He was tortured, horribly tortured. God only knows for how long, and then they executed him.'

Anna was so shocked she could barely comprehend what he had said. She reached for her tobacco and rolled a cigarette, to give herself time to think. When she was done, she lit the smoke and drew on it to steady herself.

'What proof do you have?' she asked at last.

'The two killers, they told me what they did to Petar. They were proud of it. They boasted about it. They thought it was funny that he called out my name over and over. They had nothing to lose, because they were about to do the same thing to me . . .'

'What? How did you—'

'I escaped from them, don't ask me how.'

'What about them? Where are they? Have you told the police?'

When Marin responded, his voice was cold and emotionless. 'They've paid for their crimes.'

Anna jumped to her feet, an involuntary movement.

'Does that mean what I think?' she demanded.

'Anna, these men strung me up by my hands and beat me senseless. They took me out, deep into the bush. They were going to kill me, exactly as they killed Petar.'

'You killed them?'

'I'm still alive. They were on a mission, I told you, under orders from Belgrade. It's not a game. The life I was dragged into—it's nothing you can imagine.'

Anna was in no mood to accept a rationale for whatever he planned to do. She was sickened by his story; it was a primitive tale of blood and revenge.

She had just made love to this man. She believed she still loved him. But did she really know him? What had he done? How much blood was already on his hands? She had no idea how much it had stained his soul.

'Please sit down,' he said. After a moment she did, again drawing her legs up to her chest. She felt absurdly like a child, an innocent in a violent world.

'I can't even begin to understand the violence in your life, Marin,' she said. 'But I don't want any part of it. My mother's whole family was murdered, and your own father was on the side of the murderers. You know that now, don't you? That knowledge is what drove your brother into madness. He told me as much when I met him.'

'You know Petar was a harmless boy. Those men tortured him and, while they did it, he was crying out my name. Then they blew his brains out. I can't live with that knowledge. This was all about Bijedic coming to Australia. They were sending a message in blood. I was meant to be part of that message. Do you really think I should turn the other cheek?'

Anna felt nauseated; she thought she might throw up. Tears spilled on to her cheeks.

'This is just one horror after another,' she said, struggling now to control her quavering voice. 'The Petar I met was a weak and damaged person. I'm trying to tell you where that sickness came from, Marin. After I saw him, I went to meet your father. I felt I had to tell him that his son needed help, that he was suicidal. I was alone with Ivo for only a short time, and yet he made me fear for my life. Do you know what he called me?'

'I didn't even know you'd met him.'

'*A dirty Jewish whore.* I told him things he didn't want to hear. I told him how sick Petar was, how damaged he was, how lonely—and that was your father's response? *You're a dirty Jewish whore!*'

Marin lowered his head into his hands again and, when he lifted it up, she saw despair in his face.

'I met my mother when I was in Bosnia . . . I finally found her after all these years, and she told me her version of my father's story. Anna, I know what he is, I know it now!' he said with sudden passion. 'Look, when you told me just now what he called you, those disgusting words . . . It felt like my blood was boiling. It made me want to throttle the life out of him! Please, don't look at me like that.'

'Like what?'

'Like you see something of him in me.'

'I don't. It's just . . .'

'I'm sorry, I didn't mean to upset you. I'm trying to be honest.'

'Your father has poisoned everything. Now Petar is dead, and all you can think of is some bloody act of revenge.'

'This has nothing to do with my father. Nothing. Ivo and I are finished.'

Anna drew on the last of her cigarette. She found herself longing for something stronger.

'Marin, I need to tell you something,' she said. Then she stopped, as if the words had caught in her throat. She looked down at her hands, full of uncertainty.

'What is it?'

'I don't even know if there's any point in telling you.'

'You've started now.'

She gathered herself and began again. 'I think you know that I was badly beaten by the police at the last Moratorium rally. After being unconscious for a time, I was hospitalised for a week. My father publicly claimed that I had been targeted because I was his daughter.

'Anyhow, they did all sorts of tests on me when I was in hospital. After what happened, they were worried I might have internal injuries. One morning a doctor came in to see me and told me I was pregnant. I can still remember his face. He had good news. He told me not to worry. He told me the baby was safe. That was your baby he was talking about, Marin.'

Marin slumped in his chair. The vitality that enlivened his every action suddenly seemed to have drained away. He found he could barely ask the question. 'What happened?'

'What do you think happened? I waited. I even reached out to your father for the first time, but he refused to talk to me. I waited as long as I could, Marin. But you had disappeared into thin air . . .'

Marin got up slowly and came to her, moving like a sleepwalker. She saw that his face was racked with grief. His father, his brother, his future—they were all gone. He knelt on the ground before her. He put his arms around her, his head in her lap.

Anna held his heaving body. He was sobbing like a child.

Then the door burst open.

A man with a gun ran into the room and Marin sprang to his feet. The gun was pointed at Marin's chest, but it was not steady. The man was drunk.

'Don't move, Marin!' he yelled.

'Moriarty!' Anna cried. 'What are you—'

'Shut up, Anna, stay out of this. You sit back down, Marin. N-nice and quiet.'

'Get the fuck out of my room!'

'Oh, Anna,' he said. 'C-come on, p-p-please.'

Moriarty sat down heavily on the edge of the bed and kept the wavering gun trained on Marin.

'Shut the d-door, Anna,' he said. 'You're in n-no position to argue. Harbouring a f-f-fugitive.'

'He's not a fugitive, as far as I know,' she said. But all the same, she got up and closed the door.

'This is the day of the f-fucken J-jackal, and your boyfriend here is the fucken J-j-jackal.'

'You're drunk, Tom,' said Marin. 'You don't know what you're saying.'

'Now, now,' said Moriarty. He looked at the unmade bed, pulled up the sheet and sniffed at it with a lecherous smile. 'You kids had t-time for a little f-f-fun before Uncle Tom came home, did you?'

Anna dismissed him with a disgusted shake of her head, but there was something she still didn't understand.

'How is it that you know each other?' she asked.

'We're old f-f-friends, Anna, enough said.'

Moriarty got up and walked unsteadily over to the bar fridge. He knelt with care, uncertain of his balance, keeping the gun trained on Marin as best he could. He pulled from the fridge a handful of miniatures and checked his watch.

'We've got a few m-minutes. Time for a last d-d-drink.'

He handed a gin bottle to Anna and she set it down.

'A few minutes until what?'

''Til my fellas arrive.'

'If you're planning to arrest me, what's the charge?' Marin asked.

'Conspiracy to commit acts of t-t-terrorism, for starters,' said Moriarty. 'We'll think of something to k-keep you behind b-b-bars, at least until Bijedic is safely out of the c-c-country.' Moriarty continued his scrutiny of the mini-bar. 'No *slivovic*, Marin, how about plain old b-b-brandy? I'll have the Scotch.' He tossed the little bottle to Marin and unscrewed the lid on his.

The moment Moriarty put it to his mouth, Marin was in motion. He threw the brandy bottle back at Moriarty's head as hard as he could, cracking him between the eyes.

'Marin, don't!' Anna shouted.

But he was already on his feet. He took two steps towards Moriarty. He pinned the man's gun hand down, but Moriarty managed to squeeze off a shot. The explosion was deafening in the still night.

Marin drove his forehead into Moriaty's face. The spy reeled, made a convulsive effort to get up and fell back on the bed, unconscious.

Marin then heard car doors slamming, men shouting. He ran to the window and saw two men running towards the hotel entrance. Moriarty's reinforcements had arrived. He looked at Anna, who was still frozen in her chair.

'I have to go,' he said.

He stepped out on to the balcony. The moment he saw the men beneath him rush inside the hotel, he climbed over the railing and crabbed fast along the front of the building, one balcony after another, back the way he had come.

He jumped down on to the annexe's roof and ran across the gravel, careless of the noise. He heard shouting behind him, but he didn't stop. He leapt to the ground and sprinted into the darkness.

Anna was still sitting in the chair when the door flew open and two armed men rushed into her room. One, a rangy, wolfish type, took in the scene and ran through the open door to the balcony, peering either way over the edge of the railing, pointing his pistol and shouting, 'Stop! Stop or I'll fire!'

The other man was overweight, red-faced and breathing hard. He holstered his weapon and leaned over the prone body on the bed. His first thought was that Moriarty had been shot, but he couldn't see a wound. He rolled him over. Nothing. He shook Moriarty's shoulders, undid his tie and fetched water and a towel.

The wolfish man came back inside.

'No bullet wounds,' said the fat man. 'Not that I can see. What happened out there?'

'He's gone. We've got Buckley's chance of catching him.' He then turned to Anna, as if noticing her for the first time. 'Who fired the fucken shot?'

'He did,' she said, pointing at the still unconscious Moriarty. 'There was a fight and his gun went off.'

The wolfish one turned back to his companion. 'What do you want to do?'

'That'd be up to Tom,' said the fat man. 'But he's out for the count.'

The whisky bottle had leaked its remaining contents on to the bedsheets. The fat man picked it up, sniffed it and put it on the bedside table.

Anna heard sounds in the corridor. A man in a dressing gown appeared in the doorway, but stopped when he saw the activity around what looked to him like a dead man on the bed. He stared suspiciously at the two men bent over the body and the young woman in the chair.

'Is everything all right?' he asked. 'Should I call the police?'

'We are the police,' said the fat man, moving to block the man's entry. He produced a warrant card from his breast pocket. He and his colleague, Anna would later discover, were detectives from the ACT Police.

'But what happened here?'

'Please go back to your room, sir,' said the fat detective. 'This is a police matter. There's nothing to see.'

He closed the door in the man's face and turned an accusing gaze on Anna. 'What the fuck happened here?'

'I told you,' she said. 'There was a fight. Moriarty came off second best.'

When the other detective splashed water on to Moriarty's face, the body stirred at last—still alive—spluttering, groaning on the bed. The fat man continued his interrogation.

'Who are you?'

'Anna Rosen, I'm a journalist.'

'How did that fellow come to be in your room?'

'Do you mean him?' she asked, indicating Moriarty, who was being helped into a sitting position. 'He broke in, uninvited.'

'Don't be smart,' said the fat detective, standing over her now in a clumsy attempt at intimidation. 'I mean the bloke who did the runner.'

'He's a contact of mine. I told you I'm a journalist. He came to talk to me. Woke me up.'

The fat one leered at her. 'Is that all?'

Anna stared at him with contempt. 'It's none of your business.'

'Don't tell me what my business is, missy.'

'*Missy?*' echoed Anna. 'Really? Do you have a warrant to be in my room?'

He didn't answer, but she saw doubt spread across his face.

'Do you have an arrest warrant for the man who was here?' she persisted.

No answer.

'Do you even know his name?'

'Don't t-t-talk to her,' said Tom Moriarty. He struggled to his feet, swayed, then collapsed back on to the bed.

'We better get him to hospital,' said the other detective. 'He might have cracked his skull.'

The fat one picked up Moriarty's pistol, turned it over in his hands—some kind of foreign job. He put on the safety and pocketed it without a word. He and his partner hoisted the spy to his feet and half-walked, half-carried him from the room.

Anna followed them to the door and watched as they hauled Moriarty down the corridor. They looked, for all the world, like two mates helping a drunken friend to bed.

TONY JONES

She shut the door and bolted it. She felt a debilitating lethargy come over her, as she'd seen in accident victims when their bodies shut down. She climbed, exhausted, back into the bed, still in her clothes. She switched off the light and pulled the covers over herself protectively. The sheets smelled of sex and cheap whisky.

The flesh-and-blood Marin Katich—his green eyes, the hard planes of his body, his soft insistent voice, his delicate touch— had dissolved again into a shadow, disappearing into the night. A would-be assassin; there could be no doubt of that now. He had said as much, hadn't he? The tears for his brother had been unfeigned, and so too his fierce anger. She thought about Petar and the incomprehensible idea that he had been tortured to death.

Her imagination conjured up the young man's ravaged body, sticky with blood. The air above his lifeless remains speckled with moving black dots—a humming cloud of bush flies that hovered low over him, before descending in ones and twos to crawl into his wounds to lay their eggs. And all around this terrible scene there arose the throbbing song of the countless cicadas hidden in the trees, the very pulse of the bush, rising and falling and rising again, until it became the deafening sound of oblivion.

Anna was woken at dawn by the discordant, keening cries of currawongs. Nature itself was in mourning. Marin was lost to her, lost to the history of violence that was his birthright. It had lurked in his body like cancerous cells until they found a reason to multiply. She felt resentment and a hard core of anger. He had come to say goodbye, as if she were a loose end that needed tying up. When she began to weep it was with a bitter grief.

Eventually she roused herself. It was not over. She imagined Tom Moriarty rising, concussed, from his hospital bed, to gather up his henchmen and return to interrogate her. Recalling how the spy had forced his way in and the timing of his arrival, she began a methodical search of her room. She pulled apart the bedside lamps, dragged off the mattress, examined the base and both ends of the bed, pulled the pictures off the wall, checked the backs of the furniture—and every nook and cranny she could think of.

She found it in the overhead light. The bug was concealed in the shade with a thin, dark wire running up to the ceiling inside the metal tube that held the central power cable. She cut the microphone off with a pair of nail scissors and put it in her pocket.

She imagined Moriarty sitting in a nearby room with a bottle of whisky, a set of headphones clamped over his ears, the spools on the tape recorder revolving slowly as he listened to them fucking. She packed a bag, left the hotel by the rear entrance and found the ute waiting for her with its usual ironic grin.

Somewhere along the highway that tracked the escarpment's edge above the parched plain of Lake George, a big storm came surging up the valley. She saw it coming in the distance, behind Governors Hill. It seemed to have brewed up out of nothing. The sky above her was blue and cloudless, and the same to the west; but over Governors Hill it boiled dark as doomsday and began to spit lightning into the dry earth.

Anna could have outrun it, but instead she pulled off the road, climbed out of the car and stood on the escarpment watching it come. It began with large drops drumming the tarp at the back of the ute and tapping her head like an impatient hand. Then it descended fast in a torrent, whipping and buffeting her with cold winds.

A lightning strike rent the sky in front of her, a jagged branch of electricity, merciless and elemental, searching for something or someone to earth itself on. *Go on! Take me!* she wanted to scream. *Take me!*

Anna stood there shivering, her teeth chattering as the storm swept over her. When it passed to the west and left her alive, she did not feel cleansed but emptied. She got back into the car and drove on.

32.

On Saturday morning, 17 March, the Commonwealth Police Bijedic team, still exhausted from the long hours they'd pulled accompanying the attorney-general on his ASIO raid, gathered at headquarters for a briefing from Inspector Harry Harper. Several of them were damp and bedraggled, having been caught outdoors by the fierce storm that had swept through the capital.

'Morning, Wal, you look like a drowned rat,' said Harper when Price entered the squad room.

Wally Price pulled a soggy ruin from his pocket to confirm the extent of the storm's damage.

'Yeah, caught in the bloody downpour. It soaked through a whole pack of smokes.'

'Take a seat,' said Harper. 'I'll duck out and organise a pot of tea.'

Sergeant Ray Sullivan and Al Sharp were already in the room.

'You get any sleep, Wal?' asked Sullivan.

Price threw the cigarettes in a bin and hung his wet jacket on the back of a chair.

'Yeah, I was knackered,' he said. 'Woke up to a nice morning.

Made the usual mistake of walking here and ended up in a fucken tempest.'

Al Sharp looked up at him. 'Are you not moved, Wal,' he intoned, 'when all the sway of the earth shakes like a thing infirm?'

Price stared at him, wondering if he had a screw loose. 'The fuck you say?'

'It's *Julius Caesar*, boofhead.'

'Oh, shit, and I left my annotated copy behind.'

Harper returned with a large pile of documents. 'This is all the research you'll need for today, Wal,' he said, taking up a bundle of telexes. 'This is what's accumulated in the past twenty-four hours. If anything, the threats are multiplying. We've got a shitload of reports to go through, and then I've got to write a brief for the commissioner for his meeting with the prime minister this afternoon.'

'I heard that Peter Barbour's coming up from Melbourne today to meet Whitlam,' said Sullivan. 'Is he going to make a formal complaint about our role in the raid?'

'That's beyond my pay grade, Raymond,' said Harper. 'We've just got to concentrate on keeping Bijedic safe. So, listen carefully.' The inspector picked up the top telex and began. 'Last night a bomb exploded in the Department of Supply Light Transport Depot at Woolloomooloo. It went off next to the Rolls-Royce, which was to be used to transport Bijedic during the visit.'

'Jesus wept!' cried Price.

'It was a small device and there was only superficial damage,' Harper explained. 'But there's speculation they might have been trying to plant it in the car.'

'Suspects?' asked Sharp.

'Nothing specific on that, and nothing we can do about it. It just underlines that there are people ready to have a crack.

That's Sydney. From Melbourne, we've got a report from one of our own people'—he looked down and read—'Constable Brian Devitt tells us that one Ivan Pavlovic, aged thirty-six, of North Melbourne, someone he's known for quite a while, has told him, quote: "I am going to Canberra in my car, I have a gun too and will kill the bastard myself for coming to Australia to make trouble for Croatians." Unquote.'

'I know that name, Pavlovic,' said Sharp. 'He's HOP, isn't he? Croatian Liberation Movement.'

'He is, and intel from informants, confirmed by his own statements, indicates he was a member of the group that has been planning to go to Spain this year, for the purpose of training for a further armed incursion into Yugoslavia.'

'His own fucken statements,' said Price, unable to conceal his contempt. 'He wants to be stopped. He's like a bloke looking for his mates to hold him back from rushing into a brawl.'

'I'm inclined to agree, Wal,' said Harper. 'This fellow's a housepainter with four kids, but we've had to put him under 24-hour surveillance. He's planning to drive to Canberra today for tomorrow's Croatian demo at Parliament House. He's the registered owner of a rifle so we'll have to stop him and search his car en route, and we need to find out where he's staying here. Keep him on edge and keep him quiet. Wal, I'm going to leave that to you and Ray. You'll liaise with Melbourne.'

'Okay, boss,' said Price, taking the telex.

'They pulled the demo forward to Sunday?' said Sullivan. 'I missed that.'

'Yes. Sorry, Ray—you've had a lot on your plate. The community finally listened to reason and cancelled their plans for a demo when Bijedic is here. That would have been a security nightmare. They've brought it forward to tomorrow. So there'll be an influx of angry

Croats coming to town today and tomorrow morning, and we need to keep track of the dangerous ones.'

Sharp interrupted. 'We've had a team putting together a list of houses in the local Croat community where people might be put up,' he said. 'It's a big list, I'm afraid.'

'And we can't follow everyone or raid every house,' said Harper. 'Our target list will concentrate on known militants, and especially those our informants are pointing us to.' Harper pulled up a fresh telex and continued. 'In that category is another Melbourne resident with family here. Blaz Kavran is a name familiar to most of us. He's also been overheard threatening to shoot Bijedic during the visit.'

'I know him, all right,' said Sharp. 'He was meant to have taken part in the Bosnian incursion last June, but he was arrested on another matter. He missed the whole thing because he was in jail.'

'That's him,' said Harper. 'And like Pavlovic, he has been named as one of the group of nine who are planning to go to Spain to train for another incursion this year. He's also under surveillance and he's headed for Canberra. Another one for you, Wal.'

Harper handed the telex to Price.

'We're going to be stretched thin, boss,' said Price.

'The whole of the ACT Police are at our disposal, along with elements from the army and air force. This was always going to be difficult; we can't lock down the whole city, but we can't ignore specific targets.'

'Any more of them?' asked Sullivan.

'Even without Bijedic we estimate there'll be more than two thousand Croatians here for tomorrow's demo.' Harper paused to hand the last two telexes to Sharp. 'Al, you're going to have to work with Mr Price's team. We need a complete roster of surveillance ops finished today and we need to respond to new threats as they arise. If anyone gets anything new, from whatever source, come straight to me. We'll do a triage and allocate resources where we need them most.'

As if on cue the tea lady came rattling in and they gathered around as she poured cups for each of them.

33.

At 3.30 the following morning, Al Sharp and his team were outside a Canberra house where the Melbourne housepainter Ivan Pavlovic and his family were sleeping. Pavlovic had been fool enough to boast of his intention to assassinate Prime Minister Bijedic. Now he was subject to targeted harassment. The previous day his Pontiac had been stopped and searched en route to Canberra, his family forced to sit on the roadside for two hours while police pulled the vehicle apart and riffled through their belongings.

'This is the police, open up!' shouted Sharp.

He bashed on the front door with his fist until he woke the house. When the sleepy-eyed owner, one Franjo Till, cracked open the door, Sharp demanded to know if Ivan Pavlovic was inside. Pavlovic, his family and their hosts were soon ushered out on to the driveway while the house was searched. The suspect's wife, Barbara, repeatedly shouted at Sharp: 'It is only in communist countries you can expect something like this.'

Nothing was found in the Till house, nor in any of the other residences raided that night.

By 8 am on Sunday, the day of the planned Croat demonstration in Canberra, the Bijedic team had reconvened at police headquarters. On his desk the exhausted Al Sharp found a telex that jolted him like a shot of adrenalin. It was from the NSW Police Electronics Unit, the same team he had worked with after the Sydney Town Hall bombing: Nigel Daltrey and Bob McCafferty.

The Unit had been engaged to tap the home phone of Ivo Katich, the secretive leader of the Croatian Revolutionary Brotherhood. None of the intercepted calls to and from the house had produced anything useful. It was obvious that both Katich and his callers assumed that the phone was tapped. Nonetheless, McCafferty had noticed a series of unanswered phone calls to the house, during which Katich's phone had been left to ring, on different days at different times. On the first occasion it had rung once and stopped; then twice on the second occasion; then three times on the third. On the fourth occasion the phone rang once again.

McCafferty suspected there was a pattern to the calls. His assumption was that someone was contacting Ivo Katich with a prearranged signal at prearranged times. He assumed that the caller was using public phones and that Ivo Katich, alerted by the message, would go to a public phone himself to call one of a sequence of numbers in his possession.

McCafferty had not been able to establish the phone box numbers of the incoming calls—they did not register if left unanswered. But he recommended, on the basis of his theory, that Commonwealth Police urgently re-establish 24-hour physical surveillance of Ivo Katich. If they could at least track him to a public phone, they could check the outgoing logs on that phone and find the location of the public phone at the other end.

After months without a single breakthrough, Sharp felt a surge of excitement. His lower back gave an alarming twinge as he leapt to his feet and ran to Harper's office.

'Boss, we may have something!' he yelled.

Harper looked up from the reports he'd received on the overnight raids and saw his rotund colleague, leaning against the doorframe, a hand pressed to his lower back, as if to support its crumbling superstructure.

'I'm not working you too hard, am I, mate?' asked Harper.

Sharp winced as he sat down opposite the inspector.

'These raids are just for show,' he said. 'But they take time and effort, and stretch us thin. I've got something here from the Electronics Unit that looks like real intelligence.' He handed Harper the telex from McCafferty. 'But we're going to have to act fast.'

Within thirty minutes Harper had pulled every string he had at his disposal and dispatched a surveillance team to the Katich house in the Sydney suburb of Leichhardt. Safe in the knowledge that they were securely in place at 9.30 am, Sharp went back to his office. Alongside the intelligence reports on his desk, he found a series of written phone messages sent in from the switchboard operators. There were four of them, each with the same message: *'Urgent, please call Anna Rosen'*. The messages included a number in Sydney he didn't recognise.

Sharp picked up his phone and dialled. Anna answered after two rings. Wherever she was, she was clearly sitting next to the phone, waiting for him to call back. He soon found out why.

For the next twenty minutes he took notes, stopping from time to time to clarify some puzzling point. *Tom Moriarty, you say? With a gun? And who were these armed men?*

Anna's story about the murder of Petar Katich was shocking, but he was inclined to believe it since it fitted with his own knowledge of the young man's unexplained disappearance and the dried blood on his mattress. The information that young Marin Katich had returned to Australia as the only survivor of the Bosnian incursion, and that he very likely had competence in the use of weapons, sent a chill all the way down his aching spine.

When Anna had finished, Sharp double-checked a few facts, told her that she had done the right thing, and hung up. The story was improbable but also totally believable. It fitted McCafferty's theory about Ivo Katich's coded communications. Perhaps they had got lucky—or perhaps they were too late.

Al Sharp rose gingerly from his desk and hurried to tell Harper that, despite all the false trails they had been forced to follow, he now believed he knew the identity of codename Cicada.

At 10 am, as thousands of Croats began arriving for the demonstration at Parliament House, a call was placed from the capital to the Sydney home of Ivo Katich. Not far from the Katich house, sitting in the smoke-filled rear cabin of a surveillance van disguised as a PMG maintenance vehicle, Nigel Daltrey pressed the record buttons on two tape recorders.

'Incoming call,' he said to his elegantly dressed companion, and she extinguished a cigarette whose harsh-flavoured Bosnian tobacco made her yearn for Sarajevo. Dusanka Andric, the Serbo–Croat translator attached to the police Electronics Unit, slipped on her headphones and wrinkled her brow as she listened. As always, the sound of Ivo Katich's voice—so intimate, so close in her head—triggered a wave of revulsion.

'His caller, a Croat man, is talk about raids last night on houses of Croat peoples in Canberra,' she said to Daltrey as she scribbled shorthand in her notepad. 'Many raids, he says, in middle of night. Is like back in Yugoslavia, like the communists. They hit homes in which are staying one Pavlovic, Ivan; one Kavran, Blaz; and others, too. Katich says these are bastards who do this, ones who fuck their own mothers; he is very angry. He is worried, too, I think. I have not heard this in his voice before. He has hung up now. He has cut call short and hung up.'

Daltrey picked up a walkie-talkie and spoke into it urgently. 'Mad Dog One to Mad Dog Two.'

The thing screeched in his hand like a cockatoo.

'Mad Dog Two receiving. Over.'

'Something's happening,' said Daltrey, clearly enunciating the words into the mouthpiece. 'Be alert. He just got some bad news. He may be on the move soon. Over.'

'Roger . . . Roger. We're ready. Over.'

Five minutes later the Mad Dog Two surveillance team watched Ivo Katich leave his house in a hurry. He locked the front door, pulled on a coat and strode to the big sedan in the driveway. He backed out fast, almost side-swiping a telephone pole at the edge of his drive, then accelerated down the street. The rear end slipped and slid as the wheels fought for traction.

Two cars tailed him, leaving from different locations. A third car was circling the neighbourhood ready to join the pursuit.

Katich drove only a few kilometres, stopping next to a phone box close to a public school. The nearest team pulled over to watch him from a discreet distance. The other cars took up positions out of sight at either end of the street.

Through binoculars, Katich was observed entering the phone box. He was seen to place a call and then hang up, holding down the disconnect button while keeping the receiver to his ear.

'Mad Dog Two to Mad Dog One. Over.'

In the surveillance van, Daltrey grabbed the handset again. 'Mad Dog One, receiving.'

Daltrey quickly jotted down the address of the Katich phone box as it was relayed to him. Then, crouching, he manoeuvred around Dusanka and out the back door. 'Hold the fort!' he called to her. 'Won't be long.'

Next to the van was a PMG tent, and Daltrey stepped quickly inside it and took up the phone set he'd rigged to the maintenance box. He dialled a number, which was quickly answered by Bob McCafferty, who had been waiting at the PMG main exchange.

'You were right, Bob,' said Daltrey. 'You're a dead-set fucken genius.'

'The address, Nigel, quickly!' said McCafferty.

Daltrey gave it to him.

'Got to go,' said McCafferty. He hung up and turned to the PMG technician waiting next to him. 'Mate, here's the address of the phone box,' he told the man. 'We need to find that number and put a tap on it as soon as possible. Lives are at stake, so no fiddle-arsing about.'

The man said nothing. He just looked at the address and began leafing through the directory of public phones. He'd soon found it and led McCafferty through the maze of alleys in the exchange. Each one had vast banks of wires and connections, incomprehensible to anyone except the small priesthood of techs for whom the whole system, mapped and laid out in precise order, could be interpreted by numbers such as the one in his hand.

It took time—an excruciatingly long time—for McCafferty, who could imagine Ivo Katich in the phone box, gazing out on to the empty playground of the public school next to him. Then the tap was in and McCafferty had the headphones on, and heard two men talking down the line.

'. . . there's no time, you must go,' said the first voice.

'I know. I'm going. You may not hear from me again.'

'Marin.'

'Don't say it.'

'God will guide your hand.'

'You know that's bullshit, don't you?'

'Put faith in him.'

'I don't have faith in anyone or anything. I'm gone.'

The phone hung up.

McCafferty slammed his fist on a box of wires. 'Fuck! Fuck!' he yelled. 'So close.'

'Did they say anything at all?' asked the curious technician.

'Something,' said McCafferty. 'We got something. But only if we can find the bloke he was talking to.' He pulled off the headphones and turned to the man. 'Can you get the last outgoing numbers dialled from that phone?'

'I can do it,' the man said. 'But it'll take some time.'

'How long?' said McCafferty. 'Time is what we're running out of.'

'Half an hour, maybe less if we get lucky.'

McCafferty clapped him on the shoulder. 'Get going then,' he said. 'God will guide your hand.'

Marin Katich moved swiftly through the house, gathering up his belongings. There weren't many of them—he had been ready to move, even before his father rang using the emergency code.

The rifle, cleaned and oiled, required the most attention. He took time to wrap it and pack it in its case. Then he stowed it in the boot of the car.

The woman over the road looked up at him as she watered the garden. He gave her a wave and stepped back inside for the remainder of his gear. The biggest danger was that she would be able to give a description of the car, but he was prepared for that.

Another vehicle was parked four blocks away on a quiet street. He would have to get there quickly.

He went from room to room, looking for anything he might have left behind, anything that might betray his intention. The last thing he took was the plastic bag full of rubbish. The place was clean. He threw the rubbish into the back seat, nodded to the woman still watering her garden, and climbed into the car.

He drove away sedately, past two men further down the street in adjacent houses, both mowing their lawns. He slowed down, lest he leave the impression of flight, even if he did have to fight down that sensation in his body.

A short distance away he parked under a tree and swapped cars. Again, he took everything with him and left the first vehicle as clean as he could. His fingerprints were everywhere, of course; he wiped down the obvious surfaces in the car, just as he had in the house, but he knew he would miss some.

As he drove the new car slowly along the street, Marin heard a posse of vehicles moving fast through the quiet suburb, their highly tuned engines roaring, their wheels squealing as they took corners too fast. He hoped there were no children playing on the road.

As he reached the stop sign, the posse—four large, black sedans, moving at high speed and packed with men—passed in front of him in a blur. When they had gone, he turned his car in the opposite direction and drove fast from the neighbourhood. As he did so, he imagined the woman with her garden hose and the men crouched over their lawnmowers looking up in shock as their quiet Sunday morning was interrupted by the fast-moving motorcade, the sudden screech of brakes, and the armed men leaping out even before they had rolled to a stop.

*

Harper and Sharp walked through the empty house.

'Turns out it's owned by a local Croat,' said Sharp. 'His wife's Australian and the property is in her name, so it never turned up on any of our lists. We're trying to locate the owners, but it seems they're on an overseas holiday. The woman over the road has given us a description of the man who stayed here for the past week. Tall, athletic, olive complexion. Dark hair, she thinks, but he was wearing sunglasses and a floppy hat each time she saw him. She saw him coming and going a few times. He drove a green Toyota sedan—no idea of the numberplate. She never spoke to him.'

'Now he's in the wind he'll probably ditch the car,' said Harper, shaking his head. 'Anything at all from Forensics?'

'A few partial fingerprints so far,' said Sharp. 'Looks like the place has been wiped clean. One weird thing, though: the dressing table in the bedroom is really untidy. There are open make-up bottles and powder compacts and used sponges all over the place. Maybe he's been disguising himself.'

'What as? A very tall, athletic *woman*?'

'I'm just saying that it's weird.'

'It also looks like a dead end,' said Harper. 'We've put out an alert for the green Toyota. I agree that Katich the younger is now a serious suspect, but the last picture we have of him was when he was fifteen years old. Of the thousands of Croat demonstrators outside Parliament House right now, maybe half of them match the neighbour's description. Meanwhile he's not our only worry. During the night, someone broke into a sporting goods store in Queanbeyan and stole three rifles and five hundred rounds of ammunition. This morning the NSW Police picked up another bloke in Goulburn. In his car, they found a rifle they say was set up to take a silencer, along with 150 rounds of ammo. He was on his way to the demo which, thank Christ, sounds like it's peaceful and well organised.'

'I still think Marin is the one we're after,' said Sharp. 'McCafferty says old man Katich was telling him to get the hell out of here. Told him God would guide his hand.'

'We're pulling Ivo Katich in, for what it's worth,' said Harper. 'He'll say nothing.'

'I told you Anna Rosen's story,' said Sharp. 'It all points to Marin Katich.'

Harper frowned. 'Anna Rosen is a journalist, Al,' he said. 'I've also got Malcolm Brown from the *Sydney Morning Herald* passing on info about plans to kill the attorney-general. Some fellow told him Murphy is as good as dead, that he'll be killed before the next sitting of parliament. Channel 9 has passed on info that someone's planning to hijack a light aircraft in Melbourne and use it to make a kamikaze attack on Bijedic.'

'I know Rosen,' said Sharp. 'She's been investigating the Katich family for a long time.'

'Look, I'm not saying she's leading us on a wild goose chase. There's something very odd about the set-up here. Bring her in for questioning, if you really think she's got more to tell us.'

Sharp nodded. He intended to keep Anna close. At least she would be able to recognise Marin Katich in a crowd. There was another wild card, of course—Tom Moriarty—but so far he'd been unable to locate the elusive spy.

Marin Katich's back-up vehicle was a well-maintained, hardy-looking Holden sedan. He was pleased with its ruggedness since he intended to go bush until the eve of Bijedic's arrival. There was a remote place he knew well, forty miles away, in the Brindabella Ranges. He had planned to go there anyway to test fire the rifle.

An hour's drive took him past the Cotter Dam before he wound up on the narrow road into an alpine region. Tall stands of ghost gums hugging tight to the roadside gave way to wide vistas of low, folded ranges one after the other in humped lines of drab green and khaki. Nothing, he thought, could be more different to the alpine mountains around Radusa where so many had died.

He left the sealed road, turning on to a rough dirt track ironically known as Gentle Annie's Trail. It led deep into the mountains and then down to the valley floor where he nursed the car across the shallows of the Goodradigbee River at several crossing points before following Flea Creek, one of its thin tributaries, to the flat place on its banks that he remembered. There he found two other cars and the families who had driven there to picnic by the creek. He wasn't concerned: it was Sunday afternoon and they would head off with plenty of time before dark. They paid no heed to him as he set up his small tent and crawled inside to rest.

Despite the noise of the children playing, Marin was exhausted and soon fell asleep. He had erected the tent under a tree in the shade, but as the sun moved beyond its apex it beat down on the western side, and it became hotter and hotter inside. In its stifling confines he sweated like a man who had fallen asleep in a sauna. The relentless sun cast his dreams in a red glow and he entered a kind of delirium in which he heard the sound of a boy playing alone by the creek, muttering to himself as children do, and then crying out with delight as he threw rocks into the water.

'Daddy! Daddy, where are you?'

The tent flap flew open and there was the boy staring in at him. A face he knew in his soul. Marin woke and sat up gasping for air. His clothes were drenched, his heart beat savagely, and he was overcome by a profound sadness.

*

Marin hauled himself out of the tent and found the families had gone. He knelt at the edge of the creek and splashed water on to his face and the back of his neck. Faint echoes of the boy's voice were still inside his head. The child's face was imprinted on his memory.

He rose and fetched the rifle, hoisting it over his shoulder, and headed off deeper into the bush. Soon he found an open space, wide enough for him to pace out nine hundred yards and place a target and a red flag on a ridgeline.

For nearly two hours, until the light began to dwindle, he made his calculations, calibrated the fine instruments on the rifle and shot at the target until he had satisfied himself that he was as well prepared as he could be.

34.

When four men in blue overalls arrived at 8 on the Monday morning, 19 March, Daphne Newman was there to let them into Lionel Murphy's office. She detained the foreman as his men began hauling in the heavy panes of bulletproof glass from the corridor.

'How long do you expect this to take?'

'Should only take a few hours, love,' he said. 'We'll do his office first, then your windows in here.'

Daphne was surprised; she had never considered herself a possible target. 'Really? Is that necessary?'

The man laughed. 'We can't just be protecting the bigwigs now,' he said. 'Anyway, you wouldn't want a sniper picking him off while he was having a chat in here with the girls, would you?'

'Heavens no!' said Daphne.

She had a momentary vision of Lionel Murphy pitching forward on her desk in a spreading pool of blood. Daphne remembered how Jackie Kennedy had picked pieces of her husband's skull off the boot of the black limo. She was so distracted that her usually infallible radar failed to pick up advance signals from the attorney-general.

Murphy arrived with George Negus, both of them fresh off the early flight from Sydney. They appeared behind two men carrying one of the heavy glass panes.

'Oh,' cried Murphy. 'I'd forgotten all about this.'

'What have I missed?' said Negus.

'They're building us a bullet-proof bunker, George,' said Murphy. 'Same thing for the PM's office. He feels we're at war with the terrorists. Gough'll think he's Winston Churchill. Morning, Daphne, Maureen . . . Enough tea for two more?'

'Of course, Senator,' said Maureen.

Daphne took a call as Murphy sipped his tea.

'They're in my home today, George,' he said. 'Fortifying it against an attack. They're putting a panic button in each room. It's all a bit scary. I'm worried how Ingrid will take it when she comes back with the baby.'

'She's a toughie, isn't she?'

'It's the maternal instinct, George. Imagine putting a baby to sleep in a bullet-proof nursery with its own panic button.'

'Maybe it'll quiet down after tomorrow,' said Negus. 'When Bijedic has gone.'

Daphne put down the phone and interrupted them. 'Senator,' she said. 'That was the PM's office. Mr Whitlam wants to know if you can come around for a meeting.'

'When?'

'Right now, if you can.'

Murphy put down his teacup, pushed the wayward hair behind his ears and buttoned his coat. 'Tell them I'm on my way, please, Daphne. Do me a favour, George, will you? It's Tom Moriarty's first day and I won't be here. Will you do the welcomes?'

*

When the attorney had gone, Negus took his tea into the adjacent office, where Murphy's other advisors had desks. Kerry Milte was on the phone, evidently getting a police briefing. He looked up, saw Negus and nodded.

Negus sat nearby and flicked through newspapers he'd already read. One thing he hadn't resolved yet was whether Murphy would agree to an interview on *TDT*. If only it wasn't that difficult bugger, Richard Carleton, he'd be a bit more sanguine about it. Murphy had fobbed him off when he put it to him this morning, but he hadn't done an interview since the raid and Carleton wasn't going away.

'Well, here's a s-s-sight for sore eyes!'

Negus heard the familiar voice and looked up to see Tom Moriarty wearing a pair of dark sunglasses that didn't quite manage to hide his swollen nose.

'The nation's t-tax dollars at work,' said Moriarty. 'The p-pointy tip of the spear.'

'Fuck off, Tom,' said Negus.

'And t-top of the morning to you, George.'

'Have you really left ASIO? I thought you were part of the furniture.'

'It's called a secondment, George. The Organisation's still paying my salary. I'm now a c-c-clerk Class 8 attached to the attorney-general for the d-duration.'

'They cancel your licence to kill, then?'

'It's m-merely suspended,' said Moriarty. 'I could still k-kill you in ten different ways just using the items on your d-desk.'

'Mate, you could probably bore me to death just by reading that newspaper out loud,' said Negus, throwing a copy of *The Australian* in the bin and climbing to his feet. 'The attorney's off at a meeting with the PM. I've got to go up and see some folks at the

ABC bureau.' He shook Moriarty's hand. 'Lionel said to say g'day so . . . g'day.'

Kerry Milte hung up the phone and stood, waiting for Negus to leave. 'We need to talk, Tom,' he said. 'That was Al Sharp. He says Ivo Katich's son is here in Canberra on a mission for his old man. There are multiple threats, but he's now their main target.'

'His name is M-Marin. Marin Katich.'

'Sharp reckons you know all about him.'

'I know he's hiding out here in the city,' said Moriarty. 'But it's not a m-m-mission for his father. It's revenge. He believes UDBA m-murdered his little brother.'

'What happened to your face, Tom?'

'I ran into a d-d-door.'

'Looks nasty. Nothing to do with this Marin Katich, I suppose?' asked Milte, giving Moriarty the interrogation-room stare. 'He one of ASIO's little helpers, is he?'

'I tried and f-failed to get my hands on him. Best to leave it to the c-c-coppers now. They're onto him and they've got the r-resources— the only ones who do. Now look, K-Kerry, that's a big problem, but you and M-Murphy have a b-bigger one.'

'What are you talking about?'

'The CIA's gone b-ballistic mate, that's what.'

'How do you know this?'

'I'm still t-talking to the D-G of ASIO, that's how,' said Moriarty.

'What? I thought you said they wanted your scalp.'

'Yeah, Jack B-Behm and the hardliners would put me up against the wall if they c-could. But Peter Barbour's no f-fool. He needs a c-conduit to Murphy, and M-Murphy needs a conduit to him.'

'So you're going to play both sides against the middle?'

Moriarty held up his hands, long enough for Milte to see the tremors.

'Settle down, Kerry,' he said. 'I imagine you've heard of James J-Jesus Angleton?'

'CIA's chief of Counter-Intelligence.'

'The very one!' cried Moriarty. 'The g-grey eminence, the ultimate C-Company man. Well, James J-Jesus himself has been on the b-blower to Barbour. He's got one m-message. Australia's new socialist m-masters, led by M-Murphy and Whitlam, are d-dangerous cowboys. The raid has sent him b-bonkers. He reckons that M-Murphy has tried to d-destroy the "delicate m-mechanism of internal security"—his words—the delicate mechanism that's been p-p-patiently built up since World War Two. Are you getting this, Kerry? He says the Labor P-Party can no longer be trusted with the c-crown jewels of US intelligence and he's threatening to c-cut off all contact with ASIO.'

'But that's insane!' cried Milte. 'What the fuck does he think happened down there?'

'All Angleton knows is that a s-socialist attorney-general sent in the c-coppers and raided his own security agency. You can tell him it's about C-Croats 'til you're b-blue in the face—he doesn't see the n-nuance.'

'Fuck.'

'Yeah, f-fuck,' said Moriarty. 'Now imagine the p-pressure that's gonna come down on the PM. Whitlam might hold the line for a while, k-keep backing M-Murph, but eventually he'll c-cave in. M-mark my words. My advice to you, and to M-Murph . . . This is going to get ugly. You need to c-cover your arse, mate.'

While Murphy was tied up in his meeting with the prime minister, Kerry Milte went to Commonwealth Police Headquarters to get a full briefing from Harper and Sharp. Throughout the day he tried to get an appointment with the attorney-general, but Murphy, after his morning meeting with Whitlam, spent the day flitting from one political ally to another.

Based on Tom Moriarty's intel on the CIA's anger and the growing backlash against the raid, which the US was undoubtedly helping to orchestrate, Milte put two and two together. It added up to shit. He figured that Murphy and Whitlam had done the rounds of the kitchen at their morning meeting; that the PM was indeed rattled by James Jesus Angleton's rabid response and was on the verge of pulling the rug out from under his attorney-general.

Milte knew enough about the brutal politics of scandal to know that Lionel Murphy was now busy shoring up his factional support. The best way for Murphy to keep the PM on side was to threaten a civil war within the Labor Party if Whitlam tried to abandon him. Having been blessed with a logical mind, Milte now began calculating his own chances of survival, given his tenuous position as a contracted advisor with no links to the party. If he was a bookmaker, he wouldn't put them higher than fifty-fifty.

Late in the afternoon he got a call from George Negus.

'The attorney's agreed to do a TV interview with the ABC,' he said. 'It'll be in the office. Richard Carleton from *TDT* is coming down with his crew.'

'Is that wise?'

'Lionel needs to get on the front foot, Kerry,' said Negus. 'He wants you there with him.'

When Milte arrived, the interview was already under way. Daphne Newman wouldn't let him go in, so he sat outside. He felt like a naughty schoolboy waiting to see the headmaster.

After some time, the door was flung open and there was Lionel Murphy, beaming at him like the proverbial Cheshire cat.

'Kerry!' he cried. 'Come in, come in.'

'They wouldn't let me in to watch the interview,' said Milte.

'Don't worry about that.'

'But I don't know what you said.'

'Not a problem, Kerry,' said Murphy. 'Mr Carleton here just wants to get some visuals with you in them.'

Richard Carleton's grin was much less benign than Murphy's—more like that of the *Jungle Book* tiger, Shere Khan, Milte thought, continuing the feline theme. Carleton pumped his hand and led him in front of the film camera to where Murphy had now resumed his seat behind the desk.

'Now, Kerry,' said the oleaginous TV man. 'If you'll just stand here behind Lionel, we can get the shot that says everything—since you're the man behind the raid.'

Milte pulled away from Carleton's grip. 'You've got to be nuts!' he cried.

'Come on, Kerry,' said Murphy. 'It's quite painless.'

'Sorry, Senator,' said Milte. 'I prefer an off-camera role.' On that point he was quite insistent.

Eventually, when the crew and their crouching tiger of a journalist had packed up and slunk off, the attorney-general and Kerry Milte were left alone.

Murphy went to the drinks cabinet and poured two large Scotches.

'Have a seat, Kerry,' he said, handing Milte a drink. 'I'm sorry if I made you uncomfortable with the TV crew. Sometimes I forget that we're not all politicians. You know, used to performing on camera.'

'That's all right,' said Milte, sipping the Scotch, a single malt that he was partial to. 'No harm done. I hope you didn't mind me refusing.'

'No,' said Murphy. 'But I was thinking . . .'

'What about?'

'Well, mightn't it be a good idea if you just came out in the press and said the raid was your idea?'

Milte nearly spat out the whisky, good as it was. 'I beg your pardon?'

Murphy paused, then changed tack. 'What are you going to do after all this excitement, Kerry?' he asked mildly. 'Go back to the law, I imagine.'

'That's right.'

'Wonderful,' said Murphy, savouring his whisky. 'I think I loved being a barrister even more than being a politician.'

'There are fewer compromises you have to make,' Milte observed.

'Right, right.' Murphy smiled, as if in his mind he was back at the bar. 'You know, I always wanted to be a judge.'

'Oh, really?'

'Yes. Is that something that would interest you? At some time down the track, of course?'

'I'm not sure what you're getting at, Senator.'

'Nothing at all,' said Murphy. 'It's just that, you know, your long-term interest and mine . . . might line up.'

'Well,' said Milte, 'that's certainly something to think about.'

'It is, Kerry, it is.'

Milte felt distinctly queasy. It was a subtle approach, but he thought he understood what was on offer here. He also knew that if he did take the fall for the raid, the only future job he was likely to get was as a tram conductor.

It was time to go.

35.

When daylight came on Tuesday, 20 March 1973, Marin Katich was already in the heights of the carillon. He was lying flat on his belly on the highest stage of the bell chamber's maintenance gantry. The gantry was on three levels, accessed by steel ladders. It had been built around and over the steel girders that carried the weight of the fifty-five bronze bells that were revealing themselves now in the morning light.

In their dormant state, the bells reminded him of when he was a boy hiding behind the great organ in the Town Hall. He had waited there to be summoned forth to do his father's bidding. Now here he was in another hiding place, this time waiting to do murder. And everyone would assume he was still acting on Ivo's orders.

Marin had lain in the bell chamber, stiff and shivering throughout the long hours of the autumn night. He had come prepared, with thermals beneath his clothes, but as the night grew colder the metal seemed to absorb a deeper chill that reached his bones. Eventually it had become too much for him and he'd climbed to his feet. Risking a fall from the heights, he stretched his arms skyward and paced, back and forth on the steel gantry, guided only by the pale gleam of moonlight, sure-footed as a rigger on his father's beloved Bridge.

Marin would not have slept even if he had been warm and comfortable. He thought obsessively about the details of what he had to do, turning them over and over in his head, but his grim meditation on how best to deliver death to his enemy had inevitably faltered. His mind played tricks on him. He began to see, or rather sense, moving shadows in the moonlight, and when drifting clouds covered the moon and darkness pressed in on him he thought he could hear barely audible whispers.

He imagined the hidden whisperers to be the men he had killed, each of whom he had carried with him, the manifest burdens of his conscience, from the moment of their deaths. Among them were the ghosts of Radusa and the two in Khandalah who had most recently joined their company.

What do you want from me?

He dared them to stop their incessant whispering and reveal themselves, to make themselves known by hitting the clapper of a single bell.

You want to save Bijedic? Ring the fucking bell!

They remained invisible, murmuring in the dark, purposely tormenting him until his surroundings eventually began to clarify in the first light.

With the coming of dawn, a fog had risen from the surface of the lake. If it were to hang in the air, his mission would be over, fatally compromised. But he was not concerned; he had expected a lake fog after such a clear, cold night. It would be a cloudless day and the sun would quickly burn it away.

He watched the lifting fog through the high, vertical vent in front of him. This would be his firing position. It was like an arrow loop in an ancient castle.

Then Marin saw movement on the lake. A lone sculler propelled his blade-like craft through the banks of fog. It must be an eerie, solitary experience for the man—something he himself understood, because he knew he had separated himself from the world by being here; by his intention to do murder.

He was truly alone. He would always be alone from this day on. Even if he managed to escape, the deed would follow him as surely as his ghosts.

Early in the morning on the day of Prime Minister Bijedic's visit, Anna Rosen arrived at the Commonwealth Police Headquarters to meet Al Sharp. It was the first time she had been inside the police building, and the entrance hall, with its high ceilings, polished terrazzo floors and institutional authoritarianism made her feel like a wartime informer, though neither which war nor whose side she was on was quite spelled out by her imagination.

Entering the place, she felt a deep sense of being a traitor. As one of the few people who could recognise Marin Katich, she had reluctantly agreed to spend the day with the police team whose job it was to provide close protection for Bijedic. She reconciled her doubts by telling herself that if Marin saw her in the proximity of his target he might abandon whatever mad plan he had.

At 7 am Anna crossed the hall and presented herself to the uniformed desk sergeant.

'I'm here to see Al Sharp at the Bureau of Criminal Intelligence.'

The sergeant scrutinised her with suspicion. 'Oh, you are, are you?' he asked.

'I am, as I said.'

'Do you have an appointment?'

'I do.'

'Your name?'

'Anna Rosen.'

The sergeant kept his eyes on the young woman as he placed a call to Sharp. She bore the hallmarks of the new breed of women's libbers that threatened his equilibrium—his own equilibrium and that of all other men. The tight, faded jeans; the denim jacket over a black T-shirt; her direct challenging gaze, heedless of authority—all of it bothered him. Unless she was undercover on a drugs operation, she just didn't fit. He wondered what business Al Sharp had with such a woman.

His speculation was cut short by Sharp's arrival and confounded by the warm welcome he offered her.

'Anna, thank you for coming,' he said, shaking her hand and then turning to give the sergeant the appropriate form. 'Sergeant, Miss Rosen will need a temporary pass for the day. It's been authorised by Inspector Harper, as you'll see.'

'Yes, sir,' said the sergeant. He read the form and took note of the signature, then produced an appointment book in which he carefully inscribed her name, the date and the time of her arrival before producing the precious pass. 'Here you are, miss—please sign here and make sure you return this to me at the end of the day.'

Anna signed the book, clipped on her pass and turned to Sharp.

'Deputised to join the posse, am I?' she asked.

'Something like that,' he said. 'Come on, I'll take you to the briefing room.'

As the sergeant watched the odd pair—the pudgy ASIO ring-in and the radical-chic sheila—head for the lifts, he shook his head. These were strange days and he wasn't at all sure he was up for them.

*

Sharp was watching the lights above the lift that charted its descent when Anna tapped his arm. 'So, did you speak to Moriarty?'

The lift arrived and they stepped into it.

'I did,' he said. 'He is telling us that Marin Katich is in Canberra and in his view Katich represents a serious threat—in all likelihood the most serious threat to Bijedic. He also confirmed what you told me: that Marin believes his brother was murdered by UDBA, so he has a personal motive.'

Anna nodded, wondering what else Moriarty may have confided about her own relationship to Marin.

'Did he say why he didn't come to you sooner with this new information?'

'He had a bullshit story about this mysterious "accident" that put him in hospital,' Sharp said as the lift juddered to a stop, pinged and opened. 'He's back on deck now, not that any of us find that especially reassuring. That's why you're here. Let's go meet the team.'

When they stepped into the corridor, Anna stopped him.

'Just so that you know, Al, I've told my editor that I've got access behind the scenes to report on the Bijedic operation.'

'That's your cover story.'

'It's not just a cover story,' she said. 'Whatever happens today, I'll be reporting on it.'

'That's understood,' said Sharp. 'You're about to meet Inspector Harper. He'll want to set some ground rules.'

An hour later Anna was sitting next to Sharp in the back seat of a big black Ford limo in a fast-moving police convoy headed to RAAF base Fairbairn, where the Yugoslavian prime minister's Russian-built Ilyushin jet would touch down later that morning.

The ground rules laid down by Inspector Harry Harper, who turned out to be the same straight-backed copper she'd seen accompanying Murphy on the day of the raid, were simple: no direct quotes from him or any of his team unless she ran them past him first, and she was not to report on the real reason they had asked her to join them. She had reassured Harper that she had no intention of revealing her own cooperation with the manhunt and agreed to his other terms.

Nonetheless, as she watched the familiar Canberra landmarks flashing by on the route Prime Minister Bijedic would take between the airport and Parliament House, she felt uncomfortable with the arrangement, not only because she was ready to finger Marin if she saw him, but also because she was now inside the story, part of it, rather than the impartial observer she was meant to be.

In the front seat Detective Sergeant Wally Price was talking on the two-way radio. She couldn't make out what was being said, but then he leaned over the back and spoke to Sharp.

'Bijedic's gonna be late,' he said. 'His fucken piece of shit Russian plane had mechanical problems in Bangkok—' The bleary-eyed Price stopped mid-sentence and turned to Anna. 'You quote me on that and I'll just deny it.'

'Anna won't be quoting you on anything, Wal,' said Sharp. 'So what's his ETA?'

'Sometime after 11.30.'

She saw uniformed police posted all along the route. Anna had learned at the morning briefing that Commissioner Davis had cancelled leave for the entire force. One thousand police were on duty in the capital, five hundred of them stationed at intervals between the airport and parliament. The commissioner himself had flown over the route in the RAAF helicopter, which was tasked with hovering over the Bijedic motorcade carrying Special Forces sharpshooters.

TONY JONES

The cars in Anna's convoy were the only ones on the road because all private traffic had already been diverted from the route. Sharp pointed out the distant shapes of men posted on the rooftops of adjacent buildings.

'This is an even bigger security operation,' he said, 'than when President Johnson came here in 1966.'

'It'd bloody well want to be,' said Price. 'I was in Sydney when the Vietnam demonstrators threw themselves in front of Johnson's car.'

'Run the bastards over!' said Anna.

'Exactly,' said Price.

'What?' Sharp exclaimed.

'That's what Bob Askin told his driver,' said Anna. 'The premier was in the same motorcade.'

They soon arrived at the RAAF base. Anna saw that many of her colleagues in the press were waiting beside their cars just inside the main gate, while new arrivals in a queue of cars were being stopped to have their credentials scrutinised and their vehicles searched by air force security teams.

The police cars passed into the base and reached a security marshalling area where they stopped and allowed the Bijedic team of plain-clothes detectives to spill out on to the tarmac. Most of them immediately lit up cigarettes and began chatting to the advance party.

Sharp took Anna to one side.

'I want you to go mingle in the press group, just in case he managed to get himself fake credentials,' he said. 'Take a good look at the military personnel in the area, too—and even the police.'

'Okay.'

'I'll take you to the spot where they're corralling the press. That pass you're wearing will get you to where I'll be. Make sure you come back here with plenty of time. Your colleagues, I'm sorry

460

to say, will take more than an hour getting out of here. It's been deliberately set up like that. We don't want them anywhere near the Bijedic motorcade. You're the exception to the rule, of course. We'll be in the last vehicle. So don't get lost.'

Sharp led her through a series of checkpoints manned by armed police with walkie-talkies, stopping to let each one know that Anna was to be let back through at any time. They ended up in an enclosed area on the tarmac. It was empty.

She waited another thirty minutes before the press vehicles began arriving. Then she walked around among her colleagues, feeling rather foolish as she stared at anyone as tall as Marin Katich.

'You all right there?' asked one lofty fellow.

'I'm looking for a friend,' she said.

'Who's the lucky bloke?'

'Don't worry about it.' She moved on to the next vehicle as it drove in.

'Gather round, people!' came an amplified voice. 'Gather round.'

They all turned to the source of the noise and saw a man in an impressive blue officer's uniform with a loudhailer, standing on a wooden bench that two air force subordinates had carried into the enclosure.

As the crowd of disconsolate journalists, their photographers and cameramen gathered haphazardly in front of the bench, the uniformed man—who on closer inspection bore a striking resemblance to the actor David Niven—lifted the loudhailer.

'Good morning to you all,' he said. 'I'm Wing Commander Elton and for all intents and purposes, while you are on my base, I am your commander. I'm sorry about the delays you experienced getting through security, but that was absolutely necessary. We're not doing it in splendour today.'

As he talked, Anna began moving about the small crowd,

looking at as many faces as she could. Most of them, she thought, stared back as if she was deranged.

'The security is very strict and I remind you there are a lot of nervous people carrying guns. Those are the ones you can see. There are also fifty others up in the towers and on top of buildings. They are watching for anything suspicious. So please don't run at any time. Always walk. And when Prime Minister Bijedic arrives, at no point is anyone to go within fifteen feet of him. There are trained sharpshooters who are under orders to shoot first and ask questions later. Remember that and, above all, please enjoy your visit to RAAF base Fairbairn.'

With that the wing commander stepped down from the bench, his subordinates picked it up, and they marched back into the high-security area where none but Anna could follow them.

Eventually a buzz went through the press pack. A photographer with a telephoto lens had spotted an aircraft circling high above them. She looked at her watch. 11.40 am.

In his sniper's nest, high up in the tower of the carillon, Marin Katich had returned to his meditative state. The rifle rested on a sandbag that he had hauled up into the tower. The barrel was aimed through a one-metre square hole he had cut in the steel bird screen on the lake side of the bell chamber. He checked the scope, which was locked off on the front steps and doorway of Parliament House.

The wide staircase and glass entrance doors were shaded under a portico, which was framed by two abutments. Centred atop the left abutment was the British coat of arms—a golden lion rampant and a white unicorn with a twisted golden horn carried the shield between them. Below these beasts was the scrolled motto. The magnification on the scope was strong enough for him to read the words *Dieu et mon droit*—a reference, he recalled, to the divine right of kings.

Rising above the abutment on the right side of the portico was the far more prosaic Australian coat of arms. A kangaroo and an emu, both coloured a uniform grey, held between them a shield on which were emblazoned the emblems of the six states of the Commonwealth.

Conditions were ideal for a long shot. The autumn sky was remarkably clear, as he had predicted it would be, so humidity would not be a problem. The wind across the lake would be classified as light air in sailing terms.

The flag above the front doors of Parliament House, whose pole was equidistant between the two coats of arms, was barely fluttering in the westerly breeze. He used it as a range target, calculating by eye the angle between the flag and its pole. It was no more than sixteen degrees. He divided that number by the constant four and calculated he would have to adjust for a four miles-per-hour breeze. To mark the distance, he lined up the kangaroo's head, which was silhouetted against the sky, in the crosshairs of the reticule. Using that as his target, he made fine adjustments for the breeze.

Then he subtly shifted his gaze and saw the slight movement that indicated the parallax error he knew was inevitable at this distance. Painstakingly, he moved the objective ring on the side of the scope to eliminate the parallax effect. He shifted his gaze again and there was no movement in the reticule. It was spot on.

Marin pulled back down to the shadowed glass doorway with its confusion of reflections when people came and went through the doors or lingered there. Now the doors swung open and a parliamentary official emerged and paced around under the portico. Marin followed the man's movements in the reticule, first targeting his chest and then carefully shifting up to the man's face, which wore the anxious expression of someone whose responsibilities were soon to be tested.

When the Ilyushin jet lined up for its final approach, Anna Rosen, ignoring warning cries from her colleagues, headed for the security gate to the zone marked for authorised personnel only. The armed policeman on the gate tensed, but then relaxed when she flipped out her special pass. The few journalists who were watching her and not the jet were astonished when the policeman stepped aside and let her through.

She reached Al Sharp and his colleagues in time to watch the Yugoslavians' plane hit the runway hard with a crunch of stressed undercarriage and a cloud of burnt rubber. It seemed to have barely slowed when it wheeled abruptly to the left and taxied towards them.

Sharp turned to Anna. 'Nothing to report?'

'No, just the usual suspects,' she said. 'A bunch of pissed-off journalists.'

Sharp shrugged. '*Que sera.*'

'How about that landing?' exclaimed Price. 'I thought the fucken pilot might beat the Croats to it.'

'Probably a former fighter pilot,' said Sharp. 'They like to get up and down quickly.'

With a belligerent roar, the jet rolled fast towards the official party, prompting several of them to take backwards steps, before it pulled up with a shudder. Stairs were pushed up to the front exit. The moment the hatch cracked open, the guard of honour snapped to attention and the military band struck up a martial tune vaguely familiar to Anna.

At the head of the welcoming group at the base of the stairs she saw the dapper figure of the governor-general. Continuing the Hollywood theme, he reminded her of a short, balding Clark Gable. Towering above him on one side was an army general with a peaked hat and fancy epaulettes and, on the other, the splendidly attired wing commander, now without his loudhailer. In the second rank of the official party Anna recognised the Yugoslavian ambassador.

Emerging first from the plane were two large, hard-faced men, both packed into too-small suits, peering about for potential threats. One of the men moved quickly down the stairs and stationed himself at their base, while the other stepped back inside the aircraft.

Sharp prodded Anna's shoulder. 'See the bulge under his arm?' he said, nodding at the man outside. 'We agreed to let them carry weapons. He's got a cannon, by the look of it.'

Moments later there appeared in the doorway a tall, solidly built man with silver hair and a remarkably large head. His eyes were framed by black eyebrows and bisected by a long, beak-like nose. Anna had the impression of an ageing bird of prey. She would have known it was him just from his bearing, but she had also seen photos of Prime Minister Dzemal Bijedic in the newspapers, and they captured him well, including the grim turned-down mouth, which seemed an appropriate expression for greeting a country full of existential threats.

As Prime Minister Bijedic came down the stairs with surprising nimbleness, his team of bodyguards enveloped him from behind. He shook the governor-general's hand briskly, then those of the military men and his own ambassador, who then stepped in behind Bijedic and the general as they moved on to an inspection of the guard of honour.

Anna was close enough to see the expression on the prime minister's face during the nineteen-gun salute, and while Bijedic didn't flinch he did scowl throughout the volley of shots, as if each one were a reminder of his own mortality.

Al Sharp tapped her arm. 'We have to move,' he said, ushering her to the last car in the waiting motorcade.

She heard the roaring turbines of a heavy chopper and turned to see it rise into the air in a whirlwind of dust. It moved nose-down over a stretch of tarmac and she saw the SAS men with their long rifles in the doorway, scanning the ground through telescopic sights. The clattering machine circled low over the sta-tionary convoy as Bijedic was led with his two bodyguards and the Yugoslavian ambassador to the armoured Rolls-Royce, which had already survived one attempt to blow it up.

Marin lifted his binoculars when he heard the helicopter. Then he saw it hovering low over Kings Avenue Bridge, sharpshooters in the open doorway. The convoy came into view, moving at pace on the bridge's tarmac, engines roaring. Four police motorbikes; then two high-powered black limos, packed with armed police; then the armoured Rolls-Royce carrying Bijedic. Behind that was a black van with other members of the prime minister's security detail, then another black limo and four more police motorbikes.

A small group of demonstrators had left the parliamentary fore-court and the convoy swept in to deposit its charge at the front steps. Inside the bell chamber Marin heard the faint whirring of a mechanical device as it came to life. He focused his aim on the uniformed official, whose head was now leaning through the glass doors.

It was midday and the preamble to the Westminster chimes echoed through the tower. *Bom bom bom bom* ... The falling cadence and then the rising ... *Bom bom bom bom.*

Marin blocked out the bells, aware that Bijedic and his party were on their way up the stairs. Through the scope he saw the silhouette of a large man behind the glass door. It opened. The figure emerged and the startlingly familiar face of Prime Minister Gough Whitlam was in the reticule as a target.

Anna burst out of the limo the moment it jerked to a stop. She had seen the front steps of the parliament up ahead and some sixth sense told her she had to get close to Bijedic. If Marin was out there somewhere, she wanted him to see her. She was certain he would come to his senses.

'Get me near Bijedic!' she had cried out to Sharp before throwing the door open. He was momentarily confused, then he leapt out of the other side of the car. Anna was sprinting ahead of him by the time he got around the boot and ran in pursuit of her.

The hour hammer struck the bourdon bell. The first of twelve blows reverberated in the bell chamber and rang across the lake. Marin saw a shock of white hair appear low in the frame of the scope. The top of Bijedic's head climbed into the foreground.

As the door closed behind Whitlam, Marin saw multiple confused reflections in the glass, but he had been expecting that. With each strike of the bell, Bijedic's head rose to fill the scope.

When Anna reached the bottom of the stairs, the Yugoslavian prime minister was halfway up them. She had made it up just three steps before she was hit by a black-suited wall of flesh and bone. A man took her in a bear hug, screaming unrecognisable obscenities in her face. She felt his spittle on her cheeks. She saw his mouth opening and closing, his teeth, his wet tongue, while another man next to him pulled out a pistol from under his jacket.

The breath left her body as powerful arms crushed her chest. Over the man's shoulder she saw Bijedic reach the top and beyond him, in the doorway, the Australian prime minister. She heard a shout and turned to see Sharp, yelling, holding up his police credentials like a shield as he barrelled towards her. Then she passed out.

When the silver-haired man paused at the entrance to greet Whitlam, he became a clear target. Marin let the breath slowly leave his body and the measured strikes on the great bell seemed to align with his heartbeat. Bijedic turned to face Whitlam, smiling even as the bell marked time with mathematical precision on the final moments of his life.

Marin squeezed the trigger to the first position, readying himself to apply the final pressure as the bell was struck. In the sniper's hyper-perception, the periods between the strikes slowed, as if time itself were stretched. Marin felt his heartbeat slow to match the rhythm of the tolling bell.

He saw now with remarkable clarity the man's long face, his liquid brown eyes, his thick black brows, the vertical line between them and the white hair framing the face, shading to darker grey above it. This moment of terrible intimacy with the target was familiar. He saw warmth in the man's smile as Whitlam talked to him.

Then Marin became aware of a disturbance among his ghosts in the bell tower. Petar was with him. They were lying on the beach under a blue sky. Petar climbed to his knees, pointed out at the ocean, then leaned in close.

Marin felt his brother's breath, warm on the side of his face, the salty smell of his skinny brown body, the beads of sweat, the blazing disc of the sun. So hot. So hot. The water in front of them, blue and cool.

What do you want?

He heard Petar's voice in his ear, urgent and clear: 'Don't do it, Marin!'

Petar!

'Don't do it.'

Bijedic moved fractionally in the reticule, chatting to Whitlam like an old friend. Marin made a final adjustment and pulled the trigger.

Tom Moriarty was the only one who saw the muzzle flash. It came from the other side of the lake. A moment later the crack of a rifle shot arrived. It was muffled by the tolling bell, yet he was sure he heard it.

Moriarty was in a lookout on the second-floor landing of Parliament House. From his position he oversaw the forecourt, with the lake beyond it. When the Bijedic motorcade had roared in, he had scanned down to the lake and the buildings in the Parliamentary Triangle.

The flash came from a distant tower. He raised the binoculars fast and focused on the tower on the other shore. It shimmered white in the haze. He grabbed his walkie-talkie. It was on the open channel. There was chatter and he pressed the button on the receiver and cried into it.

'Sniper! Sniper! Sniper!'

The chatter stopped.

'Sniper in the carillon!' Moriarty shouted. There was no sign of a stutter. 'The carillon!'

'Who is that?' Harry Harper's voice.

'Tom Moriarty, Parliament House roof. I saw a muzzle flash, other side of the lake. Get a team to the carillon now! Is Bijedic okay?'

There was a pause, then Harper's voice crackling over the airwaves. 'Bijedic is safe. He's inside the parliament.'

'Thank the f-f-fucking Lord.'

'There's a team moving on the carillon. I'm on my way.'

'I'm c-c-coming.'

Anna Rosen's legs were rubbery when Al Sharp wrestled her away from the implacable Yugoslavian bodyguards. He had waved his credentials in front of them, pointing at Anna and shouting, 'She's police! *Policija!*'

Sharp caught her under her arms when the huge man who had her in a bear hug shrugged and let go before running up the stairs to join the rest of his team, now hurrying into the building after their prime minister.

'You okay?' Sharp asked with concern. When she nodded, his expression hardened. 'What the hell were you playing at?'

She was about to answer when a voice crackled urgently on Sharp's walkie-talkie.

'*Sniper, sniper, sniper.*'

The words revived Anna Rosen as surely as a jolt of electricity. She and the policeman leaned into the speaker to hear the full exchange.

'The carillon!' Sharp exclaimed, staring across to the tower on the other side of the lake. Then he was in motion, running down the stairs to the black limo. Anna stumbled in his wake, willing her legs to work. The driver was standing at the open door and Sharp yelled at him as he threw himself into the front. 'Back over the bridge, fast as you can! It's an emergency.'

Anna had the back door open and was climbing in.

'You're not coming,' Sharp cried. 'Get out!'

'You can't stop me, Al.'

'Like hell I can't.'

The driver paused, hands on the wheel, the limo's engine throbbing.

'I'm part of the team,' she said. 'That was the agreement.'

'I don't have time for this,' said Sharp, turning to the driver. 'Get going.'

Sharp's limo reached Aspen Island just as the first uniformed men were arriving. He flashed his warrant card and they gathered around him like good soldiers. A handful of tourists, curious at the police action, began to drift over from the car park.

'Cordon off the area,' Sharp ordered. 'No one's to cross this bridge.' He pointed to the one officer carrying a weapon. 'What's your name, son?'

'Marsh, sir.'

'Come with me. We're going in.'

Sharp pulled out his revolver and ran across the bridge towards the carillon. He was out of breath when he reached an open door at the base of the largest tower. As he turned back to Marsh he realised that Anna Rosen had followed them across.

'Anna, for God's sake!' he yelled at her. 'You're unbelievable. Stay right here and don't move.'

Then to Marsh: 'Draw your weapon and follow me.'

Anna stared up at the carillon. It was like being at the base of a rocket launch pad. She couldn't quite believe that Marin had chosen a location as surreal as this for his final act. She waited a few beats for the policemen to climb higher into the tower before ducking inside and up the iron staircase. She heard them above her and paused out of sight when they opened a door and went in to check the first level.

'It's clear,' said Marsh. 'No one here.'

'Next level,' said Sharp. 'Stay alert.'

Anna glimpsed the two men creeping up to level two, guns raised in front of them. She was almost at the doorway on that level when she heard Sharp's shout.

'Jesus-fucking-Christ!'

Anna ran up the last few steps and stopped in the doorway to a great triangular space filled with bells of different sizes. There were massive brass objects directly in front of her, serious things heavy with weight and consequence. She looked up to see the two policemen climbing the metal ladders into the heights of the bell tower. Above them she saw what they were headed for. On the top level of the maintenance gantry was the unmistakable shape of a rifle, aimed across the lake at Parliament House, its long barrel supported by a sandbag. Until that moment she had been able to put aside the thought of Marin Katich as an assassin as some kind of bizarre fantasy. Now here it was, for her eyes to see, the instrument of death. A physical jolt of revulsion went through her and she leaned against the doorframe, unable to move. Her ears rang with a terrible and familiar sound, so like a massed, throbbing chorus of cicadas.

'What the hell are you doing here, Rosen?' a voice from behind her boomed into the cavernous space. She turned to see Inspector Harry Harper and behind him Tom Moriarty bounding up the stairs.

'This is a crime scene,' said Harper.

The inspector pushed past her into the bell chamber, followed quickly by the spy. Both of them stopped and looked up to where Al Sharp and Constable Marsh were crouched over the weapon. Sharp turned to look down.

'Anna! For Christ's sake!' he cried. 'You deserve to be locked up for this.'

Harper shook his head and mumbled, 'Bloody journalists.' Then he turned to her and issued a terse order. 'Step outside the room and stay put. I'll deal with you in a minute.'

Moriarty gave Anna his most annoying smile. 'B-b-bad girl,' he said softly as she withdrew to sit on the iron steps.

'This has been fired at least once!' Sharp called from his position, over the rifle. 'We need to search the floor down there for cartridge shells.'

It was Constable Marsh who located the single brass cartridge on the floor of the chamber where it had fallen, careful not to touch it so it could be dusted for prints. Harper and Moriarty climbed the three ladders to join Sharp on the gantry. It was a Steyr sniper rifle, which Moriarty explained was an Austrian-made, state-of-the-art weapon, very uncommon in Australia. They examined the hole, cut into the steel bird wire, through which the squat white wedding cake of Parliament House was clearly visible.

Moriarty peered through it with his binoculars. 'Must b-be n-n-nine hundred m-metres.'

'Is that even possible?' asked Harper.

'A handful of p-p-people in the world could m-make the shot.'

'This one didn't.'

'No.'

'So, maybe he wasn't one of that handful.'

'M-maybe.'

No prints would be found on the rifle, nor on the ejected cartridge. There were none on the wire cutters or on any of the hard surfaces that might hold a print. The sniper had taken great care. Then he had simply disappeared.

'We need to talk,' said Harry Harper.

Anna Rosen looked up to see the inspector standing over her.

'Outside,' he said, and led her down the staircase and out into the pleasant sunshine to a bench on the edge of the lake.

Anna sat and stared at him, as if waiting for the axe to drop. She had recovered sufficiently to realise that she was a party to the story of a lifetime. She also knew it was one that Marin Katich would never survive.

Harper spoke to her in a quiet voice. 'Moriarty tells me you were close to this man Katich, is that right?'

Anna responded cautiously. 'I knew him when I was at university.'

'I don't want to know the details.'

'I don't intend to give you any.'

Harper sighed and looked at his hands. 'Anna, this is not a formal interview. I have to explain to you what's going to happen next. I've spoken to the commissioner and he has spoken to people in the government at the highest levels. I'm sure you think that you'll be able to tell this story in the papers but you won't. As far as the public is concerned, none of this ever happened. Prime Minister Bijedic is safe. No one shot him and no one will ever know that someone tried to.'

Anna felt her face flush. Her pulse was racing. She stared at Harper as if he was crazy. 'We still have a free press in this country,' she said.

'You may think so but that's not true of matters that could damage our national security.'

'You really think you can shut me up?'

'Not me, Anna,' Harper said with surprising gentleness. 'Even as we're sitting here a D-notice is being drawn up. All information about this incident, about what we found in the carillon, about our suspicions of who was involved . . . all of it will be suppressed. No publisher will touch this, no editor, not the *Herald*, not the ABC, no one. Even if you try to get it out in some other way, no one would believe you. We'll deny it and there'll be no evidence. People will say you're crazy.'

'What about Marin Katich?'

'He's a marked man wherever he goes.'

Then Harper stood up.

'I'm sorry,' he said. 'I really am but that's the way it is. That's the way it has to be.'

'But I saw everything today.'

'I never wanted you here. That was a mistake.'

Harper turned his back on her and walked away. Anna watched him all the way back to the carillon where a team was busy removing the evidence that anything had happened. A pair of swans passed in front of her, determined that she had no bread to offer and nosed their way through the reeds to enter the lake. It was as placid a scene as one could imagine. Nothing to see here on this pretty little island, nothing out of place.

Tears of frustration formed in her eyes and she brushed them away angrily. They wouldn't be able to shut her up forever. She would find Marin Katich. She would pursue the evidence of his father's war crimes and she would find the proof of who turned a blind eye to allow Ivo Katich to come here in the first place. It all started with him.

*

It was Tom Moriarty who interrupted this line of thought. 'Anna!' he called. 'I've b-b-been looking for you.'

The spy, perceptive as he was, was insensitive to her anger. *I'll get to the bottom of you too*, she thought as he ambled towards her.

'Let's go f-find out w-what really happened,' he said.

Anna composed her face and agreed to go with him.

Moriarty drove them to Parliament House. Back at the front steps Anna helped him search the area around the entrance Bijedic had gone through, looking for any sign of a bullet strike. They found nothing. Then he led her back down the stairs. Anna followed his gaze when he stopped to look up at the glass doors, at the portico above them and to the flag, centred over the entrance, then down to the two coats of arms on either side.

'Up there,' he said. 'Let's g-g-go.'

They went back inside and climbed the stairs to the first floor where Moriarty got a security guard to let them out on to the closed balcony above the entrance.

There was no sign of a bullet strike on any of the walls facing the lake. Moriarty looked back across to the carillon, shaking his head once again at the sheer audacity of it.

'He r-really is something else, your b-boyfriend,' he said.

Anna wasn't listening. She was staring at the blank back of the Australian coat of arms silhouetted against the sky and the lake. She walked over to examine it more closely and that was where she found what they were looking for.

At first she didn't believe what she was seeing. Then she put her eye up against it and saw that it was true. She called to Moriarty. She wanted a witness to the biggest story she would never tell.

'F-f-f-fuck me dead!' Moriarty cried when he saw it.

A neat hole was drilled clean through the kangaroo's head.

Author's note

This is a work of fiction based on real events in 1972 and 1973. I have imagined how some of these events may have played out and allowed real historical characters to intermingle with fictional characters in that context. Although much of the narrative really did happen I make no claim that this is a true history.

Acknowledgements

To the incomparable Richard Walsh, who unearthed this novel—buried in a manuscript that encompassed thirty-five years of the main characters' lives—a deep debt of gratitude.

There are many others who inspired its creation. Chief among them are my dear friends Mark Aarons and Pierre Vicary, who both taught me so much. Mark set me on the historical course this novel follows with his groundbreaking ABC radio documentary series, *Nazis in Australia*, while Pierre guided me on my first tour of Yugoslavia before the conflict and also on subsequent trips there during the Yugoslav Wars of the 1990s. The work of Dorde Licina, especially his book *Dvadesiti Covjek* (Centar za Informacije I Publicite, Zagreb, 1985), helped inform the narrative of the Bosnian incursion, which features the fictional revolutionary, Marin Katich.

I would also like to thank the former policemen, ASIO men, politicians, political advisors and journalists who enhanced my understanding of the dramatic true events in 1972 and '73 that underpin my fictional story. I would particularly like to thank Kerry Milte, former Commonwealth Police Superintendent, barrister and Renaissance man, who resolutely appears under his own name in *The Twentieth Man*.

Profound thanks are also due to my wonderful and patient editors—my publisher Annette Barlow, and Sarah Baker and Rebecca Starford.

And, above all, so much more than gratitude to my beloved wife Sarah, to whom I owe everything.